A Truthful Myth

ROGER COLLEY

iUniverse, Inc.
New York   Bloomington

iUniverse books may be ordered through booksellers or by contacting:

iUniverse
1663 Liberty Drive
Bloomington, IN 47403
www.iuniverse.com
1-800-Authors (1-800-288-4677)

Because of the dynamic nature of the Internet, any Web addresses or links contained in this book may have changed since publication and may no longer be valid. The views expressed in this work are solely those of the author and do not necessarily reflect the views of the publisher, and the publisher hereby disclaims any responsibility for them.

ISBN: 978-1-4502-4180-9 (sc)
ISBN: 978-1-4502-4181-6 (hc)
ISBN: 978-1-4502-4182-3 (ebook)

Printed in the United States of America

iUniverse rev. date: 09/23/2010

Foreword

This story about an abrupt climate change and its consequences is one of pure fiction, I think. While it does begin with references to certain scientific and engineering principles that have been firmly established, the tale leads into the future as an extension of the author's imagination about the multiple worlds of science, religion, technology, politics, economics, romance, and human behavior. While it may appear otherwise, all the characters are fictitious, and any similarities to real persons are coincidental.

Roger Colley
Huntingdon Valley, Pennsylvania

Dedication

To my beautiful, loving wife, Janice, who truly inspired me to transform my thoughts and ideas for this story into a full novel. For her untiring, conscientious efforts as my "Chief Editor" I am forever thankful.

The ancient Chinese word symbol for "danger," often romanticized in Western societies as an Old Chinese Proverb:

Within each crisis lies a great opportunity.

New American Proverb:

The science is never "done."

Setting the Stage

The last ice age

Not a human could be seen. Rivers—streams of ice. The landscape—frozen solid ground. From the sky—a panorama of white; a massive ice sheet all the way north. This was "New Jersey" fifteen thousand years ago. But the repetitive climate cycle was ending, perhaps all due to the earth's wobbling orbit around the sun. Who knows for sure? The thaw was beginning. Escaping gases from the ground composed of carbon molecules began to greenhouse the planet again, or so we assume. Global warming was again in the air. This was *good* for America.

❊   ❊   ❊

Ahead

Heeding the warnings, most fled in haste; some stayed in fear, including the retired senator soon to be seen pleading desperately from the rooftop of his historic home. Amid winds and waves of fury, the massive storm was gathering energy—approaching the city. Coastal evacuations displaced a million people—the largest dispersion in U.S. history. Over twenty-five thousand residents hurried to the city's indoor stadium for refuge. The storm's sustained winds reached 175 mph and hit landfall at 125 mph—the highest rated and most dangerous of storms. Catastrophic failures of the city's floodwalls left 80 percent of the city flooded. Nearly two thousand people died in the trauma, seven hundred in the city alone. Three million people suffered without electricity at the peak of the hot summer. Television images of helpless victims being rescued off rooftops by helicopters disheartened the nation. This was New Orleans, August 2005. It was Hurricane Katrina—man's acceleration of global warming? This was *bad* for America.

❊   ❊   ❊

Bursting into the library of the professor's home, he shouted, "*Conclusive!*" and again, "It's conclusive! *Katrina* proves it! I am now absolutely, positively convinced of it." He spoke in startling words. The former U.S. senator from Louisiana gazed profoundly at his close friend and admired scientific adviser, Richard Compton.

Richard, a renowned science professor at Princeton who was well groomed in matters of climatology, smiled and replied in a soft voice, "My dear boy, please calm down. Sit down. Yes, it just took you some time. You know I have been labeling you the 'Oracle' for some fifteen years—ever since you used your fame to successfully alert America and the entire world to the rapidly rising threats to our health and to our ecological balance from Man's growing environmental pollution. Now here it is 2005—"

"But listen," interrupted the senator. "I—"

"Yes," Richard continued, not listening, "we are in a new century, and we have a new global threat on our hands. And so you are now finally convinced. The planet is in a gradual global warming cycle, and the burning of all these fossil fuels giving off massive amounts of greenhouse gases is greatly accelerating the warming process. Yes, it's true. Man is substantially contributing to climate change, and if we do not reverse the process, the quality of life on this planet will be greatly jeopardized within the next fifty years."

"Richard! No!" exclaimed the Oracle alarmingly. "I'm not talking about the gradual warming theories of you scientists. It's not *gradual*; it's not fifty years—it's *abrupt*; it's *five* years!"

*   *   *

Two and a half years later, Montecito, California, June 2008

"Oh man, I'd better hurry up. Only twenty minutes for me to get back to my room, get my gown on, and get over there," Michael Reynolds said excitedly to his dad as he hustled to wrestle his computer closed and shut down the curious apparatus sprawled across his lab bench—whirling blades over a wind-powered turbine, a two-foot square solar panel, and a hot, sweating miniature boiler with clear plastic inlet and outlet water pipes.

He needed to be at McGovern Hall at the celebrated Montecito University by 6:00 PM to line up for the anxiously awaited awarding of his master's degree in chemical engineering. The class of 2008 was a smart one, but Michael stood way out in front with his breakthrough thesis describing a much more economical way to desalinate ocean water. "Remember, Dad—it was over ten years ago when Santa Barbara mothballed its new desalination plant due to its high costs. Something new and better sure is needed—a system powered with renewable energy instead of burning polluting fossil fuels, and also with lower costs and higher capacity. Seems impossible to most people."

"Yeah, I'll walk over with you. You're right. Ever since we lost the family farm with that terrible drought, I've been thinking about it, but you've told me that boiling seawater requires a great deal of energy."

"Right, and the resulting pools of highly salty brine waters have to be somehow disposed of efficiently," replied Michael as the two scurried out of the science building.

The global warming alarm had been sounded back in 2006 by the wise man many called the Oracle. His public warnings would convince Michael and hundreds of other engineers that extreme droughts would be taking place in arid areas such as the southwestern United States. Despite the obstacles, somehow technology had to be developed to make desalination more economical. If the snow packs of the Sierras and Rockies disappeared, where would the Southwest obtain its drinking, industrial, and irrigation waters?

"Hey, I hear all these profs are laughing at your ideas, and only the dean likes them. Are they jealous or what?"

"Healthy skepticism." Michael laughed.

It had already been announced that Michael would be awarded highest honor as the dean's choice for the "Most Outstanding Engineer" of his graduating class. It was controversial within the university, yet word of his ingenious methodologies of new ways to utilize wind and solar power, more efficiently power the heating process of salty ocean water, and dispose of waste brine more easily had already reached the Departments of Environmental Protection, Energy, and the Interior in Washington. What a great spot for a smart, young, outwardly confident twenty-four-year-old to be in when the threat of global warming had become one of the key issues facing all the political candidates lining up for the 2008 presidential election. Personable, charming, and handsome, full of exuberance to help his country and mankind, Michael was raring to go.

"Get my degree and get started with that acclaimed construction engineering firm that fervently recruited me," he whispered to himself as he dashed to the auditorium.

Chasing right behind him was his dad, offering fatherly advice. "An inventive engineering career? Fine, but remember that the landscape is littered with good ideas and innovative working prototypes—but most failed at full scale. Michael, don't be arrogant; don't get overconfident. Get it right!"

*   *   *

New York City, June 2008

Some three thousand miles away from Michael's dash to his graduation ceremonies, Rose Haines and Adriana Sanchez sat back and relaxed in their small apartment in the Soho district of New York City. "This has been a great week, Ad," Rose offered happily, wine glass in hand, as another fun-filled beer commercial came on their new HDTV.

"Yeah, Rose, your graduation party last week was awesome, and we had so much fun acting like silly sixteen-year-olds these past few days, but you know—"

"Well, look, Ad, we still have another week."

"Right, but you go into the U.S. Navy next week, into that fancy job of whatever they have lined up for you, and I still have to do some dumb job for a bunch of greedy bankers on Wall Street."

"But Ad, sweetie, I'm going to be based right here on the harbor, and we'll see each other lots. And besides, you're going to meet a real nice, young guy—not like those older players you've been running around with. It's going to be right down your alley … true love next time."

The girls had met two years earlier when Adriana, a New York native, advertised for a roommate for an apartment she had just leased. It was her chance as a young twenty-two-year-old to move out of her parents' house in Brooklyn and get her own life going. Rose, on the other hand, had just matriculated into a fine science and engineering university in lower Manhattan in order to earn her master's degree in atmospheric science. She was proud of her undergraduate chemical engineering degree from a small university in her little hometown of Ryder, New Hampshire. But now she was ready for the big time. She was totally convinced that her destiny was to make an important contribution to finding solutions to the imminent threats posed to humanity by the global warming trend that had suddenly become such an important issue.

Answering a "roommate wanted" advertisement and meeting Adriana had been a blessing for Rose. Her new roommate was so experienced and knew the whereabouts of trendy bars, clubs, and restaurants. From the very start, that made the young aspiring engineer/scientist from a small folksy New England town pleasantly comfortable living in the Big Apple. They seemed so conflicted in certain values, yet they were so compatible living together. Shy, fair, pretty, and humble, socially conservative Rose dated some handsome young men from her university and through Adriana's multiple contacts, but serious romance? Neither time nor luck for that.

Flirtatious, socially liberal Adriana, on the other hand, was always in a state of infatuation with the latest "one." Her clear olive skin, big green eyes, long black hair, and beautifully proportioned figure lured them one after another. But the romances never seemed to last long.

"Rose! Right! True love—that's an illusion for dreamers like you."

With graduation, a new expertise in the exciting field of climatology, and an opportunity in the U.S. Navy to study changes in the wind and sea patterns of the North Atlantic Ocean while still based in big-time New York City, Rose was elated, excited, and ready to go. Thoughts of global warming filled Rose's mind constantly. While the so-called low-risk theory of "abrupt" climate change seemed remote from happening, she nevertheless thought we must be prepared for the worst. It was commonly known that even the top prospect to be the next president of the United States was already completely sold on all the UN reports on climate change that had been released over the last fifteen years. In addition, it was also commonly known that he was a great admirer of a former U.S. senator commonly known as the "Oracle." It was the latter who claimed that he was way out in front of the consensus findings of the UN scientists. What was not known to Rose or any others was that he had already privately conveyed his findings to this man who was to be the next president of the United States.

✻   ✻   ✻

Washington, DC, June 2008

"Still five months to go until the election, but we have this thing all wrapped up," said the campaign Chief, Thomas Barlow, in a strong, confident voice. It was late in the evening at campaign headquarters on a warm night in late June.

"Look, you know I like to call you 'Chief' because you are a master of the political game, and I have already assured you I will make you my Chief of staff if I'm elected, but let's not jump ahead. We both know that unforeseen events can happen at any moment," declared Paul Jennings, the man with the deep, golden voice who some in his political party called "the Savior." His professional demeanor, his air of confidence seemed to conquer all. Clearly this man felt himself destined to lead the nation to ever more greatness and prayed that this coming election would be his time.

"No, no," countered the Chief, his face the look of a rugged athlete sensing sure victory. "The only unforeseen event is the changing global warming mess. But as we agreed, we are keeping that issue secret for now."

"Okay, let's stick with the game plan. As you tell me over and over again, I am capable of convincing the public, with my gift of what you call 'persuasive oratory,' that I can solve both our nation's current economic problems and our health care problems. But if we alert the public too soon, before there is enough evidence about the new trend and all the bad effects of a sudden increase in global warming. ..." He paused, and his voice dropped into a somber tone. "We will just scare them too much and potentially damage my credibility."

"Right on," said the Chief quietly. "Let's stay on course. The public may be completely skeptical of predictions of a devastating event forecast for late 2012 or of the Oracle's concerns of near-term global warming impacts ... but let's not reveal that *we believe them*." The Chief, a man of obvious strong ambition, liked the idea that a crisis of some kind could be the means to catapult him to a position of great political power, even if behind the scenes.

✻   ✻   ✻

Paris, France, June 2008

The middle-aged man from the Middle East walked briskly into the hotel lobby looking for a young Frenchman who would also be wearing a red handkerchief in the lapel pocket of his blue blazer. Their eyes met and both nodded.

"Aazim," the Frenchman called. "Come sit over here where it is quiet and we can talk privately."

"Antoine, at last we meet."

Sitting alone in a corner of the large lobby, the two men gazed at each other for a moment as though their glances would accurately size up the other's integrity and somehow the other's intentions.

Antoine spoke first of the subject at hand. "So we both know what each other does for a living. You represent your government in purchasing advanced weapons, and I work for a private bank that negotiates and facilitates such dealings. But isn't this more?"

Aazim leaned forward in his chair and in a direct, firm voice answered his new acquaintance. "This is delicate. Our telephone conversations need to be confirmed. I am discontented. You are too. The Second World War, peace, the creation of the United Nations to prevent more bloodshed, but, you know, nothing but failures since. The world is crazy—we need to stop this madness. I know how."

"Yes," Antoine replied. "We need to stop the killing—once and for all."

After a long pause as the two continued to stare at each other, perhaps searching for and finding that empathetic feeling in their hearts and minds, Aazim continued, "My friend, let's talk."

※　※　※

Princeton, July 2008, Setting the Science

Richard and the Oracle together again, reviewing their extensive research— three years after Katrina. It was the UN mandate issued in 1988 to create the Intergovernmental Panel on Climate Change (to become known as the IPCC), followed up with its Earth Summit in 1992 that first got the ball rolling. Concerns expressed at that meeting by scientists studying changes in climate conditions called attention to the rising world temperatures over the course of the twentieth century. They labeled it "global warming," an increase in temperature perhaps due to increases in atmospheric gases that trap heat rising from the earth, keeping such radiant heat from escaping into space. These gases are known as "greenhouse gases," or GHGs, and include carbon dioxide, methane, nitrous oxide, and water vapor. Since the rate of temperature increase was accelerating during the second half of the century faster than the first half's increase, perhaps man's activities were responsible for the faster warming through greater industrial and commercial use of fossil fuels, deforestation, and pollution.

Scientists engaged by the climate panel, the IPCC, were to provide assessment reports and technical papers at regular intervals. Three years later, in 1995, the IPCC's second assessment report "Climate Change 1995" stated that "climate change will lead to an intensification of the global hydrological cycle and can have major impacts on regional water resources. Models project that between one-third and one-half of existing mountain glaciers could disappear over the next one hundred years. The reduced extent of glaciers and the depth of snow cover also would affect the seasonal distribution of water flow and water supply for hydroelectric generation and agriculture. Climate change is likely to have wide-ranging and mostly adverse impacts on human health, with significant loss of life." Scientists noted that carbon dioxide stays in the atmosphere a long time compared to emitted aerosols, which have a cooling effect. Hence, industrial buildup of emitted CO_2 will last several centuries. They concluded that immediate stabilization of the concentration of carbon dioxide at its present level can only be achieved through an immediate reduction in emissions of 50 to 70 percent and further reductions thereafter.

"Richard!" exclaimed the Oracle. "It's the middle of 2008 and we're sitting here in your library poring through these UN reports again, but enough is enough. I already put all the pieces together three years ago."

"No, no," replied Richard. "Let's read on. We still have to be sure your conclusions are correct. You know, I'm still a little skeptical. But Senator, I do clearly recall the amazing conversation we had back then, right after Katrina. It went something like this:"

"Well, Richard, it's almost 2006. We have to do something about it … fast!" exclaimed the Oracle.

"What? Write another book?" Richard snickered facetiously, looking for something less alarming in his friend's reaction.

"No, something more dramatic, like a way of changing complacency into action on a worldwide basis … but at least starting here in America where we are the biggest contributor, or should I say polluter, because in a short time we will have to convince the EPA and the Congress and the public that carbon dioxide is a pollutant to be regulated."

"Even though we all emit it with each breath we take?" The Oracle pretended not to hear Richard's last comment.

"Richard, perhaps if I can condense all this solid evidence into a convincing documentary—because, you know, a picture is worth a thousand words—we can use my reputation as an avid environmentalist and my contacts as a former member of the U.S. Senate to create a grassroots movement to gain public *support. At the same time, you and your colleagues, me, and the UN reporting team all start making presentations to Congress. It's Congress that will have to appropriate the funds to change the ways we produce energy. Eighty percent of the world's energy is produced by fossil fuels whose burning emits greenhouse gases. We'll need to go solar and wind as quickly as possible—urgently!" His deep strong voice raised again in volume and tempo.*

After a long, silent pause as the two momentarily sank into deep reflection, Richard offered quietly, "Better yet, why not run for president? If, three years from now, you can win in 2008, and you are correct in your prediction, you would be in the key leadership position to show the way—to save us and the planet."

Another long pause. "Good idea, Richard. You have an ingenious mind ... but I have been removed from politics for too long—you know, in order to study the global warming issue. Now other possible candidates are way out in front in the public eye. Here's another idea. In a few months, in December, for the first time since the Kyoto Protocol was adopted in 1997, all its signers will be attending a UN climate change convention in Montreal for the purpose of agreeing to extend the treaty and to develop tougher emission limits. It is expected that ten thousand delegates will attend. Of course, I'll be there, and I've been invited to chair one of the important new negotiating sessions. If I can manage to be one of the keynote speakers, I can get myself into a leadership position fighting for much stronger action."

"And just how would you get things moving?" Richard asked.

Look, we have to get India and China into the game. They are excepted from inclusion now as 'developing' nations, yet they are in fact just behind the United States as the biggest total emitters of CO_2. And then us ... we have to stimulate—no, alarm the American public about the imminent threat. You know full well, Richard, that our U.S. Senate would not ratify the emissions treaty unless every country was in the deal."

"Yes, I know," Richard chimed in, now raising his voice and beginning to show more emotion than his usual calm demeanor. You're the person to sound the alert—right, get the convention delegates riled up in December, and in early 2006, let's get that documentary up and running."

✻　✻　✻

The Oracle's documentary released in late 2006 about the coming impacts of global warming and its adverse affects upon the planet and its inhabitants was a smash success. Dramatic in its production, it captivated hundreds of government leaders and millions of ordinary citizens. The Kyoto Protocol was justifiable, and new evidence of the threat would compel even stronger steps by Man to reverse his emissions of greenhouse gases, the "GHGs." The Green Revolution was on, but the Oracle was way ahead of the IPCC scientists. Could the Oracle be right? Richard's unspoken thoughts raced to other dire predictions from the past. So many had been accurate, and astonishingly he was now face to face with today's most credible oracle. Memories of past oracles were conjured up in Richard's racing mind—the Romans' Cybil, Greece's Delphi, the Middle Age's Merlin the Prophet with predictions of polar shifts, and the Holy Bible's Book of Revelation predicting the Apocalypse. Then there was Albert Einstein suggesting that many millions of years ago, before the mammals, there had been a major pole shift from what we now view as the equator to their present position as the North and South Poles. He speculated that any new sudden pole change would be disastrous.

Richard continued thinking to himself—recollections of the prophets of doom, even thinking of the WebBot Project on the Internet site called "web-bot.com" predicting that something "hot" will happen to the planet December 21, 2012, coinciding with the doom predicted at the end of the Mayan calendar. Perhaps something about polar shifts, a la Einstein. Almost all of the scientists working on the IPCC assessment reports and technical reports, however, believed that global warming would be "gradual" through the twenty-first century and that its potential adverse effects could be mitigated and abated through substantial GHG emission reductions and through the development of new non-fossil-fuel energy sources. Confusingly, doubts lingered in Richard's mind to that consensus opinion as he listened to the Oracle constantly beseeching him to accept the near certain possibility of the so-called "abrupt" change.

In IPCC Paper IV, in 1997, it was stated that holding emissions at the current levels would have no substantial impact on reducing the year 2100 levels of GHGs, the greenhouse gases. By 1997 it was already determined that shrinkage of ice in the Arctic areas was at a faster rate than previously predicted. Resulting increases in carbon dioxide in the ocean would produce more acid and would lower sources of food for fish. To mitigate the adverse effects of global warming, the UN-sponsored Kyoto Protocol of 1997 pointed toward furthering emission reductions from those agreed to at the 1992 UN Earth Summit whereby industrial nations were to reduce GHG emissions by 5 percent by 1997 compared to 1990. While 160 countries representing 55 percent of global greenhouse gas emissions signed the treaty, the United States did not ratify it, primarily because industrializing China and India were deemed exceptions from the protocol as "developing" nations.

The next meeting of all the parties to the Kyoto Protocol of 1997 occurred at the UN climate-change convention in Montreal in December 2005. Its purpose was to extend the life of the protocol beyond its 2012 expiration date and to negotiate deeper cuts in GHG emissions. Also in 2005 the European Union adopted its emission trading scheme, a cap-and-trade system established for the purpose are reducing total emissions from the EU countries. The IPCC Technical Paper V, 2002, stated, "The atmospheric concentrations of greenhouse gases have increased since the preindustrial era due to human activities. Globally, by the year 2080, about 20 percent of coastal wetlands could be lost due to sea level rise."

On November 17, 2007, in Valencia, Spain, the IPCC released its fourth assessment report, confirming that warming of the climate is unequivocal, that over the last fifty years there has been more melting snow and ice and rising sea levels, fewer cold days and nights, more hot days and nights, more frequent heat waves, and a high frequency of heavy precipitation events. "Global GHG emissions due to human activities have grown since preindustrial times with an increase of 70 percent between 1970 and 2004." IPCC scientists noted that the rate of growth of CO_2 emissions was much higher during the ten-year period 1995 to 2004 than the entire twenty-four-year period 1970 to 1994. "The atmospheric concentration of CO_2 exceeds by far the natural range over the last 650,000 years. During this period the sum of solar and volcanic forcing would likely have produced cooling." Thus, the scientists concluded, it is "very likely" that temperatures were up due to an increase in greenhouse gases caused by man.

"Okay, Professor. We know for a fact that we have accelerated warming, and we know that we have polluters who are causing it, but let's go on to what bad things are going to happen if we don't take immediate action."

The IPCC pointed out that big climate changes in Africa would occur by the year 2020 and in low lands in Asia by 2050 and that the worldwide global warming trend of the first half of the twenty-first century would be at twice the rate as occurred in the twentieth century. The IPCC scientists pointed out that warming should be slow and gradual but thought that there was some risk of *abrupt change* if ocean circulation patterns change.

"Richard, *this* is what I'm talking about!" the Oracle now exclaimed, jumping out of his seat. "Climate change, hmmm, they say *'gradual*

11

probably … *abrupt* possible, but improbable.' These are the words of the IPCC. I know for sure about my hunch that it's going to be 'abrupt.'"

Richard nodded with a look of concern and continued to spread the reports out on his large desk.

Noteworthy in the 2007 assessment report was Table 3.2 contained in Topic 3, entitled "impacts." The table portrays the likelihood of selected trends and the impact of such trends on agriculture, ecosystems, water resources, human health, industry, and society. Of the twenty-four likely impacts, only two were deemed "beneficial," while the remaining twenty-two were termed "adverse." However, it is noted that the adverse overall global warming impacts should be slow and gradual through the twenty-first century, even though warming could be twice the rate of warming of the twentieth century, perhaps a consensus average forecast of plus four degrees Fahrenheit in the twenty-first century versus a plus two degrees Fahrenheit average for the twentieth century... unless: *"If a large-scale abrupt climate change were to occur, its impact could be quite high."* The abrupt change IPCC scientists most worry about is a sudden change in ocean circulation patterns combined with a sudden speed-up in the melting of Arctic ice. As a consequence, the melting permafrost, those land areas frozen for tens of thousands of years, would release vast amounts of greenhouse gases into the atmosphere in a very short period of time. Other scientists worry that if in addition to sudden ocean shifts and permafrost melting, the North and South Pole positions were to change their relative tilt, as they possibly had many millions of years ago, the resulting calamity would be mind-boggling.

"Now then. We're finally to the table I wanted to review with you. Based on some other data I have received, my conclusion—well, it's all leading me to believe that these adverse impacts will be upon us sooner rather than later." Richard listened intently as the Oracle continued.

"This table of the six trends, these twenty impacts—they are alarming on their own, but catastrophic if they turned from "gradual" to "abrupt." Heat waves of much more severity … much more frequent and highly intense heavy rainfall in certain areas … more severe droughts over wider areas in other regions … and the strongest categories of cyclones and hurricanes. Higher sea levels would be devastating for the millions of inhabitants living along or near coastal areas. Factor in all twenty-two unfavorable impacts and consider if they were to happen suddenly …" The Oracle's voice dropped off.

The two sat in quiet contemplation staring at the reports now filling Richard's desktop.

✻   ✻   ✻

Yes, the Oracle and his closest adviser, Richard Compton, were certainly well aware of conclusions pointed out in the April 2007 IPCC report: food and water shortages; a sea level rise from seven to twenty-three inches by the end of the century (just a four-inch rise could flood islands and coastal areas of Southeast Asia); Louisiana and Florida at high risk of flooding; stronger natural disasters; expansion of desert areas; millions of species facing extinction; alterations of the oceans' wind and circulation systems potentially causing a mini ice age in Western Europe; the unlocking of the GHG methane from melting permafrost; freeing up carbon trapped under sea ice thereby causing increases in evaporation of warmer water. (Water vapor is actually the largest GHG, 36 to 70 percent, then CO_2, 9 to 26 percent, and methane at 4 to 9 percent.) CO_2 levels could soon be the highest in twenty million years. Two months after the 1997 IPCC report, *National Geographic* magazine reported that world temperatures were up nearly two degrees Fahrenheit since 1880 with the rate of increase accelerating. The Arctic temperature effects were accelerating at twice the global average rate; glaciers and mountain snows were melting; Montana's glacier national park had 27 glaciers now vs. 150 in 1910; coral reefs were dying off; and there was an upsurge in extreme weather events such as wildfires, heat waves, and strong tropical storms. Clearly, humans have been putting CO_2 into the atmosphere at a faster and faster rate.

The evidence seemed clear. The IPCC work was endorsed by more than fourteen scientific societies, including all the national academies of science of the major industrial nations. The estimated temperature rise in the twenty-first century could be as much as an astounding eleven degrees Fahrenheit despite releases of aerosols into the atmosphere, which have a cooling effect by reflecting sunlight. Scientists debated other warming factors such as the variations in the earth's orbit around the sun and solar activity such as sunspots, but believed that these facts could not account for what is to come if Man were not to dramatically decrease his output of CO_2. But the specific words that caught the attention of the Oracle and his trusted adviser were contained in an IPCC statement referring to the melting of the permafrost in the Arctic region. The area has been frozen since the last ice age over ten thousand years ago. The striking statement

13

in the 1997 report: "A catastrophe lies below the permafrost." What could this mean? The Oracle knew.

✻   ✻   ✻

America, 2009

Reactions to global warming disclosures kept pouring in beyond the 2005 UN-sponsored meeting in Montreal. In April 2009, *Foreign Policy* magazine reported, "Climate change and a rapidly growing middle class are putting pressure on the Earth. Unless we innovate ourselves out of this dire situation, the planet is in peril." During the same month, the newly appointed U.S. Secretary of State remarked, "Climate change is a clear and present danger to our world that demands immediate attention." Shortly thereafter, the Secretary-General of the United Nations added, "We have less than ten years to halt the global rise in greenhouse gas emissions if we are to avoid catastrophic consequences for people and the planet. It is, simply, the greatest challenge we face as a human family." An ABC television special on June 2, 2009, entitled "Earth 2100," vividly depicted extremely dire consequences for the entire United States during the second half of the century with the only possible salvation through taking immediate steps to remedy the situation. A fully attended UN-sponsored climate change convention held in December 2009 in Copenhagen resulted in an "accord" to work toward substantial carbon reductions by the years 2020 and 2050. Accepting the dire predictions but also accepting the "gradual" nature of the climate change, the major carbon-emitting nations of India, China, and the United States were still reluctant to jeopardize their growth economies by signing a legally binding reduction agreement. The job of the Oracle was not nearly completed.

Despite strong warnings from the UN about adverse conditions forecast for the second half of the century, what was not generally known in 2009 was that the information the Oracle had linked together predicted that the situation was going to be much worse, much sooner, than originally thought—*global warming impacts were going to be abrupt, not gradual.*

Chapter One

Imminent Persuasion

Summer 2010

"**I** know it's only July, Richard, but we have to really press our case with him now. The year 2009 was a fluke, as were the freaky snowstorms last winter. We only saw modest signs of global warming impacts, but you know that our new guy has been in office a year and half now, and time is fleeting. It's coming." The Oracle looked concerned.

"Look," Richard calmly replied to his impassioned friend. "Your documentary worked so beautifully that not only do we have all the key leaders and their followers from all around the world clamping down their nations' output of greenhouse gases, but we also have a new president completely won over. I mean, how fast do you think 'abrupt' change means? Your predictions for 2010 could be quite premature."

"Okay, yes, our meetings with the president have been productive. He stepped up last month by pressing Congress into passing stronger alternative energy legislation. Sure, and we are now clamping down on the greenhouse gases, but he doesn't quite see the *imminent catastrophe* as I do."

"Well, you know, he's a former retail business guru and was a motivational speaker as a consultant, so what does he know about science?" Richard replied.

"True, but I thought the secret we told him just before his election would do it. That's almost two years ago. Does he get it, or is he afraid of being an alarmist?"

"He will get it, he will," murmured Richard. "I believe he already knows—just in case you're right."

☆   ☆   ☆

The warm and humid months of August, September, and October in the Caribbean region and the southeastern states of the United States are commonly referred to as "hurricane season." It can be a delightful time; it can be a scary time. Looking back, Hurricane Katrina in August 2005 was a very powerful storm that caused devastating damage to thousands of homes in Louisiana and Mississippi. It was the costliest hurricane in American history, causing nearly $100 billion in property damage, and nearly 2000 people died. From a mild start in the Bahamas, it crossed Florida in the least severe category, Category 1, but increased to the most severe category, Category 5, in the Gulf of Mexico. It hit land in Louisiana as a Category 3 storm, with sustained winds of 120 mph. When the federal levee protection system failed in New Orleans, 80 percent of the city flooded. Despite the relative calm to the U.S. mainland during the 2007, 2008, and 2009 seasons, Katrina was the big prelude to the increasingly more violent storms forecast by the believers in the gradual but accelerating global warming trend caused by man.

✻   ✻   ✻

Now in early August 2010, it started. Hurricane Alice intensified as it headed on a direct path toward San Juan, Puerto Rico. It was rated the most intense, Category 5, as it inflicted incredible damage upon the most populous city in the Caribbean. Thousands were dead; there was property damage in the hundreds of millions; and acres of farmland were destroyed. Hurricane Bruce, also a category five storm, missed major population centers, and another Category 5, Clara, left the sugar cane fields of Haiti in utter destruction. David—another Category 5—headed for Miami. Wind damage was moderate against Miami's strong building codes, but high seas left the harbor's vast fleet of boats in shambles. All electricity in the city was out for two weeks. Then, in late August, came the worst. It was Hurricane Edna—five in a row at Category 5. Never before in recorded history were there five hurricanes in one season rated as the most intense, let alone five in a row. It was worse than Katrina, as the rebuilt levees in New Orleans did not hold. When the season ended in mid-November, the region had experienced a total of sixteen hurricanes. Eight were rated Category 5 just prior to reaching land. In the entire region of the Caribbean islands and the southeastern states of the United States, property damage was incalculable by the insurance industry. The death toll exceeded ten thousand people. Local economies came to a standstill. The federal response was woefully inadequate to the needs. The hurricane season had been truly catastrophic. Alarmingly and perversely, the rest of the United States remained in a prolonged drought, and agricultural output slumped. Wildfires in California burned out of control for weeks. By Thanksgiving, national television coverage had fueled a general fear in the American public that all the publicity about "gradual" global warming over the rest of the century may be wrong. Perhaps something "abrupt" was indeed happening.

✻   ✻   ✻

The secret Camp David meeting took place the day after Thanksgiving. Richard Compton had been meeting privately for weeks with scientists assigned to the IPCC assessment reports. He met with climatologists, physicists, oceanographers, and atmospheric scientists. He was left more startled than ever before by what he learned at these meetings. Arctic ice was melting much faster than projected. Contrary to any gradual warming scenario, carbon dioxide and methane from the melting permafrost was entering the atmosphere at a much faster rate than forecast. The average ocean temperature by mid-2010 exceeded the highest end of the forecast range as reported in the 1997 IPCC assessment report. While not yet possible to measure, the scientific consensus that Richard noted in his individual meetings was that a significant shift in ocean currents was taking place abruptly in the North Atlantic Ocean waters, where the major wind pattern is clockwise. This factor alone could account for more severe hurricanes being formed at the equator.

Not certain was the complex interplay among shifts in ocean currents, changing patterns of wind currents, rising sea levels, rising ocean temperatures, and rising air temperatures. What would be the total outcome of all these changing relationships? What was certain to Richard was that the total interplay of these forces together was causing an "abrupt" as opposed to a "gradual" climate change in North America. Puzzling, however, was that although the rest of the world was also experiencing record high temperatures, adverse impacts elsewhere were not yet moving into the "catastrophic" range. Forecasts containing this disturbing information had been presented by the Oracle and Richard Compton to the incoming president months before his election but had been kept secret. No other knowledgeable parties to the global warming scenario were able to put the incomplete puzzle together other than the Oracle. Now, two years after his election and after the devastating 2010 hurricane season, what was to be done? What was to be revealed to the American people by the president about the Oracle's startling conclusions?

After exchanging pleasantries, the Oracle opened the meeting in an even-toned voice. "Mr. President, five years ago I became convinced that global warming was heading our planet toward a catastrophe within just the next five years. That's now. My alarm and its publicity helped prompt even the three biggest contributors—the United States, China, and India—to begin measures to reduce greenhouse gases significantly over the next twenty years. The IPCC may be happy with that, and their consensus, as you know, has been that with *gradual* warming we can all work toward mitigating adverse impacts of the trend and also adapting to gradual global warming with a gradual change in our habits. The planet would still be in a general gradual warming trend, but we will at least have removed Man's substantial contribution, which had been clearly greatly accelerating the trend. We would have prevented the world from going over the edge, past the tipping point. … However, you know now that the public is very anxious after this last devastating hurricane season. From all that I could gather, and with Richard here grudgingly confirming it, I have been disputing the 'gradual' theory and have been a firm believer in the fallacy of the theory that an 'abrupt' climate change would be 'very unlikely.' You have known our secret data for some time now; you know the issue of the permafrost. Most of the UN climate panel's top scientists believe that this devastating hurricane experience we just witnessed in the United States and the Caribbean was of a freak nature and didn't really have much to do with any kind of abrupt climate change. The reason I believe the opposite—that is, that an abrupt climate change is already upon us—is that we have used the data to figure out that many apparent independent events are actually so interrelated that now we have a confluence upon us, and—"

"I'm sorry to interrupt," the president said politely, "but it's not easy to follow all this—wind, currents, shifts. I know that I was elected two years ago to save our country from the impacts of inadequate health care, poor quality education, and excessive dependence upon the use of imported oil, and I know that you had shared your conclusions with me back then. But are you about to tell me—you the incredible forecaster; you who is known as the Oracle—that I now may have to save America from the adverse impacts of an *abrupt* climate change?"

"No, Mr. President," spoke the Oracle with a sudden tone of strong emphasis. "Not *may* have to save, but *will* have to save!"

No one noticed the grin on the face of the Chief at that moment. Any issue that could possibly enhance the leadership opportunity and image of the Savior was a blessing. To the Chief, the president's right-hand man, the name of the game was power—sustained power to control people and events to his own permanent advantage.

The president, after turning in his seat to face the window, remained still for several long moments and then turned back and spoke. "Well then, it is my duty to put Americans first. All those problems overseas can wait. We are already on our way to an improved economy here at home. My programs for universal health care, new mileage standards to reduce gasoline consumption, and increased educational scholarships have already been passed by the Congress. Tell me again, Senator, slowly, in layman's language, exactly what the melting permafrost and the change in ocean currents and the change in wind currents mean to our country … and why this is *so urgent.*"

✻　✻　✻

It was the autumn of 2010—two and a half years after graduation. Michael could not believe how time had flown. His engineering firm in Los Angeles held very lucrative contracts with the State of California Water Department. Based upon his work ethic and sharp mind, Michael had been assigned as lead project manager on his firm's most important contract of all—the study of the state's interrelated system for transporting water from the Colorado River and from Northern California to the heavily populated areas of arid Southern California. The study was all-encompassing, including the useful life of existing systems, their shortcomings, and projected needs for the next twenty-five years to provide suitable systems for drinking water, industrial water, commercial water, and irrigation water. It was an important task for young Michael, a mighty challenge in a projected era of warmer and drier climatic conditions.

Michael worked long hours. His apartment in Encino was only a fifteen-minute drive from his office in Burbank. He found his social life limited, but that was fine since he kept his lifestyle in healthy balance. He did some light weightlifting in his small living room before going to bed about 11:00 PM, took a short jog in the morning before breakfast at 6:00 AM, and participated in bike-riding sessions with several associates from the office on Saturday mornings. On most Saturday evenings, he enjoyed dinner or movie dates. Michael was so handsome, friendly, and polite that any young lady would be glad to have a date with him. For the twenty-six-year-old, though, there would be no lasting attachments. Pursuing his exciting career came first. There would be plenty of time for marriage and kids later on.

"Rather curious," Michael thought to himself. He had enjoyed a wonderful Thanksgiving dinner in Santa Monica with his parents. Despite his office being closed for the long holiday weekend, he had stopped in Friday morning to do some quiet research pertaining to chemical discharges into the state's waterways. He immediately noticed a memo sheet lying on his chair with the name of the firm's CEO, George Blake, imprinted on top. Below it read in neat handwriting, "Michael, I'll be back in the office from a trip at 1:00 on Monday. Come to my office then. GB."

"Uh oh," Michael murmured out loud. "I hope I haven't done anything stupid." To himself he thought, "Why was the boss in on Thanksgiving Day? It must be important. Why would he leave such a mysterious note?"

✻   ✻   ✻

Sunday afternoon's long, lonely drive back to New York City from a chilly but pleasant Thanksgiving break in her hometown gave Rose plenty of time to reflect. The two and a half years since graduation sure had been hectic—and confusing. Sure, the social life keeping up with Adriana and her male companions had been fun. Certainly the navy training and all those excursions out to sea from her small science lab at the tip of Wall Street had been exciting. "But what is really going on?" she repeated out loud to herself as she navigated the traffic flow. Her task for the navy was to study the currents of air and water in the North Atlantic as well as record air and sea temperatures and then compare such data against past recordings over the last century. Obviously, the Defense Department was very concerned about changes in climate and how any potential major shifts might affect naval coastal facilities and at sea operations. "Those hurricanes," Rose said to herself "Five in a row at category five. Yet the scientific consensus is that they are just an offset to the mild last three years. But here the press has the public alarmed that global warming may have suddenly descended upon us."

Rose recalled the vital statistic that over half of the U.S. population—51 percent—live in or near coastal areas. That sure is an alarming number, she mused, after one reads the recently updated report from the MIT Integrated Global System Model. That report, issued in May 2009, stated that if no changes were made to Man's current rate of emissions, the earth's average median surface temperature could increase by as much as nine degrees Fahrenheit by 2100 over the 1980–2000 period and a potential twenty degrees Fahrenheit increase in the Arctic region. Of particular alarm to Rose, however, was the small print from that report that much of the adverse impact would be mitigated by Man's actions unless an unexpected confluence of events caused a massive melting of the Arctic's permafrost. That little detail stuck in her mind. If anything like that were to happen, how could she be of help? Young, beautiful, athletic, and intelligent—Rose had it all. But none of that mattered compared to her sense of compassion for humanity. She had a role to play, an important role. She had to get to the bottom of this nagging concern. Just before reaching her tiny apartment at the harbor naval station, she reached for her cell phone.

✻ ✻ ✻

The mood at Camp David was somber. "Okay, enough!" said the president forcefully. "I have the picture. The Arctic permafrost, all that frozen ground north of Canada, is rapidly melting and at a much faster rate than the UN boys have presented. The ocean temperatures are rising much faster than expected. The oceans and trees cannot absorb all of the excess greenhouse gases. The ocean winds and currents are pulling the tides in faster than anyone imagined. We have half the U.S. population areas under water in fifteen years. We have stronger hurricanes every year from the hotter temperatures below us. We have hotter desert temperatures, droughts and fires in our Southwest. ... So, so ... what do we do?"

"We move to the middle," responded the Chief, half jesting.

"*Bingo*! Chief, you may have the solution. Listen, I recall being told that the worst natural disaster in recorded history was in 1931 in China. The drought there followed by the floods killed four million people. I am not going to allow that kind of catastrophe to happen in America. Gentlemen, we've been sitting here for three hours. Let's go have lunch. We have it."

The Oracle, Richard Compton, and the Chief of staff looked startled at those last remarks from the president, but they all immediately stood up and followed their leader out of the room with no hesitation.

✻ ✻ ✻

"Michael! Come in," said George Blake. It was exactly 1:00 PM Monday. One could not be anything but on time at a top-notch engineering firm. "Sit down, Michael; how are you?"

"Fine, sir," Michael replied politely, somewhat surprised that this first-time, private meeting with the big boss had started out so cordially.

"I have some great news," said George, his voice expressing a strong tone of enthusiasm. "We have the funding. The higher-ups in Sacramento are really concerned now about the potential impacts of climate change. Someday we may lose those snow packs in the Sierras, and—you know ... well, a lot can happen to our water sources."

"Right, I sure know," piped in Michael. "I wrote my senior thesis—"

"Yes, yes, I know. That's why you're here, Michael. You are an expert on the desalination of seawater. Your thesis has been read by the head of California's Water Board and by the Department of Defense ... and the Department of the Interior ... and the Department of Energy in DC ... and I even hear by the president's new environmental adviser."

"Well—" Michael tried to inject a humble acknowledgement into the conversation, but George continued.

"So here's what's happening. The feds and the state have combined to ante up three million dollars for us to reactivate that mothballed desalination plant up there in Santa Barbara—you're familiar with it—and to test your new technologies for feasibility and cost effectiveness."

"Wow!" interjected Michael excitedly, a glowing smile now replacing his prior look of anxiety.

"And you, Michael; I'm obviously going to pull you off the aqueduct project and name you supervising project manager. We'll have the first funding dollars in hand by April. In the meantime, start drafting in outline form how you would scope the project, and, say, spend the three million dollars over a two-year period. If your pilot program looks good, I'm certain of a big increase in dollars toward a larger full-scale plant in the LA area. This is incredible for the future of California, and maybe even the United States."

"Right!" jumped in Michael. "All this concern about water shortages. Three-fourths of the planet is ocean. We're loaded with water. We just have to get the salt out cleanly and economically and efficiently transport it to where it's needed."

The two men then just sat there, quietly staring into each other's eyes with the glow of satisfied amazement beaming across their suddenly warmed faces. It wasn't until his drive home that evening that Michael heard the echo, his dad's forewarning: "Scale up ... failures ... get it right." At that moment, Michael felt very small indeed.

✽   ✽   ✽

"Jane," Rose spoke into her mobile phone with one hand on the wheel. "So glad you answered. I'm almost back to the big town from having turkey with my parents at home in New Hampshire. I just have to talk with you."

Jane Stricker was a forty-year-old PhD in climatology living in Seattle and performing special consulting assignments for the University of Washington's Department of Environmental Sciences. She had earned quite a reputation as an expert in climate change while assigned a UN task to investigate the permafrost. Her scientific findings ended up as important detail in the UN's epic 2007 IPCC report. The two women had met at an environmental symposium while sitting at the same dinner table the first night. Beyond sharing similar ideological sentiments to help save humanity from environmental disasters, they had immediately become good friends.

"Permafrost" is a new word to many outside the world of geologists. It refers to soil that is below the freezing point of water, thirty-two degrees Fahrenheit. Most of it is found in the considerable areas near the North and South Poles. A portion of the outer layers may melt in summer seasons and is typically two to twelve feet thick. While there are many variations in the permafrost areas—some continuous, some discontinuous, and some sporadic—its melting causes concerns to climatologists primarily because of the vast amounts of carbon stored in such soils. Releases of carbon products to the oceans and to the atmosphere obviously would accelerate the global warming trend and exacerbate its dire consequences for humanity.

"Jane," repeated Rose. "You know I'm an atmospheric scientist and don't know too much about ice, glaciers, and the permafrost soil, but I need to know your thoughts on something. You're the expert."

"Go ahead, Rose dear," Jane countered with a touch of pride in her voice, sensing her friend's admiration.

"Look, Jane. I am so confused about this. I'm seeing in my data in the North Atlantic a strong trend upward in air and water temperatures. This could obviously be the combination of more greenhouse gases in the atmosphere along with melting ice and melting glaciers, but the soil thing—is all this massive frozen soil up there in the Arctic really melting more than anyone thinks, or is your 2007 report right on? I mean ... I don't mean to dispute ..."

"No, no, that's okay, Rose. It's been almost four years since I wrote that report indicating that the melting of the permafrost was slow and gradual, but Rose, they *were* my words footnoted at the end of that report. I mean ... any sudden change was not out of the question, and if that happened, we could have an environmental disaster ... all that carbon ..."

"But, Jane, are you updating your work?" Rose asked with a high excited pitch in her voice.

After what seemed like a long pause or a lost connection, Jane Stricker's voice came back in a strident tone. "Rose, I'm not privy to tell you this. It's confidential, but as my friend and colleague—not for you to repeat—yes, not only have I been asked by the IPCC to quickly update my data by the end of the year 2011, but I have been approached by Richard Compton, the scientific adviser to one of our former vice presidents of the United States, He's working on a special project to determine if the climate change we're experiencing—that is, global warming—is, to use the words of the IPCC, possibly becoming 'abrupt' as opposed to 'gradual.'"

"But," jumped in Rose, her driving hand tightening on the wheel amidst all the traffic, "which is it?"

"Rose. Again, this is confidential. I'm afraid that it may be 'abrupt.' The permafrost is going fast."

☆ ☆ ☆

The 2010 Christmas season came and went with great calm. For most Americans, the beginning of winter ended all thoughts about those prior hot droughts and disastrous hurricanes; except, of course, for those hundreds of thousands in the South faced with the grim prospects of rebuilding homes and businesses. The government was finally getting on top of the situation.

In the White House, however, the president and his Chief of staff moved at a hurried pace. Plenty of public appearances during the day touched on all kinds of issues, but in the evening hours after dinner, the two met for extended periods on what they called "The Abrupt Issue." For the president, the imminent threat of experiencing the serious adverse impacts of climate change meant the opportunity to use his impressive skills of persuasion to the common good. He never liked certain political and media personalities either admiringly or sarcastically referring to him as "the Savior." But perhaps now there was a divine calling to become just that—a savior to his people, to lead them away from an impending disaster.

For the Chief of staff, however, the situation meant something else. He had always been a student of history and had expended many hours in the White House library searching in vain to find the true "benevolent" dictator. He thought democracy was too full of constant haggling among the uninformed. It seemed that strong, wise, and intelligent elected leaders who know what is best for the people just could not get enough time in office. They get dragged down by a vocal opposition and by restless, fickle voters.

History had shown the alternative form of government—the central party group led by a strong man—to be inefficient, self-centered, and corrupt. He thought to himself, "If there can be no benevolent dictator found, then what we need is a popular leader with all the right ideas who can be reelected for life—one who can be so good that all political and media opposition would be drowned out." Now with the Savior at the helm and an overriding critical issue at hand, the Chief saw a bright light. The way forward was clear.

"Here's what I have, Mr. President, from all these nightly sessions," said the Chief on a warm evening in March 2011. "Beginning each Monday night, after all the weekend sports and before all the weekday events really get going, you will have a fifteen-minute "chat" with the American people, after their prime-time shows and before they go to bed, touching briefly upon all the important issues of the day, but—"

"I know what you're going to say, Chief. … It's *Bingo* time," interrupted the president.

"Right on! The last five minutes of the fifteen will be devoted to our big issue … and then you will slowly but surely, calmly and confidently, express your vast knowledge about an impending situation related to climate change, a situation that—"

The Savior jumped in again. "A situation that will have dire consequences within the next ten years unless the American people listen to, understand, and follow my plan."

"Yes," said the Chief. "A plan that will be outlined to them in detail between Thanksgiving and Christmas. A plan that will save America!"

"So, Chief, we have thirty of these chats to line up over the next thirty Monday nights. Each one will slowly but surely build a case—no need to panic, my fellow Americans; just understand the predicament we're in and follow my lead."

"Okay," said the Chief. "I'll line up the speech-writing team and get going. But at the same time, we need to converse on a regular basis with the Oracle and Richard Compton to gain their input of what the ultimate—shall I call it the Master Plan?—will be."

"Hmm," mused the Savior. "The Master Plan. Sounds good. I agree. We'll get the country ready to follow and then announce the Master Plan between this coming Thanksgiving and the year-end holidays. Let everyone enjoy the season. Everyone will watch bowl games New Year's Day, and then we commence on January 2, 2012 with the Master Plan."

It seemed as though the two men breathed a sigh of relief simultaneously as the White House lights dimmed for the night.

Chapter Two

Bingo!

Spring 2011

On April 2, 2011, the "chats" began. "My fellow Americans, this chat with you is the first in a weekly series that I hope will allow you the opportunity to know and understand exactly what your president is doing in the office to which you elected him. I will cover all the major issues that you and I pay particular attention to each and every day, and I will also disclose in these fifteen-minute sessions my position on a matter that is critical to all of us in the coming years." Ten minutes later, the president moved forward in his chair and turned quite serious. "Fellow citizens, I wish to close with comments on an issue that is most important to our future welfare. You have all read and heard much about the issue of climate change and what it might mean to our common future. I know that there is some controversy about the potential impacts of climate change—that is, climate change we have called 'global warming'—but one thing is clear: by burning fossil fuels that emit waste products into the atmosphere that then trap heat within our atmosphere, all of us have been accelerating the general trend toward global warming. I am sure you have heard repeated warnings about our global need to reduce these so-called 'greenhouse gases' in order to mitigate the potential impacts of this trend.

"While it no longer seems controversial that Man is greatly accelerating this natural trend, it has not been clear as to how severe the impacts might be and when they might be upon us. To illustrate the complexity, were the tragic events of last summer's hurricanes anomalies, or were they part of an accelerating trend? Over the course of these Monday night sessions in the coming months, I will try to enumerate these potential impacts and make clear to you that we as citizens must soon take greater action. Thank you for tuning in tonight, and I will speak more on this subject at the close of each of my Monday night chats with you. I look forward to addressing you again next week. May God bless America."

The Monday night "chats" went extremely well over the course of the next three months. The Savior was brilliant in his touching upon the global warming issue toward the end of each weekly address. The sessions were warmly received by the American public as they were quite convinced that their president had their best interests at heart. He understood and was on top of all of the key issues of the day, and he was going to continue to be an effective leader in whatever the cause.

"Well done, Mr. President," said the Chief after each of the sessions as springtime progressed. Behind the scenes, the Savior and the Chief were in constant telephone contact with the Oracle and his advisor, Richard Compton. The four eager men established that just after the Fourth of July holiday, a special team would be assembled to provide detailed input into the plan being devised by the president. Until this point, it had only been informally termed "Bingo" among the four and pleasingly referred to as "the Master Plan" by the Chief.

"I have come up with a team," declared the Chief. "Mr. President, it will consist of the four of us plus the expertise of the secretary of the interior, Arthur Schnell; the secretary of energy, Hank Abrams; the top economics professor in the country from the number-one business school in the country, the Wharton School, John Heyward; and H. D. Stewart, the chairman of the Federal Reserve. The expertise of these four gentlemen, in addition to the wisdom of the Oracle and the scientific knowledge of Richard Compton, will allow the eight of us to put all of the final touches on your general plan. I have been astonished that your general thinking has been so distinctive. Your idea sounds so complicated, and yet so simple. If over half of our population live near the coast, and the sea is rising and coming in on us, then we must move everybody back inland. It's quite logical."

"Yes," countered the Savior, "but, you know, I told you months ago, when I said 'Bingo,' that I was simply thinking of moving everyone back from the coasts. Since then I'm thinking—you actually said 'middle.' So why not temporarily move our entire population, except the military, to a central location that makes sense? Why not, say, to Denver, Colorado, where on the plains side of the Rockies we can grow food for everyone and the climate is fairly mild?"

"Wow!" exclaimed the Chief. "Does that sound brilliant or does that sound outlandish? Hmm ... let's get the team together to discuss." Upon deeper reflection, the Chief began to relish the thought. What greater power than to have our benevolent leader put all followers directly under his thumb, in one location? "I think I might like this," mused the Chief.

*　*　*

Coincidental with the first chat to the American public by the president was the arrival of the government funding George Blake was promised for the Santa Barbara desalination project. Michael was already at the plant when he received the text message that the funding was in and that he could begin. He had established a great rapport with officials from the city of Santa Barbara, including its Chief engineer responsible for the mothballed plant. Progress on restarting the plant went smoothly. By the end of June, Michael was ready to begin converting the plant's power source from oil-burning furnaces to his greenhouse-gas-free sources of energy. The wind-powered electrical generators were being moved into positions adjacent to the oil rigs in the Santa Barbara Channel. To supplement the wind-powered sources of energy, a large field of solar-powered electrical panels had been moved into place in just three months at a site ten miles over the mountains in the hot, dry Santa Inez Valley. Wind and solar power efficiently generating electricity to heat ocean water to near boiling in Southern California and replacing an objectionable fossil fuel—how brilliant!

While the electrical lines were being installed from the wind and power source generators to the desalination plant in Santa Barbara, Michael kept reading over and over again the solicitation he had received in the mail to attend an environmental symposium in Seattle, Washington, at the end of July. The topics and speakers looked extremely interesting to Michael since the "hot subject of the day" among environmentalists was how to reduce the costs of wind and solar energy and thereby replace fossil fuel energy in an economic way. Still to be proven, of course, was Michael's theory outlined in his university thesis that he could substantially reduce the costs of energy through the redesign of the electrical turbine generators and the use of a new metal alloy, which would greatly enhance the flow of electricity from the generators to the point of use in a much more efficient and economical way. If any of the speakers at the symposium had come up with anything close to Michael's approach, or perhaps even something to enhance his approach, he had just better know of it.

"George," Michael said into his mobile phone, "it's Michael calling from Santa Barbara. As you know from my weekly reports, everything is going very smoothly up here. We're right on target with our costs and scheduling, so I would like to head up to an environmental meeting in Seattle, July 27 and 28. They will be addressing the costs of wind and solar power energy, and I think I had better be up to date on everyone else's thinking."

With no hesitation at all, George's reply was affirmative: "Of course, Michael, go ahead, and put your travel expenses on our general account rather than the funded desalination project account. Learn all you can, and let me know what's up."

☆　☆　☆

Poor Rose. As the months passed since her astonishing conversation with Jane Stricker, she was in a constant state of mental turmoil. She spent her evenings during the week doing extensive research on one issue: What in heaven's name was going on when it appeared over and over again in all the technical climate reports that the overwhelming opinion of the world's leading scientists working on the climate change issue expressed belief that its adverse impacts would take place gradually over the course of the twenty-first century? And if man acted quickly and prudently, most of the adverse impacts could be greatly mitigated. All scientific references to an "abrupt" change seemed to be hypothetical references only and to be deemed very remote. But then again, a few nonscientists, such as the former senator known as the Oracle, had been dropping public hints that global warming was going to be disastrous in the very near future. And then there was Jane's last comment that she was asked by the UN's IPCC to expedite her research update on the precarious condition of the permafrost. But even so Jane apparently already knew the outcome of her conclusions with data she had already collected. She was simply spending month after month attending to the confirmation of her early findings. And then there were Rose's own findings that the ocean temperatures in the North Atlantic were being recorded at higher numbers than any of her navy colleagues thought might possibly have been the case. It seemed curious that none of her superiors reading her monthly reports had yet responded back to her that her temperature numbers seemed to be surprising. Rose was puzzled ... and concerned.

And then there were the Saturday afternoons and evenings with Adriana. How many times would Adriana say to her bewildered friend,

"Come on, Rose. I keep telling you to stop talking and worrying about all of this global warming stuff. The guys in the office keep saying it's a bunch of crap. We're slowly but surely going to get away from importing foreign oil, and they say that we have enough coal in this country for four hundred years and that they are coming up with ways to clean the coal exhausts so that it will not be a problem. And they say that we're smart enough to adjust. This thing is not like a sudden flood, hurricane, tornado, or earthquake. They tell me global warming takes place very slowly and gradually. What is the big deal, Rose?"

"The big deal, sweetie, is that global warming may just turn out to be more like the flood, hurricane, volcano, or earthquake if it were to take place so quickly that not only my little naval station at the tip, but you and all your boys on Wall Street would soon be up to your knees in seawater."

"Ha! Anyway, why would you think that I would want to know what is going on with all this stuff you're doing? I'm just an administrative assistant to all these fancy bankers. Besides, it sounds as though your technical jazz could just turn out to be in the realm of science fiction. Hey! It's Saturday—let's go out and have a good time."

"Okay, Miss Adriana, I agree. Let's just relax and have fun and see what happens. I hope I find the man of my dreams and fall madly in love."

"*Love* again. Rose, honey, do you know what it is?" Adriana paused and tried to think of a clever answer herself.

Rose quickly answered, "Love is when you look a guy dead in the eyes and know that there is some magic there. Some warm feeling. Your heart flutters and you know in your heart you would do anything for this guy, and him for you. … Have I experienced it? Well, no, sorry to say."

"Yeah, true love. I guess like you, Rose, I'm not quite there yet."

"Well," said Rose, "I guess we're in the same boat—except for one thing. I just feel that sex should equate with love … and true love equate with marriage."

"Wow! That sure is a noble thought in this day and age."

"Listen, who am I to judge the right or wrong of the moral or immoral state of your affairs relating to the opposite sex? Maybe it's just your preference versus my preference. Sure we have argued about politics and abortion and lots of other issues, but our backgrounds are very different … so obviously some of our values may be different. In the final analysis, we like each other and respect each other."

Adriana broke out in a smile. "Enough now," Rose continued. "Who are you fixing me up with tonight, and where are we going? I'm getting very hungry. Let's have a glass of wine and get ready to go to dinner."

The weekend had been great. Dinner at a neat restaurant in the Village with a polite, handsome date. The foursome had a good time. Of course at midnight, Adriana and her date were nowhere to be found. Rose, after being escorted by taxi to her little navy apartment, politely thanked her date and gave him a nice kiss goodnight. Perhaps a future call?

On Sunday, prior to taking the subway up to Central Park to take a leisurely walk, Rose opened Saturday's mail and noticed a flier describing an environmental meeting coming up at the end of the month in Seattle, Washington. Her commanding officer allowed her to attend any type of educational meeting that she cared to attend, so long as the time and cost were reasonable. While Seattle was a six-hour flight from New York, the topics to be covered at this meeting really seemed pertinent to the one big issue that Rose was so completely committed to: the timing and perils of global warming. She jotted down a note to call her commanding officer first thing Monday morning to obtain permission to attend. While all the previous educational meetings she had attended pertained to the subject of the environment, this one described a session dedicated to rising ocean temperatures.

✳   ✳   ✳

The president opened the first meeting of his new advisory group. It was in the Oval Office in late July 2011. "Gentlemen, the eight of us represent a new team, an important one. Anyone who knows we're meeting will have no clue as to what we're up to unless they link the fact that our regular meetings may tie into the last few minutes of my Monday night 'chats' referring to climate change. You have already been privately briefed by Richard Compton on the subject matter. Please, I am requesting that we keep the content of our meeting discussions confidential. We—that is, myself, the senator, and Richard—are firmly convinced that global warming is coming upon us not in a gradual manner, as most scientists believe, but rather, that it is coming quite abruptly. My job is not to create panic but to deliberate and create a Master Plan that will move Americans away from the dangerous impacts outlined in our climate forecast. Do not fall off your seats, gentlemen, but within a few short years, we will have very serious impacts harming over half of our population—those who live along and near coastal areas and those in the arid Southwest. We're going to have flooded cities, impossible conditions, and strong storms along the coast. Remember the last hurricane season in the Southeast, and the severe drought and hot conditions. It was hotter than ever in our Southwest. So we could simply move people to higher ground, or to cooler areas. Move the people of New Orleans up to the mountains of Northern Arkansas; the people of New York to the Adirondacks; the people of Philadelphia to the Appalachians, and so on, but that would be chaotic. How would they live? Instead it is my vision that we have an orderly plan to have our military take charge of all the major cities of the United States in order to preserve order, property, and security while we temporarily move everyone—and I mean everyone—to a sensible location ... and by sensible location, I mean Denver, Colorado." The president paused and slowly gazed around the room.

The Oracle looked on sternly. Richard Compton appeared calm. The Chief of staff looked amused. This all sounded quite incredulous. The Chairman of the Federal Reserve, H. D. Stewart, not only looked puzzled but wondered to himself why in the world he was there. Professor John Heyward looked on quizzically as well. The Secretary of Energy, Hank Abrams, could not wait to hear more as he edged forward in his seat. Arthur Schnell, the Secretary of Interior, understood instinctively that he was going to be a big deal in this mysterious, perhaps preposterous, undertaking.

"Gentlemen." The president started speaking again in his straightforward tone of voice. "Let me outline a role for each of you. Just think, if we are to move nearly three hundred million people to one general location, how much space do we need? What type of housing complexes would we utilize? If we take up the entire eastern half of Colorado, will we still need more space? How would we feed everybody? If we want to stop methane gas from exacerbating an abrupt global warming situation, do we stop all beef production and reproduction, and eliminate the cows? Again, how do we feed everybody? Arthur, that's your task. Hank, if we're not going to burn fossil fuels any more in order to eliminate carbon emissions, how do we provide enough energy for three hundred million people in such a small space? John, how do we disrupt our massive economy and make something temporarily work that is absolutely unprecedented? H., if we close all the local and state banks and people have to suddenly change jobs, how do they get their money? How do they get paid?"

Now the four newcomers edged forward in their seats with their puzzled looks turning to sheer anxiety. The Chief still displayed a slight grin. John Heyward spoke first, "No disrespect, Mr. President, but are you serious?"

The Oracle fielded the question instead, speaking his first words: "Dead serious, John. The coming impacts of global warming are dire. Outside this room, only a few people understand that within ten years we will have an unbelievable catastrophe in this country unless we act immediately. We will share all this data with you. As you leave this meeting, you must keep this information confidential for now."

"Correct." The Chief jumped into the conversation. "You have been listening to the president referring to this subject each Monday night over the last three months. So far we're simply trying to alert the American public that there is a situation out there, that there is a problem out there. The plan is to continue a general disclosure until close to year end when the president will then begin to reveal how he will save our country. The purpose of this group is to provide intelligent inputs to us so that we can formulate a well-thought-out Master Plan that can truly be put into practice at the beginning of next year. And even if it takes ten years to fully implement, we—I mean the president, the Savior—will have rescued the American people from disaster."

What the Chief neglected to say was that in the Oracle's opinion and in Richard's opinion, the Master Plan would be *temporary*, and that in time, as long as the coastal cities were properly protected by the military, people would be able to eventually return to their original homes. That is, they or their descendants. On the other hand, he rather liked the idea that he and the Savior would rule over three hundred million people attached to one city in one location. That's fifteen times the population residing in the high valley of Mexico City. No need for a "benevolent dictator" since saving the populace from sure disaster would be an automatic ticket to lasting adulation, and of course, unlimited power for the "noble leader."

The president took command of the meeting again. "Okay, okay, let's get a working order here. This group will meet every Monday at dinnertime starting the first Monday in August. That way we will not disrupt my regular schedule and create too much speculation by others in the administration or the media. Each one of you will stick with your specialty. Richard, you will continue to provide the technical data on the global warming situation, particularly the rising ocean temperatures, the higher sea levels, changing currents, and of course, the all-important melting of the permafrost. Our renowned former senator from Louisiana, whom we love to call the Oracle, will continue to review the data and all your reports and challenge my thinking and give us his best forecast as to how all this will play out. I tremendously respect his incredible sense of vision.

"Arthur, you'll create a ten-year plan on how we live and eat after you figure out how to get everybody there on an orderly basis. John, you will create the ten-year plan on how the economy functions. H., you will focus on the money supply and how workers and businesses and all others will be paid. My part will be a matter of persuasion and gaining acceptance and of giving hope. Everyone will have to be convinced that the Master Plan needs to be implemented and that it will work to everyone's advantage. I know enough about human nature to feel that while it is nice to say that everyone should love and be nice to everyone else, many of us can also be very competitive by nature. In the final analysis, everyone must act to their own or to their family's own best advantage. I will transform that self-interest to the larger group's advantage—to all Americans collectively. I will make sure that we create, and that I present, a Master Plan that does just that for the advantage of *all* of us here in America.

"If other nations recognize a similar problem, hopefully they will follow our lead. You know, last year, before Congress finally took action on greenhouse gases, the rest of the world still thought we were not doing enough. After all, it's not just *America* warming, it's *global* warming. We will work as closely as we can with the United Nations, and while the Chief and I have moved from what we had called 'the great issue' to 'the Master Plan,' for now, let's just temporarily give it the code name 'Bingo.'"

✻   ✻   ✻

Seattle, Washington, was the perfect place to be in the month of July. Sunny, dry, low humidity, beautiful mountains, perfect seas—the ideal location for an environmental symposium. The title for the meeting was "Progress and Challenges—Our Changing Environment." It was a two-day event with eight sessions scheduled—four of them related to climate change, including one dedicated to the subject of the permafrost. Leading environmental scientists from around the world were scheduled to attend. Of course, Jane Stricker was listed as moderator of the permafrost session; it was her specialty, and the conference was right in her own backyard—Seattle.

Michael flew up in two hours from Santa Barbara on Alaska Airlines. He had reserved a room at the downtown Marriott hotel where the symposium was to be held. Rose arranged a nonstop flight from New

York's Kennedy Airport to Seattle and booked a room at the same hotel. She looked through the advance materials at the names of the prominent scientists who were attending but did not pay too much attention to the others once she saw her friend, Jane Stricker, listed. Excellent. She was to be the moderator of that all-important session—the permafrost. During her flight, Rose wondered over and over in her mind, "What in the world will she say? She has not yet released her report to the UN on the rapid melting of the permafrost, and she asked me to keep her disclosure to me confidential." During his flight, Michael was thinking to himself, "I don't know if I'm going to learn anything new, but I'd better keep an open mind. There will be some pretty smart people there."

The first day's sessions went quite smoothly. There was little controversy. Avid environmentalists were talking to avid environmentalists. The subjects under discussion covered what was already commonly known—the need to slow or stop the reduction of the rainforests in Brazil, which was occurring as a result of increased land clearing for agriculture and bio-fuels; the further tightening of regulations for automobile and factory emissions; the need to be sure no toxic materials leach away from the nation's growing landfills; and so on. Global warming issues were to be covered in the second-day sessions. The cocktail party and socializing at the end of the first-day sessions were to begin at 5:30 PM, with dinner set for seven o'clock, right at the Marriott.

Destiny. It must have been a little past six o'clock when two hands both coincidentally turned and reached out for the same last glass of wine on the waiter's tray.

"Oops, I'm sorry," said Michael. "I didn't see you there."

"Oh, that's all right," replied a startled Rose. "Guess I was so eager for another glass of wine I just went for it—my fault." She giggled with that comment but then turned to look directly at Michael, and that's when it happened. She looked directly into his eyes. He looked deeply into hers. The crowd around pressed them closer. The energy field between their eyes blazed alive in vibrant rapport, and their two bodies were now only inches apart amidst the gathering. The two said nothing for what felt to them an eternity. Awkward, since after all they were both engineers attending the same technical meeting. They must have a lot in common, professionally. Surely they could discuss something!

Michael finally went first. "Hi, I'm Michael … here from Southern California. Chemical engineer. I'm doing some work on water systems."

"Hello, Michael," responded Rose softly, her cheeks getting warmer, her heart beating faster. Was it the wine, or was this the feeling she and Adriana had been trying to describe? "I'm … Rose. … Nice to meet you. Ah, well … I came all the way from the Big Apple; you know—New York. I'm a chemical engineer too. Well, now an atmospheric scientist in the navy; not in uniform obviously," she blushed. "We're very much interested in learning more about the rising air and sea temperatures in the North Atlantic. I'm really looking forward to tomorrow's sessions."

"Oh, sounds interesting. That's great. … Yeah, tomorrow; me too," replied Michael.

"So what exactly is it that brings you here, Michael?"

"Oh … right," Michael paused as he wasn't quite sure what he was talking about as he couldn't take his eyes off of Rose's now glowing face. "Yes, rising temperatures … yeah, right, me too. It's been getting much hotter and drier in the Southwest recently. We have a lot of people living in Southern California and on out to Phoenix, and we are afraid there may just not be enough good water soon. So I'm actually in the middle of leading a project to restart a seawater desalination plant in Santa Barbara, and—"

"Wow, that's cool," interrupted Rose. "What a great thing … like the rich Arabs do in Saudi Arabia, but isn't it incredibly expensive? The Arabs have their oil profits."

"Right, but that's the point. I've been working on some—well, in college I worked on some mechanics and chemistry and electricity, and maybe I've found a way to make it all more efficient. I hope so. That's what I'm in the middle of right now."

Their exchange had been rapid fire until their gazes locked again as a comfortable silence took over. A dozen questions were in the mind of each as their comments and interests had been so compatible. Two professionals with strong interests in the threats of climate change. But something else was going on. Why the long looks in the eyes? Why the quickened pace of two hearts beating? Why the four glowing cheeks?

After what seemed like an eternity but was actually a pleasant interlude, the professional chatter resumed. "Sounds fantastic, Michael. I wish you the best in getting your project accomplished. I guess an engineer follows the tried and true, but it sounds like you have some scientist in you as well, coming up with new ideas and checking it out. What is the time frame for your project looking like?"

Michael must have gone on for fifteen minutes straight explaining the State of California water project he had started with and then the sudden switch to the desalination project, including starting up the plant, getting all the wind and solar equipment in place, adding all his enhancements, running new electrical lines to the plant, working out the details on his novel way of disposing of the highly salty waste brine, the comparative cost expectations, the schedule, and on, and on. Rose listened to every word intently until Michael finally caught himself.

"Hey, I am sorry. I have been selfishly lost in my enthusiasm for my own work. What about your project? What is the navy up to?"

"No need to apologize, Michael. What an exciting and worthwhile project you are working on. ... Uh, well, let's see; where do I start? Are you sure you want to hear this?"

"Absolutely," said Michael. "Please."

"Okay, well, it started while I was earning my master's degree at the Manhattan School of Science and Engineering. I studied atmospheric science, and in all my extensive reading I had this nagging feeling that global warming could turn out to be much worse than anyone imagined. I lost sleep, and then I happened to notice that the navy was advertising for atmospheric scientists to sign up for four-year hitches, and I thought maybe this is my chance." Then Rose went into a long monologue describing what she was doing in the navy and why the navy needed the information. She admitted, however, that with all the experience she was gaining, she was still worried about whether global warming would be coming soon—"abrupt" they called it—or would it be "gradual" as most scientists believed. She was determined to learn as much as she could. She went on to describe to Michael her relationship with Jane Stricker and why she was attending the upcoming session. Michael listened intently. What seemed like only a few minutes together actually turned out to be over an hour. As dinnertime was announced, attendees began to scramble for seats. Michael had arranged to sit with some engineering colleagues he knew from college while Rose had planned to sit next to her friend Jane Stricker.

"Well," said Michael. "This was so fantastic meeting you. I would love to hear more about your work and the navy and perhaps—"

"Michael," Rose interjected, "me too. I would also love to hear more about your project as time goes on. Can I see you after dinner for a moment to give you my e-mail address?"

"Ah, great," Michael said. "I'll see you later."

Although the two sat at dinner tables some thirty feet apart, it was easy to steal glances at each other. Their smiling eyes could not be anything but unintentional flirtations. After dinner Michael could not wait to jump to his feet and approach Rose. She politely introduced Michael to Jane Stricker.

"Nice to meet you, Jane. I just met Rose for the first time before dinner. She told me so much about you and your work. I am really looking forward to your session tomorrow."

"Well, thank you, Michael. It also happens that during dinner Rose mentioned your project in Santa Barbara. What a great advantage it would be to arrive at a more economical way to desalinate ocean water. A super project, Michael. Good luck."

Then came an awkward moment for Rose. She did not know whether to say good night to her friend Jane or to continue their earlier conversations. Sensing her hesitation, Michael interjected.

"Rose, here, let me write down my e-mail address, and if you'd kindly let me have yours—or better yet, here's my card with my address, phone number, and e-mail address. Please keep me informed of your project."

"Yes, okay, Michael that's a good idea. Let me find my card and then I'll do the same." They seemed so preoccupied with exchanging cards that they didn't stop to think they would both be in Jane's session the next morning.

*   *   *

With this new acquaintance on his mind, Michael looked in vain for Rose at the breakfast tables in the ballroom next to the conference rooms. "Hmm … I guess she doesn't eat breakfast," he thought to himself. As it turned out, Rose had gone down earlier so that she could get back to her room and catch up on some phone calls to the East Coast where it was three hours later in the morning. As a healthy, balanced woman, she never skipped a good breakfast.

Moderating the 10:30 AM session on the subject of rising ocean temperatures and melting permafrost, Jane Stricker played it right down the middle. She made sure all the panelists had the opportunity to fully finish their presentations and answer questions, but never did she challenge the presenters or inject her findings that the rising air temperatures and rising ocean temperatures were helping to melt the permafrost at a rate far beyond what was previously thought. She was communicating that sensitive information directly to only Richard Compton, and she was holding back publicly until her final report was issued to the IPCC.

As Jane's session ended, it was now Rose's turn to rise quickly and approach Michael. She had sighted him taking his seat when Jane's session started. "Hello again, Michael, I just thought ... uh ..." She wanted to ask him to have lunch with her since she was thinking she would probably never see him again, but she could not get the words out. She just could not take her eyes away from his, and like last evening, she again felt her heart fluttering. Returning her gaze, Michael quickly blurted out, "Rose! Hi! Can we have lunch together?"

"Yes! I would like that," she enthusiastically replied.

During lunch, however, with eight persons around a table all talking loudly and 150 people in the room talking at once, Michael and Rose just could not say what they really wanted to say, which was, "Where do you live? What do you do in your free time? How about your family? You're not married, are you? Are you in a committed relationship?" No engagement or wedding rings were worn, but one never knows. As they prepared to head to the next and last afternoon session, Michael turned to Rose, hesitated, but then said, "Look, Rose, ah ... I'm heading out at four to catch a six o'clock nonstop flight from Seattle to Santa Barbara. When do you leave for New York?"

Rose felt a surge of excitement but then disappointment. He would be leaving before the end of the symposium, and she probably would never see him again. Rose responded to his question, saying ruefully, "Well, I'm staying one more night in beautiful Seattle, which I haven't even really seen yet. I'm flying out at nine tomorrow morning."

"Oh," Michael responded. "Well, I know there's a late flight to Los Angeles at ten tonight. I could cancel my six o'clock flight and then stay with my parents tonight in Santa Monica, near the LA Airport. Rose, if I did that, would you like to do some sightseeing and have dinner together this evening?"

Rose's feelings of disappointment evaporated. She again felt a surge of excitement. Her answer was immediate and seemingly automatic: "Great, great; that would be great."

"Well," said an elated Michael. "I'll check it out. Hopefully I can change flights. I'll see you at the coffee break at three."

With that, Rose felt as though on a cloud as Michael quickly disappeared.

✿　✿　✿

That evening there was no doubt—he thought it was the best of his life. Michael knew it simply because he could feel it. Strange, since he always thought as an engineer, a scientist. How could he figure this out? He had learned back in college from a friend who was going to be a neuroscientist that our five senses, whether touch, smell, sound, taste, or sight, create electrochemical signals that first put our emotional system into action—the familiar "fight or flight" theory. Now he was pondering. In humans, those signals subsequently go to the front part of the human brain—the prefrontal cortex—which is larger and more developed than in other mammals. It is in that region where we reflect and think, but then most of the time those messages head back to the emotional system located in the middle of our brain. Our resultant behavior simply ends up following a mix of those emotional feelings and those rational thoughts. But right now, his emotions were fully in charge—and it was not too difficult to imagine that Rose was experiencing identical feelings and thoughts.

Drinks at an outdoor bar along the sparkling water, dinner upstairs with a perfect view of the harbor; a beautiful couple. It was a perfect setting. On a July evening in the Northwest, it seemed that twilight never ended. Yet, as nine o'clock approached, "reason" half returned. Michael started looking nervously at his watch. *I never want this night to end*, he thought to himself. I had better grab a taxi fast and get to the airport quickly in order to catch the ten o'clock flight. Should I stay over and go back tomorrow? He questioned himself again and again. Normally a clear-thinking engineer, suddenly his mind was in a cluttered state of turmoil. What part of his brain was in charge? She might think it is much too bold if I tried to stay over, and where would I stay? Certainly I would not try to stay with her; or would I? I know that this is supposed to be a professional situation, yet I have these feelings that I have never experienced before. His mind raced. Again, the nervous glance at his watch. It was now one minute before nine. Time was running out. Then …

"Rose, it's been so great being with you that I've lost track of time. I'd better hustle and get out to the airport."

"Oh, my gosh … I lost track of time too. Michael, I am so sorry." They both jumped up from the table and again looked into each other's eyes. It was the moment of truth. Does he run for the taxi? Does he kiss her goodbye? Does he offer to stay overnight? Does she say, please stay? Did she tell him how much she enjoys *him* or should she just say how much she enjoyed talking about their environmental projects? What were these feelings she was having? Alas, the responsible engineer and the rational scientist prevailed. The inhibiting, deep thinking part of his brain won. And so too for hers.

"Well, Rose, this has been fabulous. It was so great meeting you. I've learned so much, and I'm so glad I came to this meeting."

"Me too, Michael. I've had a great time. I wish you the best. You'd better run," she said, knowing that was really the last thing she wanted to say. After shaking hands warmly and a last look deep into each other's eyes, he was gone.

❊   ❊   ❊

The flight back to Santa Barbara was smooth except for what was going on in Michael's mind. *What just happened?* he kept thinking to himself. *Climate change, sure. It is happening faster than we had thought. My project is ever more important. But that girl ... beautiful.* He imagined that he had kissed her goodbye. He imagined that she kissed him back and that the embrace lasted for minutes. New York, California. *This could never work,* he thought. *How? When could I ever see her again?* Upon landing, he turned on his cell phone, pulled Rose's card from his pocket, and hastily typed the text message "It was great meeting you, Rose. Have a safe trip home." To his pleasant surprise a text message came right back to him. She must have left her phone on before going to sleep, but yet she was still awake. The return message read, "Thanks. It was nice meeting you too; take care." Michael thought to himself *Okay; it's okay.* He felt good all over.

Rose had tried to get to sleep by eleven. She had to get up at six to catch the flight back to New York. But she tossed and turned. She could not fall asleep. She had left her phone on as a backup alarm and when she heard the ping for a message received at 12:30 AM, she jumped up, turned on the light, and felt a rush of excitement as she read Michael's message. As she turned off the light and snuggled again into her pillow and covers she thought to herself, *Okay; it's okay.* She felt good all over.

❊   ❊   ❊

"What am I doing here?" Arthur Schnell said to himself on a warm Sunday night in early August in Washington, DC. He laughed to himself and thought, "It's vacation time and I should be on my cool ranch in Montana right now, but ..." his mind went blank. Consternation. Arthur was a strong environmentalist. After a distinguished career in educational administration and a former presidency of the Sierra Club, he had been tapped by the new president in early 2009 to become secretary of the interior. "Piece of cake—right up my alley," he had thought. But now he was sweating over a long list of questions he had jotted down on his notepad. He was preparing for tomorrow night's dinner meeting with the president to review all the items that were to be covered if he was going to satisfy the president's impossible, improbable plan to move all of our population to Denver, Colorado, within the next ten years.

His notes read, "How would we secure everyone's homes and businesses that would need to be vacated? Schools we can close and reopen, but what do we do with hospitals, nursing homes? Bus and rail systems, we could mothball." He remembered that Richard Compton gave strict instructions "not to worry about the economics; concentrate on how we leave everything in place and have the military protect everything, move three hundred million people, eliminate the burning of any fossil fuels, eliminate meat production, and eat only fish that would be grown on fish farms." Arthur continued jotting down on his notepad, "Mobile homes, high-rise condos, townhouses, all of them in Eastern Colorado and maybe the southwestern corner of Nebraska and the northwestern quarter of Kansas—everybody must fit. All electric cars, only electric power plants sourced from nuclear, solar, and wind.

"Denver—perfect location, mild climate, lots of sun, strong winds along the ridge of the mountains to the plains as a result of temperature and pressure differentials, sufficient grain protein from corn, wheat, and soybeans grown nearby. Housing—feasible. Food—feasible. Keep present fish farms open along the coast even with rising sea levels; transport mature fish to New York and fly them into Denver. Keep the vegetable farms in California open if a water source can be found. Use the snow melts from the Rockies for drinking water until ..." Arthur Schnell was finding answers until this one. The aquifers in the Midwest and local rainfalls could irrigate the crops for a while, but "how do we provide drinking water and domestic water for three hundred million people located within sixty thousand square miles?" Arthur reviewed his scratched notes over and over and pondered this last question long into the evening. Dare he mention it to the president at dinner tomorrow? Before falling asleep, a revelation came to him. He remembered a summary of a report written by a young engineer who thought he had a way to desalinate seawater in a much more efficient way than current technology. His theory had come to the

Department of the Interior a couple of years ago and had circulated widely among senior staff. He vaguely recalled that some government funding was going to take place to test the young engineer's ideas. Arthur found comfort in these thoughts and fell asleep much more peacefully than he ever thought he would. Perhaps the improbable could be transformed into being feasible.

✻   ✻   ✻

Hank Abrams faced a similar situation. Coming into Washington from his summer home in the quiet Chesapeake Bay seaside town of Saint Michael's on an early Sunday afternoon in August was no treat. He much preferred enjoying his family's Sunday evening dinners by the water and commuting back to DC early Monday morning. He went directly to his office at the Department of Energy, arriving by 3:00 PM. He was alone, but at least his office was air conditioned. How could he prepare for tomorrow evening's dinner with this new team appointed by the president to accomplish the impossible? Eighty percent of the nation's energy is produced by burning fossil fuels; coal-fired electric plants, gasoline-powered cars and trucks, and gas-fired industrial boilers. "Change all that in ten years?" he repeated to himself over and over again. His mind raced. "How could we eliminate the burning of fossil fuels in this, the greatest industrial nation in the world, within ten years?" Well, at least the economics is not for him to think about, he mused. That will be John Heyward's problem.

For Hank, the challenge was to come up with a practical way to have three hundred million people located in the Denver, Colorado, area become dependent on their energy requirements from sources other than oil and coal. Even producing corn to burn ethanol would be out since that technology also releases CO_2 into the atmosphere. That leaves nuclear plants to produce electricity—quite safe but not a popular choice with the public. Always that fear of the invisible. Then hydroelectric plants, but they require a great deal of water flow—not something to be found near the Denver area. So we turn to the hype of wind and solar. Certainly a lot of case studies had been performed about placing electric turbines on wind propellers along the coasts—not feasible, for the electricity would have to be transported too far and the oceans will be in turmoil with global warming. Local wind power—that may be it. The mountains of the Rockies reaching top peaks of fourteen thousand feet compared to the plains east of Denver at five thousand feet create a pressure differential and a temperature differential that combine to produce high and steady winds. That can be feasible.

Solar power—that could also be feasible. The hotter and drier Southwest could provide a home for hundreds of thousands of new solar panels that could produce plenty of electrical power that could be transmitted in new high-voltage lines built through passes of the Rockies over to the plains. The Denver area also has plenty of sunshine on an annual basis so that every home, office building, and business location can have solar panels on their roofs for generation of electricity. Also, since the climate in the Denver area is generally mild, that form of electrical generation to produce home heat could be conserved by limiting usage to early mornings and evenings. In the summer months, there is enough fresh air of low humidity that a great deal of power would not be required for occasional air-conditioning needs. Perhaps this is feasible after all!

Almost out loud Hank said the words, "Hmm, I wonder how the president came up with Denver in his plan? He's not a scientist. He's not an engineer. He is a politician. Is he that brilliant?" Hank continued to scratch out his notes. "Utilities—what to do with the existing enormously complex electric power grid spread throughout the United States? Oil and coal plants—moth ball or continue the development of technologies that remove carbon from their smokestacks? But no foreign oil. If we're not going to use gasoline in our cars and trucks, let's just eliminate oil altogether. Coal—workers working underground is just no longer an occupation for Americans. Too unhealthy; coal mining underground is out, but strip mining is okay. Keep open using carbon removal at the end of the burning process in coal-fired electric plants where transmission lines can efficiently reach the Denver area. "

Hank's now voluminous notes were scattered all over his desk. The realm of possibilities seemed endless, but he felt energized. He was thinking about things he had never imagined before. Normal dinnertime came and went and not a pang of hunger.

"Transportation—electric cars, buses, trucks, and trains—we can do it. We could keep the ports of New York and San Francisco open to import efficient, low-cost electric cars from Europe and Asia until we can make enough ourselves. The military could supervise those ports. We would have to provide housing and sufficient food supplies for the military and the civilians working there under their control. It looks like the military will have a big role to play. If the sea levels rise too much and those ports are no longer operable, we will have to stop importing and more quickly establish factories in or around the model city that can produce these modes of transportation. But metal and plastic production? We could establish assembly plants, but where would the basic metals and plastics be produced if we shut down production plants in coastal areas?" Hank noted that this last question would be for John Heyward—that is "economics."

By 10:00 PM Hank finally turned off the lights in his office and slowly headed to his Arlington, Virginia, apartment. He felt somewhat satisfied that what started out to be an impossible task perhaps may have some ways of producing realistic results. The cost of making such radical changes in such a short period of time may be out of the question, but again that would be Arthur's, John's, and H.'s worries. As he turned off the light by his bedside at 11:00 PM, Hank stared into the darkness for nearly two hours before falling asleep. His mind raced with what seemed like a million thoughts. Crazy, he thought, but wonderful.

✻　✻　✻

John Heyward's train from Philadelphia arrived at Union Station at 2:00 PM Monday. He checked into the downtown Marriott Hotel, sat down at the desk, and started preparing his notes for the 6:00 PM dinner meeting with the president and the so-called "Bingo" project.

He had been so perturbed the last week over what had been requested of him. He had studied and taught economics his entire career. At seventy years of age, he should be retiring and spending his time with travel and grandchildren. But now he has been asked by none other than the president of the United States to think about and come up with solutions to a situation that has no precedent in economic history. Until now, he had written nothing down. Nothing in his mind made any sense. The notepad on his hotel desk so far only had the time, the date, the subject, and the number "one." By 5:00 PM his notes read nothing more. He simply could not conceive of a feasible economy being built by attempting to transform a two-hundred-year-old functioning economy spread 3,000 miles wide by over 1,000 miles long and moving it to an area only 250 miles wide by 250 miles long. As he pushed the elevator button and waited for the ride to the lobby to take the short taxi ride to the White House portal, he asked himself, "What in the world am I going to say?" As he stepped out of the taxi that had been screened at the White House gate, he was greeted by a staff assistant to the president. Trying to feel important in such surroundings, he calmly kept repeating to himself, "Only if this is temporary; only if this is temporary."

✺   ✺   ✺

For H. D. Stewart, the position of being chairman of the Federal Reserve Board was easy. With the economy now humming along, fully recovered from the 2008–2009 recession, his job was simply to read the weekly economic reports to ascertain whether prices were climbing, and if so to raise the Federal Reserve interest rates to its member banks in order to dampen the prospects of inflation. Since the economy was growing nicely, he did not even have to think about the other side of the coin, which meant lowering interest rates to encourage economic activity.

He had not come back to Washington early from his summer home at the Hamptons in Long Island, New York. He thought that his contribution into this one really crazy scheme would only come at the end of everyone else's input. And he was certain by that time that the president's plan of centralizing America would be overwhelmingly rejected by the new team. Therefore, he would not have to provide any input. Surely there were more down-to-earth solutions to the handling of higher temperatures inland and higher sea levels along the coasts than disrupting everyone's lives with a hare-brained directive from the government. Certainly H. had been selected for his lofty position because he was socially progressive with strong fundamentals of banking responsibility. He had been president of a profitable, community-involved bank in Montclair, New Jersey, for over twenty years. He was open to tight regulations being imposed by the state and federal governments. Despite the extensive reporting requirements and a wide number of social programs financed by the bank, he ran a tight ship and showed nice profits that were rewarding to the bank's public shareholders. He had been appointed president of the New York Federal Reserve Bank prior to his appointment as chairman of the parent Federal Reserve Board in Washington. He was a responsible, model citizen.

Although feeling quite honored as he made his way to the dinner meeting at the White House Monday evening, he also felt relaxed and at ease. Just the formalities of entering the White House can appear as overwhelming, but H. moved swiftly and confidently with his escort to the dining room. He enjoyed all the baseball talk during dinner and figured that the serious talk would quickly turn from the preposterous to the practical. How wrong he would be!

✺   ✺   ✺

A wonderful salad and then perfect, medium-rare filet mignon surrounded by grilled asparagus and cherry tomatoes, finished with vanilla ice cream topped with fresh raspberries; lots of talk about the current baseball season and the poor Washington Nationals in last place; certainly an enjoyable dinner in a beautiful atmosphere. But the pleasantries went fast. The dishes were cleared. Bottles of brandy, port, and sherry were spread on the table along with three pots of coffee. It was now 7:00 PM, and in another three hours the president was due for his popular televised fifteen-minute "chat" with the American public. His presentation had been well prepared and well rehearsed that afternoon. He could spend at least two hours now with his new team discussing the all-important "Bingo" project—surely the most significant since the secret 1944 "Manhattan" project designed to produce an atomic bomb that could provide a means for ending World War II. A simplistic name—"Bingo"—but it means, "I suddenly have a winner," and that's what the Oracle and the Savior both thought.

As the president politely called for the group's attention, the room turned completely silent. "Let me start by saying to all of you—the newcomers to the team, Arthur, Hank, John, and H.—that you have probably been in a state of disbelief this past week. Let me begin by telling you to relax; we're not going to come up with answers tonight or next week or next month. This is just the beginning of our thoughts and ideas. Again, the targeted date for producing a Master Plan is at year end. Let me count. ... We have twenty meetings before then to coalesce our ideas into a plan—yes, the Master Plan. This is certainly going to take quite a bit of innovative thinking on our part. I'm the politician. Ninety percent of politics is perception. I have the PR machine. Listen, the Chief here even calls me the 'Savior.' Don't worry about having the American public accept something they might initially think sounds preposterous. I believe that my challenge will only be the last 10 percent of skeptics and the last 10 percent of those out there who never liked me or my politics or my ideology. That's my challenge.

"But the reason you have been chosen is that your backgrounds are so impressive that I have confidence that you will come up with detailed parts of the plan that are practical and feasible." He gazed around the room, trying to judge whether there was any comprehension to be read in the eyes of the new members of the team. He saw nods from the heads of Arthur and Hank but looks of concern on the faces of John and H. Sensing and understanding that, the president spoke, "John, H., do you have any initial questions before we go around the room? My plan tonight is to list all the issues that we should put out on the table; not answers, just a list of issues from each one of you so that we have an orderly path forward toward finding the right answers."

"Sir!" John said forcefully and then coughed and said, "Mr. President, I must admit that in thinking about all of this over the last week, I have no organized way of attacking the problem unless I ask you this question first."

"Sure" said the president. "Shoot."

"Okay." John proceeded to speak in a strong, clear voice. "The idea that you have expressed is so complex, so unprecedented, that I must ask you … is this truly a temporary situation? That is, in time either global warming will reverse itself or we will have so adapted that we can go back to a more normal economic society—I mean, utilizing the entire United States." He paused and then looked down, almost embarrassed that he had interjected such short-ranged thinking. Everyone except the Chief looked directly at the Savior for his response and waited. The Chief squirmed in his seat and looked away. Deep in his mind was always the thought that since all the "saving America" talk began, this "moving" idea was not a temporary solution. This was the dawn of a New America; a new political system; a new economic system; a new social system; and, the birth of a new ideology. He almost blurted out loud at that moment, "We control everything!" Thoughts of "free men" and "the pursuit of happiness" never entered his mind. At the same time, H. Stewart was privately thinking the opposite—that this was the beginning of the whole fantasy falling apart.

The cool demeanor of the president was obvious. He calmly looked directly at John and issued his answer with the utmost sincerity in his voice: "John, a good question. My intentions are to do the best for the welfare of all Americans. Certainly we would take all measures to preserve our incredible infrastructure of roads, housing, factories, schools, hospitals, and office buildings throughout the land. Not even Richard here can promise when global warming will begin to reverse itself or when our efforts to diminish it will completely take hold. … But yes, certainly we should view the implementation of our Master Plan as temporary. I will present it that way and promise all Americans that their lives and the lives of their children and grandchildren will return to normal as soon as possible." Everyone was sitting back now, feeling somewhat reassured, except a still skeptical H.

"Thank you, Mr. President," John said. "That makes me feel better. Economically, the costs of anything close to the plan you envision would be so high that we would need a brand-new economic system and banking system to accommodate anything other than a very short-term temporary relocation."

Now it was Richard who jumped in and began to speak. "Gentlemen, as the technical representative in this group, I confirm again the seriousness of our situation. We must take very, very drastic measures. I can assure you of that from a technical standpoint, and as the Oracle has not missed a forecast yet, we must find a practical way to create and implement the Master Plan. I can also assure you that from a technical point of view we can eliminate the burning of all fossil fuels in a short period of time."

It was the Oracle's turn to jump in and expound. "I agree that everything we are talking about is technically correct and technically feasible. Gentlemen, time is of the essence. This is urgent. We have to find a way to put the solution into play as quickly and as practically as possible. I dislike being the bearer of bad news, but in my honest opinion, the word 'temporary' should not be in our private jargon—only for the public when they first learn."

The president sat back in his chair now. He was beginning to enjoy the interplay now taking place among his team members. John Heyward lost the better feeling he had enjoyed a moment ago. Arthur chimed in, "Ah ... I have a long list of issues here for us to review as a start. But as I am thinking about it, I concur. I believe that having all of our population in Eastern Colorado, having enough food and housing ... you know, gentlemen, that I think it can be done. I think it is feasible. My biggest issue will be water supply, but I'm working on that right away."

Hank added a resounding, "Yes, and I also have been thinking that it can be accomplished—we can provide enough energy into that section of the country. Lots of hurdles, lots of issues to be worked out ... but I think it is feasible."

What other description could fit the faces of the two team members on the economic side other than looks of astonishment. John Heyward had come to the meeting room with no notes, and H. D. Stewart had come to the meeting with not the slightest doubt that this fantasy bordered on the fanatical. Now the two were hearing that the other six are serious about this. And so their meeting progressed with Arthur Schnell, the secretary of the interior of the United States of America, and Hank Abrams, the secretary of energy of the United States of America, reviewing for the group in deadly seriousness all the issues that they were going to tackle. No outside parties were in the room. It was assigned to the Chief to take notes, have them recorded by his secretary under an oath of strict confidence, and hand deliver meeting minutes to each of the eight members of the team. That was the protocol established and to be followed for the next five months.

As the time approached 9:00 PM, the Savior knew he had to end the meeting. Yet there had been no input from John Heyward nor H. D. Stewart.

"John, H.," the president stated. "I know this is not typical analysis for you. Populations have moved historically to find food and energy, but not to find a new banking system. They may have moved to find better economic systems for them to thrive in … but to one that has never yet been created? Please try your best." He looked at them appealingly, and his eyes appeared to be begging. He tried not to reveal his private thoughts—that beyond the unknown issue of water, the economic side could be by far the weakest part of his "Bingo."

Chapter Three

Feasible

Summer 2011

The day after that incredible meeting at the White House, John Heyward's first telephone call of the morning was from a rather frantic banker, now the head of the Federal Reserve. Of course, it was H. Stewart, calling from his office in Washington.

"John, I still can't believe what I heard last night. Can we meet as soon as possible?"

"H., well, I'm back home in Philadelphia, and my calendar is really tight this week. But … you know, I'm also really concerned about what went on last night. They're serious about this."

"John, are you free this weekend? Can you get up here to my home in the Hamptons?"

"Well, let me see … yes, I think so, H.," replied John. "They all seem so sure of everything, but how can we possibly make any sense of this economically?"

"Right," said H. "I think this is all a bit of fantasy, but it sounds like we have to come up with something."

"Yeah. I did think of a few things while on the train last night. It was late and I was tired—the perfect time to dream about the impossible. Okay, tell me where, and what time, and I will be there."

"Thanks, John. That will be great. My wife is away this weekend … but you're welcome to bring your wife along. We have a nice pool, and we're only a block from the beach."

"Okay, yes, I'll ask her. Thanks," said John.

Four days later, after a long five-hour drive from Philadelphia, John and his wife, Helen, arrived at H.'s home in the Hamptons. It was a beautiful property, especially at the height of the summer season. John and Helen wished that this could simply be a relaxing summer getaway, but after a pleasant lunch on the patio, H. turned serious and was ready to talk. Helen got the hint and conveniently disappeared toward the beach. Pouring more iced tea for them both, H. got right into it.

"What the heck are we supposed to do? I've thought about it. If this is a fantasy being acted out by the president of the United States, then let's create a fantasy economy. Let's concede that the nation is facing a true catastrophe if no action is taken. I always thought that any bad effects of global warming would come on slowly and that we would have plenty of time to react. But if they're right … okay then; let's concede that point. Can you imagine what it would cost to move virtually everyone within a few short years to a centralized location? What would they do for work, John?" H. studied John's face and searched for a serious reaction from the famed economist.

To the contrary, John's quiet, somber demeanor suddenly turned into roaring laughter. "H., I'm with you. This is crazy from an economic point of view. How in the world would we finance everyone basically quitting their jobs and moving to Denver? Our economy would die. What are they thinking?"

After a long silence, their conversation continued. "Okay, let's play their game," John went on. "Let's assume that everything they said from a technical point of view is 100 percent correct. Let's then assume that the president is so gifted that he first convinces everyone that we are facing an imminent threat of disastrous proportions, and secondly he convinces everyone that he has a plan to save the day, and thirdly that his plan, most importantly, is feasible … and last but not least, he convinces everyone to follow it!" John again succumbed to loud laughter before turning serious. H. did not see the humor. "You and I know that the outline of the plan that we have been listening to makes no economic sense, So H., let's create our own myth and sell it as the truth. …"

And so it began.

✽   ✽   ✽

Michael's progress in Santa Barbara continued unabated. Going into the second week in August, Michael reviewed all his prior notes over and over again:

- Review the project with plant personnel who have been rehired from its brief operation over fifteen years ago.

- Train new personnel as to the plant's operation.

- Achieve optimum results of removing salt from Pacific Ocean feed stock using Michael's special distillation process and compare to the prior reverse-osmosis process.

- Provide an adequate fuel supply until such time as the plant can be converted over to Michael's new energy sources.

- Transport the waste brine to holding ponds down the coast until Michael's new disposal method can be set in place.

- Have the upgraded windmills securely set in place outside the Santa Barbara Channel.

- Lay the electric transmission lines under water, secure to the plant, and meet all electrical safety standards.

- Set all the required solar panels in their proper positions in the hot, sunny valley over the mountains.

- Run and test all the transmission lines to meet safety standards.

Michael was gratified that all the needed equipment had been ordered and delivered expeditiously. The project funds were timely. He was on schedule. His plan was to accomplish the setup in a year and half and then utilize six months operating time to collect data and prove expected results. That would take the project out to the spring of 2013. Michael had been so excited about the project that he never once thought that his ideas were patentable. If it all worked as he had thought, he could end up a billionaire. George Blake had never given that aspect a thought either. This was pure engineering for the benefit of humanity.

But that was the daytime. Each evening, without fail, Michael's attention turned to another matter. He could not stop thinking about Rose. She was so different from all the girls he had dated. They were all very nice. He always had a good time. But he had never felt the warmth that had enveloped his entire body and soul as he had during his brief encounters with Rose. It was a feeling of yearning, wanting to be with her. Could this be something special? Could she be something special? Where would it go from here? He is busy. She is busy. They are three thousand miles apart. It could be a long time for another environmental symposium to take place where they might meet again. He thought to himself late one evening, "Why not at least have her as a special friend?" So Michael opened his cell phone, pressed the text message icon, and typed in a message for Rose. "Thinking about you in New York. Are you under water yet? Ha! All going well here with my project." Michael completely forgot, after waiting impatiently for a possible response, that in New York it was three hours later. He then realized that at 1:00 AM in the morning Rose was probably asleep with her phone off.

✳   ✳   ✳

As soon as Michael's alarm sounded at 6:00 the next morning, he quickly shut it off and hurriedly reached for his phone. He was elated to see Rose's response. "Hi. Yes, we are completely under water here, but luckily I have my navy boat! Ha, Ha! Send e-mail & tell me how your project is progressing."

Rose's routine kept her very busy. Up early, quick breakfast, hurried workout, and fast walk to the dock to check her vessel. It was a rather odd-looking boat—short and squatty and, of course, painted navy gray with black identification letters. Secured to the stern was the American flag along with a dark blue flag flying underneath. Its big bold letters in bright gold read, "NAVY." Rose never knew whether that was an official flag of the U.S. Navy or was borrowed from an Army/Navy football game. She dare not ask. With a wide array of exotic equipment both on deck and below, it was obvious that this strange-looking craft was a research vessel. On weekdays they left from the dock quite early, charted to reach different areas in the vast North Atlantic Ocean. The crew's mission was to record a wide variety of measurements. Sometimes they were at sea for three or four days, sleeping in tight quarters. The sailing crew was only four in number, while the research team numbered six. Each member of the research team had a different task. Rose's job was to measure air and water temperatures as well as wind velocities and directions at each fifteen-minute interval while recording exact longitude and latitude readings. Her recording chart indicated the date and time of day. One might think that this job would be a bit boring other than on those days when the seas were rough or the air quite cold. Although the information attained was sketchy, Rose had already done considerable research on what these temperature measurements were over the course of the last thirty years.

She was perplexed to learn that her measurements over the last two years appeared to be significantly higher than measurements recorded just ten years before. Those measurements ten years ago had only been slightly higher than measurements twenty years prior. But now, everything was accelerating rapidly.

After her prolonged conversations with Jane Stricker at the environmental symposium in Seattle, Rose was now convinced of her prior suspicions that global warming was occurring at a much faster rate than the consensus opinion. Of course, this information would be very important to the U.S. Navy because of its extensive bases along the coasts of the United States. Rose felt a strong sense of commitment to her job because she knew that her reports were going to be very pertinent to future decisions made by the Department of Defense. On the other hand, she was beginning to feel quite helpless in that she was in no position to find a solution to the imminent threat. She felt like a small pebble in a big pond. At least her new acquaintance, Michael, was doing some real service by helping the arid Southwest develop an additional source of drinking and irrigation water. Thank goodness she had Adriana on weekends to take her mind away from these weighty matters. Even so, not a night went by that Rose didn't have thoughts about Michael—that cool guy she met in Seattle. And while Saturday afternoons and evenings were fun with the dates Adriana fixed up for her, she just could not seem to experience the heart throbs she had felt during those brief encounters with Michael.

On September 1, she finally received that first e-mail that she had requested from Michael. Disappointingly it read like a professional engineering report describing Michael's project in Santa Barbara. The only personal words mentioned were in the opening: "Hi Rose, How are you? I wish I could tell you all of this in person." And then the closing: "Take care of yourself. I wish another environmental symposium could be on our calendars soon! Best regards. Your friend, Michael."

With that, Rose laughed out loud and said to herself, "Well at least we've established that we're friends." Then she realized in thinking about him so much over the past four weeks since they had met that maybe it is not the best idea to strike up just an e-mail relationship. "I must already have regular e-mail correspondence with over fifty people," she thought. "Somehow, I just think this guy is something special. Do I have the nerve to call him?" She felt that impulse was a good idea. Maybe on Saturday at noon before teaming up with Adriana. It would be 9:00 AM his time and might be a good time to catch him. "Maybe I could just say 'good morning' to him," she thought out loud.

On the other side of the continent, Michael was thinking to himself: "I hope she answers my e-mail. She had asked me to keep her up to date with my project. I wonder if the 'friend' bit was a little too corny." Nothing arrived for a few days, but then Friday evening—it must have been close to midnight in New York—he heard the message ping on his cell phone. He opened it, and much to his chagrin, it read "DesalPlant" in the "Subject" space and simply "Hi friend, good work, regards, Rose" in the message space. Reaching for a glass of wine and swallowing a big sip, Michael thought to himself, "I know text messaging is very brief and e-mail messaging is not too flowery compared to the old practice of letter writing, but I had sure hoped for more." Little did he know that Rose was teasing with her short message and planned to call him the next morning.

✻   ✻   ✻

By early September, the president had already given twenty of his brief Monday night chats. As a public relations effort, they had been well received by the general electorate. The president was doing a good job communicating. The country was rolling along, other than in the Southeast where tens of thousands of citizens were still recovering from those disastrous hurricanes and in the Southwest where hot, drought conditions persisted. When the president alluded to climate change in the last few minutes of his Monday evening chats, the thought of how much turmoil those hurricanes caused a year ago made it easy for him to get his point across. Unless everyone pulled together, global warming would become a more serious issue. Of course, so far the president had not yet tried to describe those impacts in detail or outline how severe they might be or when they will arrive in full force. His official policy dated back to a document released by his administration in June 2009. Its theme was one of possible dire consequences over the course of the century, but it left much hope that as long as carbon emissions were substantially reduced, global warming impacts would be quite moderate. The president was adept at raising the issue and keeping it in the forefront yet not creating alarm.

"It's early September, Mr. President," said the Chief. "I think we are right on target, sir. You have cast an umbrella over our big issue, and it is creating the aura of concern that we wanted, but certainly no panic. I really think we can get this plan together within the next three months and be ready to go by the start of next year."

"Chief," the Savior responded calmly. "Uh … I guess I have to agree with you, but I do feel very uneasy. Certainly there are no historical precedents for what we plan to do. I trust I will have confidence in the plan that the team comes up with and enough confidence in myself. But … you know."

"Yeah … but don't worry. You will pull it off. You're the best ever. Maybe you don't realize it, but you appear to exude an air of superiority, and yet at the same time you can easily relate to the common man. That's a great combination, and Mr. President, your oratorical skills are so great that you really should have the utmost confidence. I know you are telling the team that you are completely confident in selling the public, but privately, between the two of us, you must gain the confidence that you can really do it." In the quiet that followed, the two men's eyes wandered around the Oval Office, their sparkling minds not sharing their private thoughts. The Chief was thinking to himself, "Oh no, he'd better think that he can pull this off. He has to believe it, not just say he believes it. This is going to be my dream come true." The president was thinking to himself, "The Chief is right. I can do it. I know I can do it."

"Chief, how about arranging lunch this Friday with the senator and Richard? We need more of their private input before the team gets together next Monday. I know that John and H. have really seemed to come around the last couple of weeks, but my sixth sense is still telling me that they are having difficulty coming up with the economics on all of this … and let's have lunch with Arthur and Hank on Thursday. I need to give them a little stronger push again, privately."

"Sure," replied the president's loyal Chief of staff. "I agree. A pep talk for everybody. I'll take care of it." With years of experience as a shrewd political operative working behind the scenes for two different powerful governors in his home state of New York, the Chief was relishing this job more and more each day. The two men in the Oval Office clearly played off each other's strengths perfectly.

✳   ✳   ✳

Michael was just putting on his running shoes for his Saturday morning jog with some new friends in Santa Barbara when his phone rang. He noticed that the caller ID did not give a name but only a New York area code. He hesitated, but then the image of Rose flashed through his mind. He immediately pushed the green light on his phone and softly answered, "Hello?"

"Good morning, Michael. It's Rose," she said cheerfully. After a brief pause—was it surprise, or shock, or delight?—Michael responded in a much emboldened tone:

"Hey … Rose! What a pleasant call. How are you?"

"Good, good … how are you?"

"Terrific, just terrific … and the weather here is beautiful," Michael bragged. "I assume you are in New York? All okay there?"

"No, Michael, actually I'm up in the Santa Ynez wine country, very near you. I was wondering if—"

"Really?" Michael replied in an obviously surprised tone. "Fantastic. Can we—"

"No, no, Michael, I'm just kidding. I wish I were there because I remembered that night in Seattle drinking a beautiful Pinot Noir from Santa Barbara." Rose was having a good time with this line and waited patiently for Michael's response.

And after a lengthy pause, with Rose pressing her ear close to the phone, Michael whispered, barely audible, "Now I know why I like you, Rose. You are a very serious engineer and scientist but with a great sense of humor. You must have known I was a little down after receiving your e-mail yesterday—it seemed a bit impersonal, but this phone call …" Rose continued to be quiet with her ear still pressed to the phone waiting for Michael's further response. He knew that he was opening the door for possibly something beyond a professional friendship, and gathering his thoughts he consciously stepped through. "Rose, I … ah … you know … I have been kind of thinking it would be really neat if we could somehow get together again … that is, if you have not developed any serious commitments since we—"

Rose could hold back no longer. She was delighted to hear Michael's voice and the words he spoke. She thought it was time to interrupt. The door was open.

"Michael, I do have one serious commitment—to the U.S. Navy. However, I do have a one-week furlough the first week in October. Do you think there might be another environmental symposium somewhere that week? Like in Los Angeles?" she teased.

Now in complete command of himself, Michael jumped right in. "Better yet, I can show you what this beautiful environment is like out here that week and at the same time find that fabulous Pinot Noir at one of the forty vineyards that lie just over the mountain in the Santa Inez Valley. Of course … uh, well, I have an assistant here whose roommate is moving out of their two- bedroom condo. She is really nice. I'm sure she would be pleased to accommodate you."

Rose's face was now aglow. "Well, I ..." thinking quickly to herself, "that may be ideal." Departing Seattle the two had at least established that neither was married nor living with anyone. Maybe this was a chance without getting too daring to have some fun and see where this relationship was going. It sounded like an irresistible offer. "Well, okay, yes; that sounds good."

"All right," responded Michael. "Let me check things out. Call you later this afternoon. It might be evening your time. I take it this is your private cell phone and not the number you have on your navy card. Will you be there later, or shall I just leave a message?"

"Of course ... call me. I do have several heavy dates later this afternoon and this evening, but I'll try to make time," Rose said lightly but followed with a hearty laugh.

"Right, so I'll call you before my dinner date with Miss California."

"Sounds good, Michael. Have a good time."

"You bet. Talk to you later. Bye."

"Okay, bye." As Rose pushed the "END" button on her mobile phone, she felt elated. The warmth was flowing again. It was a good feeling.

✵　✵　✵

A luncheon at the White House is a rather formal affair. It took a while for all the assistants and messengers and waiters to leave the room before the four men could begin their real conversation. Arthur Schnell and Hank Abrams never missed the president's cabinet meetings, nor had they ever missed one of the Monday night dinner meetings taking place before his Monday night chats. So actually they were a bit apprehensive as to why they were called to the White House for this luncheon meeting. It was a first.

It was the Chief who turned the conversation from the lighthearted, especially the jabs at the White House media and the opposition political party, to, "Gentlemen, the Master Plan. The president and I believe that everything is on target, but we do have some concerns as we move down the homestretch. Specifically, after appearing bewildered at the first couple of meetings it now seems like John and H. are getting on board with the game plan ... but we still detect some signals from them indicating great uncertainty."

"Right," interjected the president. "They seem to have really come around. Now I know that this is very difficult for them on the economic side. The senator and Richard and you two are quite confident that we can put together a Master Plan that makes sense technically and administratively, but we need something quite new and novel to make the economics work. Of course I'm the first to admit I am a complete novice when it comes to economics. That has not been my background, but I do believe that John and H. have the smarts to come up with something— something feasible. Ah, I guess what I want to say is that you two have to be very firm and confident when we meet on Monday evenings to show John and H. just how serious the consequences to the nation will be if we don't take immediate, drastic action … that the total plan has been put together soundly… that it can work, it can be done, it is feasible. So I'm requesting that you be very forceful at our meetings, advocating that their economic side of the equation move along in tandem with the technical part; that all the pieces of the strategic parts of the plan fit together; that it will work. It must all tie it together in sync. Are you following me?"

Of course by this time Arthur and Hank were well along in the strategic decisions to be made in their areas of logistics and energy. It was exciting, and they both knew that their inputs into the Master Plan were the most important career decisions ever to be made in their lifetimes. Arthur spoke first. "Mr. President, rest assured that I think about this night and day, and I believe that the steps I have suggested so far are absolutely doable. I give you my pledge that I will be sure to firmly convey to John and H. that this plan will work for the benefit of all the American people, that it will save lives and fortunes, that the nation's assets will be protected, and that we will certainly get through this crisis with minimal adverse impacts."

"I, too, Mr. President," added Hank. "Certainly I will express the strongest confidence in accomplishing our future energy goals and impress upon John and H. the necessity for them to keep up with us, step by step, and help make this plan coherent. We have the technology to make it work. We just need the right economic scenario to finance it." In this bravado comment intended to please his president, Hank neglected mentioning his one great concern, more critical than energy and logistics, the most basic of all human essentials—water.

"So be it, gentlemen. Well done. Have a great weekend. See you Monday for dinner." The president smiled. The Chief smirked. "Smooth— like oil on glass," he thought of himself and his president.

✵　✵　✵

The Oracle had spent most of the summer in the temperate mountain airs of Colorado. He particularly enjoyed the three daily performances at the Aspen Music Festival, the Jeep rides to abandoned mining towns, and the intellectual climate at meetings sponsored by the Aspen Institute, a renowned think tank. Flying from Denver back to Washington each Monday for the president's special team meetings was quite all right, but he was a little annoyed that the Chief had asked him to come to a Friday meeting at the White House in hot, humid Washington. The Chief did not want to discuss the subject of the meeting in advance but did mention that Richard Compton was also invited. Thankfully, Richard invited the former senator to come to his Princeton home after the meeting and then spend the weekend at Richard's summer home along the beach at the pleasant resort town of Beach Haven, New Jersey. They then could take the train together Monday morning from Princeton to Washington for their weekly meeting with the president.

"Thank you for coming. I know everyone tries to leave Washington on Fridays, and yet I asked you two to arrive," said the president after he had cleared everyone else from the luncheon room. "Okay, let's get started. First, I want to bring up the point that what I think we have learned so far is that the logistics of what we plan to accomplish are quite feasible, but our Master Plan must have an acceptable basis in an economic sense. If politically, technically, and socially it works, but there's not a sound economic foundation under it … it just would not be feasible. We have the top two economic brains in the country on our team here, and you saw their disbelief at the beginning of all this followed by their eventual lukewarm support. Well, what we need, I think, is an impetus to turn their tepid support into genuine enthusiasm. We need their best creative thinking, and sometimes I just think they may be wondering how this is all going to work out. We need them to be truly diligent, and I am asking you two to help provide that support at our upcoming Monday meeting—"

"Mr. President, don't worry about an impetus," interrupted the Oracle. "Richard and I have been following the situation all week. … Richard, go ahead."

"Yes, thank you. Gentlemen, I have direct contacts at the national hurricane center. We are all aware that the most violent storms have remained at sea this hurricane season compared to last year, but Hurricane Mary at this moment has now turned into the Gulf of Mexico and is approaching Category 5 wind speeds. Its latest heading could be directly toward Houston. If the storm center remains at its current speed and direction, she could hit Houston by Monday noontime. Now it's only Friday and a lot can change. Regardless, there is sure to be some major damage somewhere along our coastal areas ... and if that occurs at the moment we're all together for dinner on Monday ... well, I think John and H. will get the point."

While the president and his Chief of staff were staring intently at Richard, the Oracle then added, "What's more, gentlemen, is the story of the past tornado season. Through June of 2009, there were over eight hundred tornadoes in the Midwest ... in fact, eighty of them just in one week in June. Worse, through June of 2010, the number was up by 10 percent, including a commensurate increase in property damage. This year through the month of June, the end of the tornado season and the beginning of the hurricane season, we had another 10 percent jump to nearly one thousand tornadoes. In July and August of this year, we had three more hurricanes than the eighteen of last year, but fortunately, until now all remained at sea. Well, the current one might be the first to hit a major landfall. Then there is the heat. For instance, the average summer temperature in Phoenix is running 4 percent higher this year than last year, and last year was 2 percent higher than 2009. Phoenix has experienced temperatures over 105 for one hundred straight days now, without a drop of rain. The wildfires raging now in California are the worst in recorded history." The president and the Chief looked on even more intently now. The Oracle continued, "What I'm saying is that the adverse impacts of global warming upon our country are already getting more severe. How could John and H. not possibly believe that their brain trust is absolutely essential to creating the Master Plan as quickly as possible?"

✻   ✻   ✻

Saturday was a beautiful beach day. Nevertheless, the two men could not help checking the weather site on Richard Compton's mobile phone. The storm had skirted the edges of Jamaica and Cuba without major damage and seemed to be tracking in a northwest direction, most likely missing the tip of Florida. Richard's repeated calls to the National Hurricane Center still confirmed that Houston could lie in Hurricane Mary's path. Television coverage indicated that striking Houston was a possibility, and the mayor of Houston was already reviewing evacuation plans.

On Sunday, another perfect beach day along the coast of New Jersey, the mayor of Houston directed that the city's evacuation plan be put into effect at noon. The exodus was on. It had happened before in Houston, in 2007—just four years prior. That year, wind and water damage were severe but not devastating. This time, however, the intensity of the storm was projected to be stronger. On Monday morning, Richard Compton and his weekend guest, the Oracle, could not wait to drive back to Princeton and board the Amtrak train to Washington. The anticipation of a dreaded event taking place at the same time that they were to meet with the president and his team further heightened their feelings of anxiety. This was global warming.

☆   ☆   ☆

Energized by their private luncheon meetings at the White House the prior Thursday and Friday, Arthur, Hank, the Oracle, and Richard all arrived an hour early for their usual 6:00 PM dinner with the president and his Chief of staff. While waiting for the president, their entire conversation revolved around the news that the center of the hurricane directly struck Houston, Texas, just three hours earlier. The hurricane's force was rated Category 5, roaring through the Gulf of Mexico, and was downgraded to Category 4 after making landfall, but it was still incredibly powerful. Television coverage in the hallway outside the president's dining room was providing continuous reports of extensive wind and water damage. Fortunately, the evacuation plan worked well, and there were no reports yet of loss of human life. All four men thought the same thing at the same time: *evacuation with no loss of life—that is the essence of the Master Plan.* When John Heyward and H. Stewart arrived, they appeared to have little knowledge of what was going on in Houston.

There was no talk of baseball or politics or the media during this presidential dinner. Hurricane Mary was the sole subject. Speaking somberly, the president asked Arthur, his secretary of the interior, for an update of the situation and whether federal emergency response people were on the scene. It appeared that the local, state, and federal response was as good as could be expected, but of course there were severe limitations upon any direct assistance until the storm had passed and all the damage was assessed. Evacuation plans seem to have worked efficiently.

"Gentlemen, this is why we're here," the president said. "This is not a drill. We're not creating a contingency plan. This is happening … and it is happening now. You have provided me with information that in each of the last three years the hurricane season in the South has been more severe, the tornado season in the Midwest more severe, and the heat and drought in the Southwest more severe. The trend will continue … and in fact will accelerate. The Oracle is predicting that within ten years these conditions will make human life in these areas uninhabitable. If we also lose the coastal areas of Boston, New York City, Baltimore, San Diego, Los Angeles, San Francisco, and Seattle due to rising seas, then we will have panic and devastation. Virtually our entire nation is in jeopardy, and the only answer is to do what Houston has just done—evacuate!" There was silence in the room for a long moment as everyone appeared to be buried in their own deep reflection.

"Sir! Mr. President." John Heyward, the renowned economist, broke the silence. "Now, more than ever, I do understand the problem. Can it make any sense? I know that you are calling for a complete evacuation, other than the military and security, to the Denver area … but it might make it a little easier. Uh …" It was that obvious John was nervous about his impending question. "What would you think if we left some satellite cities—I'm thinking from an economic point now; in places away from coastal areas, like Atlanta, Dallas, Minneapolis … where there is room for continuous expansion … where evacuees from the coasts could establish temporary homes and the economic resources there could be maintained."

The Chief cringed and tried not to show his consternation. "Too difficult to control. No renegades," he wanted to shout out, but he kept his thoughts to himself.

The president reflected for a brief moment and then responded, "Well, John, that hasn't been the plan, as complete consolidation seemed to make the most sense to be fair to all … but am I still open to that?"

The Oracle immediately jumped into the debate in a serious tone of voice, looking directly at John. "No, no, John. That wouldn't work. Atlanta will be subject to strong hurricanes alternating with drought, the same with Dallas … and with warming moving up the Great Plains, Minneapolis will be directly in the stronger tornado corridor, as will Chicago, which also faces a potential for flooding. Even the Great Lakes will be rising as the melting Arctic gives them a new source of water. There is no habitable safe haven other than Denver and just to its east. It is out of the hurricane and tornado paths. You'd possibly need that northwest piece of Nebraska and the northwest quarter of Kansas. Those areas are on the outskirts of the tornado belts—those quarters should be reasonably safe. We will have lots of grains and beans from the increasingly warmer areas of the Great Plains. No, our technical problem is water. None other."

Richard Compton nodded his concurrence. "I agree, 100 percent," he said in a strong voice. John Heyward sheepishly backed off. H. Stewart stared ahead with no expression on his face. "Incredible!" he thought to himself.

The president's regular fifteen-minute "chat" that night at 10:00 PM was delivered in the opposite order from its usual arrangement. The first ten minutes usually referenced health care, the growing strength of the dollar, overseas diplomatic efforts, education, and the like. The last five minutes then discussed the issue of climate change. This time the president reviewed his normal issues for just the first five minutes and then grimaced and put on a very serious face.

"My fellow Americans, I have been speaking directly to you for a number of months now about the concerns we all share facing our planet's change in climatic conditions. The world's scientific community has been unanimous in calling for us all to take immediate actions to drastically reduce the amount of carbon that we emit into the atmosphere. I trust I have adequately explained to you over the last several months that carbon-based gases trap heat in our atmosphere and create the so-called 'greenhouse' effect. With stability, of course, there is no problem. We need our atmosphere to hold in the sun's heat and provide a habitable planet for us. But as explained, if there are more greenhouse gases going up into the atmosphere than can be circulated and absorbed back into the oceans and into our plants and trees, then that excess is overheating the planet based upon our existing living conditions."

The president then went on for another ten minutes explaining in layman's language about the cycles of climate change and its adverse impacts. He concluded, "As you know, Congress has taken steps to reduce these greenhouse gases back to levels emitted many years ago in order to diminish or eliminate man's impact upon a general global warming trend that, as I have attempted to clearly explain to you, is part of nature's cycle. But there are some scientists who believe that even after these steps have been taken by all of us good citizens of the planet, we may already be in a cycle too difficult to repair in the short term…. As previously announced to you, I am gathering and assessing this disturbing information and will be reporting back to you. It is clear that recent climatic conditions have been worse than many scientists expected. We are on top of this. And it is exactly the reason why I have been dwelling on this subject each week with you in these updates. It is in this regard that our attention tonight is on critical news coming out of our Gulf Coast. Like last year, the hurricane season has been very severe, but the difference, until today, has been that the strong hurricanes have not reached landfall as they did last year, a time when we experienced more devastation than in any other hurricane season in the history of this nation.

"However, I'm sure you all have followed the television coverage today and this evening of the strong winds and racing waters now being experienced by our good and brave citizens of southeast Texas. Fortunately our forecasts were accurate, our warnings were timely, and our citizens in the path of the eye of that storm have safely evacuated. The storm is now decreasing in size and intensity as it heads north, and in the morning surely we will be able to fully assess the damages. Preliminary reports are revealing incredibly extensive property damage. The Houston Ship Canal, as many of you know, is the heart of our American oil-refining and petrochemical industries. Plant closures in that area have the possibility of creating a severe economic hardship on many of us.

"I can assure you tonight that all federal, state, and local governmental officials are on the alert to provide the best possible support and services as the situation requires. As your president, I can also assure you that the United States is now, and will be in the future, a leading force to do everything that it possibly can to reduce and mitigate any and all potential adverse impacts of the global warming trend. While it may be possible to eliminate man's contribution to the trend and thereby give credit to our willingness to reduce and mitigate its negative impacts, it is conceivable that we cannot reverse the underlying trend of nature and that we may surely have to arrive at new means for our citizens to adapt to it. In this regard I plan to continue these weekly updates about this extremely important issue…. Meanwhile we wish everyone living in the path of this dreadful storm to be safe and to know that every American stands by to assist you. May God bless America. Goodnight."

✻ ✻ ✻

Arthur Schnell, Hank Abrams, and H. D. Stewart had all retreated to their Washington, DC, apartments after the White House dinner to watch and hear the president's speech. John Heyward called home and told Helen that he would be staying over in Washington that evening and would be back to Philadelphia the following afternoon. He had nothing urgent on his calendar Tuesday. Before departing from the White House, he had arranged to meet H. early the next morning in H.'s office at the Federal Reserve. H. had assured John that he would postpone all his calls and morning meetings to keep the time free for a meeting with him. As they departed Monday evening with that arrangement in mind, their eyes said it all. The president was serious. They had better start crossing some *T*s and dotting some *I*s in the economic myth they were about to create.

✻   ✻   ✻

It was 8:00 AM in H.'s ornate office at the Federal Reserve. A perplexed John sipped his third cup of coffee of the morning. "Maybe there's a chance we can do something really different. We seem to have been given a blank slate. Basic economic principles under any kind of historical system just won't work. We are talking about creating a mythical system and having people think it will work. We have to hope it is temporary. The mythical gods of the ancient Greeks represented the 'truth' until the breadth and depth of philosophy advanced, science discovered, and the new god of Abraham, Jesus, and Mohammed revealed. Greek mythology was temporary and worked until something better came along. So, my friend H., what to do? Do we create a myth that a combination free-market system with one strong governmental body overseeing the system for three hundred million people in one small location will work when we know it won't? Do we dream up a new system to fit those circumstances knowing that it will soon collapse? Or do we really put our heads together and try to come up with something that we truly believe could work?" John paused and reached for his coffee cup again.

H. was just letting his colleague talk on and on, but when John paused, H. broke into the first smile that John had seen on his face since he had first met him last spring. "I … phew … had thought this whole thing crazy," H. said. "But now … okay, let's get serious. You throw out three options. First … no way. I see no way a free-market capitalist system could possibly work in the type of environment the president envisions. Second, I don't even envision a mixed economy, part free, part socialistic—it won't work in those conditions. Third, I cannot envision an authoritarian government directing a centrally controlled economy if we are to have foreign imports and an international currency … a la a modified Communism, or whatever. So that leaves me to think that we do have to create something new. Your question is whether that something new will work temporarily or will collapse in no time flat. Hey, what if we dreamed it up and it worked and worked well for a long, long time? How many Nobel Prizes in economics is that worth?" John wasn't quite getting this sudden change in H.'s attitude. Where was this sense of humor coming from all of a sudden?

"Okay, that's good," said John. "Let's start with the premise that nothing ever tried historically will work in this situation. Sure, we could study the economic system of a functioning isolated city-state such as Athens back in the time of the ancient Greeks, but today's society is much too complex and materialistic, and our technology is way too advanced to even relate to what might have succeeded for them. Okay ... let's start from scratch. Can we meet next Monday and bounce some ideas off each other that we can take into the dinner meeting with the president next Monday night?"

"Yes, I'm with you. Let's do it," replied a now more relaxed looking H. Stewart. "This global warming stuff could be quite interesting after all."

*   *   *

On the following Monday, the opening of the weekly dinner meeting found the president in a very upbeat mood. For a whole week, the media had been steadily reporting the president's clear reassurance that he had everything related to the global warming issue under firm control. While state and local resources were obviously inadequate, the federal emergency response to the Hurricane Mary damage along the Gulf Coast had been swift and effective. There had been no reported deaths as a direct result of the hurricane. Property damage, of course, was extensive, but the federal emergency response team and the insurance companies were well coordinated with plenty of officials at the scene. The biggest downside was damage to thousands of residences and to the large Texas oil-refining capacity. The president faced a major housing crisis with no immediate answers yet at the same time appeared very strong with his public messages that he would help with the people's housing problem and not tolerate any price gouging by the oil companies. They had been making plenty of money and had ample cash reserves.

Following the president's pleasant introduction in opening the meeting as dessert arrived, Richard Compton asked if he could give his report first. As he started to speak, the mood in the room quickly darkened. "I flew out to Seattle this week to meet with Jane Stricker. As mentioned to you before, she is the expert on the all-important status of the permafrost. Her report assessing the rate of melting and its impact is to be issued to the IPCC one month from now, by mid-October. I think that her report, when made public and compiled with an official IPCC report, will rock the scientific community. For a number of years now, we have all felt that retreating glaciers and melting ice would slowly but surely raise average ocean temperatures and contribute to the problems of the global warming trend, but now…" With that pause, the other team members all leaned forward in their seats straining to hear the next words spoken by this renowned environmental scientist.

The melting permafrost had been mentioned several times in these meetings as one of the most critical factors in the greatly accelerating global warming trend. What was Richard about to reveal? He continued, "I have revealed data to you previously that certainly underlies the major reason why we're here creating a Master Plan in order to avoid a national crisis—that an abrupt climate change will create a catastrophe in less than fifteen years as opposed to the common scientific perception that a gradual change will occur over the next fifty years.

"The updated confidential data supplied to me by Jane, which cannot be disclosed outside this room until her report is formally issued to the IPCC—and the press gets a hold of it then—is that the rate of melting of the permafrost in the last three years is five times the rate publicly reported for the three prior years. Jane does not believe that even an immediate elimination of our burning of fossil fuels would slow down this process. It's too late. The melting permafrost is putting a huge amount of greenhouse gases up there right now. The damage has already been done … and while most of us fault Man's excesses for this phenomenon, it is not pertinent right now whether we blame Man or whether we blame nature for this happening. The fact is that it's happening even faster than my good friend here, the Oracle, had predicted just a few months ago. In the next few years, we are going to witness constant devastating hurricanes and tornadoes, flooding, drought, heat … throughout the whole country. And no one knows when it will stabilize and reverse. Gentlemen, the beginnings of a catastrophic climate are upon us now."

Silence filled the room. All were reflecting upon Richard's startling revelation. "Jane Stricker," thought the Chief. "I have to meet this woman."

"Well, gentlemen," said the president somberly. "Thank you Richard. That explains a lot. This means we move on with our planning. We have three months. Before the start of the new year, we must have the Master Plan complete. I will have to convince the American public that we have to begin to implement it as quickly as possible, and it will have to be fully implemented within five years, not the ten years we originally envisioned, but is it feasible? Can we move to the economic side, the area most troubling to me because I understand it the least? I know that John and H. have taken a while to adjust their thinking to this new reality. Last week you were getting in tune. Where do you fellows stand?"

"Mr. President. Mr. President." Both men started to speak at once. John quickly proceeded, and H. sat back in his chair, waiting his turn. "Mr. President, I think I have given more thought to the situation this week than I have in the prior two months. And now with today's grim news—I apologize; this is a difficult situation to grasp—I have studied the strengths and weaknesses of all the economic systems that we have known about over the last three thousand years. As all of us in this room know, no economic system has ever created more wealth for more people for a longer period of time than our private enterprise, free-market-driven system operating under a truly democratic government imposing fair rules and regulations.

"Witness the incredible economic engine of the United States and also the systems we imposed on Germany and Japan after we defeated them in World War Two. Witness the failures of the Communist systems. It is only recently that China has created some wealth for a segment of its population because it has allowed capitalism to thrive in certain designated areas, like Hong Kong and Shanghai. Witness the economic stagnation that took place in countries in Europe. Some went overboard with socialism and then became more balanced with a combination of capitalism and government involvement. Witness the economic problems in many of the less-developed countries, which depend so much on aid funds for development from the more developed nations, even where they have a vast supply of natural resources and a ready source of labor. Insufficient and poorly allocated capital, inadequate education, radical religious control, and certainly a vast corrupt business and government climate all contribute to a lack of sustainable economic growth and in fact stagnation without support from the developed world.

"However, H. and I have agreed that the free-market system—a capitalistic system—would not work in the Denver scenario. Capitalism thrives on the principles of private property, ready access to a variety of resources, and free-market opportunities. Fair, open competition and wide consumer choices best allocate available resources to the best advantage of all, except for those who are somehow personally handicapped within the system. In our new scenario, in order to save millions of people from the adverse impacts of the coming global warming crisis, we simply cannot devise such a complex, open system for so many people in such a small area. Now maybe it could happen over a period of many, many years through the innovative nature of our people adjusting to the situation, but we're doing this so quickly, and as you said, Mr. President, hopefully it is temporary. So H. and I have been setting up a number of models in devising something never seen before—never done before—but a system that we believe can work under the circumstances. ... H.?"

"Right, John, thanks. I completely agree, Mr. President, that we are on to something brand new. I feel confident that we can lay out a full report for you to review by Thanksgiving. With any adjustments you and the team would like to make, we promise that we will have a plan ready in full detail by year end to fit into your Master Plan."

No one looked more relieved than the president after listening to those comments. After months of meetings, they were the first positive comments provided by his economic team members. Across the table, however, the Chief suddenly had a worried look on his face. He just had to have a strong hint of what John and H. were thinking. Their economic plan simply had to conform to his vision of a completely centralized control mechanism over the entire economic system. He made a note to himself to set up a private meeting with them before next Monday's dinner meeting.

✳   ✳   ✳

In this new world of e-mail correspondence, Rose was not accustomed to receiving much mail from the post office, other than from her parents in New Hampshire. The letter of Admiral Stansky's from naval headquarters at the Pentagon was very brief and right to the point. "Your commanding officer has been informed that your presence is requested in my office on next Thursday, September 18, at 9:00 AM. Call my assistant Lillian Rhodes at the number below to arrange quarters for your stay the night before and for directions to my office. Bring with you any reports pertaining to your assignment that have not yet been formally submitted to the department."

Rose was puzzled by the seeming urgency of such a request. As she thought more about it, she felt energized that perhaps her work was being recognized as an important concern not only to the navy but perhaps to the whole East Coast of America. In her excitement, she immediately called Adriana. Her vivacious friend was working with those glamorous investment bankers just blocks away from Rose's little office building and dock space, properties leased by the navy at the tip of Manhattan.

71

"Ad, I have some exciting news. I have just received a written request from one of the top navy admirals to meet with him personally in Washington this Thursday. He apparently wants to review the data I have collected. I think it's important."

"Hey, Rose, that's great! I'm sure you won't get seasick on that train ride to Washington," Adriana said facetiously, obviously referring to the fact that over the last few summer months so many of the ferocious hurricanes that turned out to sea had Rose's little navy boat incessantly tossed about by big waves, playing much havoc with her stomach.

"Okay, Ad, I have to run. See you Saturday. Can't wait for an update on the guys. Bye."

✳   ✳   ✳

It was fun for Rose, all decked out in her dress uniform, riding the train for the first time to Washington. It would also be her first time visiting the widely photographed and famous Pentagon. Crowded, noisy, exciting—that is, until she entered Admiral Stansky's office. Three other top navy brass introduced themselves without smiling and curtly asked her to sit down. On top of Admiral Stansky's desk was a stack of monthly reports that Rose had previously submitted. With no personal chatter about her trip or the weather or other pleasantries, Admiral Stansky immediately got into the matter.

"Lieutenant, or Rose, if I may call you by your first name … you see, this may appear to be a very formal meeting, but I would like you to relax and be as informal and as open as possible. Your data is startling. We never expected such a rapid rise in temperatures of the North Atlantic Ocean nor in surrounding air temperatures. If this trend continues at this rate, our naval facilities along the coast, such as our huge operation in Norfolk, Virginia, could be in jeopardy in a very short period of time. Due to the seriousness of this matter, we need additional verification that the equipment and methods—no offense, Rose; we know that you are a competent engineer and atmospheric scientist, but we plan to assign an additional scientist to team with you so that the two of you can verify each other's readings. This is all so important. But now let's review the data together so that we are on the same page."

Rose listened to Admiral Stansky in rapt attention and could not get much more out of her mouth than a cough. "They don't trust my work!" she thought to herself. But then remembering his introductory words of informality gave her comfort, and she finally proceeded to review her data with complete confidence in a clear and calm voice. In closing, the admiral remarked. "Rose, this work is so important that before we even continue with your assignment and supply you with your scientific cohort, I want you to know that we plan to condense this information and get it to the president of the United States. I'm sure you're aware of his continuing Monday night talks with the American public about global warming. We understand that it is the highest of his priorities. Thank you, Rose, and good luck."

As she journeyed back to New York, Rose accepted the admiral's decision. Her water and air temperature recordings were so unexpected that it made good sense to verify the data.

✻   ✻   ✻

The following Monday, the Chief arranged for John and H. to arrive at the White House an hour earlier than usual. He had to rid himself of a nagging feeling that the economic team was not coming up with a plan suitable enough for his concept of complete centralized control by a strong national government.

"Thank you, gentlemen, for arriving early," the Chief said from behind his large desk, clearly conveying a look of importance. "Sometimes at our weekly meetings we don't have the time to go into substantial depth ... and I know that over the last two weeks you have been giving considerable thought to what your economic system might look like under the Master Plan. I don't mean to jump ahead or to steal your thunder as you will be addressing the entire team, but I am concerned that under very trying times in what basically is a national emergency situation, I believe the national government, in its executive branch, must have absolute power."

"Chief." John spoke up with a very calm voice, attempting to peel away the tense look of anxiety on the face of the Chief. "H. and I fully understand the situation. Trust us. We understand that this plan, no matter what it might be called when introduced to the public, truly is an emergency plan. We will be operating under a national emergency, and in such case, the executive branch of the federal—or if you want to call it 'national'—government must have unlimited authority over all functions of society."

"Chief," a smiling H. added, "Don't worry about our economic plan not giving the president sufficient powers to properly execute it. I think your worry should be—to be perfectly blunt, and it's rather peculiar the question has not yet arisen in our weekly meetings—under what provisions in our Constitution can the president execute the powers that we are coming up with in our Master Plan?"

There was a long pause as the Chief stared at his two visitors. He thought to himself, "How are these guys so smart? Of course I have a plan to amend the Constitution, but that is not a subject for the president's team of economic advisers. That's my role." Dropping his anxious look and beginning to show a slight smile, he answered, "Good thinking. That's very astute. Now it is your turn not to worry. The president and I and our White House legal counsel have been on top of that issue for months. It may appear to be a thorny legal issue, but I am confident that I have the answer." The truth of the matter was that the president was extremely concerned about this issue. The Master Plan concept had not yet been revealed to his White House legal counsel. The president was resting his case solely upon the opinion of his talented Chief of staff. It would have to be the Chief who would skillfully navigate this delicate issue to a successful resolution.

During the team meeting that evening, the Chief felt relieved that the issue of acting within the Constitution did not arise. The main issues revolved around the president's demand that the Master Plan be upgraded to a shorter implementation period and be finished on time. He constantly expressed concern that it was important for him to lead the country on a timely basis and with a sound plan. All the members of the team repeatedly assured the president that their inputs to the plan would be timely.

✽　✽　✽

The first week of October was rapidly approaching. Two hearts, three thousand miles apart, were beating in sync. How incredibly exciting for Rose—finally she was to have a week off. Her work was being recognized by the top brass at the Pentagon, and her new colleague to be assigned by Admiral Stansky was not scheduled to begin work with her until November. So here was a whole week to relax, to see beautiful Santa Barbara and its fabled wine country, and to drink some great Pinot Noir—but most importantly to find out what this Michael was truly all about. Her imagination ran wild. Michael too was getting flush with excitement. He had arranged for Rose to use the extra bedroom at his assistant's condo near downtown Santa Barbara and was jotting down numerous notes for all the things to do with her. His imagination soared, but just like the last night in Seattle—overriding his feelings—he thought it wise to go slowly despite his desires. "Better not rush things—just let it happen."

✻   ✻   ✻

Most people in the South believe that hurricane season is over by the time October arrives. On rare occasions, a hurricane does strike in October or November. On even rarer occasions, meteorologists track hurricanes on a course heading toward the northeastern coast of the United States. Occasionally a weaker hurricane force or the remnants of a stronger hurricane strike areas such as Delaware, Pennsylvania, New York, or on up into New England. So it was a bit unusual that during the beginning of October the National Hurricane Center was tracking a massive storm center that was gaining momentum just northeast of the larger islands in the Caribbean. In this case, it was not giving any indication of veering off farther east as most of the larger hurricanes had done earlier in the season of the year 2011.

While Rose was gathering together civilian clothes she thought appropriate for her flight to Los Angeles on Saturday morning, she recalled how rough the seas were getting earlier that afternoon. Her navy vessel had experienced unusually high seas returning to its New York Harbor port. She managed to put those thoughts out of her mind as anticipation was building for her trip west and what would hopefully be an exciting week with Michael. Then the news came—not good news—as she reported to her office at 7:00 Thursday morning. It was two days before her furlough was to begin. Her commanding officer informed the entire crew that their mission that day was canceled. Navy headquarters had informed him that a new hurricane was building in the South Atlantic and appeared to be headed toward the northeast coast. Rose and her crewmates spent the rest of the day following the news and gathering all the weather reports that became available to them through the navy and on television. On Friday, the news grew worse. The storm had intensified from a Category 2 hurricane to Category 4. It was still well out to sea. Nevertheless, because of the curvature of the northeast coast toward the North Atlantic Ocean, it was likely that the hurricane might hit full force anywhere from southern New Jersey to lower New England. The second piece of bad news for Rose was a bombshell. Her commanding officer abruptly informed her Friday afternoon that all navy furloughs for the following week were canceled. All personnel were required to be on hand to safeguard navy vessels and facilities and to possibly help out with any public emergencies. Rose nervously grasped her cell phone.

"Michael, I'm glad I reached you. I am so sorry. I don't know if you have received the news. My trip for tomorrow is canceled," Rose lamented in rapid-fire seriousness.

"Hey, Rose, whoa—slow down. What's happening?"

"So you haven't heard yet of the huge hurricane headed our way? Right toward New York City. Would you believe it? All furloughs have been canceled."

"Oh, no! I've been so busy this week planning on some time off next week when you're here that I haven't followed the news at all the last couple of days. That's terrible—a hurricane directly hitting New York? I've never heard of such a thing. But you ... you're not coming ..." Michael was flabbergasted. Rose was devastated.

Neither was aware that a Category 4 hurricane actually did flood lower Manhattan in 1821, or that a Category 3 hurricane was responsible for six hundred deaths in Long Island in 1938. Rose was only aware that the U.S. Army Corp of Engineers, collecting data for the National Hurricane Center in 2006, predicted that the sea level around New York City would rise three feet by the year 2080. But that conclusion was reached before the new permafrost melting that Jane Stricker and Rose and only a few others knew about at this point. The rare hurricane hits on New York City were now about to become a common occurrence.

"Oh Michael, I'm so disappointed. Can I please just keep this roundtrip ticket for another time? Yeah, a hurricane in this area is highly unusual. But of course we're all thinking about what has been going on lately with the strength of hurricanes. Michael, I should tell you. Actually the work I am doing for the navy is indicating that the change in wind patterns in the North Atlantic as well as the currents is ... well, the data indicate that more hurricanes will be heading toward the Northeast rather than veering out to sea. The meteorologist on my team agrees with that thinking, and so we have been quite surprised this season that so far all the big hurricanes, other than the one that hit Houston a few weeks ago, have been heading out into the North Atlantic. This climate change thing is sure difficult to figure out, but no doubt, Michael, everything is getting worse."

Their conversation turned quieter and more somber during the next few minutes. No fluttering heartbeats this time. No flushed cheeks. Just sheer disappointment.

✻ ✻ ✻

The storm was swift and severe. New York City had ample warning and was braced. No one thought of evacuating the city. This was not New Orleans or Houston. Lots of solid concrete, and everyone huddled indoors. It was all over in eight hours. Rose's commanding officer made sure the entire crew tied down their research vessel as tightly as possible. It remarkably survived the huge waves. Many of the other ships in the harbor area were not so lucky. But that was not the major problem. The high seas and crashing waves pushed by one hundred mph winds entered the subway system. Millions of rail and subway commuters would be finding some other way to travel in the next two weeks. There were few fatalities and little property damage other than at the harbor areas. But in the money capital of the world, there was a great deal of disruption. Was this another rarity, or was it part of the president's constant drumbeat about global warming?

Chapter Four

Master Planning

Autumn 2011

George Blake's call to Michael one early morning just before Thanksgiving caught him by surprise. Since beginning his desalination project in Santa Barbara, Michael had been communicating with George through weekly e-mails and monthly written reports. George's voice sounded excited. "Listen, Michael, I know that you're on target with setting up your new power sources, wind and solar, and that you're well into the process of getting your special techniques set up at the plant, but I have some news. The secretary of the interior in Washington, Arthur Schnell, called me yesterday and told me about recent developments in making desalination more efficient but that none of them compare to the ideas presented in your graduate thesis. I don't know what this is all about, but he was in a hurry to find out what you are doing at the Santa Barbara plant, and what our timetable is."

"Wow!" is all that Michael could blurt out.

*　　*　　*

Most environmental scientists and engineers are quite aware of the advantages and shortcomings of processes that desalinate seawater. The greatest advantage is the supply of drinking water to populations that live in arid regions but close to seawater. In other areas, the greatest disadvantage to desalination is its high operating costs compared to all other means of obtaining drinkable water. Seawaters contain salt content far in excess of what humans can tolerate. Ocean waters typically contain 130 grams of salt per gallon, while humans require drinking water of less than 2 grams per gallon. Two desalination processes are effective in achieving this standard: Since the days of Aristotle in ancient Greece, Man has found various ways to boil seawater, condense the steam, and thereby remove the salt—distillation. An alternative to modern distillation plants that boil and condense seawater is another method—reverse osmosis. This second technique utilizes very fine membrane filters to remove the salt.

Worldwide, in the year 2009 there were thirteen thousand desalination plants producing three billion gallons of treated water per day, only about 1 percent of the world's daily consumption. Desalination plants in the Middle East provide 75 percent of this total world capacity. Obviously this land area is arid and close to seawater and has countries with substantial oil revenues to pay for the expensive plants. The Jebel Ali distillation plant in the United Arab Emirates produces eight times the amount of treated water that the largest plant in the Western Hemisphere produces, the one located at Tampa Bay, Florida. The Arab plant produces two hundred million gallons per day, while the Tampa plant produces twenty-five million gallons per day. The largest plant designed for the arid Southern California region is a plant north of San Diego, which will produce fifty million gallons per day, enough for one hundred thousand homes. Due to their high relative costs, desalination plants account for only two-tenths of 1 percent of the world's treated water.

Even though seawater can be boiled at lower temperatures than normal by using low-pressure techniques, the energy costs of boiling water in the distillation process are still relatively high. Alternatively, the high energy costs of pumps to force water through the membrane process make that technique relatively expensive as well. In addition, the costs of transporting treated water to consumers away from coastal areas can be prohibitive. Furthermore, these processes are only 50 percent efficient; that is, half of the seawater becomes treated and usable while the other half, obviously very high in salt content, becomes a waste product. This brine waste has to be disposed of so as not to cause harm to marine life. It is estimated that to provide desalinated water for half the U.S. population, one hundred new electric power plants would have to be built, each at a huge one-gigawatt capacity.

Michael was well aware of all these facts. The Santa Barbara plant was built in 1992 as a result of a severe drought experienced in Southern California in 1991. It operated for only a short period of time with a design capacity of seven million gallons per day of treated water. Plentiful rains came shortly thereafter at the same time the city of Santa Barbara approved a much less expensive connection to the aqueduct system flowing from Northern California. The plant was then converted to a backup system. When running, it had operated as a reverse-osmosis process using electric power purchased from Southern California Edison to drive the pressure pumps. Michael was also aware of new technologies under development utilizing nanoparticles and biological particles that would enhance throughput of membrane filters and make them perhaps 30 percent more efficient, but those improvements paled in comparison to his breakthroughs.

Michael's plan was to restart the filters but at the same time install a small boiler to run the distillation process side by side. He believed that his inventions would be much more practical using the distillation process. The latter eliminated downtime for cleaning the filters. It would also be much more efficient and economic the larger the system configuration. He was thinking big. If his ideas were to really make a mark and help the vast population of arid Southern California in the coming days of global warming, his process had to work efficiently with very large volumes of water. And the cost, at least initially, would have to be competitive with the cost of transporting water from Northern California. Not lost on Michael was the irony of his environmentalist friends' preferences: the desalination costs of the shuttered Santa Barbara plant had been approximately $3.00 per thousand gallons of high-quality water, while at the same time many Californians were drinking bottled water that cost them up to $6,000 per thousand gallons!

"Anyway," George continued, "he is arranging roundtrip tickets for us to fly from Los Angeles to Washington on Monday. Michael, have a nice Thanksgiving with your family and pack up all your notes; I will meet you at LAX Monday morning at the United ticket counter at 8:00 AM. Our flight is at 9:30. We will review your whole program together during the flight."

"But George," Michael said, "you know that we are only eight months into the project, and we have no data yet on how good it is going to be."

"I know … but your writings apparently have been so logical that there must be a high degree of confidence even before we prove it out. Either that," continued George, "or maybe they want to change the scope of the project before we're through. After all, they're funding it."

"Okay, sir. I'll do my best," Michael said in a not-so-confident tone as the conversation ended.

☆   ☆   ☆

Michael had never been to Washington before. He was awestruck as their taxi from Dulles International Airport crossed the Potomac. For the first time in his life he had a view of the Washington Monument, the White House, and the Capitol at the end of Pennsylvania Avenue. George and Michael arrived at Arthur Schnell's office at the Department of the Interior right on time at the appointed hour for their late afternoon meeting. The secretary of the interior greeted them at his receptionist's desk and escorted the two into his ornate office. Two other men were in the office waiting to shake their hands and introduce themselves. One was Hank Abrams, the secretary of energy, and the other was Richard Compton, who introduced himself as an environmental scientist teaching at Princeton University.

Michael felt a twinge of anxiety, as everyone looked incredibly serious. They took seats around Arthur Schnell's desk. Richard Compton spoke first. "Mr. Blake has spoken very highly of you, Michael. You have executed beyond expectations every assignment he has given you, but let me get right to the point. Why would we bring you all the way here today?" Michael squirmed in his chair, clearly wondering where this was leading. "We have read your university thesis on desalination. We are up to date on your pilot program at the Santa Barbara plant. Now, we know that you are still months away from running your program and collecting data, but compared to all the other new developments we have been studying regarding improvements in the technology ... well, I'll be frank with you. Nothing else compares with your potential for large-scale clean water volume." Michael now looked quite uncomfortable. He glanced at George, who also looked especially edgy.

He thought to himself, *"What am I doing here? I'm twenty-seven years old. George Blake is a renowned engineer. The secretary of the interior, the secretary of energy, the professor from Princeton—they must all be twice my age and have ten times the experience."*

Richard continued speaking; his voice pitched was low and his tone steady, "Michael, we informed George before you boarded your flight that we are working on a highly secret mission regarding global warming. I'm sure that you have been listening to our president over these past many months informing the American public what global warming is all about and hinting about its adverse impacts upon the United States. And I am sure you know that all Americans have been worried about the strength of the hurricanes that have slammed into the United States the last two seasons." "New York!" flashed into Michael's consciousness. Richard Compton paused and looked down for a moment as though weighing the gravity of his statements. The other men stayed quiet and still in their seats. All seemed quite serious.

Richard began again, "Let me describe a hypothetical situation and ask you a question, Michael. Let's just say that at some point the adverse impacts of global warming become so severe that we would have to move all of our populations on the West Coast inland. Let's just say, so far inland that they would have to be close to a major food source, like, say, Denver, Colorado, next to the Great Plains. And let's say the snowpack in the Rockies has melted and there is less rainfall. How do you suppose we could get vast quantities of drinkable water to that area? Think about it. Could we desalinate billions of gallons of Pacific Ocean water and transport it a thousand miles uphill, from sea level to mile-high Denver? What do you think?"

Michael squirmed again in his seat but was intensely aware that the eyes of four senior men were looking directly at him. "Uh … you want me to answer that? Well, okay, the first thing I would think about is building a very, very large pipeline from the Great Lakes—that's fresh water of course—and if we are talking about out in the future when we could use vast wind farms across the Great Plains to generate electricity to power multiple pumping stations, ones big enough to push the water from a few hundred feet above sea level—let's say at Chicago—all the way to Denver, that would be more economical." Michael thought that was quite a clever answer.

All of a sudden, Arthur Schnell smiled and appeared suddenly relaxed behind his large desk. "Good, Michael; that's good." He spoke for the first time since they sat down. "Now suppose they needed twice that much water in Denver, and you are the expert in desalination; what else?" Now Michael caught on.

"Sure, okay … I get it. We use my new desalination technology to create a number of huge plants in Los Angeles, California, build huge pipelines to Denver, and power all the water uphill through openings in the mountains using the vast power of solar energy that would be available in the arid Southwest."

Everyone looked directly at Michael, eagerly waiting for him to say more. "Ah, but gentlemen …" Michael paused, knowing that this hypothetical situation was a little ridiculous despite the serious setting enveloping him, and then let it out. "It could be done. Technology is not the problem, but surely you must know that the cost of desalinating and transporting so much water, or even just the cost of transporting water from the Great Lakes, would be outlandish. Prohibitive!" Other than the weak smile now breaking out on the face of George Blake, the other three men brushed Michael's comment aside. Michael looked sheepish.

It was now Hank Abrams' turn to say his first words. "Let's forget the costs for now, Michael. We just want to talk about technical feasibility. Remember that Americans enjoyed low-cost energy for sixty years by buying cheap oil from the Middle East while also depleting the oil fields in the United States. And we have been using low-cost energy from coal for a couple of hundred years. The point now, Michael, is that we do not want to use these fossil fuels anymore. We have someone else to worry about the costs. Today, we just want to know about the technical feasibility of producing and transporting hundreds of billions of gallons of treated water one thousand miles. I think you have given us the answer. Incidentally, keep all this to yourself, Michael. Speak to no one outside of this room."

Silence. Private thoughts flowed at hype speed. Bewildered, Michael wondered, "I thought this was to be hypothetical."

Despite his prior utterance, a perplexed Hank Abrams asked himself, "Looks like plenty of water and energy technically, but how are those economic gurus going to handle the costs in our Master Plan?"

Satisfied, Arthur Schnell thought, "My biggest worry—water—yes, we'll be okay."

Grinning, Richard Compton said to himself, "Feasible!"

"Unbelievable!" exclaimed George Blake as he opened the taxi door for Michael as they headed to the nearby Marriott Hotel for the night.

✣   ✣   ✣

Back in his room after a dinner with George reviewing that most peculiar of all meetings, Michael couldn't wait to call Rose. They were finally in the same time zone. Michael was sure Rose would be amazed that he was so close to New York, yet he knew from their recent exchange of e-mails that there would be no way to see her. She was headed to sea Tuesday, and he was to be back on the plane to LA with his boss.

"I can't believe it, Rose," Michael lamented. "We are so close but yet so far away. Would the navy allow a civilian out on your boat tomorrow?"

"Oh, I do wish," Rose replied dejectedly, all the while trying her best to speak in an upbeat tone. "So ... how was your meeting there? Was it good? What's happening?"

"Well, it's all rather strange," replied Michael. "I can't believe my boss and I met today with such high-level people. It's exciting. Would you believe the secretary of energy and the secretary of the interior—great that they want to know more about my desalination theories, but … well … for whatever reason, they asked that I keep the details of our conversation confidential. Oh, how I wish I could tell you the full story Rose, but I think it's all about the concerns the president has been expressing for some eight months now about global warming. I guess from what I'm observing everything seems to be happening faster than anyone thought …"

"Michael, listen. It *is* happening faster. You met Jane Stricker in Seattle. Remember, I told you that she is the expert on the melting permafrost … and remember that I mentioned that I visited a very important admiral at the Pentagon who is very concerned about the observations I've been making about—"

"Right, right, I remember," Michael cut in. "Yeah, something's going on. Why would our president be talking about this on national television every single week for months and months? How come both of us are called to Washington? Why are we so important? There sure are loads of scientists and engineers much more experienced than we are about this global warming situation."

"Yes, but Michael, that means the work the two of us are doing must be pertinent. The arid areas are going to need water from the sea. We're going to have to vastly improve the efficiency of wind and solar power. You're on top of all that, Michael. Look, sea levels are rising, ocean currents are changing, and storms born at sea are getting worse. They want to corroborate my readings … but this is what we signed up for in life, Michael. We're in the game!"

"Well, I think you're right, Miss Rose," Michael said, now for the first time adopting a pet name for his comrade in the world of rapid climate change. "We're in the game. This is what we both wanted, but it sounds like the game is being played at a much faster pace than we imagined." After a pause, Michael continued softly, "So anyway, what are you doing for Thanksgiving? Are you on duty or home to see your folks?"

"Yes, so cool. The navy is generously giving me, and in fact our entire crew, Thanksgiving, the next day, Friday, and the weekend off. I guess they don't want a research ship wandering around the frigid North Atlantic while New Englanders are all eating turkey in their warm homes. If there is any snow up there in New Hampshire, I will try to catch a few ski runs, although the way temperatures are going I wonder. But wait, before I wish you Happy Thanksgiving, Michael, listen to this. I just received the advance materials on the Annual International Water Week Conference.

Would you believe, Michael, that it's going to be held in Palm Springs in February?"

"Awesome!" Michael's tone of voice suddenly jumped up a dramatic notch. "Man, I can be there from Santa Barbara in just a four-hour drive. Have you ever been to one? Will the navy sponsor you? Can you go?" Michael asked excitedly.

"Yes, yes … I can go. I will go! There will be no hurricane hitting New York this time," said Rose, matching Michael's excitement.

"Fantastic!" Michael exclaimed again.

Two hearts in perfect harmony—beating faster than ever with the excited anticipation of their next meeting.

✻　✻　✻

The Chief seldom spent time at home, even on holidays. His wife, a litigating attorney, spent most of her time at her downtown Indianapolis office, in court, or in her home office. Their two teenage sons were away in boarding school and typically spent holidays vacationing at resort homes owned by their friends' families. Aggressively active in the art of politics—that was the substance of his entire adult life. Now as Chief of Staff of the President of the United States, he was spending sixteen hours a day in the White House. He believed that the path to political power was to have as much knowledge as humanly possible about the political motives of both friends and foes and as much knowledge as humanly possible about all sides of pertinent political issues. At this instance, he simply could not sit still without learning more about the scientific subject of the melting permafrost. It seemed to be the overriding issue now promoting climate change. It was going to impact the political future of the country. It also seemed to be his path to the greatest jewel of all—absolute political power.

"I could simply call this person, this Jane Stricker, but maybe that's not enough," he thought to himself. Alone in his office late Monday night, after the meeting of the eight insiders and after the president's usual Monday night "chat," he conceived his plan. First thing Tuesday morning he would schedule a flight to Indianapolis for Thursday morning and arrange to take his wife out to dinner late Thursday afternoon for Thanksgiving dinner. Next, he would book a flight to Seattle for early Friday morning to personally meet with this famed Jane Stricker, the world's number one expert on the melting permafrost, the expert who was now sending her updated information to the UN's climate panel—the IPCC. Yet, who

knows how long it will take the IPCC to issue its next technical report. In fact, they may not accept her startling information without doing a double check to corroborate her research and her unexpected conclusions. Now this Jane Stricker will just have to see him Friday no matter how busy she might be at the University of Washington or whatever she might be doing over the holiday. One cannot turn down a visit from the Chief of Staff of the President of the United States.

*　*　*

Jane Stricker was happy to open the door for an important visitor at her small office on the nearly deserted campus. It was a four-day holiday weekend. Virtually everyone was gone. Jane maintained a nice apartment just off campus and enjoyed walking there and back. She was not married and lived alone. At age forty, she had enjoyed male companionship from time to time, but these relationships never lasted for long. Her love of research and her busy quest to be the world's top expert in the environmental conditions measured from her post in Seattle all the way to the North Pole kept her fully occupied. Jane knew that another environmental professor from Princeton, Richard Compton, was closely following her recent work and that her confidential reports were getting to higher-ups in Washington, DC. But for the Chief of staff of the president of the United States to come three thousand miles personally to see her, then obviously her work was part of something big. Interesting that the president of the United States had been discussing the issue of climate change for many months in his weekly evening chats. "This is suddenly so critical. I guess they really want to know firsthand how the rapid melting of the permafrost is going to influence the government's environmental policy," she thought to herself as the 3:00 meeting time approached.

"Very pleased to meet you Professor Stricker," the Chief offered to Jane as he shook her hand just outside the doors to her office building. "I trust I have not inconvenienced you too much on this holiday weekend."

"Oh, no," replied Jane pleasantly. "I'm very close by and had no special plans over the holiday. Research reports, research reports, and more research reports … you know." For some reason, Jane expected a very stern older man as the tone of the Chief's curt telephone call a few days earlier seemed so blunt and businesslike. Perhaps it was the political expertise of this man, but he seemed very nice, very courteous, very handsome, and indeed younger than she had imagined. Scholarly, wearing her large eyeglasses, her hair somewhat askew, with little makeup on, Jane suddenly felt slightly embarrassed that she had not better prepared herself. "Anyway, please come down to my office. Can I get you a cup of coffee, tea, water? And please just call me Jane. That's what everyone around here calls me ... from the students to the president of the university."

"That's fine, Jane. I would love some coffee if it's not too much trouble. I was up pretty early this morning to catch the flight here ... and by the way just call me 'Chief.' I've almost forgotten my real name. That's what everyone has been calling me these last few years working for the president."

The two were having a good time exchanging pleasantries in this very quiet setting. It seemed like no one else was in the entire building or to be seen outside Jane's windows strolling through the campus. It was their world alone. Finally, her visitor brought up the issue. "Jane, certainly I do not have to tell you that you are the expert in understanding a most important element within the global warming situation. I want you to know that your report—your information—that is now in the hands of the UN regarding the melting permafrost had been previously conveyed on a regular basis through your confidante Richard Compton directly to me and the president of the United States. I'm sure you're also aware that the president has been alluding to the global warming issue during his weekly 'chats' to the American people over the last eight months."

"Yes, Richard Compton calls me on a regular basis, and yes I have watched and listened to the president a number of times."

"Jane, this is extremely important. It's urgent. Are you sure of your data and conclusions? Could it be that sudden sunspots or something else could be causing the melting beyond what anyone expected? Is it temporary and will soon be ending?" The Chief was very adroit in challenging Jane, even knowing her answer in advance.

"Sir ..."

"No, no ... again, please call me Chief. I do not in any way want to dispute you and your data. It's just that it's all so incredible. The reason I'm here is that I just have to hear it directly from you, and I would like you to tell me in layman's language just what the permafrost is ... what's happening to it and why. What are its impacts, and when and how severe will they be? Thank you so much, Jane."

With that reassuring calmness, Jane went on to explain the essence of her recent life's work, her passion in life. "Yes, it's always theoretically possible that some other factor tipped the melting into this rapid acceleration state—solar activity we don't understand or whatever, but we scientists are pretty united that Man's fossil fuel emissions over the last fifty years tipped the scale. Now there is so much carbon going up there that we may have a doomsday cycle that can't be stopped."

Two hours later, it was dark outside. They could not believe how fast the time had gone, and it seemed like they were just getting started. Not having eaten all day, the Chief suddenly felt hungry and looked at his watch. "Wow, it's nine o'clock at the White House and I ... uh ... I haven't had anything. I'm a bit hungry, but Jane, I'm so sorry. Am I holding you back from your dinner plans?"

"Oh, no ... I ... uh ... don't have any plans tonight. Probably just going to try to find a movie on TV," Jane sheepishly replied. That was too fast a response, Jane thought to herself. "Golly, he thinks I'm a big-shot scientist, but I wonder what he thinks about me personally—a lonely egghead?"

"Well then, would you like to pick a restaurant and have dinner with me? I haven't even thought where I'm going to stay tonight. ... Maybe you can also recommend a hotel. My plane back to Washington is not until eleven o'clock tomorrow morning."

Acknowledging that this visitor was the Chief of Staff of the President of the United States, Jane picked an exclusive restaurant not too far from campus. Next she called the Ritz Carlton Hotel in downtown Seattle to book a deluxe room for him with guaranteed late arrival. She then excused herself and in the faculty ladies room managed to quickly fix her hair, put in her contact lenses, and added some makeup. At dinner—must have been the holiday weekend that meant that few other diners were to be seen—the two continued their technical discussion in nontechnical terms, just as the Chief had mandated. How did the evening go so incredibly well? Jane was delighted that she had accepted his invitation. How pleasurable—vodka cocktails, steak and fish, a nice bottle of wine, and port after dinner. It was suddenly three hours later.

"Jane, this has been a wonderful afternoon and evening. Forgive me for not knowing in advance that intellectual college professors—research scientists—could be so utterly charming. You said it's a long taxi ride to the Ritz downtown. It's gotten so late. Maybe, I ..." His voice trailed off, his eyes pleaded with hers. Was the Chief getting tired or was he remembering all the extracurricular activities he enjoyed in his off hours before he accepted this overwhelmingly busy job in the White House? For Jane too, the last few years had been almost all work and no play. She thought to herself, almost embarrassingly, "Here I am alone feeling no pain with the

Chief of Staff of the President of the United States only two blocks from my apartment." The words flowed out, "Chief! Are you thinking we should just let our hair down?"

✦   ✦   ✦

The Monday meeting on December 5 of the eight esteemed participants in the master planning process was rapidly approaching. The Chief was back in action. For several reasons, he had been feeling quite elated ever since his surprise trip to Seattle the prior week. He was now completely confident of the Oracle's predictions that global warming would soon be a catastrophe if dramatic action was not taken immediately, and he now understood the causes why. For more reasons than one, he now had a new confidante in his pocket—Professor Jane Stricker. But he also knew that to keep his president moving ahead and staying on target, more time would be needed than merely the two-hour dinner this Monday evening. It had taken the Chief only a few moments to call the Oracle, Richard, Arthur, Hank, John, and H. and request that the dinner meeting start two hours earlier over cocktails and appetizers. All obliged.

As usual, the president was the first to move away from the political and media chatter. He started the serious dialogue by 4:30. "Gentlemen, let's get going. We're getting close to our year-end deadline, and I'm delighted that the Chief arranged for all of us to get together earlier this week. ... So, Chief, why don't you start the order."

"Right. Gentlemen, I actually would like to start with myself in today's order of proceedings. A little unusual as you six are the experts, but let me tell you—as support for what the Oracle and Richard have been telling us for some time now about the incredible impact coming from the melting of the permafrost, I actually wanted to speak with Jane Stricker personally. I really wanted to grasp the gravity of the situation. It's unbelievable. As Richard has informed us, the permafrost covers 25 percent of the land area in the Northern Hemisphere and holds up to 30 percent of the world's carbon. The UN's IPCC scientists have been estimating that 90 percent of it could melt by the year 2100. However, as Jane informed you, Richard, that 90 percent melting could come within twenty years and not ninety years. We're soon going to experience a tremendous increase in sea levels, but worse, huge increases in air temperatures as a result of all that carbon. A climatic disaster ..." The meeting grew solemn.

"Not only that," interjected Richard, "but a lot of that carbon also released into the oceans will destroy the ecological balance as we know it,

89

and the millions of people who rely upon fish as their primary source of protein will no longer have that food source."

"Richard," said the Chief, "what's your take on how the scientists at the climate panel are going to interpret Professor Stricker's data?"

"Good question," responded Richard. "As you know, they have the data and Jane's conclusions right now. My inside sources tell me that the scientists working on the next technical report, to be released mid-January, are beside themselves. They are dismayed. They don't know whether to suppress the information and quietly seek corroboration or include her data in the report but downplay her conclusions about the imminent impacts. These scientists are not politicians, and as such they always have a fear of overly alarming the general public without a lot of proof confirming just one person's theory. Of course, as you know, the Oracle and I fully believe it, and no matter how the Intergovernmental Panel on Climate Change writes its report, it all ties together. The president's buildup over the last eight months now leads to the Master Plan, which is going to offer salvation to get us through this coming crisis."

The Oracle jumped in. "All right now. We have been through this before. Good that you all feel the sense of gravity about the situation, but come on. We need to spend this time getting the Master Plan devised and completed. We have no time to lose. Forget the IPCC."

"Okay," said the Chief. "Let's go. ... Arthur, you have the biggest volume of input. Please get started."

✻　　✻　　✻

And get started he did! Arthur Schnell had a massive task. The operational and geographical logistics to be contained in the Master Plan had at first seemed overwhelming. Gradually, however, Arthur grasped all the major issues brilliantly and proceeded without hesitation.

The first issue was security. All overseas military personnel would return to U.S. soil gradually over a period of two years. Manpower would be substantially increased by requiring all high-school graduates to spend the two years after their graduation in the military service. Their primary mission would be to protect the vast properties that would be left vacant by everyone's move to Colorado. All real estate property would be under constant camera surveillance, utilizing the most advanced electronic equipment yet devised. Police officers would have the option to move to Colorado with their families or join the military. The federal government in Washington, DC, would move to new quarters in Denver with the exception of the Pentagon, the military command center.

The next issue was moving almost three hundred million people to Colorado—a huge challenge. This task was not the Houston hurricane situation of evacuating one million people a short distance in one day for a short stay. Adequate housing must be rapidly built in Colorado. Hank must have adequate electricity to meet new power needs while at the same time balancing the difficult task of scaling down power capacity to those not yet moved from their current locations. Arthur estimated that a complete move would require five years. He hoped that time frame would allow sufficient time prior to the most severe climatic devastation sure to come to America. This meant moving about two hundred thousand people per day into about twenty thousand new residential buildings per day. The populace would have to be moved by all available means—cars, trucks, airplanes, and trains. Next, all vehicles unable to be converted to electric power would be transported to locations in the Rocky Mountains for materials recycling.

Thankfully the big issue of housing seemed an orderly undertaking. The first new inhabitants of what Arthur was dubbing "New America" would be carpenters, roofers, electricians, and plumbers, along with paving contractors for all the new streets to be built. Arthur calculated sufficient space for housing, commercial real estate, light industrial parks, streets, and open areas for recreation. He estimated that dwellings would be two stories high with an average of three persons per family, on two floors, or six persons on average per residential building. That would require fifty million dwellings. Each lot would be ten thousand square feet holding a fifty-foot-by-fifty-foot building, which would give a very comfortable twenty-five hundred square feet per residence and leave a nice twenty-five feet of open space on all sides of the building to the street and neighboring properties.

For fifty million dwellings on ten thousand square foot lots each, a total of five hundred billion square feet would be needed. With twenty-five million square feet in each square mile, twenty thousand square miles would be needed. The State of Colorado to the east of the Rocky Mountains measures 250 miles by 180 miles, or a total square mile area of forty-five thousand square miles. Factoring in room for streets, Arthur calculated an additional ten thousand square miles needed on top of his twenty-thousand-square-mile housing requirement, which would then leave fifteen thousand square miles for government, commercial, and light industrial buildings, and also for recreational parks, all in Eastern Colorado.

To test his mathematics, Arthur made a few calculations about population densities. The northeastern quarter of New Jersey is one of the most heavily populated areas in the country— approximately forty by fifty miles, or two thousand square miles, containing an estimated population of six million people, or three thousand people per square mile. That includes a lot of commercial, industrial, wetland, and park areas. A more strictly residential area would be the San Fernando Valley section of the City of Los Angeles, containing approximately 1.8 million people in an area only 10 by 25 miles, or 250 square miles, meaning a density of 7,200 people per square mile. The Colorado calculation would be three hundred million people divided by a thirty-thousand-square-mile residential area or ten thousand people per square mile. Arthur was delighted with his calculations. The San Fernando Valley calculation included parks and businesses and mostly one-story housing. The Colorado calculation excluded businesses and was based on two-story housing. Everyone could fit.

The issue of food was the easiest one for Arthur to handle. The large plateau known as the Great Plains runs from North Texas up through Kansas and Nebraska and the Dakotas and into southern Canada. The area was once a sea and has a huge aquifer running underneath, mostly under Nebraska and Kansas. Some 133 million gallons per day is withdrawn from the aquifer, three-fourths for agriculture. Rainwater from Colorado's Rocky Mountains replenishes the aquifer, but not sufficiently to prevent a net depletion of water. Global warming means less rainfall in the region. However, one major advantage of the warming will be a large increase in fertile land running north, thereby stimulating the already massive growing of beans and grains. Arthur's idea, as an ardent environmentalist, would be to eliminate the production and consumption of dairy and beef. This would eliminate the methane-producing greenhouse gases from farm and ranch animals. Meat protein would be replaced by fish raised on aquaculture farms and by soy protein derived from abundant soybeans grown on the plains. The other staple foods would be wheat and corn.

For health reasons, Americans would be expected to consume large quantities of fruits and vegetables. They also would become heart healthier from eliminating high-fat meat and dairy from their diets. Some of their fruits and vegetables would be grown locally and some imported from South America through the protected port of Baltimore and then transported to Denver by electric trains. In the small space behind each residential building, good soil would be added, and each family would have a small garden to grow their own fresh vegetables. In the spaces between the homes, the only trees planted would be fruit trees. Since his conversation with Michael, Arthur took comfort in the thought that the depleting aquifer of the Great Plains could be replenished by water transported from the Great Lakes.

As long as Hank provided the energy, then Arthur's main concern— providing enough domestic, commercial, industrial, and irrigation water—would be alleviated by not only the transportation of fresh Great Lakes water but also by desalinated water from the Pacific Ocean. Until those sources were ready, New America would obtain its drinking water from the reduced snowfalls and rainfalls of the Rocky Mountains along with transported water from rivers to the east. It was anticipated that the Colorado River would run dry in less than ten years. The only point of uncertainty in Arthur's mind was whether sufficient capacity could be built in time. The average American consumed between eighty and one hundred gallons per day of domestic water, often up to five hundred gallons per day per household. Even if that were to be reduced to an average of fifty gallons per day per person, three hundred million people would require fifteen billion gallons per day of treated clean water.

Other challenging issues would be the provision of soft goods like clothing and of hard goods like televisions and phones. Arthur imagined that the economists, John and H., would be determining which products could be assembled in Colorado and which might have to be imported from overseas. Obviously, the more that could be produced in Colorado the better, in order to provide more meaningful jobs for the people. Every residence would be provided with the latest computer technology for working at home, and every home would be provided with a modern sewing machine for assembling personal clothing. Some raw materials such as cotton and wool for clothing and exotic metals for appliances would require initial production overseas and then final assembly in Colorado. Arthur trusted that John and H. would arrive at a means of paying for any imported goods. Arthur was certain that, if required economically, substantially more gold and silver could be mined from Colorado's mountains. For any required importation of raw materials, again the Baltimore port with train service to Denver would be utilized. In addition, it would be feasible to move the port of Long Beach, California, further inland if it would be required to import raw materials from Asia. Again electric train service would be provided from there to Denver.

Petroleum-powered airplanes would be grounded and maintained at hangars around the country for potential future use. A New America airport necessary for the military and top government officials would be maintained in Denver.

The other important product requiring an adequate supply would be medicines. Arthur's plan outlined specific priorities for locations designated as pharmaceutical-production centers. The practice of good medicine would receive priority attention. Health-care reform would no longer be an issue of contention. The national government would be in charge of free universal health care.

Arthur did think about the people's welfare beyond basic needs of food, water, clothing, and medicine. Certainly, education would be a top priority. For lack of space, the government would set up home-schooling programs as well as special satellite locations for those unable to participate at home. A limited number of medical centers and hospitals would be provided for the critically injured or ill. The government would provide medical services at people's home locations whenever possible. He also thought about people's basic needs for diversion, such as sports, music, and entertainment. Space would be provided for these activities at multiple parks that would be constructed throughout the residential areas. Outdoor recreational areas for biking, hiking, and camping already located in Colorado's Rocky Mountains would be greatly expanded. Arthur thought that drawings on a lottery basis would be a smart way for the winners to enjoy vacation time.

The Chief then pointed silently at his watch. Arthur knew that his time was up at this special meeting. There was a lot more to cover from him and all the others, but he looked at the Chief, begging for just one more comment. "Gentlemen, let me just make one last point in my brief review of all these pertinent issues. Obviously, the nucleus to make this work is a centralized national government. What we would do is take over the state capitol building in Denver and all the other state offices as well as all the present offices now located in downtown Denver. The departments of the federal government would fill those spaces. But there's more— the brilliant intellectual minds in this country must be brought together to collaborate on how the Master Plan would continue to work, in case our now conceived temporary plan has to run longer than say five, ten, fifteen, twenty years. Oracle, you have yet to make it clear when global warming will begin to reverse—after we eliminate greenhouse gas emissions, the permafrost stabilizes, and America returns to normal?"

The Oracle simply stared at Arthur and said nothing. The Chief tried to hide it, but there must have been a slight smile on his lips. "So," Arthur continued, "my strong suggestion is to build a large university complex right next to the Air Force Academy. We would fill it with the top professors from every discipline as well as the elite engineers and scientists who are intimately involved in our project."

A brief pause ensued, and then the president spoke. "I like it, Arthur. I like it."

✼　✼　✼

It was now the energy czar's turn to review his topics. Hank Abrams, the president's secretary of energy, was a renowned expert in the power industry. He was never one to foster growth in the scary nuclear power industry, but now conditions had changed. No more burning cheap imported oil or exploiting America's abundant coal reserves, which pollute the atmosphere with greenhouse gases. His first step would be to reconfigure the nation's power grid so that electricity generated by existing nuclear plants would be sent to Colorado. These plants emit no carbon, so why not use them while no population centers are nearby? In addition, most of the existing plants are near the oceans, where the military would require electricity in its role as protectors of the nation's assets. What would have to be examined would be the impact of rising sea levels upon their efficient operation. Sea walls might have to be constructed to protect them. Some would have to be closed.

As the group had discussed many months before, Eastern Colorado was the ideal location for "New America," since its five-thousand-foot altitude kept the general climate cool enough that little air conditioning would be required in the summertime. It was not part of the hot Southwest. The area also received abundant sunshine in the wintertime. Accordingly, every residential building and every commercial and industrial building would be designed to hold a maximum number of solar panels on their roofs. Along with a maximum configuration of wind turbines up and down the corridor just east of the mountain range, Hank figured that all local requirements for electricity could eventually be met by wind and sun. The extreme temperature differentials from the nearby mountain peaks of the Rockies to the plains produce a constant windy condition. Wind experts calculate that an average eighteen mph wind speed is necessary to efficiently drive the turbines that generate electrical current.

Colorado looked ideal. Windy conditions are also prevalent in the wide-open Great Plains states, so the idea of using wind power to drive water through pipelines from the Great Lakes uphill to Colorado also appeared feasible. Likewise on the western side of the Rockies the vast deserts all the way to Los Angeles could conceivably provide a feasible solar energy configuration for transporting vast quantities of desalinated water from the Pacific Ocean uphill to Colorado. Hank's job of generating abundant power looked easy. His department had already bought thousands of large turbines produced by General Electric over the last several years. Many of these had been standing idle as Americans had found it much less expensive to buy electricity produced from traditional sources than the more expensive wind farms. For example, the press had reported that back in 2008 T. Boone Pickens, a legendary Texas oil tycoon, had already purchased two billion dollars worth of giant turbines—687 of them to be mounted on structures four hundred feet tall in West Texas—but found them to be uneconomic at the time. The Interior Department bought them at a 10 percent discount in early 2011. "But now, how quickly economics can change," Hank said aloud.

Hank noted that just a couple of years ago at a meeting in Italy, leaders of the industrial world had vowed to reduce their carbon emissions by 80 percent by the year 2050 in order to reduce average world temperatures by four degrees Fahrenheit. With the advent of the new crisis, under the Master Plan the United States amazingly would reduce its carbon emissions to near zero by just the year 2020. Richard Compton smiled to himself and hoped no one brought up his silly notion that we humans all breathe out carbon dioxide with each breath and that God forbid if this new powerful central government decides that each of us is a "polluter."

*　　*　　*

Now it was time to turn to the last participants in the Group of Eight to get onboard with the plan to save America from the ravages of global warming. It appeared that the renowned economics professor from Penn's Wharton School of Industry and Finance and the prestigious Federal Reserve banker were now convinced.

"Gentlemen, we have come a long way," said John Heyward forcefully. "The economic part of the Master Plan is going to appear quite radical, we know … and although we are convinced of its feasibility, we will proceed publicly on the premise that all of this is 'temporary'—an emergency—necessary to save our nation. Let me start with the all-important subject of real estate." John went on to discuss a number of property issues. "Outside of Colorado, title to all existing real estate properties will be recorded into a national database. Titles will be frozen in the owners' names effective the date the Master Plan becomes effective and at the appraised value as of the date of January 1, 2012." John wanted no speculative fluctuations past that date. "In other words, existing ownership rights will be preserved. Inside Colorado, all undeveloped land and all developed properties including the new residences will be temporarily owned by the national government. Approved occupiers will use the property free of charge.

"All records of local and state governments will also be preserved. The military will provide security. To allow the economic plan to work, America's normal political and legal system will have to be put in abeyance. Only one government entity will be in place during the temporary emergency—that would be the 'national' government headquartered in Denver. The federal judicial system will continue in place to settle disputes, but Congress will be given a long 'vacation.' With respect to intangible assets such as stocks, bonds, marketable securities, and cash, again values at January 1, 2012, will be inventoried and preserved. In order to have funds available until each person moves to Colorado, I will ask H. to explain the new monetary system in a minute," John interspersed in his presentation.

"At the effective date of the Master Plan, every industrial company in America will start reducing its output by 20 percent per year so that all future production will be taking place in Eastern Colorado by the end of the fifth year. Each company will be reimbursed by the national government for its loss of business profits during that transition. American consumers will continue to purchase both domestic and imported goods until the move to Colorado, at which time a new system of commercial distribution will take place utilizing 'new' money.

"In Colorado, the national government will control all means of production and distribution. During the time of the 'temporary emergency,' consumers will have little choice." Nevertheless, John promised that "homes, home furnishings and all the comforts of home will be of the highest standards. Clean streets and clean properties will be maintained by a work force of government employees." In fact, John's greatest challenge was to devise a plan that would keep everyone busy with productive work and would provide a supply of goods and services that would be adequate and of high-quality standards. Ideally, most work would be performed at home, except for personal services required for others. For everyone who was mentally and physically capable of working under prescribed government standards, he believed that his goal could be achieved. As Arthur had indicated, whatever goods could not be produced locally would be imported under strict controls.

Obviously, a national government economics czar would have to be appointed with a huge and competent staff, but John was certainly not positioning himself for that job. He did point out the fact that current skill levels of working Americans would not exactly match the skill levels or the numbers required by the economy of New America. Another government agency would need to be established to handle retraining so that each capable person would be a contributor to the new economy. John laughed when he pointed out that "just a couple of years before there had been a lot of talk around America about creating 'green' jobs. Well, here it was in fact—100 percent."

H. picked up the monetary part of the new economic plan. He noted that money, or currency, had for thousands of years been the intermediary for traders exchanging goods. In free markets, the quantity of that money and who held it determined the allocation of resources through the pricing mechanism. Sometimes in closed societies, a central government printed money and discovered that too much money chasing too few goods caused massive price inflation. In modern societies, central banks of sovereign nations were created to regulate the quantity of money and to influence interest rates on borrowed money in order to stimulate economic output without causing inflation. Whenever governments imposed price and wage controls to dampen inflation, typically the supply of goods would fall dramatically, making the situation worse. In other words, a confusing mix of government control, free-market choice, and a semi-controlled money system rarely resulted in economic stability for very long because of its complex mix of differing objectives. On the other hand, if the government stayed out of the equation altogether, then private industry over-exuberance and excessive self-interest would typically take over, and without regulation the system would boom but eventually crash in its own overindulgence.

So H. figured that neither Adam Smith's "hands off" theory nor Communism's "from each according to his ability to each according to his needs" theory would work. And there would be no mix—not part socialism, part capitalism. No mix, no compromise. The only economic system that would allow the president, the Savior, to exert complete stability in this temporary national emergency would be one where money is completely controlled by a central bank. Accordingly, as of the Master

Plan effective date, all banks would close and all bank deposits and loans would be frozen. A new denomination of money, called the "new dollar," would be created and pegged to a set gold and silver standard. Therefore, America could continue to import goods from overseas and pay for them. All citizens in Colorado would have an account with the national bank and be paid through direct deposit—the same new dollar amount for each hour worked.

Since the government would be providing free housing, free education, free medical care, and free electric automobiles, the only use of such money would be for food, clothing, personal and household goods, and amenities. The amounts to be paid for assigned work would be standardized without variance. Minimum working hours would be at least high enough to be able to purchase a reasonable quantity of food necessary for good nutritional balance. It may have sounded as though Hank was proposing a repeat of past failures—a powerful central government printing money along with wage and price controls to prevent inflation, but in this case there would be a fair allocation of resources; there would be no production of unwanted products. There would be the proper production and distribution of the right products required for this particular economy. There was no need to create wealth for anyone in this temporary economy. Everyone was equal. It appeared to be ingenious.

✻ ✻ ✻

The Chief looked at his watch. It was nearing 8:00 PM, and the president would have to start preparing for his ten o'clock weekly "chat" with the nation. "Okay, Hank. Let's stop there. Good work. Mr. President, I suggest we start at four o'clock again next Monday. We have to quickly get all this information into concise order, and then I suggest we allow time to review the possible objections we will be hearing as you announce the plan in early January. Emergency or not, temporary or not, our country has a history of free speech and open debate. I'm sure there will be many who disagree that we are handling the situation in the best way."

"Chief … Chief," said the president, breaking into a wide grin. "You know, that's my job, and there will only be a handful of dissenters. Don't worry. I'll get them." That was exactly what the Chief wanted to hear. The evening ended with everyone in a good frame of mind and looking forward to next week's meeting. Little did they dream of the political turmoil soon to be facing their president. After all, the Savior was the Savior, and the best evidence of dreadful things to come was that for the first time on record there had been no snowfall during late November/early December anywhere in the country. Not one flake. This was global warming.

*   *   *

In the days that followed, John and H. were constantly on the phone together. They knew that the Chief would be putting their handwritten notes into draft political narrative as an important part of the Master Plan. They knew that the meeting next Monday, December 12, might be their last chance for revisions or new ideas before the Chief finalized a document for the president by Christmas. From the beginning, the Chief's demand had been to complete the Master Plan by Thanksgiving and give the president a few weeks' time to digest it and prepare for his announcement of the plan by Christmas. The timetable now was amended to announce it the day after New Year's Day, January 2, 2012. The Chief's latest consideration had become: when would the plan go into effect? Just think of the political challenge to amend the U.S. Constitution so drastically, even if the president were to successfully mesmerize the entire country with his rhetoric. John and H. were worried. They wanted to be sure both the general public and the nation's economists would buy into their part of the plan.

That week found everyone else in the Group of Eight busy as well. The president and his Chief of staff huddled often between meetings and speeches in the Chief executive's busy schedule. Their conversation focused over and over again on the subject of how to best transition the country from nine months of verbal warning, the "chats," to a course of direct physical action. A monumental task—motivating a new direction in human behavior for America. The Master Plan had to sound voluntary, not like an act of coercion. This was not to be like the old China regime forcing people to move to farmland back in the 1970s backed by a strong military under central command. The Savior would have to be at his very best. All week long he and his Chief spoke only in the most positive, optimistic tones, pumping themselves up, but not one word was mentioned of their private, internal doubts.

At the same end of the spectrum of cautious optimism were the words and thoughts of the Oracle and his scientific advisor, Richard. They found time for hours of phone conversations between themselves during the week. It sounded something like this: "All this time in preparation … we face an imminent catastrophe, and we finally have a good solution," the Oracle repeated over and over again, "But can the president pull it off?"

✢ ✢ ✢

On Friday, December 9, the Chief e-mailed everyone that the Monday meeting of eight would start at its normal 6:00 PM time—no early four o'clock start. The president seemed to be in a jovial mood during the dinner. No talk of the plan came up until 7:00 PM when the Chief passed out a thick notebook. Then the mood turned serious. There were no words on the outside cover, but the first page inside had the words "**MASTER PLAN**" in huge black letters. "Okay," started the Chief. "Would everyone please open to the first page—CONTENTS—read it, and then read the second page—SUMMARY." Everyone seemed quite amazed that what would appear to be about a three-hundred-page document had been so neatly organized into major chapters by key issues with subtitles clearly marked for every subject discussed during the many preceding weeks. It was detailed right down to a precise description of the fruit trees to be planted on every residential plot of land in Eastern Colorado.

The Chief had done a miraculous job. He had kept all the notes submitted by the participants, had recorded meticulous memos of the verbal comments, and had just one administrative assistant put the whole package together under strict confidentiality. It was absolutely amazing that no word of an action plan in the works had been leaked to the press all these months. Despite the strong hurricanes of 2010 and the 2011 Houston and New York hurricanes, the increased number of tornadoes, and the severe heat and drought in the Southwest, the president and his Chief of staff had deftly led the press into thinking that the president's eight months of referencing climate change was nudging the public into a gradual change in habits and getting Congress to pass additional legislation—further reducing dependence on fossil fuels, moving at a faster pace toward wind and solar power, electric cars, green jobs, conservation, environmentalism, and the like. Panic was to be avoided.

The regular Monday evening White House visitors had parroted that same line when occasionally asked what they were doing there. In fact, the president had done such a good PR job that polls overwhelmingly showed that America's Chief executive was right on top of this important issue. His responses to the major hurricanes of 2010 and the Houston and New York City hurricanes of 2011 were considered "perfect." The "chats" had worked.

But as the Oracle, Richard, Arthur, Hank, John, and H. in their immense curiosity were quickly scanning the large, heavy notebook after reading the summary and before the Chief could command them again, three thoughts were racing through the mind of the president: "I've prepared my audience, but there will be dissenters. An overwhelming majority does not mean unanimous." Secondly, "How do I suddenly transition my people from thinking 'gradual' to 'abrupt,' from 'concern' to 'crisis'?" And lastly, "Thank goodness Chief didn't include the issue of constitutionality. We need to think that out."

The Chief knew that everyone would be scrambling through the book at this first sighting, so he calmly restrained himself and took pleasure in watching the commotion. When the shuffling finally began to diminish, the Chief continued, "Okay, next, here's the plan: We have about forty-five minutes left. All your prior inputs, which of course are represented in the material in front of you; if you have any changes or amendments you would like to make, jot them down now and give them to me before we break up. I'll get them into the document tomorrow and then get revised copies of the book delivered to you on Wednesday. I would like to have everyone read the document before the weekend and call me with any additional revisions or corrections by Friday at 8:00 PM. I plan to have a final copy to everyone by Sunday afternoon.

"Then, that's it. We will have had our last meeting on this document, gentlemen, next Monday, December 19, just to review everything in logical, summary form. The president's last 'chat' will be about two minutes long, just to wish everyone a Merry Christmas and a happy holiday. After that the president and I will be drafting his January 2 speech, presenting the Master Plan to the American people. Please mark your calendars to be here for luncheon on Monday the second of January at noon. We will need to brief the entire cabinet and certain congressional leaders and then spend some time reviewing everything again before the president's eight o'clock address to the nation."

The scene was eerie—eight mature men of the highest intellect and fame sitting completely still around an ornate dining room table in America's White House in complete silence, each holding onto a large book with a blank cover, each staring off into nowhere with his own innermost thoughts, hopes, doubts … and perhaps prayers.

* * *

The next two and a half weeks went like clockwork, just as the Chief had planned. Intertwined with his tremendous personal drive and ambition, his thirty years of experience since his college days as a backroom organizer were now paying huge dividends. The six outside members of the Group of Eight were in complete alignment now. This was not just an exercise in getting a new and different piece of legislation to the floor of Congress in front of a raucous membership of many different political persuasions. This was a radical plan to place extreme domestic emergency powers in the hands of the president in order to survive an upcoming catastrophe to the nation—and to do so in the land of cherished personal freedom.

The dinner meeting on Monday the nineteenth went smoothly. The holiday week between Christmas and New Year's was a joyous reprieve for those parts of a nation trying to recover from those disastrous hurricanes and a severe drought in the Southwest. The Chief's daily sessions with the president were perfectly productive. The forty-five minute address to the nation was sounding comprehensive and convincing during its drafting, polishing, and rehearsals. The meeting with the White House counsel and Vice President Graham set for 9:00 AM on January 2 was all set, as was the luncheon briefing meeting to follow with the president's full cabinet, his vice president, the Chief Justice of the Supreme Court, the Speaker of the House, and both the Senate and House majority and minority leaders. The television networks and the press would not be told about the president's address to the nation until late Sunday night January 1. Any media speculation occurring on Monday was fine, as it would build up viewing intensity for the evening's address.

✵   ✵   ✵

"Rose, please!" screamed Adriana. "Please go home, get dressed, and come to the party with me. It's New Year's Eve. We're going to have a blast."

"No, no. Thanks, Ad ... there's just too much on my mind. I can't settle down. I sense something very ominous going on in our world right now, and anyway, I want to talk to Michael tonight. Just think, with the three-hour time difference, we can talk from midnight here 'til three in the morning when it's midnight out there."

"Huh?" responded Ad, not understanding Rose's logic at all. The two had enjoyed a nice early dinner together at Adriana's apartment. It was now approaching nine o'clock. "Yeah, okay, but before you call him, why not just come for a couple of hours and get your mind off all that stuff for a while ... relax ..."

"Ad, sweetheart, no. I can't relax. Let's just have one more glass of champagne, and then I'll help you look like a knockout. Me? I just can't get myself together; I'll just park right here."

Michael's call came three hours later as Rose was beginning to doze on Adriana's couch. "Miss Rose. Hi, you know I just can't stop thinking about you."

"Michael, I think about you right in the middle of my temperature calculations onboard my rocking chair navy boat," she giggled. "But listen, my mind is in turmoil. Jane is right. Something big is going on. I called my parents a little while ago to wish them a Happy New Year. It still has not snowed up there in New Hampshire. That's never happened before ... and then my ocean readings are going through the roof. I know out there where you are it still has not rained, and the temperatures in Phoenix are still over a hundred degrees, and—"

Agreeing with Rose's concerns but struggling to change the subject momentarily to try to enjoy the holiday spirit, Michael interrupted her: "I know. You're right, but you know something? I have two tickets to the Rose Bowl tomorrow in Pasadena, and all I can think about right now is you there sitting by my side."

Chapter Five

Turmoil

The Oval Office at the White House, 9:00 AM Monday, January 2, 2012

The president's chief counsel and his two assistants looked on in astonishment as the president and his Chief of staff rattled off in precise dialogue a perfect description of the nation's imminent crisis and their solution to it. A large white book was placed on top of the president's desk, large black letters in gold trim emblazoned across the front cover: "**THE MASTER PLAN.**"

"But here's the challenge," said the Chief. "We have three hours now to research and draw a strategy before we face constitutional objections at our important luncheon meeting at noon. We have three equal branches of federal government, and we're going to ask two of them to sit tight for a while, although the Supreme Court could be active in judging interpretation of our emergency rules. So the question is the legality of our executive branch powers during a national emergency."

"How about Lincoln at the start of the Civil War?" the president interjected. "And how about FDR during the Great Depression and World War II? Our founders must have left leeway for the Chief executive to act at his discretion in times of a national emergency. And look at how the 'general welfare' clause has been liberally interpreted the last eighty years."

"Right. Now I'm sure," continued the Chief, "that we—I mean, our president, our Savior—will absolutely convince ... I mean one hundred percent ... the other two branches of government and all fifty state governors and all the American people that we are facing an imminent, unimaginable catastrophe of untold tragedy unless he takes bold control of the situation himself. There can be no dissent, no naysayers. We must have one leader, one vision, one voice to guide us through." The White House Chief counsel could not get a word in.

At 10:00 AM, the president closed the meeting with his legal staff. "Let's take a break, gentlemen, and do a little research. We'll reconvene here at 11:30. Let's have some answers."

*　*　*

The noon luncheon meeting commenced with the usual pleasantries among representatives of the three branches of government, but only for a few brief minutes. All the invitees looked nervous. Why was the former senator from Louisiana there? And who was this John Heyward, or this Richard Compton? They were not Washington people. Climate change, yes, climate change; that's it. The president had been pressing the issue for months. While there had been no leaks from the White House, and the president's "chats" had not been unduly alarming, the whole country sensed that something was happening much faster than they had previously been led to believe. And those disastrous hurricanes during the 2010 and 2011 seasons, the tornadoes, the droughts, the heat, the lack of snowfall—something was up.

Even before the crab salad appetizers had been fully consumed, the president opened the meeting. "Ladies and gentlemen, yes, I know what you are thinking. This is an unusual mix to have been brought together. Let me introduce Richard Compton and John Heyward to those who have not yet met them."

Just at that instant, the brilliant master of political art interrupted, "Sorry, Mr. President," the Chief said forcefully. "The vibrator signal in my mobile just won't stop. My staff is telling me that the mayors of New York, Houston, and Phoenix are on a conference call together and will not get off the White House line until we communicate with them." This was opera at its best. The Chief's plan and its execution were perfect.

"I know they're panicked," said the president. "But can they please wait for a couple of hours?"

Everyone outside the Group of Eight swirled nervously in their chairs, wondering what in the world was going on. "Sorry, everybody, but I am being besieged by the mayors of New York City and Houston about the continued shutdown of their ports and the mayor of Phoenix about its drought."

Luckily, the major hurricanes of 2011 had surprisingly veered off to sea except for the two that centered on Houston and New York City. While ample warnings of the coming blasts of wind and water served to minimize the loss of life, property damage had been extensive, particularly in the port areas. In addition to the temporary chaos in New York as a result of the shutdown of the city's subway system, hundreds of thousands of jobs were directly or indirectly lost as a result of the ports' continued closures in both regions. Despite massive federal aid and insurance company payouts, physical damage was so immense that it would be several months before import/export goods would be flowing again. In Phoenix, on the other hand, the problem was the continuing scorching heat. Summer temperatures over one hundred degrees Fahrenheit continued unabated. Water from the Colorado River and other sources had slowed to a trickle. The city's electric power supplies were being severely rationed as power sources could not handle the heavy and sustained air-conditioning loads. Life was in disarray in the entire Southwest.

The Chief nodded back. "Yes, Mr. President, they will wait for your callback at three o'clock."

"Well then, let me continue. We have a grave situation confronting us. Climate change, more specifically 'global warming,' is not the concern of the twenty-first century. It is *the* concern for all of us *right now—* today!" The president then went on for about twenty minutes in a perfect cadence reviewing the last nine months of warnings he had been giving the American people. But now, however, he had learned that the adverse impacts of global warming would not be occurring gradually. As scientists like Richard Compton described it, the climate change was considered "abrupt." The luncheon guests listened intently, now transitioning from comprehension of the seriousness of the situation to next waiting for the president's proposed course of action. That's when jaws dropped.

"Yes, that is exactly the plan of action—evacuation! There's no choice. It is the only action we can take. The safety of the American people takes precedence over every other factor. As Chief executive, that is my number one responsibility. I know your first thoughts, and believe me I have considered all options and reviewed them with my advisors numerous times. But just moving people back from the coastal areas is not sufficient. The problem is much bigger. It affects virtually the entire United States. Now remember; we pray that the situation is temporary and that by reducing air carbon emissions to virtually zero we will be able to see a reversal in the situation in a few short years.

"Let me be perfectly clear. You might be thinking—wait for the full impact of the crisis when everyone is clearly convinced and then move. But we cannot wait until then. It would be catastrophic. We first thought it would take ten years to make the transition to a safe area. Now we believe that the crisis will be in full force within five years, so we have moved our time table for reaching safety to half that time—full evacuation to middle America within five years."

The message was now beginning to sink in. The president's elite audience was now beginning to accept the need for a radical plan of action. Just imagine—moving everyone to a safe area in the middle of the country and having the military protect all other properties until the crisis passed. Perhaps not such a preposterous plan after all. Perhaps brilliant.

But now the stunning statement: "Now, ladies and gentlemen, to set this plan in motion—I am going to be very frank with you—we need strong leadership with a clear message and a solid plan. I have that plan. I believe I can deliver a clear message tonight in my address to the American people. But the all-important ingredient is strong leadership! We cannot allow for extended debate or haggling or even dissent. At the same time we cannot turn the American presidency into a dictatorship, so I am seeking this covenant: I must be granted temporary emergency powers similar to what is granted in our Constitution to the Chief executive during the time of declared war. If this requires a minor modification to our Constitution, then so be it. We must get it accomplished. Now here's what I am specifically requesting of you."

In a brilliant monologue, the president continued to speak without hesitation for the next ten minutes about the executive powers he required. At the same time, he needed to have the Congress and the state governors and the state legislatures enter a so-called time warp until the national emergency had passed. Obviously this phase of the president's appeal to his luncheon guests was quite hard to swallow, but it took only a few minutes longer for the overwhelming thought "Savior" to be at the forefront in their minds. This man was truly someone very, very special—gifted! Nevertheless, how could it ever be possible that most members of Congress or the governors of the states would go along with such a concentration of power in the hands of the Chief executive of the federal government? It requires two-thirds majorities in the state legislative bodies and both federal legislative bodies, ratified by three-fourths of the states, to amend the federal Constitution. Certainly constitutional amendments have a long history of taking place—twenty-seven of them—but never one remotely close to what the president was now seeking. Surely the super majorities would have to be firmly convinced that a national crisis was underway and a national catastrophe imminent. True, it was clear to everyone in the room that the climate change of the last two years had been much more dramatic than what was anticipated, *but evacuate virtually everyone to Colorado?* Brilliant maybe in its simplicity, but suddenly it began to sound like science fiction if everyone of status was going to be on the sidelines except an all-powerful president.

The luncheon schedule was extended an extra hour to three o'clock in order to allow the cabinet members, congressional leaders, and the Supreme Court Chief justice to ask questions. The Chief White House counsel was also in attendance. No one could mistake the solemn tone of the Oracle warning that the coming days would be truly catastrophic for American civilization without dramatic, immediate action. The luncheon guests left the White House with that message clearly understood. The perplexing bone of contention centered around the president's request for absolute power. After all, these were powerful people in their own right.

Knowing the president's former 10:00 PM brief "chat" had been changed to a prime-time formal address to the nation, the press was beginning to clamor for explanations. It was impossible to hide the fact of who was attending a special luncheon at the White House and that it did not end until 3:00 PM. This situation was just what the Chief wanted. The anticipation of the president's address and its almost obvious reference to global warming was building an incredible level of national anxiety. Probably every television set in the nation would be on tonight—perfect for the Savior. The next few hours seemed like an eternity. The Chief paced around the Oval Office, his heart racing. The president, nervous on the inside, calm on the outside, reviewed his address to the nation over and over again. His secretary opened the door every fifteen minutes. "Is there something I can get for you?" she asked. "And Mr. President, your private telephone line is ringing off the hook."

"No, no calls. At this time I want no outside interferences," he responded. "Just bring us more coffee and doughnuts ... and fruit. At least, Chief, I did speak with the mayors you lined up."

As the time approached eight o'clock, the Chief again reviewed the follow-up plan after the address. "We will return to the Oval Office here, and I will place calls for you to select members of Congress and governors. These are the most powerful. This will take us past midnight. Skip your usual workout tomorrow morning." The scrambling Chief finally let loose a hearty laugh over that remark. "I will schedule a 6:00 AM taping of an interview with you right here in the Oval Office with ABC News. Let's say twenty minutes. Excerpts of your address and your interview showing you clearly in charge of this emergency will be repeated all day long on all the news networks."

✳   ✳   ✳

It was time. "My fellow Americans. I will get right to the point. I address you this evening on a matter of extreme urgency for each and every one of us. Without immediate effective action taken by all of us, our great nation and its great people face a grave national catastrophe. The threat is beyond imminent. It is beyond a possibility. It is actually happening—right now.

"For the last nine months, I have been speaking to you every week about our changing climate. I have explained why it is happening and how the warming of our atmosphere is accelerated by the excessive burning of fossil fuels for our energy needs. I have explained how the waste chemical—carbon dioxide, a gas emitted from the burning of petroleum products and coal—helps trap the sun's heat in our atmosphere and warm the planet." Serious, somber, but in a clear, strong tone of voice, the president continued at length to review and explain the history of and the reasons for the planet's global warming.

"My fellow citizens, during my first two years in office, my administration along with close cooperation from the Congress did our best from the information we had at the time to mitigate the adverse impacts of this situation and to protect our form of civilization through the rest of this century. Legislation was enacted to eliminate 80 percent of the burning of fossil fuels by the year 2050. However, the premise behind such legislation was recognition that average global temperatures rose two degrees Fahrenheit in the second half of the twentieth century but would be expected to gradually rise by more than four degrees Fahrenheit in the twenty-first century; that is, without restricting the burning of fossil fuels. Most important as a factor in influencing climatic conditions in that average four degree forecast was the estimate by the world's leading scientists that average temperature increases in the Arctic areas would increase by more than *fifteen* degrees. Such drastic warming would lead to our experiencing at least twenty adverse impacts upon our way of living. Let me enumerate them." And the president did, describing each one in detail.

"Accordingly, it had been our best judgment following the recommendations of the world's leading scientists that we would substantially mitigate these adverse impacts by eventually eliminating man's contribution to the buildup of these greenhouse gases in the atmosphere. But unfortunately, we are too late. As I come before you this evening, after studying the stunning number of the recent hurricanes rated highest in severity—that is, Category 5 with winds in excess of 150 miles per hour -- the ones that pounded our southern states in the year 2010 and the two that recently hit our Houston and New York City areas—it has been determined that these were *not* freak happenstances in the normal course of weather history. It has also now been determined that the 112 degree temperature you might expect in Phoenix, Arizona, in July … that it is *not* a freak of nature that we experienced the same temperature there—in Phoenix—this afternoon! Yes, in the wintertime, in the Northern Hemisphere. Nor is it an unusual blip on our weather maps not to see one ounce of snow on any mountaintop right now, *in January*, anywhere in the United States." The president paused for a moment, dropping his eyes down as though in pain, and then continued forcefully, more emotionally now, looking squarely at the camera and its invisible adjacent teleprompter.

"My fellow citizens, this is only the beginning. We are swiftly facing a national crisis. Without immediate bold action, we are facing a national catastrophe. Let me explain what has recently happened that has dramatically changed all of our prior thinking. Let me talk about something called the *permafrost*," the president continued, one minute the articulate science professor, the next minute the strong effective commander-in-Chief. It was brilliant theater in a real setting with a completely captive audience. The other seven members of the Group of Eight had been sitting with and listening to this man for many months, but their rapt attention at this moment was amazing to behold. All of them had years of experience in the art of presentation and persuasion, but this performance exceeded all expectations. Even the Chief, after all the repeated rehearsals, stood in awe at how masterful the Savior was articulating his message, creating the required sense of urgency and skillfully preparing his immense audience for the knockout punch at the end of the address—the Master Plan.

Forty-four minutes had gone by—on target for the forty-five-minute planned address. Conveyance with a strong sense of urgency, emotionally charged, but with no sense of panic. Informative, but not overly intellectual. Mastery of the facts, eloquently delivered. The essence of the Master Plan had been brilliantly revealed in clear language. The Chief was ecstatic with the performance of his articulate boss.

"Now let me be perfectly clear. I am declaring a *national emergency*, but at the same time I wish to convey to you that there is no need for panic or hysteria and that we have ample time ahead to implement this plan in an orderly fashion. The overriding factors for this action—let me repeat, the overriding factors in this entire operation—are for *your safety* and for the *security* of the properties and possessions of every American.

"In the coming days, I will be briefing the Congress and your governors about the details of the Master Plan while at the same time continuing to keep all of you fully informed. And at this very moment, I want to assure you that the full attention of your government's emergency response resources is directed toward aiding the damaged areas of the Northeast and our Gulf Coast as well as the heat-stricken entire Southwest region. My fellow Americans, rest assured that I will be expending my entire energies in the coming days to making America safe for all of you. Have comfort. With your unfailing courage, together we will succeed in this bold endeavor. May God bless you, and may God bless America."

*   *   *

At that moment electronic America was in full gear. There was no rushing to the streets. No alarms sounded, but the media was broadcasting that every home telephone, every mobile phone, and every online computer was going full blast. "What's happening? What do we do? Is this for real? Did you hear the president? Evacuation? For how long? Is he kidding? What happens to my house?"

And now human behavior nurtured over millions of years of biological evolution and thousands of years of cultural evolution was coming into play. A land of three hundred million people with three hundred million genetically different physical brains with three hundred million individually different-thinking minds and personalities; no two of us exactly alike; immigrated into America from hundreds of different foreign cultures of differing values. In America, the most common cultural value Americans would come to share is a *love for freedom in a land of opportunity*. In rich America a few basic biological traits inherent in human nature had become taken for granted. The big three of those basic traits over 99 percent of our evolutionary timeframe relate to our genetic needs for nutrition to provide our energy, for procreation to maintain our species, and for a secure space to protect ourselves. The president had to take care of those three. He did mention that ample food supplies would be available from the Great Plains, and he did mention that families would be kept together. However, his reference to housing in Eastern Colorado was somewhat vague. The American home was sacred. Attainment of security in one's own home had always been the American dream of every adult person. The destruction of thousands of homes in Louisiana and Mississippi as a result of hurricane Katrina was indeed traumatic. However, the prevailing thought then was that evacuation away from the storm would be temporary. Displaced residents would soon return to their own rebuilt houses. What was the president saying? Horrific hurricanes are coming, but we cannot soon move back? My home is my home. My neighborhood is where I live. It is my own secure space—a basic human need.

☆　☆　☆

The Oval Office, 9:00 AM, January 3, 2012

It was unplanned, but the Chief had quickly assembled the entire now-renowned Group of Eight. He had cautioned John and Richard not to head home to Philadelphia and Princeton the night before. "Incredible," the Chief said. "Your speech was perfect. We had congressional leaders lined up; your calls to the key governors last night went smoothly; response into ABC News was positive after this morning's interview, but—"

The Oracle jumped in, "But what? It's obvious. Everyone accepted the president's buildup over the last nine months. Everyone accepted the president's brilliant address last night and his follow-up interview this morning. So it's not the messenger. It's the shock of the message. That should be expected."

"Right, I agree," said the increasingly loquacious John Heyward. "Mr. President, look how shocked and surprised we were when we first started meeting with you last spring, but it did not take us long to get on board with the message and the solution."

"Yes, John, but with us, the president was dealing with a rather informed audience," interjected Arthur Schnell. "We're all well educated and in tune with the great issues of the day. The statistics were that on any given Monday night during the president's "chats" last year, the tuned-in audience averaged 30 percent of all the television sets in the United States. That leaves the majority of Americans watching sports or entertainment or not watching TV or going to bed worried about their jobs or family or whatever. They're not focused on some possible future threats of global warming ... or carbon emissions ... or greenhouse gases ... or rising tides if they live in Austin, Texas, five hundred feet above sea level. So I agree that it was a shock."

Excited, everyone around the president's desk wanted to get a word in. These seven were now the trusted cohorts of the president of the United States in the boldest endeavor since the secret making of the world's first atomic bomb. But this was different, vastly different. Then, the American public was in the dark and remained in the dark until after the dropping of that awesome weapon upon foreign soil. And the motivation then was to bring a devastating war to a quick end in order to save American lives thousands of miles away. Now, it was different—again to save American lives, but on American soil. No secrets this time—it's all out in the open … it's feeling the fear, and it's knowing that there might be no quick end to the crisis.

"Wait now!" The normally soft-spoken, cerebral Richard Compton jumped into the animated discussion. "New ball game. On the way in, the news on the radio is that the whole nation is tuned in. Every radio station; every newspaper this morning; every TV station; the top of the Internet news. Everyone now knows what's going on. There is great concern, mental turmoil, yes … but fortunately no panic, no hysteria. That part, at least, is encouraging."

Secretary Hank Abrams was quick to his point. "Listen, by now everybody in this country knows that we have to start producing electricity from the wind and the sun. What the president is asking is that we simply have to do it much faster to avert a crisis."

"That is not the point here, Hank," countered H. Stewart. "That is obvious and logical—two challenges that are truly unique face us in this country. We have had crises before—two World Wars, the Great Depression, 9/11—but the closest situation to this is our Civil War nearly 150 ago. That situation challenged our Constitution. Were we going to be one union of many states united into one country or were we going to break apart into two separate countries? If the South had prevailed, of course there would be no slavery today, but we could be looking at two constitutions of two countries now, not one.

"So at present we have another constitutional crisis, but different from the one that took place back then. We are really talking about an unknown. In wartime, the president does have supreme command of the military, but this time the executive branch of the federal government will operate supremely, not only over the military, but over the other two federal branches of government, as well as over all states' rights. Can we pull that off? During the Civil War we pulled hundreds of thousands of young men away from their homes—Americans fighting Americans—and those beloved homes were no longer secure and resulted in a great deal of trauma. But not close in numbers to *everyone's homes*, as will be the case here. So our president is facing two gigantic hurdles: Even if 100 percent of our population agrees that we surely have a grave crisis upon us and that our president must exert a powerful new form of leadership, there is going to be a huge constitutional challenge. And I also suspect—okay, right now no panic, but an incredible reluctance about asking hundreds of millions of people to voluntarily leave their cherished homes, especially those already living inland."

The president listened intently, wanting to hear from everyone, but before he could express himself, the Chief exclaimed, "Okay! Good points. But don't worry. The president will be holding a press conference at 11:00 AM. We certainly will stress this issue about Americans' 'love of home.' But now, on the Constitution side, you gentlemen don't know it, but the president and I have already met with the White House counsel, and we think we have a clear-cut route toward amending the Constitution. We have a strategy, but I have suggested to the president that we low-key that subject publicly right now and work behind the scenes with the key leaders of Congress and the state governors."

"Gentlemen," said the president calmly and softly, "I appreciate all of your thoughts and comments. Politics is the art of the possible. If a nation like ours operates on the principle that government leadership succeeds only with the consent of the governed, let me repeat the reasons I dreamed up the Master Plan. Our citizens are facing an imminent threat to their safety. I am skilled in the art of persuasion. I can persuade them that I can lead them to safety. I will gain their consent to the plan. I will have their consent to be their strong leader. Secondly, if politics truly is the art of the possible, then again I must use my considerable powers of persuasion and oratorical skills to make it possible for our other branches of government to voluntarily bend to this temporary situation, this crisis, this potential catastrophe. 'Fear' is a great motivator—you know our primitive 'fight or flight' instinct." The president smiled confidently. "So I am the one to fight while the Congress and the governors temporarily take flight."

For as many times as the Group of Eight had met in the prior six months, the other seven, yet again, stared at the president, their Savior, in absolute awe.

✢ ✢ ✢

The noise level in the press room before the president's televised conference at 11:00 AM was boisterous, yet within a second the din turned to absolute silence as the president entered the room. Just moments before, the president's mercurial press secretary, still in a state of shock as he had been left out of the Group of Eight meeting matters, gave the president a quick update. "The press corps is in an uproar. They accept a crisis but cannot believe the scope of your plan. Congressional leaders on both sides of the aisle are astonished at the idea that Congress would not be an integral part of creating any kind of Master Plan. People living in interior cities are flabbergasted; they don't know what a hurricane is. Organizations at the opposite ends of the pole—the ACLU and the NRA—have already issued press releases that they are opposed to the plan on constitutional grounds. Their pitch is that a mandatory evacuation order by the government has always in fact been voluntary. Government cannot force those ordered to leave their homes. 'Mandatory' just means that the government would not come to your assistance should you elect to stay behind."

"Relax, young man." The president smiled, striding confidently as he approached the noisy press room. "I am declaring a national emergency, but it's not like with the military where I can issue mandatory orders. You'll see—they will follow voluntarily."

Quickly walking to the podium, he pulled out notes from his jacket pocket. Looking straight out to the middle of the room, he started, "I'm sure you all heard my address to the nation last night and my follow-up televised interview early this morning. I know I'll be facing a thousand questions, so let's get started." It seemed like every hand in the room rose simultaneously. In unison came the shout "Mr. President!"

"Joseph, *New York Times*." Remarkably, the president seemed to show no trace of worry, no grimace, no concern on his face; just a warm, receptive, confident glow as he pointed directly at Joseph O'Rourke.

Finding it impossible to slow down his speech, the newsman blurted out, "Mr. President, how can you do this? Can't we just pull back each time a hurricane is forecast?" A dozen hands rose as though getting to their question was more important than the president's answer.

Patiently, the president calmly responded. "Let me be clear. This is not just a question of hurricanes. On that issue let me also be very clear. You have already seen the beginning. Not only will the hurricanes striking our Gulf Coast and Eastern seaboard become more severe in intensity, but they will be happening more often and reaching further inland, and finally, they will be striking year round, not just in the summer months. I also made the point in my address last evening that inland tornadoes as a result of rapidly changing climatic conditions will be increasingly devastating to the entire Midwest from the Mexican border to the Canadian border and will also extend all the way to the East Coast as never before. In the Southwest, we are all aware of summertime temperatures in excess of 100°. Today, January 3, in Austin, Texas it was 101°, in Phoenix 110°, Las Vegas 115°, Escondido just east of San Diego 101°, Riverside in the Los Angeles Basin 104°, the San Fernando Valley, the northern part of Los Angeles 101°, Walnut Creek just east of San Francisco 101°, Sacramento 104°, and all the way up to Portland Oregon 100°."

Astonishingly, the restive press corps now seemed quieted, riveted to the president's recitation of climatic conditions. "So there's more. Let me address sea levels. The rapid melting of the permafrost is releasing the greenhouse gases methane and carbon dioxide up into the atmosphere at such a fast rate that sea levels in all of our coastal cities are rapidly rising. Already the levels in Los Angeles, San Francisco, and Seattle are causing hazardous conditions at high tides. This situation will become progressively worse. ... So where do you want to go—Idaho, Montana, Wyoming, Colorado? I believe we should all stick together ... close to a food source. That's my plan."

The hands went up more slowly now as the president pointed around the room and ended up at Verna Paul, *Washington Post*. "Mr. President, I believe we understand and feel the gravity of the situation and have empathy with your good intentions for the American people, but our capital here, our functioning central government here in Washington— isn't our city relatively safe? Even facing an occasional tornado or severe hurricane? Don't you need these centralized established resources?"

"Yes, Verna, a strong, functioning central government is vital, but I have every confidence that it is portable. As you know, there have always been contingency plans that in the event of an enemy attack upon the United States, the central government is designed to operate out of a command post in the Rocky Mountains. With today's modern electronic means of communication, we are easily up to the task. And climate? Come on, Verna, you thought it was hot and humid this past summer here in Washington? You haven't seen anything yet," the president replied, momentarily breaking out into a wide grin, trying to relieve the tension in the room.

By now not only was the White House press corps completely mesmerized by this remarkable figure, but so were the overwhelming majority of those listening and watching on television. The turmoil was going to come down to just a few—but how powerful those few.

✻   ✻   ✻

"Michael, hi. It's Rose. Did you watch the press conference?"

"Yeah, as we expected, the situation is critical. Only in Santa Barbara do we have a perfect climate." Michael tried a weak laugh to break the tension. "Only problem is that the high tide hit the streets this morning."

"Yes, here too. So we're under orders not to leave our little office until we receive orders from the Pentagon. Michael, we were well aware of the abrupt change in climate, but what do you think of this evacuation stuff?"

"Unbelievable, Rose. I can't imagine an evacuation of such scope, but I do understand now why those big shots in Washington wanted to see me—wait, can you believe it? Here's a call from the interior secretary now. Call you later, Rose. Take care."

Arthur Schnell's administrative assistant was on the line to alert Michael to be available for a 3:00 PM conference call with Michael's boss, George Blake, and the secretary.

"Listen, guys. You two know what's going on. I want you to proceed as fast as possible. No limit on spending. First, Michael, run all your tests for your new system as quickly as you can. Second, Arthur, put your entire firm's resources on designing water pipelines from Los Angeles to Denver and from the Great Lakes to mid-Nebraska. Again don't worry about costs. Third, design Michael's desalination plants—"

"Sir," Michael interrupted. "What kind of production and carrying capacities are you talking about?"

"Three hundred million people, Michael, three hundred million. Drinking water will be chlorinated at treatment plants in Colorado. We'll have an engineering/construction firm in Denver design and build those plants. And the irrigation water from the Great Lakes. Now, no treatment; capacity to be what the Great Plains aquifer would lose each year if there was no rainfall ... got it? Be ready with those design plans so that construction can begin by September."

"Rose! I can't believe this," Michael voiced into his mobile phone as evening approached the West Coast. "I'm supposed to go all out with my desalination process as quickly as I can and then help design ... oh ... I forgot to ask about confidentiality, but you know, the president already announced—"

"Right, I get it, Michael. Evacuation to Colorado at the same time the snows on the peaks are disappearing means your water—"

"Yes, it means the impossible!" How can we ever desalinate that much water and then transport it one thousand miles uphill?" And let me be honest. I may have faith in my technology, but who knows whether it will work at full scale, especially at the scale I'm thinking they want." His voice dropped off.

Rose was silent.

"Well, I'm the one who so confidently described an incredible efficiency of my fancy process, and I'm the one who told them we have enough solar and wind power to move it through pipelines. So what have I done? Am I crazy?"

"Now wait, Michael; be calm! Just sit down and rough it out. Maybe it can be done if they don't care about the costs."

"Well, maybe. I pray you're right. They told me not to factor in costs ... just design and build; engineering and construction feasibility, not economic feasibility. But still—"

"Oh Michael, I knew when we met in Seattle last summer that we were destined for something like this. I just can't believe it's happening so fast ... and Jane Stricker knew ... and the Oracle knew ..."

"Yeah, I wonder if the Palm Springs meeting will still be on."

"Well, it should be; it's all about water. And besides, Michael, I want to see you." Rose's voice dropped off softly.

"And Miss Rose, I want to see you. ... Sometimes I think all I can see is salt coming out of seawater, but that thought of that evaporates as quickly as it appears ... I can only tell you that in my mind I see you always."

"Now that's quite flattering, Michael." Rose's unseen face flushed. Flirting, she added, "And what am I wearing, if anything, when you see me?"

With nervous anticipation welling up inside, Michael excitedly replied, "I'll tell you when you're finally in my arms."

✵ ✵ ✵

The White House, 6:00 PM, January 3, 2012

Another dinner meeting with the Group of Eight; this one spontaneous, but this time the table was set for twenty-one. For the first time, the president's press secretary and House counsel were invited to attend. From now on—transparency. The other eleven included the Supreme Court Chief Justice, the Speaker of the House, the majority and minority leaders of the House and Senate, the chairmen of the House and Senate energy committees, and the cabinet secretaries of Environment, Commerce, and Health. The current vice president, Alexis Graham, remained outside of the city for reasons of security, but she was keeping herself fully informed of the meeting by texting with the press secretary. The new guests appeared nervous, excited. The Group of Eight's six outsiders appeared confident. The president remained calm. The Chief was agitated—he just wanted to get all this "persuasion" over with and to move on with the plan.

"Please, everyone … sit down. Let's get started," the president opened as he approached the head of the dinner table. "This has been a momentous twenty-four hours. The message is that just about everyone agrees with the impending disaster to our nation. The proof is out there right now—rising tides, unbearable heat, no snow anywhere in January, drought, storms—but the issue is that obviously not everyone is at first going to agree with my solution and will challenge my leadership. Now, ladies and gentlemen, of course you all know that in nations governed by authoritarian rule, leadership is challenged at the risk of military reprisal and is legitimized by the rule of law as the leader decrees it, while in our free, democratic system of government, leadership is freely challenged and is legitimized by the rule of law only as the people and their elected representatives see it."

No one at the table moved. There was silence, except for the sound of silverware touching the plates of those finding the White House chef's selections too delicious to ignore. The president calmly and deliberately continued. This was not the campaign trail—no need to shout.

"Accordingly, I am asking for consent … voluntary consent. America is and will remain a democracy, and evacuating our people to safety must be a voluntary act, even under a declaration of national emergency."

On cue, the president's Chief of staff responded to his boss's brief monologue, "Understood, Mr. President. So what is it you are asking for?"

"What I am asking for is a week for the public to digest all this. Then I will make an appearance, ten days time from now during prime time, to address the Congress and make a formal announcement that as Chief executive of this great nation, I have officially declared a state of national emergency, *but* by the following day, I need to be given a supermajority vote from both chambers of Congress for their consent to implement the

Master Plan; in other words, a form of instant ratification. Then behind the scenes, with written public disclosure as we progress, but no speeches, my executive branch will work with the federal and states' legislative branches within view of the Supreme Court to pass an amendment to the Constitution to allow me certain enumerated powers during the emergency. Simultaneously, my legal staff will be working with the legal staffs of all fifty states to have their state constitutions held in abeyance during the emergency period. I will be setting up White House conferences to meet with all the governors personally during this period, and I would expect everything to be completed by April."

Where was all the backroom bravado of the congressional leaders now? Before coming to the White House dinner, the Congress was in a state of upheaval. Since the end of the president's morning press conference, virtually every member of Congress was flustered, outspoken, unsettled, miffed. How could a president come up with some radical-sounding Master Plan without their input? Phone calls and e-mails poured in. Many were relieved to know that the president had a plan for everyone's safety, but to move from home? Buzz, turmoil, mental hysteria, but no physical panic across the land.

"With all due respect, Mr. President, I admire your fortitude, your foresight, your first duty to protect the American people, but ..." The Senate majority leader spoke in a barely audible voice. "Do we not have time to run this through channels? To deliberate your suggested legislation in the Congress and finalize a plan that meets the full needs of our people in their time of crisis?"

"Yes, I agree," said the House Speaker, the second in line to succeed the president under the Constitution, boldly raising his voice now that one of his compatriots had finally spoken up. Until now they had so meekly accepted everything this captivating Chief executive had said. "We are the representatives of the people to make the laws of the land. We are indebted to you for submitting such an inventive plan to us, but we now need to take the time to—"

The Chief edged forward, repeating almost out loud to himself, "Come on, boss, come on. Don't let him get away with that. It would be chaos to allow debate in the raspy halls of Congress."

"Mr. Speaker. I repay the respect, but no, there is no time. Our founding fathers deliberated and debated quite a long time to forge the Declaration of Independence. It was eleven years later before we had our Constitution. We are a nation of deliberation ... of debate ... of compromise … of consensus. … But as soon as the tests proved the theory, our president Truman had the lone decision in 1945 to drop a horrible new weapon of mass destruction upon two large cities of civilians. In a time of an emergency, his interest was in saving the hundreds of thousands of American lives that would have been sacrificed to invade and conquer the entire Japanese mainland. It was them or us." All around the dining room table, faces were blank. He now had an audience, not a forum.

"Fortunately, in this case, our war is against nature, not a people. *No one has to die.* Until the climate shifts again, we are at war against global warming. We are now being besieged, as I speak, and we have no time. I must act. I must act now!" The president then grew quiet. The room was silent.

The Chief broke the silence. "All right then. Let's go with the president's request. I would like to make it a point that our Savior—I mean our president—will make the time to meet with any congressional delegation you would like over the next week. Let's make them breakfast meetings—9:00 AM, one hour max. He is going to have a busy schedule."

✻   ✻   ✻

Busy it was. Details of the Master Plan emerged: Twenty-five-hundred-square-foot residences with fruit trees and gardens, furnished. Free medical care. Protection of all private, personal, and real estate property during the temporary emergency period. Parks and recreation nearby. A good climate considering everywhere else. Safety and security.

A strong element characteristic of our human natures was at work. Entwined with the basic desire for one's own secure space is another strong motivating factor governing human behavior—to seek an advantage or to avoid a disadvantage regarding one's own comfort. The president was offering the advantage of a nice lifestyle and protecting personal property while avoiding the disadvantage of facing the hardships of a horrific climate. Playing on fear; raising hope. Avoiding suffering; creating comfort.

By January 4, the president had a new forum in conducting his "chats." He would allow one reporter from each major newspaper and one newscaster from each major television network and cable news show to conduct a fifteen-minute interview each morning at 11:00 AM. He would do this until Friday January 13, when he would appear before Congress that evening to make his emergency declaration official and consensual.

Meanwhile, static about the plan was becoming concentrated exactly where the Group of Eight had anticipated it to center: the far liberal left;

the far conservative right. The editors of the *New York Times*, every writer associated with the *Nation*, and the executives of American Civil Liberties Union had new friends at the *Wall Street Journal*, the *National Review*, and the National Rifle Association. The major TV networks tried to be objective despite the pained grimaces on the faces of their well-recognized anchors, but the cable stars on the right and those on the left suddenly became new compatriots. This is America, the land of the free and of the brave. Emergency or not, we have the right to think; the right to free speech; the right to make our own decisions. But what message, what salvation, were these pundits expressing? "Every man to himself?" They offered no solutions but at the same time never budged off their harsh criticisms of the Master Plan.

✻   ✻   ✻

The president remained calm throughout the verbal and written onslaughts from the fringes. His Chief hated the ordeal. "Idiots!" he shouted periodically to his loyal administrative assistant, the one who so diligently typed all his confidential minutes from the Group of Eight meetings, the trusted one who prepared the first printing of the Master Plan. By January 11, the Chief had grown increasingly agitated and alone.

"Sir, I don't like the feedback I'm getting. Voices on the left and the right—maybe they will eventually run out of steam since it looks like, from all the polls, we have about 80 percent of the public supporting us."

"So what's the problem, my friend?" the president said in a comforting tone.

"The problem is this: You told the House and Senate leaders you wanted a supermajority vote consenting to your authority to declare a national emergency and to implement the Master Plan. You were clear that you do not want legislation raised, debated, and passed spelling out a new 'law' for the plan, nor debating your authority there under. Well, my sources tell me that with one day left they don't have the necessary 75 percent in either the House or the Senate."

"What's the count?" The president grew more serious. He had not wanted this battle.

"It looks like ten short in the House and two short in the Senate."

"Okay, Chief. Give me the list of definite 'ayes,' definite 'nays,' and those on the fence. Let's skip dinner and start calling. If necessary, I'll stay up all night calling the 'nay' list. But I'm not going to play any politics and make any special promises."

"That's it, my man!" The Chief gulped, knowing he had overstepped his bounds. He enjoyed a close friendship with the president, but it still meant calling him "sir" or "Mr. President" as the proper name tags for his White House superior.

✻ ✻ ✻

Meanwhile, there was no plan for the Group of Eight to meet with the president prior to his appearance before the Congress. It was an appearance surely to be watched by nearly every adult person in the United States. The outside six had done a heroic job over the last ten days. They had been requested by the Chief to make themselves available to the media and to hammer on two simple themes: one—the climate crisis unfolding right now under the eyes of the American public is going to grow worse at an accelerating pace; and two—the president's Master Plan is feasible in all respects. He, and it, will save us.

The group had done a great job despite their personal exhaustion and the unrelenting sour notes coming at them from the far left and the strict right. The Oracle was at the pinnacle of mental strength aligned to the message. No critic could move him one inch away from his forecast of doom to our civilization unless immediate, drastic action was taken. Naturally, the two professors almost slipped from time to time into accepting counter points of view. In their noble Ivy League traditions, they had been trained in debate, commentary, and listening to see if another point of view held merit. But they remained steadfast to the plan. If Princeton's Richard Compton were to debate, it would be only with the Oracle. If Wharton's John Heyward were to debate, it would be only with H., his fellow economist.

✻ ✻ ✻

The calls were made, the persuasion turned on. By Friday, the president was ready. The nation was now well prepared and eagerly awaiting his next address.

"Michael, are you watching the president coming on? Or is it past your bedtime? You work so hard," Rose teased, trying to remove the tension in the air.

"Miss Rose, now you know it's three hours earlier out here," Michael responded, not knowing whether in the drama Rose had her time zones correct or not. "But, hey, first … did you get those devices out there?"

"Right! Mission accomplished. Despite the rough seas this week, we secured over one hundred sensing devices over a ten-thousand-square-mile area. Our recordings will now be by radio transmission. That's fine with me—those overnight boat trips were no pleasure excursions and were getting worse every time."

"So now that you're grounded, you can roam the Big Apple with your friend Adriana." It was now Michael's turn to try to lighten the tense scenario.

"Yeah, ha! I couldn't keep up with her for all the tea in China. Listen, if I'm grounded by the heavy seas, I'll have even more time to think about you. ..." Silence. The seriousness of the situation returned. Two twenty-eight-year olds; studying, training, working—always diligent in their quest to help humanity. Idealistic, but practical; building foundations under their dreams. Who would have even dreamed that their world could turn upside down so fast, and just when that one magical evening in Seattle together would introduce a new passion into their lives. A parting handshake; voices on the phone—is that all there is? Where is *love?*

✶   ✶   ✶

Congress, 8:00 PM, Friday, January 13, 2012

It was time. The president had given the nation the promised ten days from his startling announcement of the Master Plan—his solution to saving the people—for it all to sink in. His follow-up had been superb, with constant explanations and rationale of the impending threats to personal safety and how to reach a safe haven, leaving a little time for any initial hysteria to calm down but not too much time to reflect on alternatives. The remaining hurdles were how much influence the liberal left and the conservative right would have in challenging the uprooting of the entire population to a government-selected location and how many congressmen and congresswomen would rail up against his limitation on new legislation during the period of the national emergency.

✶   ✶   ✶

"Members of Congress, Justices of the Supreme Court, Vice President Graham, my fellow Americans, I stand before you this evening ..."

Chapter Six

Triumph

The Oval Office, 9:00 AM, Saturday January 14, 2012

The president's speech the evening before was eloquent, moving, persuasive, and all that he had hoped it could be. His audience had remained in their seats in rapt attention. At the end of the twenty-minute address, every last member of Congress stood up, and the applause was profuse. Television analysis continued nonstop for three more hours after the president left the chamber. Opinion polls placed reception right down the same lines again—80 percent favorable, 10 percent from the left critical, and 10 percent from the right critical.

"The applause meant nothing, Chief," the president said, finishing his morning coffee and doughnuts. "Congress always stands and applauds. Before my address, I was certain that we had well more than 75 percent of the votes in each the House and Senate. But, you know, they can be strange ducks. Yeah, how well I know; I was there myself not long ago, and I often didn't know exactly how I would vote until it came my turn, and on this issue … well, I know it's quite radical for them."

"Hmmm," murmured the Chief, "but they now know the seriousness of the situation. I bet there will be only a few holdouts who will want to do it the traditional way. Look, they're convening at ten o'clock. I'm sure they're all running around right now, chattering, complaining, and in full disarray getting it off their chests. But it won't take more than ten minutes for them to settle down and vote, Mr. President, and they will vote in favor of your emergency declaration as the temporary law of the land."

"Okay, let's just see how good I am," replied the president, rising from behind his desk and turning toward the door. "Come in, come in." He had requested the presence of his White House counsel and his press secretary at 9:00 AM. "Well, guys, your reviews were good last night. What do you think this morning?"

"Awesome, Mr. President, awesome," responded his Chief counsel. "I thought it impossible to pull this off without a protracted legal battle. You know, my legal advice to you has been a bit tenuous, and there is no historical legal precedence for what we're doing. There have been national emergencies declared before, but there was clear legislation to back it up. You have a right under the Constitution to ask Congress to declare war. You have a right under the Taft Hartley Labor Act to declare a national emergency in the event of a strike closing down an industry essential to the nation's welfare, but in this instance, I have tried to carve out a new rationale. I pray that Congress accepts it, and I pray that we do not have a dozen petitions to the Supreme Court challenging your authority. The big question that we have left is this: is it the 'president' alone who declares the end point to the national emergency and no one else?"

"No, Mr. President, no challenges. Your address was fantastic. We will not need the power of counsel's prayer." The White House press secretary was a young, energetic disciple brought out of major media at the start of the president's term. He had been temporarily miffed by his exclusion from the Group of Eight, but he later realized that his inexperience and lack of seniority kept him as a minor player. Now he had his chance. He had been sitting on cloud nine the entire prior week, briefing the press about the overriding merits of the Master Plan. Each night he had assiduously studied the document until having it virtually memorized.

✴   ✴   ✴

Saturday, January 14, at 10:00 AM

Both the House of Representatives and the Senate of the United States of America convened in their separate chambers to discuss, debate, and vote on the president's proposal. The entire nation was waiting for the outcome. Would the Congress go the traditional route as an equal partner in the federal government with the executive branch and take days, weeks, or months to produce its own version of a law for the president to sign, or would it submit to the president's request for immediate passage of an emergency declaration that would immediately grant the Chief executive immense power? Congressional members are responsive to their constituents. They knew full well that the overwhelming majority of Americans were on board with their popular president—the engaging man commonly called, and now even more so, the "Savior."

Now it was fifteen minutes past eleven o'clock. The president, normally the perfect representation of the description "calm, cool, and collected," was on his feet pacing around his desk. Only one of his many television sets was tuned in to the congressional process. He was alone with his thoughts. "Have I gone too far? Can I really pull this off? Is it too much for my people to take? What if something happens to me? What if 'temporary' turns out to be longer than imagined— who will succeed me?"

As the Chief stepped back in from a short break to retrieve messages from his office and stop quickly at the restroom, he scratched his head and blurted out, "Why are they taking so long? They did the right thing the first moment they convened and voted to limit debate, but it's over an hour now, and I think a few of them just want to be seen on national television looking important. Oh no, now the two majority leaders want to go into closed session without the TV cameras on. What's up?"

"The vote shouldn't be too close," the president said. "Why don't they just get to it?"

"Okay, they're back. It looks like they're ready to vote in both chambers—finally. It's almost noon."

The rolls were called. The president and the Chief expected over 80 percent approval in both chambers to ratify the declaration to be followed by a bill on the president's desk within moments to have him sign his approval. The Chief nevertheless jotted down the math on his notepad. With 435 members in the House, the 75 percent supermajority the president had promised the nation to carry out his mandate would require at least 327 "aye" votes. With all of the president's last-minute phone calls and arm twisting, the Chief confidently thought votes for approval would be over 400. Recalcitrant members of Congress appeared to be those from the very independent mountainous states of Idaho, Montana, and Wyoming—areas that did not appear to be in much harm's way in the coming crisis. In the Senate, "aye" votes needed to tally at least 75. If those independent thinkers in Maine sided with Idaho, Montana, and Wyoming, and possibly Hawaii and Alaska, then the approvals should at least total an overwhelming 88.

The vote was in. Included now in the Oval Office watch around the president's television set were the Chief White House counsel, the White House press secretary, and for the first time, the current vice president. The president, standing with arms folded, surprisingly displayed an unusual appearance of defiance. The Chief, sitting restlessly and leaning forward in his chair across from the television, looked miffed. The gregarious young press secretary was the first to speak, "It's done! We have it! The 329 votes in the House is our supermajority, two more than we needed. Right on our supermajority with 75 votes in Senate. The bill will be on your desk for you to sign within an hour. Do you want the press in?" The Chief put his head down into his hands.

The president walked slowly around the room, his arms still folded, in deep thought. Everyone waited. He finally sat down behind his desk, leaned forward, and spoke softly. "Right. It's done. Yes, bring the press in as soon as the congressional leaders bring the bill in. No, wait ... let me have ten minutes alone with the legislators first. I want to know what went on behind closed doors and why the vote just barely made it. At the signing, I'll make a few short comments about how pleased I am that we can quickly move on with the Herculean task of making everyone safe. You can schedule your own press briefing later on this afternoon and handle things from there. No appearances tonight. I'm going to rest and think, but I want you all to know that while I have this great mandate, I really want it to be unanimous. I want to triumph—I mean, carry on—with *everyone's* approval. I'm going to find a way." The Chief mused to himself, "Isn't it wonderful to win and yet feel extreme disappointment that the performance wasn't perfect?"

"Mr. President, you know that for security reasons, as your vice president, I cannot stay in the White House for very long, but I request a few private words with you."

*   *   *

Alexis Graham had been an exemplary U.S. senator. Some had described her as the typical progressive liberal from California, but on most matters she had been extremely objective, not blindly dogmatic. More than just popular with those who favored "big government," she appealed to moderate voters with her insistence on fiscal responsibility and that all the people's problems could not be solved by big money programs alone. She had always believed that an active, empathetic government had to be combined with individual responsibility as equal partners. Almost everyone needed some kind of help, but no "nanny state." It didn't hurt her politically that she was not only disciplined, eloquent, and intelligent but also quite attractive. She had been selected for the election ticket four years prior for all those reasons, plus her assurances she could bring in the big states of New York and her native California. How could she have turned the position down? For security reasons, she knew that as second in command she would be in the background, mostly out of sight as the nation had a loquacious, eloquent new president in the limelight. Yet, in this present scenario, she thought that there was something very, very wrong. Certainly the president had to take strong action and lead the nation in this coming crisis. However, this Master Plan seemed rushed to her, and the president was going to try to implement it with no input other than from this very small group he had been secretly meeting with over the last six months.

"Mr. President, I respectfully request an explanation. As your second in command, I was never consulted about the creation of a plan to move the American people to safety. Even while you were giving all your 'chats' last year with constant reminders about the adverse impacts of global warming, you never advised me what you were thinking. So naturally I am hurt. You told me we are going to operate as a team. With your persuasive skills, you have won a nice majority with your plan, but in the rush I am afraid I see many flaws."

"Ali," said the president softly. "I am truly sorry. In my heart there were so many people I wanted to bring into the inner circle, but I decided that if I opened that door, too many would rush in, and it would confuse me. I kept my advisory team to of course my Chief of staff, but then only six outsiders who could provide me with expert technical advice on the key issues of the science of global warming, the implications of our interior, and our energy situation ... and finally an economic system to make it all work."

"Well, sir. I understand that," she countered. "But the point is that if something happens to you I need to be in the know in case I have to take over. I understand your position, but now that the Master Plan is out in the open, I respectfully request that I be kept informed on a regular basis from now on."

"Okay, Ali, I will have the Chief—"

"But that's just the point," she interrupted. "I know the Chief. He's very guarded about his position. I often have the impression that he thinks he is more powerful than what his position calls for. The position of Chief of staff simply means that he is in charge of all your White House assistance—your household, administrative assistants, scheduling—not your political or statutory assistance, such as your cabinet and myself. I feel that the Chief is—"

"Enough said, Ali," retorted the president. "You're right, but I rely on the Chief far more just than the person in charge of all my administrative matters; I depend a great deal on his political acumen. I also have that relationship with you, Ali, and I have leaned on your advice many times over the past four years. But I just felt that I had to take the ball on this issue. We are facing an imminent catastrophe. The Chief fundamentally lives in my office, and you know for security reasons that you have to keep your distance. But I'll try, and I'll keep you informed … and seek your advice as the need arises."

Ali's cool blue eyes turned into a deep stare. "Fine, Mr. President. I will play the role publicly as your loyal vice president, but I will be blunt. There are parts of this plan that seem ominous … and frankly, I simply don't trust your Chief."

★ ★ ★

Midday January 14, 2012

A field day for the media. Late-edition newspapers were on the presses getting ready to hit the streets in the late afternoon. The typical headline read: "PRESIDENT DECLARES NATIONAL EMERGENCY—CONGRESS APPROVES BY LANDSLIDE VOTE." Radio talk shows had no other subject up for discussion. Major television networks and news networks were scrambling to find climate scientists, environmentalists, and congressmen to interview.

Except for the far right and the far left, the media was hailing the president as a genius. He was now truly earning his "Savior" nickname. The popular mainstream media so overwhelmed the air waves with praise that the words of dissent were beginning to get drowned out. But behind the scenes, those dissenting voices were beginning to fuel anger.

In the back halls of Congress, the 25 percent "nay" votes in both chambers gathered into luncheon groups and communicated with each other by mobile phones. The only way to slow down this radical scheme was to form a united coalition across party lines. True, the country could be facing a sudden worsening of climatic conditions, but are there not more sensible ways of avoiding disaster?

Meanwhile, the Chief requested that the Group of Eight plus the Chief counsel and press secretary to meet for an early dinner at 5:00 PM.

★ ★ ★

"Gentlemen," started the president. "Sit down, please, and relax. Let's start with a cocktail. I know I've been wearing you out, but let's see where we stand and how we should proceed."

"Right," said the Chief. "Let's go around and have input from everyone. Let me recap: I think we have accomplished more than we could have imagined. A week of expected turmoil has been converted into a day of triumph. The president set the tone over the last nine months. Then, climatic conditions dramatically worsened, and we backed up the president's ideas for evacuation with lots of specifics. We went public with the Master Plan for the safety of our citizens with the president's address to the nation. His subsequent request to Congress to obtain consent was close in historical analogy to prior crises but yet unprecedented in the particular nature of this one. Gentlemen, we have three-fourths of Congress with us and four-fifths of both the media and the public with us. We can proceed."

The more cautious Yale Law School–trained White House counsel squirmed in his chair. "Yes, but Chief, that minority can be very vocal, and more than that, they can cause significant discord if—"

"If given a chance," the president retorted. "I agree with you. I believe we should remove that chance."

The Oracle joined in. "Look, I have been in politics for over thirty years, and I know that a 51 percent majority is a great thing in a free-spirited democracy. That's the beauty of our system; everyone has a different opinion, but by majority vote the majority rules, as long as they don't trample on the minority's human and legal rights. Now we have 75, 80 percent … that's fantastic. We have an unimaginable crisis upon us, so let's go!"

"Yes," Richard Compton chimed in. "We have a supermajority. There is no way to silence the minority. They are not going to take to the streets with arms in protest. This is the United States of America."

"Yes, but some in America took to the streets in arms. Remember 1776?" H. Stewart countered.

Now there was a pause in the conversation. All were in deep contemplation as the Chief signaled for the waiter staff to come in and remove the appetizer plates.

"Okay, but look." It was the usually taciturn Hank Abrams' turn. "Maybe I don't know much about anything other than polluting energy and clean energy, but I would argue that a small minority can throw us off course. How do you think we can get everyone on board?"

The Chief's cell phone, set on vibration mode, kept shaking. He had also been keeping watch on the muted television screen nearby. He was finding it difficult to contain himself. Multiple thoughts were flashing through his emotional mind, attempting to reach his rational mind. "We could do nothing and just let the dissident chord fizzle out with time. We could continue on the offensive against those dummies; keep the president out in front every day; sit back and just continue planning the evacuation. Hmm, remember that guy, Chavez, in Venezuela? He got rid of term limits with just some limited vocal protests that did not stop him. But then that President Zelaya in Honduras tried the same thing and was thrown out in a coup. And Israel continues to build settlements despite the minority protests. Crazies! Unpredictable! What if here in the United States—what if this rises to the Supreme Court?" The Chief looked perplexed.

The discussion continued. "Mr. President," said the economist John Heyward, "since the time of your announcement last week and continuing through late this afternoon, my colleagues, my fellow economists, and my close friends have been calling me. First they congratulate me for being on TV so much last week," he offered with a weak smile. "Then they tell me that virtually no one in my profession can see how the country can finance this evacuation, and they also can't understand how we can duplicate our present gross national product all crammed into Eastern Colorado."

"How do you answer them?" asked the president.

"Well, sir, I tell them that the details of the Master Plan have all been worked out. We will freeze all existing assets at current value, back the new dollar in New America with a gold standard, stabilize wages and prices, and return to normal directly after this temporary emergency condition."

"And their response?" asked the president again.

"They are dubious, but they understand the need for a flight to safety, to protect assets, and most importantly, that this is all temporary. The climate has to swing back."

The Oracle grimaced. In his mind, a "swing back" might be measured in the hundreds of years. The Chief also grimaced. He wanted no part of a "temporary" transfer of pure power to the presidency.

"Arthur," the president said. "What are you thinking? Beyond the economic foundation, the essence of this plan is geography."

"Well, gentlemen," Arthur Schnell, nationally acclaimed as one of the best interior secretaries ever for his stance on environmental priorities balanced with economic feasibility, tried to recap the situation in very measured terms. "We have a crisis, but we have a good plan to avert the loss of life and to continue a viable society. We have sold the overwhelming majority of our people on our solution and that we have an able leader to execute it. We also have some dissenters who feel that their input is neglected or that the plan is too radical. I suggest the following: First, take all of us off the air and let's speak now with one voice—his." He pointed to the president. "Second, have the president conduct a weekly press conference with a five-minute opening statement and only fifteen minutes of questioning. We're sure we have a closed deal with the public. When the president is confronted with questions about the dissenters, he can simply state that 'this is a free society and our folks can express their deep feelings, but I have the ultimate responsibility for our citizens' safety, and I have to move on with the approved plan.' Third, the president meets with or telephones the most influential detractors and tries to privately persuade them that we barely have enough time to move ahead with this very feasible plan, and that it's only temporary. They will like that latter part. Fourth, we move ahead as quickly as possible with the detailed construction design plans for building the infrastructure we will need during and after the evacuation—water and solar structures; electrical transmission lines; streets and housing. Begin to make visible progress that it's happening. That's it."

"Wait, but Arthur," John interjected, "we have yet to determine how we move or compensate all those present property owners in Eastern Colorado. And how about states' rights?"

"Eminent domain, John, eminent domain. Private property taken for the public good," the Chief White House counsel calmly stated. As the only lawyer in the group, his role was becoming increasingly important to the challenges ahead. Still not clear was the potential for lawsuits on constitutional grounds challenging the president's expanded authority. Could they be taken right to the Supreme Court despite the wording in the national emergency? Also not clear was how the president could convince fifty governors to even temporarily give up their own state constitutional duties to protect their citizens and their properties. "And the states ... well, we'll have to see. I've told the president that a declaration of national emergency supersedes all states rights."

"Good, very good," said the president, then becoming silent.

Again, the Chief called for another pause as the group fell into a deep reflective mood for the second time. "Let's have dessert," he declared.

"Okay, well then," the president resumed, "what do I have to worry about? You all go ahead and move ahead with the plan. I'll sign executive orders tomorrow giving you authorizations over everything. I'll worry about the vocal minority and the governors. I'm not going to worry now about any challenges being taken to the Supreme Court until they happen. Go home everybody and get a good night's sleep ... and please turn off your phones and TVs."

✻ ✻ ✻

That same day Michael had little time to listen to the radio or even glance at a TV screen. He was aware that Congress had passed a bill to authorize the president to move ahead with his evacuation plan. But Michael was now working sixteen hours a day on the dual tasks of running the Santa Barbara plant using his new technology and designing greatly scaled-up versions for the Master Plan. On his accelerated project schedule, he was three months ahead of his original timetable. So far, all phases were working as Michael envisioned. He was deeply relieved, but the challenge of a huge scale-up seemed daunting.

Rose, on the other hand, was confined to her small office at the tip of Manhattan. Local and city officials were growing increasingly concerned about harbor water rising up above dock levels during periods of high tides. There was no questioning the president's claims of rapid climate change among these citizens.

"Michael, it's eleven o'clock here, and I know you probably haven't even had dinner yet, but I'm going to bed soon, and I just wanted to touch base with you. So much is happening—even Adriana is exhausted. Well, it sure looks like the president's plan is moving ahead. You know Congress gave him the green light."

"Yeah, I heard, Rose. Wish you could come out here and help me."

"Very cool, Michael; I'll ask the navy brass first thing Monday morning for a transfer. You know how grounded I am right now, just following radio signals from my sensors. But listen, I got word late this afternoon to be prepared to head to the Pentagon again on a moment's notice."

"What do you think is up?" Michael asked perplexed, not understanding much about the U.S. Navy's position in this upheaval.

"Well, I'm guessing the navy has a big sudden uptick in concern about all our coastal naval bases. Maybe they think that as an atmospheric scientist, I'm going to give them all the answers," Rose said facetiously.

"Don't downplay your role, Miss Rose. Look what the big boys did with little me."

"Michael, are you frightened at all? I don't know about your friends and family, but mine … well, my family lives in what they thought was secure New Hampshire. Now they are terrified. They accept the idea of the president's plan to evacuate to safety, but to actually do so is frightening … and what would happen if they don't move?"

"Well, honestly," replied Michael, "I haven't focused on that yet, although my parents too are incredibly concerned, living near the coast in Santa Monica."

"Okay, let's just see what happens. Right now you and I have our jobs to do, so let's just do them." And so Rose closed the conversation. There was no romance in the air on this dramatic day.

✵   ✵   ✵

Over the next week, the loud vocal dissent seemed to be wearing out. Maybe the strategy of letting the dust settle was working. Or was it just that the small percentage of dissidents were getting organized into a more formal protest? In the general populace, the mood was one of resignation to the need for dramatic action yet one of unspoken fear at the unknown. It was unsettling to all.

Unknown to the president, his Chief of staff, or the media were the quiet conversations going on among the 131 representatives and senators who voted against congressional support for the president's emergency declaration. They were meeting behind closed doors. The congressional dissenters were preparing alternative legislation to bring safety to the American people without moving anyone except those living within twenty-five miles of the two oceans or the Gulf of Mexico.

Also unbeknownst to the White House or the media was the quiet coalition of state governors forming to stand up for states' rights. The president had his initial victory, but trouble was brewing while the president and his Chief of staff were preparing for his annual State of the Union speech before Congress—scheduled a week later, on Tuesday, January 31. While at week's end things seemed surprisingly calm, the president's gut kept churning with the same feeling and with the same message he had experienced after learning of his supermajority win in Congress: "I need—I want—unanimous support."

✵   ✵   ✵

Normally, the National Hurricane Center is fundamentally closed in January for the off-season. One technician remains simply to keep the many sophisticated instruments in working order. It was certainly peculiar that on January 23 the technician noticed a tropical storm gaining strength a few miles off eastern Cuba. He called a superior in to review his observations. Sure enough, this looked the same as an August storm. Based upon recording devices located on small islands in the Caribbean, it was rapidly gaining wind speeds and was on a northwest coarse heading toward Florida. It appeared to be reaching hurricane speeds of seventy-five miles per hour as it neared Jamaica. It missed that island head on but continued to gain wind speeds as it continued its journey. How could this be? The south Atlantic needed to be very warm to great depths in order for a hurricane to spawn.

Twenty-four hours before the storm slammed into eastern Florida just above Miami, the center cautioned the Florida governor to consider evacuation of coastal areas. The situation presented a huge challenge as all the Florida coastal areas are jammed with winter visitors in January. Where would they all go if evacuated? The hurricane was now tracking a zigzag course in a general northwestern direction. It was pure guess work where it might hit land and go from there. It slammed right into the crowded city of West Palm Beach. It was rated as the most severe in wind speeds—Category 5. It continued an undulating path across Florida and hit the large city of Tampa Bay as a category three storm. From there it went directly north along the Gulf Coast and began its journey inland toward Atlanta. It was downgraded by that time to Category 2 but still packed devastating winds when it ravaged central Georgia.

This hurricane was different. Last-minute warnings were given, but few people were prepared. Similar to the strong hurricanes of 2010 and 2011, property damage was extensive. However, this time too many unprepared people were in its path. By the time the storm dwindled to a mild tropical storm in normally snowy Buffalo, New York, the death toll was estimated at seven hundred while the injured toll was estimated at ten thousand. The scene was chaotic.

Meanwhile, with no snow in the Sierras and the Rockies, the Southwest continued to boil. In almost every inland city, electrical power was breaking down and air conditioning curtailed. Irrigation supplies dwindled, and drinking water became a rationed luxury. Hotels and golf courses closed. Las Vegas suddenly became a ghost town. Many within the massive population of Phoenix began to flee somewhere north if friends or family could accommodate them. Over three hundred heat-related deaths were reported there.

If these implausible wintertime happenings were not enough, the next event was the final straw to prove the Oracle's case. The anticipated "gradual" global warming was indeed suddenly "abrupt." Three days before the president's State of the Union message, the pestilence broke out—seemingly from nowhere, but apparently carried by tropical winds blowing north. These winds had completely overpowered the normal northwest to southeast arctic winter winds coming down from Canada into the middle and eastern United States. These tropical winds carried pests, half the size of a fly, numbering in the hundreds of millions. By the afternoon of January 31, 2012, at 5:00 PM EST, just a few hours before the president's speech at the Capitol Building, the pests had already blighted a substantial portion of the evergreen vegetation reaching from central Texas east to Savannah, Georgia, north to St. Louis, and northeast through Tennessee, Kentucky, Virginia, and into Pennsylvania.

In identifying the insect, the Center for Disease Control did not believe any bites or stings sustained by humans would cause serious illness, but its warnings to the public stated that it couldn't be certain if the "immune impaired" were safe.

✻ ✻ ✻

One person in America, one hour before the president's address, was completely at peace with himself and with the State of the Union. What a change in temperament from two weeks prior. The White House Chief of staff was glowing. Reports were flowing into his office in the past week, and especially in the last few days, that the left-wing media and the right-wing media had gone completely silent. There were no more public outcries against the president's "radical" Master Plan or against his massive temporary powers or his alleged trampling of the U.S. Constitution. Similarly, the secret plots of those dissident congressmen, plots that had somehow leaked out to the Chief, suddenly seemed to evaporate. And finally, those state governors who seemed to be colluding behind closed doors to stand up against the federal government had suddenly gone public in support of the president.

The Savior had been right. "Fear" is a great motivator. It prompts emotionally driven behaviors that could possibly be unpredictable, but if one can "persuade" the "fearful" through a balanced combination of an emotional appeal with a reasoned approach, then one can "lead them all to safety." They will follow their leader. An impossible hurricane, a prolonged devastating drought, and a completely unanticipated pestilence all converged to create enough *fear* that the president now had the complete right-of-way. His State of the Union speech was now narrowed to dwelling on the massive federal response to the multiple locations across the country in desperate need of aid.

"I say go for it," the Chief said as he closed the door to the Oval Office after entering briskly. It was fifteen minutes before the president was to depart for the Capitol Building. The television networks already had their programs on, cameras viewing the floor of the hall where the president would give his State of the Union address. The typical smiles were missing from the normally boisterous members of Congress standing in the aisles and rows.

The president stared hard for a few moments directly into the Chief's eyes as though he were attempting to read his mind. "You have been very loyal to me, Chief. I know what you are thinking, and you know what I have been thinking these last two weeks. I have achieved my goal, but still there is risk. I wanted unanimous support ..." The president continued in soft measured terms. "In my wildest imagination I couldn't foresee the type of devastation that has taken place this week. It's exactly as the Oracle foretold ... and he tells us it can only get worse over the next ten years. Yes, I have to go for it. At the end of my address, I am going to ask for a unanimous vote for my Master Plan under a state of national emergency fully sanctioned by the Congress. I'm not going to wait until tomorrow for their convening and voting again. I'm going to ask them to stand up and be united. If they all rise, I'll tell them that move indicates unanimous approval. The entire nation will be watching, and after this week's unanticipated devastation, how can any one of them not stand up?"

"Brilliant, sir, brilliant," the Chief replied, breaking into a wide smile. From turmoil to complete triumph.

✻   ✻   ✻

The truth is that the president did not have to say much in his State of the Union address. Not one citizen was unaware of the most unusual and dramatic climatic conditions affecting the North American continent since the Europeans' first visit over five hundred years earlier. Sunspots, melting permafrost, fossil-fuel emissions—no one cared at this point what was to blame for the sudden acceleration in the global warming trend. People were dying. Let no one in the Congress hinder the president now. They all stood up. The Declaration of National Emergency - 2012 had unanimous congressional consent.

✻   ✻   ✻

"Rose, I've told you and the IPCC and a Princeton climatologist working for the president of the United States that the permafrost is melting so quickly from our emitting excess GHGs that climate change is accelerating rapidly. You know that this is my area of expertise, but late at night—or maybe it's in my dreams—I keep conjuring up an additional explanation. You're an atmospheric scientist; I need you to help me."

Listening carefully to her friend Jane Stricker some three thousand miles away from New York City, Rose interjected, "Jane, what is it?"

"Well, let me gather my thoughts, and then I'll try it on you," Jane replied. "In the meantime, let me tell you something else that I just have to get off my chest. ..." Rose waited patiently during the pause. "Rose, a couple of months ago, the White House Chief of staff, the right-hand man of the president of the United States, would you believe, came all the way to Seattle to privately interview me. He wanted to confirm the data and conclusions I had sent the IPCC and also what I had told the Princeton professor. He seemed satisfied. I was 100 percent certain at the time, but ... uh ... you know ... there was more. We were alone for hours. We had had dinner together. He is altogether charming. We ... well, we had a lot to drink, and it was late and we ended up at my apartment and ..." Another long pause, but this time Rose interjected.

"It's okay. Don't be upset. So what's wrong?"

"Well, he has a call in to me now. I don't know how he can have the time. The president just gave his State of the Union address last night, and you would think he would be much too busy. Rose, I'm telling you because he may want to see if I'm still standing by my theories and observations, and I don't want to tell him I now have a few doubts."

"And maybe he wants to see you again?" Rose teased to break the tension.

"Oh sure, I'm so beautiful." Jane laughed. "Okay, I'll keep you posted. Take care. I think he's calling again. Bye, Rose."

✻   ✻   ✻

"Hello."

"Hello, Jane. This is Chief. It's been since Thanksgiving. How are you?"

"Well, I'm fine. It sure has been a dramatic two months," Jane replied cordially. "How are you?"

"Terrific. We have gained a complete victory—I mean, the president has. He has secured a green light to get everyone to safety. Look, Jane, I … I know we will be seeing each other again soon. We are drafting a plan to create a national university in Denver staffed with the smartest professors in America. I'll see to it that you are awarded a prime spot. I—we—need your ongoing expertise as to what's going on with the permafrost situation. Sound okay?"

"Well, ah … sure. Count me in," Jane replied softly, trying to contemplate what it meant not only to experience an abrupt climate change but also an abrupt change in the place and manner of living. As the phone call ended, she stared ahead at a wall decorated with her diplomas and awards and pondered what this unanticipated new relationship with a guy called "Chief" could possibly mean.

✷   ✷   ✷

The energized Chief rushed back to the Oval Office for lunch with the president. The Savior looked tired for the first time, but relaxed, satisfied. There was no time to savor or celebrate his complete triumph. He had persuaded everyone. It was time to move on with the Master Plan; that is, unless an unsuspected constitutional challenge surfaced in the days ahead. Or unless some state legislators wanted to champion states rights even though all fifty governors the president had called in the last twenty-four hours had cast their lots with his "temporary" authority.

"Well, why not? Why not go for it while at this moment you are invincible?" the Chief pleaded.

"Well, because I think this is stretching it too far. If my leadership endures through the evacuation period and the plan goes well, then I'll be reelected in November for a second term. That takes us to January 2017."

"Yes, but suppose the plan is not fully implemented at that point, or climate conditions get worse than even the Oracle is predicting, or something goes wrong with John and H.'s economic scheme. I say we go for it again—for a constitutional amendment to eliminate your term limits. We did offer Congress the concession that there will be no congressional elections during this emergency period while we hold their offices in suspension, that their individual terms will be frozen in time. They will retain their treasured seats."

The president, now feeling quite fatigued but knowing that all the stars were aligned for him at this point in history, reflected on the Chief's brazen push. His own ongoing leadership and vision were essential to the initial and ongoing implementation of the Master Plan. Little did the president suspect that half the reason his subordinate wanted his boss in charge indefinitely was the Chief's own strong ambition for unencumbered power. Imagine such an ulterior motive—the Chief of staff for the rest of his life. At fifty-two years of age, he was in excellent physical condition. His eighty-five-year-old parents were healthy; he had good genes. He could be the man behind the scenes running the show in Denver, in New America, for a long, long time.

"All right, Chief. You never know when to quit. That's what I like about you ... my right-hand man. Let's go for it, but make it orderly. Get the full White House legal staff involved and do it the right way so there are no legal technicalities to trip this up. Chavez did it in Venezuela, but in the Honduras the Supreme Court and the military threw Zelaya out!"

Suddenly, the fatigue was gone from the president's face. He let out a laugh. His shoulders no longer slumped. This was exciting.

"Once a 'Savior,' always a 'Savior,'" he mused to himself.

The Chief sat back in his chair across from the president's desk. "Triumph for him; triumph for me." He smiled, fully contented.

Chapter Seven

Implementation

America, 2012 to 2016

Three years earlier, in late 2009, the Hollywood movie *2012* had been lots of fun to view. Since 2012 was the year the early Mayan society's calendar ended, it was good entertainment for those with a vivid imagination to watch civilization come to an end on the big screen. Subsequent to that movie, there was great hype in the land, as so many people worried during 2010 and 2011 that the severe hurricanes of those years were preludes to the Apocalypse. Now, however, it was no longer hype; it was reality. During late spring in 2012, the nation's extreme weather conditions continued. Within the United States it snowed absolutely nowhere the entire winter. The oppressive heat and drought continued in the Southwest. Severe punishing storms continued to pound the Gulf Coast and the entire Atlantic seaboard. High tides continued to flood coastal areas throughout the country.

For sure, neither the Oracle nor Richard Compton dreamed that the "December 21, 2012, Apocalypse" would be coming true—that was pure fiction—but certainly fear had gripped the nation enough that the legislators of all fifty states voted in the majority to suspend their constitutions during the "Temporary National Climate Change Emergency" period. They further voted to approve passage of a federal bill to grant the current president unlimited terms of office under the U.S. Constitution. The U.S. Senate and U.S. House of Representatives passed the constitutional amendment by unanimous vote. The critics had been silenced. Trepidation was in the air. The only hope was the Savior's Master Plan.

☆   ☆   ☆

Michael and Rose never did meet in Palm Springs in February. The International Water Conference had been cancelled. Foreign visitors had stopped flying into the United States. Palm Springs, California, continued to register winter temperatures above one hundred degrees Fahrenheit. Nevertheless, the city was jam-packed as its underground aquifers still had plenty of water. Without normal replenishment, however, the aquifers were likely to run dry within five years.

Rose and her group were no longer in Manhattan. She and her scientific team along with their small vessel had been moved to a safer inland area at the Philadelphia navy base. Storms and high tides had lead to periodic flooding in Manhattan, often shutting down the city's subway system.

Adriana, now for the first time truly terrified, called her dear friend weekly with the same begging question: "I'm still following the news, Rose, looking to see when we evacuate New York. No one knows yet whether it's one year, two years, or what. My firm says that residents of coastal areas will be the first to move to Colorado. Do you know yet?"

Rose had been called to the Pentagon again. She was asked to keep close observation over her remote sensing devices and report back weekly on sea temperatures, current sea patterns, air temperatures, and atmospheric patterns. However, she knew nothing about who moves when, nor did she know anything about the navy's plans for protecting its bases along the coast.

✳ ✳ ✳

"Michael, I have to tell you. The entire pattern of ocean currents is changing quickly and dramatically. You know that the prevailing winds blow in a clockwise fashion in the northern hemisphere, but those patterns are moving north. I think that's why the hurricanes have gotten worse. The warm spawning area is farther north, along with higher sea temperatures. It's not good."

"What about the Pacific side?" Michael asked.

"My counterparts say the same thing is happening there. That's why the Southwest is becoming a Sahara desert."

For the past several months, Rose's weekly calls were devoted to the whining of Adriana, to her serious naval commander in Washington, to hard-working Michael in distant Santa Barbara, to confidante Jane in far away Seattle, and to her worried parents in New Hampshire. The latter were mystified at the lack of snowfall in their home state but were relieved that climate conditions were still quite good. They were puzzled why they should be asked to evacuate, but at the same time they understood that climate conditions were getting worse everywhere. The president knew what was best for them.

"Rose, you know how busy I am, but I just have to find a way to see you," Michael said, as though pleading with some omnipresent force. George Blake had postponed all vacations for his entire firm's personnel. Everyone had to be focused full-time in helping Michael design the scaled-up versions of his desalination plants, power sources, transit pipelines, and brine water disposal. On the other side of the continent, navy headquarters at the Pentagon had postponed all leaves for personnel working on critical missions, and that order included Rose.

"Michael, I know. I feel the same way. I hope you're feeling the good vibes I'm trying to send you."

✻ ✻ ✻

By the end of August, the Master Plan was in full gear. Within an absolutely incredible period of seven months of the president winning approval for his grand scheme to flee to safety, arrange decent living, and create a functional economy for his followers, the basics of the new infrastructure were in a final design phase. Every major architectural and design engineering firm in the country was assigned a portion of the gigantic project. Every major construction management firm was engaged to review the plans and the construction timetables. Fees were being paid weekly by the Treasury Department in "old" dollars until such time bank accounts would be frozen and conversion to the "new dollar" would take place.

John Heyward took a leave from the Wharton School and was given an office right next to H. Stewart's at the Federal Reserve. Richard Compton took a leave from Princeton and was given an office next to Arthur Schnell at the Department of the Interior. Strangely, the Oracle was mysterious as to his whereabouts. The best guess was that he was spending time in the Colorado Rockies—in his favorite town of Aspen—communicating only by e-mail and quietly contemplating how nature would behave in the coming months and years.

At the Department of the Interior, half of Arthur's Washington staff was working overtime expanding the Master Plan's description of how essential services would be established and distributed in Eastern Colorado. The other half was assigned the complicated task of scheduling and transporting three hundred million people to "New America." The original idea was to make the transition evenly over five years, but now the president was pushing for everyone within one hundred miles of the coasts to move within two years—that is half the U.S. population—and then the rest within four years. Even more daunting was that the Chief insisted that this new time table begin from the start of the current year, 2012, so that by the beginning of the year 2016, the Master Plan would be fully implemented. Not clear yet was how to handle the pressure from inland cities such as Phoenix, Las Vegas, and Tucson to get their more vulnerable citizens moved out of the hot, dry desert heat as soon as possible.

At the Department of Energy, Hank Abrams felt at ease. The use of solar and wind energy was already commercial in some small communities in the United States. The engineering and construction firms assigned to Hank simply had to designate areas that would accommodate a vast increase in solar panels and windmills. Similar to the efforts in World War II where American automotive companies were engaged by the federal government to build tanks and military transport vehicles, Hank signed contracts with General Motors, Ford, and Chrysler to shift half of their manufacturing to small electric vehicles and half to building solar panels, windmills, and electricity-generating turbines. Hank also signed contracts with all the larger metal-working companies to construct transmission towers and cables to transport electricity from the solar panels and windmills, the clean-energy power sources for New America. Discussions were also underway between Hank and the largest pipeline manufacturers in the United States. This time, however, the pipelines transporting water would be ten times the circumference of the size of pipelines currently transporting petroleum.

* * *

Autumn came and went. While the doomsday date of December 21, 2012, passed without civilization coming to an end, there was little joy during the holidays. Dramatic adverse climatic conditions continued. Afternoon temperatures above one hundred degrees continued from Austin, Texas, through the West all the way to Portland, Oregon. Hurricanes pounded the Southeast and Middle Atlantic states. Tornadoes were numerous in the Midwest all the way to New England. The saving grace for those who had watched ABC television's dramatic production in June 2009 of the adverse impacts of global warming was that in real life America had a savior. In that fictional production, it had been depicted that without taking immediate mitigating steps to reduce carbon emissions, "gradual" warming over the twenty-first century would lead to violence and mayhem. Examples depicted included violence over water rights in the Southwest and flood barriers in the New York Harbor waterway that could disastrously fail in a big storm. Fortunately, the Savior would prevent those fictional traumas from becoming reality.

During this period the president maintained his comforting demeanor. His weekly "chats" were reassuring about the future. At the same time, he pointed out the positive steps the federal government was currently taking to provide emergency relief to storm-damaged areas as well as water and electricity to torrid drought areas. Diligently concentrating on his duties, he felt greatly relieved that recent amendments to the Constitution waived the federal elections otherwise scheduled for November 2012. He was to remain in office, and not one lawsuit was filed to contest it.

The Chief commanded, in the president's name, that all the engineering, construction, and manufacturing companies engaged under the auspices of the Master Plan send written summary reports directly to his office by each Friday evening. The reports were to summarize the status of their work in progress for that week. He insisted that there be no deviation from schedule, and there was none. By mid-January 2013, construction was ready to begin for "national" government buildings, the new national university, secondary schools, streets, parks, medical centers, nursing homes, and the millions of new residences required in Eastern Colorado. Small electric-powered cars, vans, and buses were streaming out daily from multiple production centers.

Arthur Schnell called the Chief with one problem. "Listen, we have to build a contingency into the plan, Chief … I—"

"Whoa," replied the Chief, "Everyone knows we are sticking with the plan. No deviations."

"No, no!" exclaimed Arthur. "Not deviation, but compliance. With the demands to get people out of storm-damaged areas and heat-wave stricken cities so quickly, we need to stay on target and move a quarter of our people to Colorado by the end of this year. We can only do that if we create tent cities to house them until enough residential buildings are constructed."

"Okay, okay, I get it, Arthur, go ahead and contract it out … every tent you can buy. But be sure to make them clean and comfortable."

And so the great move began.

*   *   *

While most aspects of the plan were comfortably on target now that the tent cities' addition had been initiated, one very critical component continued to be of major concern to Arthur Schnell and Hank Abrams: water. The plan had been built around the premise that a combination of Great Lakes water, desalinated Pacific Ocean water, and some local rainwater would take care of the needs of three hundred million people squeezed into less than fifty thousand square miles as well as the farm irrigation needs of another hundred thousand square miles.

Initially the large aquifer under the Great Plains would handle most of the irrigation load, but without replenishment, the Great Lakes water would be critical. Could the wind farms being constructed from the Rockies to Chicago generate enough electricity to power all that water uphill for hundreds of miles? More uncertain, yet—could Michael's barely tested engineering marvels desalinate enough water and find enough solar-powered electrical energy to push all that water uphill one thousand miles?

☼   ☼   ☼

It was early morning on a typical hot, dry day in Los Angeles when George Blake received a phone call. Hank Abrams was on the other end. "George, listen, Arthur and I are satisfied with your written reports—you seem to be on target—but nevertheless … well … we would like to have a direct word with you and Michael here in Washington." His voice trailed off at the end, giving away a signal that perhaps complete confidence was lacking.

"Hey, sure," George quickly replied in a strong reassuring tone. "Are you suggesting changes to what we are doing?"

"No, no," Hank said. "Just want face-to-face dialogue to make sure we are all on the same page. You know, written reports and conference calls are fine, but in such a critical area, there's nothing like a quiet setting to generate full understanding."

George understood, but upon ending the call he reflected upon the gravity of his assignment. His firm's complex engineering studies and construction designs, the unproven workings at full scale of a young engineer's new process—could there be flaws? Yes, understood. "Washington must be deeply concerned," he thought to himself.

Michael's new process in Santa Barbara was working like a charm. The small plant was running twenty-four hours a day. The reverse-osmosis method of removing salt was eliminated in order to avoid any downtime in cleaning filters. Michael's new process of generating sufficient heat to separate salt from the seawater at a much lower temperature and pressure using the clean energy of his superior solar and wind devices was working

148

as planned, without a hitch. Even his new method for dispersal of the huge amounts of brine water without harm to the marine environment was operating as designed. Obviously local environmental concerns, once so prominent an issue in California, were now taking a distant backseat to the immediate safety concerns of California's large human population. But the big question remained: could the process be scaled up hundreds of times larger and still work? Beyond the concern of the planners in Washington, that question tore away at Michael's inner being every waking moment.

*　*　*

"Hey, how are you?" Rose welcomed Michael's call. Despite busy schedules, the two were relentless with at least an e-mail, a text message, or a phone call each and every day.

"I'm fine, but is this crazy, Miss Rose?"

"What's crazy? This world? This planet we're living on?" she asked with a giggle.

"No, I mean us … I mean, why do we keep this up? Are we two souls that simply need a friend to talk to in all this madness?" Michael paused. "Clever," he thought to himself as he waited for her reply, which took a few agonizing seconds.

"Michael, that hurts. The way we talk to each other … miss each other. I thought maybe … that maybe someday we might be more than just friends. Am I presumptuous? Are we just engineering, scientific buddies? Maybe so. I'm sorry …"

"No, I'm sorry. Forgive me. I want to be more than your technical colleague … much more. I'm sorry, I should not have baited you like that, but I just needed to sense your reaction because I have some good news."

"Oh! Okay, what … what is it?" Rose elevated her mood a notch, completely forgiving him for leading her into that uncomfortable exchange.

"Okay, sit down. Listen. My boss and I are flying to Washington next Monday. We get in mid-afternoon and then have a meeting with the heads of Interior and Energy. We think they need some personal reassurances that we are going to produce enough water for Colorado. Yeah, I'm worried about that too, but here's the deal—I'll have to have dinner with my boss, but I can make sure to break away by eight. We leave for California early the next morning. Can you … can you get down to Washington that night?"

Rose jumped to her feet. Her heart must have doubled its heartbeat. It had been a year and a half since they had met and reached for that same cocktail; a year and a half since they had dinner together and parted without even a kiss goodbye.

"Michael, Michael! I'll call you back in an hour. Michael, oh my God, that's great!" Joy, excitement, anticipation—emotions Rose had not felt in a long, long time.

☆　☆　☆

Another conversation was taking place at the same time, this one between Washington and Seattle. "Jane, I uh ..." the Chief started. "You know I want you to help me with the design of the new national university in Denver ... and hey, you know you're soon going to be one of the top professors on the staff. I've taken care of that. How about arranging to meet me Friday afternoon in Denver and reviewing these final plans with the architect joining us. Okay? And hold your flight back to Seattle until first thing Sunday morning. What do you think?"

"I think I can do that," she replied without a pause. "But you know, it's three times over the past year. Are we safe with this?"

"Jane! Don't worry," replied the Chief. Still, at the end of this conversation she sat at her desk in her small university office for a long time, staring out blankly, as if looking for an answer written on the wall. Each time they talked, each time they met, Jane wondered what this relationship was all about and what would come of it. Of course, she felt honored that she would be among the elite at the new national university. The majority of college professors across the country would be relegated to teaching courses via electronic mail in the New America. Did the Chief simply want to stay directly informed of the important "permafrost situation" through a special relationship with her, and did it have to be so intimate, or was he truly interested in converting this romance into something more permanent as he was vaguely promising—or was it both? What could she trust about this man? And what about his wife, whom he seldom saw and never wanted to talk about? Where did she stand in this trio?

Jane had found it hard to believe how quickly the permafrost was melting. In the back of her mind, and only partially revealed to the ever-inquisitive Rose, was the thought that the tremendous release of carbon from such a rapid melting might be only part of the reason for the abrupt surge in global warming and the resultant dramatic climatic changes taking place across the United States. She had another possible reason, but it was much too early to discuss it further with anyone. She had to learn more.

✵ ✵ ✵

"Okay, all right, listen," Rose said excitedly. "I have good news and I have bad news. Which do you want first?"

"Oh … okay; give me the bad news first," Michael said, pressing his phone tightly to his ear, not knowing what to expect.

"Well the bad news is that I have to be up at 6:00 AM Tuesday morning for a seven o'clock meeting with our entire staff and a visiting commander from the Pentagon." There was a long pause. Rose waited for Michael's response.

"Yeah, okay; tell me the good news."

"The good news, Michael—no, the great news—is that I can be to your hotel at eight o'clock. *But* I have to catch the last train from Union Station back to Philadelphia—at ten thirty."

Trying to make the best of her exclamation of "great news," Michael raised his voice and exclaimed back, "Two and a half hours together, Rose. Wow! That's fantastic! I would give anything to spend even two and a half minutes with you!"

✵ ✵ ✵

During the plane trip to Washington, George Blake and Michael reviewed their notes assiduously. Scale-up design for a dozen ultra-large desalination plants—on target. Michael's pilot program in Santa Barbara was running perfectly. It was only natural that Arthur Schnell and Hank Abrams, far away in Washington, would have concerns as to whether a full-scale operation would be feasible. After all, with the lack of snow in the Rockies and limited rainfall, water was the most critical commodity essential to the success of the entire Master Plan.

The meeting in Arthur's office was scheduled for 3:00 PM. George and Michael's taxi dash to the Department of the Interior was accomplished just in time. "Michael, Hank and I are up to date with your progress through your monthly reports and our monthly conference calls. Our purpose in requesting that the two of you be here today is for you to give us a firsthand account as to what might *not* be in those reports and calls. What can go wrong? What is your confidence level in achieving satisfactory scale-up? Have your calculations been peer-reviewed as to how much electricity must be generated from your wind and solar designs in order to transport so much water one thousand miles uphill to Denver? Will you have enough solar and wind power in the Los Angeles Basin to run the dozen desalination plants that will be constructed along the coast? Where are you going to put those plants since the sea level is rising so rapidly? We don't think we'll be able to run the coastal nuclear-powered electricity-generating plants out there for more than three more years. Will you be completely ready by then?"

Michael had anticipated every one of these questions that Arthur was reciting from his prepared list. On the outside, he calmly reassured Arthur, Hank, and George that all objectives would be met timely and efficiently. Inside, however, Michael's stomach was churning. Despite the smooth running of the small Santa Barbara operation, there was no precedent for what he was attempting with his new technology. Would his small success scale up? The engineering world was replete with large scale-up failures after much pilot-plant fanfare—something about mechanical limitations and the laws of physics. Michael felt the gravity of what was being asked of him. On the one hand, he felt challenged and wanted to be confident; on the other hand, he felt overwhelmed by the burden being placed upon his young shoulders.

Never a very religious person growing up in the increasingly secular state of California, images began flashing through his mind of all the recent prayers being said by so many people in churches spread throughout the country and being shown daily on mainstream television. Obviously, a nation founded on religious freedom was still holding onto and cherishing those roots so very dearly. Religious leaders everywhere were in complete harmony with every request the president had made to date. Some had even hinted at his possible divinity.

Michael wanted to believe that a divine force was helping him along. There was so much at stake in his project, yet he just could not quite make up his mind for certain. He equated hope with prayer, and so he both hoped and prayed that if there was a divine being out there, "Please help me through this incredibly difficult challenge I am now facing." All these thoughts raced through his mind as he tried to grasp the meaning of his presence in that room that day.

Three hours later, at 6:00 PM, Hank was growing quite tired and called an end to the meeting. "Okay, enough," he said. "George, your young Michael is wearing us out. I'm satisfied. Let's just make sure the financial team is responsive and up to date with his needs to secure every piece of equipment he requires on a timely basis."

"Well, I agree," added Arthur. "You have satisfied all my questions, Michael. I can only repeat again how critical your project is to the success of the Master Plan. Continue reporting, and in a few months Hank and I will come out to California for a firsthand look at your progress. Gentlemen, thank you for coming. All the best for continued good work."

During dinner at the Marriott Hotel, an ecstatic George Blake downed his second vodka on the rocks and applauded Michael repeatedly for a job well done. Suppressing his inner uncertainties, Michael acknowledged the compliments. More importantly, he kept the waiter hustling so their soup-to-nuts meal could have a timely ending. It was ten minutes to eight when George signed the tab. "Good night, George. Thanks. It's been a long day. We're both tired. See you here for breakfast at seven." George started to respond, but Michael was already gone.

✻   ✻   ✻

The elevator couldn't go fast enough. When its doors opened on the ninth floor, Michael glanced at his watch. It was exactly eight o'clock. He ran through the elevator lobby and turned into his hallway corridor.

There she was, waiting outside his room. She looked so beautiful—just like he remembered her. She wore a tight-fitting casual dress cut just above her knees, revealing her perfect figure. His heartbeat surged as he approached her, his magnetic room key in hand.

"Hi," Rose said softly with a faint trembling smile on her lips.

"Hello, Rose," Michael responded, nearly out of breath as he slowed to greet her.

He gazed into her eyes for several seconds, perhaps to be sure that this was indeed the girl he had met a year and a half ago and the one he had been communicating with so closely ever since. It was. Michael then reached out and hugged her as tightly as he could, Rose squeezing back in return. He partially turned and opened the door to his room.

No words were spoken. It wasn't necessary. Michael dimmed the lights low. He wanted intimacy, but he wanted to see her face, her hair, her body. At long last, their first kiss, finally. It was as perfect as they had so long anticipated. Then a second and a third, again and again. No wild scene of torn clothes and runaway passion. Gentle, warm, exploring; excitement building. Soon they would both experience and understand for the first time in their lives the real feelings and meaning of ecstasy. Man and woman—the way it was meant to be.

Rose turned to look at the clock by the bed. Her eyes were moist. "It's five minutes to ten. I have thirty-five minutes to be on that train."

"I know," Michael responded. "I'll go with you in the cab. It's only ten minutes to Union Station."

They held hands together in the back of the taxi. Both stared at the nearly empty street ahead. Something seemed surreal. They were both quiet.

Still tightly holding hands through the door and into the station at 10:20, Michael suddenly stopped and turned her toward him.

Looking directly into her teary eyes, he said softly: "Rose, the world is upside down. I don't know where all this craziness will lead us, but I've never been as happy as I've been tonight.... Darling, I love you very much ... I love you so very, very much, you know."

"Oh, Michael... and I have loved you from the moment we met, and I will love you forever. Whatever perils lie on the road ahead, our love will guide us through. You'll see."

✧   ✧   ✧

It was three months later, the spring of 2013. Early phases of construction and assembly for New America were continuing on schedule and with few hitches—an engineering marvel. Everyone was cooperating as climatic conditions continued in their severity. It was still the custom of national security measures to limit the time the president and the vice president could be together. As busy as the president was keeping his citizens calm, dispatching aid to areas of suffering, and monitoring progress toward timely implementation of his Master Plan, the vice president felt that her talents were being wasted. She was beginning to believe that her only role in holding such an esteemed position was to be there in the event the president became incapacitated or died. Her only contact with central command was the voluminous reports she received weekly from the Chief's administrative assistant regarding the current status of the plan.

"Enough!" she said out loud to herself, squirming in her office chair. She dialed the president's private line.

"Sir, in all due respect, I think you can surmise that I am out of sorts. You need me to participate." The president just listened. He didn't need any complications. She resumed: "I know that your so-called Group of Eight, from which I am still miffed about being excluded, still meets occasionally. Mr. President, I would like to attend those meetings."

"Uh … Ali," the president responded coolly, trying to find a polite way to cut her off as he was now feeling a bit agitated.

"Sir, let me be honest and direct with you. I think you need a voice that respectfully challenges what we are doing. Of course, you have a complete mandate—our people are fearful. But there are always alternate routes to take to get to a desired location."

Now he was agitated. "But that's what we don't want!" His voice was now rising in what was going to become an unwelcome debate.

"That's what *you* don't want, sir, or what your Chief of staff doesn't want?"

The president paused. "Okay, here's the point. We don't want a thousand voices suggesting a thousand different routes—we would never arrive. But maybe one more inside voice? Well, all right, Ali. Join us, but let's keep it civil. I know all too well that you and the Chief don't see eye to eye. The next meeting is our six o'clock Monday dinner."

☼   ☼   ☼

And at the start of that next meeting, there she was. The Chief gulped and thought, *What is she doing here?*

"Hello, Chief. How are you? You don't know how glad I am that the president is now including me in these meeting. I must be kept fully informed, you know, in case something happens to him." Ali's smile seemed to reach from ear to ear.

"Uh … can I show you something in my office for a minute? We have ten minutes before the dinner meeting starts," a very startled Chief blurted out. The president had not mentioned to his Chief that the eight were now nine. He wanted no agitation.

"Geez, Ali. Why get involved? My assistant is sending you timely reports, so you are fully informed."

"Calm down, Chief. I know you don't want dissent. There can only be one leader in the time of crisis. I understand and support that, but the president has no experience managing anything but the political landscape—just like you. The others in your group have expertise in certain niche areas. What I think I bring to the table is experience in a broad array of disciplines. Granted, everything has gone smoothly so far, beyond the wildest expectations, but your New America is not New America yet. Don't think things can't go wrong. You need me."

No time to argue, the Chief thought. Only time to give her a long cold stare. "Let's go to dinner, Ali."

✽   ✽   ✽

After their absolutely wonderful public relations performances during that special first week in January 2012 announcing the Master Plan to the citizens of the United States, the Group of Eight stayed pretty much in the background during the next fifteen months. While now well known to the public and the media, the group kept their personal interviews to a minimum. Whenever there was an appearance, they kept it brief and parroted exact details as spelled out in the Master Plan. Behind the scenes, of course, they continued to update the president and the Chief regarding the status of the dramatic climate changes now being witnessed by all Americans.

The president opened a Spring 2013 dinner meeting with an observation that even the most erudite climatologists found puzzling. Another winter had passed, and again there had been no snowfall anywhere in the United States. He queried no one in particular, "How can it be? This dramatic a change so quickly? All those fourteen-thousand-foot peaks in the Rockies and in the far West—I am told that normally they receive over three hundred inches of snow a year, and now all of a sudden ... nothing. Can you please review this again for me? Where are we headed? Can it get any worse? If so, how and when?" The Chief grimaced. He thought that at this point the president was beyond questioning the awesome climate change taking place. Like the others in the group, wasn't he simply expecting that conditions would continue to deteriorate for an unknown period of time? Or perhaps the president was experiencing one of those nagging doubts that often arise periodically in a rational mind during periods of momentous decision making. A long pause ensued.

"Well, I am your resident climatologist, I suppose, so I can start on that," Richard Compton said. Richard was still on extended leave from his normal duties and teaching at Princeton. The university recognized the important work he was doing and gave him special privileges to study the science of abrupt climate change. "As we have discussed several times before, the unexpected phenomena that triggered all this was the very rapid acceleration of the melting permafrost across Northern Canada and the Arctic land mass. We told you that the land mass holds high amounts of carbon that when released results in added methane and carbon dioxide to both the surrounding oceans and to the atmosphere. The resulting warming effect exacerbates a problem already there—too much CO_2 emitted from the industrial and automotive buildup during the second half of the twentieth century. The circle got bigger, like a balloon being blown up faster and faster. But you already know that. So what have we learned in the past year? As the Chief knows—he has interviewed *the* expert scientist in this, Jane Stricker—what circumstance slipped past everyone other than Jane and the Oracle that prompted this acceleration?"

At this point both the Oracle and the Chief sat back in their chairs with their arms folded, enjoying their recognized expertise. The others listened intently as Richard continued, "We know that the oceans comprise 75 percent of the earth's surface area and that water holds its temperature much more evenly than air masses or land masses. In other words, once heated, oceans dissipate that heat at a much slower rate than air or land release their heat. So in order to have an *abrupt* change in climate we have to first relate it to air and land-mass temperature changes. What Jane Stricker discovered, and the Oracle picked up early on, is that the extremely rapid melting of the permafrost over the last four years had a sudden cause. The result was an enormous increase in carbon gases released to the atmosphere that more than tripled the greenhouse gases that Man's fossil fuel emissions had thrown up over the prior fifty years. The combination, that one-two punch, quickly became disastrous—"

"Okay, okay, but what was this sudden cause?" the president said forcefully, leaning forward in his chair like an inquisitive schoolboy learning some new startling revelation.

"Well," Richard continued, "the GHGs—that is, methane, carbon dioxide, and water vapor—all contain carbon and oxygen molecules mixed together. Now it's a little difficult to understand and quite difficult to explain. It's sort of a point of no return. It's sort of where a cubic meter of air contains a certain amount of free carbon and a certain amount of free oxygen, both elements alone, but not yet the heat-trapping carbon dioxide gas. This phenomenon is not yet clearly defined by the laws of physical chemistry, but under very exact conditions of temperature and pressure, an almost sudden explosion takes place in the creation of carbon dioxide gas. You might think, where two molecules become four become eight become sixteen—a geometric expansion rather than a simple arithmetic expansion. Exponential. Do you follow?"

"You know, Richard," the president sat back, laughed, and retorted. "No, I really do not, but in political jargon we sometimes talk about a synergistic effect where two strategies come together and have much more impact in combination than the sum of the two strategies acting independently."

"Good! That's it, sir—the synergistic effect. It applies in the world of chemistry as well," Richard affirmed.

So the meeting went.

✻　✻　✻

By mid-May 2013, the Group of Eight was informally now nine with the addition of Vice President Graham. But even Ali, while still suspicious, could not help but be impressed by the cohesion, cooperation, and knowledge displayed among the group's members. For the next three months, all aspects of the Master Plan showed continued progress. Everyone was ecstatic. It wasn't until their meeting in mid-August that circumstances became unexpectedly grim.

A natural phenomenon associated with short-term weather conditions but not a factor in global warming considerations is what is commonly called the jet stream. However, in the summer of 2013, the jet stream did indeed become a complicating factor. It had taken on an unusual curve, much like a statistical bell curve, over the entire West instead of its usual long, smooth, undulating shape.

The jet stream is a very fast-moving flow of west to east air currents that travel in a meandering course anywhere from one thousand to three thousand miles long but are only one to three miles wide. It exists at altitudes of approximately seven miles high, or thirty-five thousand feet, in the tropopause, which is a narrow transition area between the lower troposphere and the higher stratosphere. The former is where temperatures decrease with height, and the latter is where temperatures increase with height. There are two main jet streams: the stronger polar jets and the weaker subtropical jets. On the globe, they are located at the boundaries of adjacent air masses that have significant differences in temperatures. They are caused by a combination of these primary atmospheric heating differentials and the planet's rotation.

Their meandering path moderately influences weather every few days in the United States when they move slightly north or south or slightly change their shape. They are also influenced by Pacific Ocean oscillations, changing currents of warm and cold waters coming to the surface sometimes referenced as El Niño and La Niña. Then they can become stronger and in a more northern flow or conversely stronger in a more southern flow. These movements can affect weather conditions from Southern California up through the Pacific Northwest. It is even thought that the infamous Dust Bowl of the 1930s was caused by the polar jet stream moving farther south in a prolonged weakened condition thereby not permitting moisture to rise from the Gulf of Mexico to the Great Plains.

During the hot months of June, July, and August 2013, the prolonged bell curve over the entire Southwest and Pacific Northwest worked to aggravate the already severe heat wave in the West by allowing more hot air to flow up from Mexico all the way to Vancouver. The impact of this combination of heat factors further strengthened the public's belief in the Savior and the credibility of his Master Plan. Both drinking water and irrigation water were running short. Power outages were becoming increasingly common. Air conditioning became a luxury. Death rates were increasing for those unable to tolerate extreme heat—the health-compromised, the lung-impaired, and the elderly.

Before even finishing his appetizer that August evening, the president started in, showing considerable impatience: "Richard, Oracle, you have been telling me that climatic conditions will worsen over the next ten years until we begin to see things level out, and then perhaps a reversal might not take place for even fifty years from now. Arthur, this complication with the jet stream in the West is even making things worse, and all the hurricanes and the pestilence is getting worse—the tornadoes won't quit. Can't you speed up construction? Hank, water and electricity… Can you speed it up?" The president, clearly agitated, continued uninterrupted.

"Gentlemen, Ali, if things are even worse now than we thought and we might not see a reversal of all that carbon dioxide up there for another fifty years, how can we better protect our citizens now … and how in the world can we be telling the Congress and the public that this is all 'temporary'?" Another one of those long pauses ensued. There was no experience to use as a guide in this crisis. Nothing in the lessons of history could help. Only the Chief looked amused, but he hid it well, except perhaps from the glances of Alexis Graham.

Finally, the president sat back in his chair and started eating again. The silence was broken. Arthur Schnell tried his best to speak calmly and confidently, sensing the downward spiral in the group's mood from just a month ago: "Mr. President, gentlemen, Ali, do you recall the contingency that I ordered inserted into the plan and that the Chief approved? Well, beyond the nearly one million people that we have already moved to safety from the ravages of the recent hurricanes and from the heat in Phoenix where every single nursing home had to be closed, I have already warehoused three million tents and have ten million more requisitioned. We have plenty of room to expand our so-called 'tent city.' And my recommendation is to allow me to expedite the process, get the people with immediate needs into the tent city, and show the public that we are taking serious steps in insuring their safety."

The president responded, "Yes, Arthur. As much as I did not like the concept of a 'tent city'—it reminds me of refugee camps in faraway places deep in squalor; children crying; mothers begging—once the Chief told me about it, I did approve your contingency plan. It makes sense, so yes ... go ahead at full speed."

The Chief jumped in forcefully, "Listen, Arthur. I will back you up with all the resources you need. This is important. You must make these tents comfortable. You have to have decent bedding. You have to have adequate sanitary facilities. We cannot afford to have any breakout of disease. You must have recreation for the children and TV with movies for the adults. We do not want people complaining or depressed. We need to have the public stay on our side. Completely! Got it?"

With that, everyone around the table perked up. The mood was lifted. There was not a single pause in the Chief's strong directive. "That's my boy," the president said to himself, now appearing measurably more relaxed.

"He's going to be a challenge," the vice president said to herself with a sharp glint in her eye.

"Yes, of course. Got it," humbly replied the now overwhelmed secretary of the interior.

✻ ✻ ✻

Poring through reports in her new national university office, Jane Stricker was in the worst of moods; she was in the best of moods. She wanted above all to be a dedicated scientist. It was the essential meaning to her life; her fulfillment. How exhilarating, yet paradoxically depressing, that her work was now so involved in the destiny and welfare of her country. She never bargained for that much responsibility. On top of that, how complicated it had become to be sharing her scientific work with a married man with whom she had become intimate during her monthly trips to the new national university being built in Denver. Her rational mind constantly reminded her that it was wrongful behavior, but her heart found him irresistible. She was on an emotional high every minute she spent with him. He was charming, polite, complimentary, and intelligent. Moreover, how intriguing that this man sat with the president of the United States each and every day. And then to top off that internal conflict, another deep nagging thought kept tugging away inside. A great anomaly, the carbon explosion and the abrupt climate change. She could explain that science to the IPCC and to Richard Compton, but something else was going on as well. She had hinted to Rose that she would need her assistance as an atmospheric scientist, but it was still too soon to inform her of her early findings. Once more, she thought it would just confuse Rose until she obtained more facts. Similarly she thought it too soon to confide with her romantic partner until she knew more.

"Hello, is it Jane?"

"Hi, Rose. How are you? I can't believe it's October already. We haven't spoken in months."

"Well, I'm good. I don't like being stuck here at the navy base in Philadelphia. We're still not going out to sea. The oceans over here in the Atlantic are still too rough, and all I'm doing is writing down recordings from my sensors out there."

"Are temperatures and wind speeds still going up?" Jane asked.

"Yes, both water temperatures and air temperatures are still rising each month, but not wind speeds except during storms. What I am noticing is that ocean currents are moving in directions I cannot find in any of my reference books."

"Rose! That's exactly what I want to talk to you about—but not yet. I'd need lots more data. As I mentioned, I'm going to need your help. The reason I called—you did tell me that your initial enlistment in the navy is four years. After that, is enlistment year by year?"

"Yes. Navy enlistments are normally for another four years, but in my scientific group, it goes year by year. So before June 2014, I have to decide what I'm going to do. If I re-up with the navy, I'll be stationed somewhere along the East Coast. So Jane, what would I do if I go civilian and had to move to Denver?"

"Here is your answer, dear Rose. I've told you about the gallant Chief of staff and my appointment to one of the highest scientific positions at the national university, now being built in Denver. I want you to come and be my colleague. I can appoint you as an associate professor directly assigned to my research project on the permafrost. I do truly need an atmospheric scientist to help me with some of my new findings."

"Wow! I don't have to even think over your offer. Fantastic!" Certainly a meaningful continuation and connection with her scientific endeavors, Rose thought. But a second overwhelming thought quickly raced through her mind: two thousand miles closer to beloved Michael. She couldn't wait to call him.

✻ ✻ ✻

"Hi, my darling stranger. Do you remember when we made love ten months ago and I first called you with some good news and some bad news?"

"Come on, Miss Rose, you know I think about those two hours every moment of my life. Don't you tantalize me."

"Michael, listen, but first respond: do you want the good news first or the bad news first?"

"Yeah, the good news is that you're coming as a civilian to Santa Barbara to be with me for three hours, and the bad news is that it's going to be four years from now when you're out of the navy."

"Michael! Which is it?" she demanded.

"Okay, again, give me the bad news first."

"All right. The bad news is that the navy is not transferring me to a West Coast base where I can be near you." There was a long pause as Michael remained silent. "All right, Michael, you're waiting for the good news. ..." Continued silence. Michael loved her antics. "You may have forgotten, but after the initial four-year enlistment, my navy reenlistment is year by year, so I will not be reenlisting in the navy for another four years. My current time ends next June." Michael's interest heightened, but he remained silent. His mind raced to the inconceivable notion that she could move to Santa Barbara as a civilian while all the other civilians were moving to Colorado. "Am I boring you, Michael?"

"Rose, come on, hurry! I want the good news."

"Okay, okay," she replied now in a more serious tone. "I will be moving to the new national university in Denver and becoming an associate professor working on climate change with none other than Jane Stricker. She has been appointed the top climate change professor. I'll be right there, Michael," she said, lightening her tone again, "waiting for you with all your water."

"This woman—funny. What am I to think?" Michael wondered to himself and calmly replied, "Rose, don't take this as corny. Listen, we both have two loves in our lives—our projects and our concerns for the welfare of humanity. But the second is the most important one to me——my love for you—anything, anything that gets you closer to me."

*　*　*

Christmas 2013 was not very merry, and the holiday season not very happy. The nation was saddled with despair but also graced with hope as all the design work had been completed and construction was well underway for New America. Salvation was coming. The tent city program was running smoothly. The sick, the injured, and the elderly were being moved to Colorado by the thousands every day. But for the rest of the nation it was becoming increasingly difficult to bear the hardships. Continuing hurricanes, severe storms, unrelenting heat and drought, untreatable pestilence, and sudden fearful tornadoes were beginning to tear at the American people's patience with the implementation of their Savior's Master Plan. Only the calming, confident tone in the president's voice during his weekly televised "chats" maintained the people's fortitude.

"Oh Rose, I'm sorry to call you at this late hour, but I just wanted to say a traditional 'Merry Christmas' to you."

"No it's fine, Ad. I'm awake. Michael and I were just trying to do our best to be cheerful on this Christmas Eve. How are you doing?"

"I guess I shouldn't talk to you about it now, but ..."

"No, go ahead, Ad. I don't think I can sleep tonight anyway."

"Well okay. But you know, other than going out with the guys once in a while, I'm sitting in my apartment most of the time. The flooded subways don't run, and I'm getting severance pay. My company has shut down. I'm bored, Rose, and you know what they're telling me? When I move to Denver next year, I'm going to be in a residence with two other girls, and we're going to be given sewing machines. Sewing machines! Everything is going to be free, but we have to earn our keep by sewing clothes eight hours a day. I have no idea where the guys are going to be. Are there going to be bars, clubs? Am I going to be able to see you?"

"Hey, wait, calm down," Rose replied. "I agree. For you that does not sound too cool. But look, remember that I told you that I lucked out and will be working at the national university on my specialty. I'm sure that we will need a talented administrative assistant. Or hey, you know ... my mentor is very close with the Savior's Chief of staff. Wouldn't that be neat? If I can't get you a job with me, how would you like to work in the office of the president of the United States?"

"Rose ... I knew I loved you. My best friend."

*　*　*

The pace was fast and furious during the year 2014. New America was a boomtown on a massive scale. The Department of the Interior did an incredible job in quickly obtaining millions of tents and providing adequate services, just as the Chief had directed. At the same time, residential construction kept up with the aggressive schedule established in the Master Plan. Nearly five million residences had been built in 2013. Over twenty million residences were to be built in 2014, and everything was on target to build the remaining twenty-five million residences in the year 2015. Just about every paving contractor, electrician, plumber, and carpenter in the entire country was already living in the first residential structures built. They were working twelve hours a day, six days a week.

At the Department of Energy, the task was more difficult and the timing uncertain. Those not yet moved to Colorado required energy, while at the same time the electrical needs of the millions moving into Colorado had to be met. Outside of Colorado, the original concept was to wind down the fossil-fuel-burning plants month by month and meet all power needs by utilizing the electrical energy from the nation's existing nuclear plants. Inside Colorado, the plan called for a weekly increase in electrical power generation from the widespread construction of windmills and solar panels.

However, climatic conditions, particularly the strong hurricanes, continuously disrupted the nation's power grid. It had become routine for homes, stores, and businesses to experience daily power outages. The worst human suffering was in the South and Southwest, where air conditioning units were commonly in a state of failure. Hank Abrams just could not wait until everyone arrived in Colorado. Then he could shut down all power outside New America except for what the military needed for protecting property and guarding the coasts.

One critical resource common to the concerns of both Arthur and Hank, of course, was still the issue of water supply. It had been nearly two years since they had called Michael to Washington to review his plans for the desalination of an enormous quantity of Pacific Ocean seawater and transporting it one thousand miles to Colorado with an incline of five thousand feet. To keep abreast firsthand, the two had been visiting Michael's projects in California every six months, flying privileged on military aircraft. Construction of the dozen massive desalination plants on higher ground in the Los Angeles area appeared to be on target. So did the construction and laying of dozens of the large twenty-five-foot diameter pipelines that would transport huge quantities of water. So did the hundreds of thousands of windmills and solar panels positioned along the way that would provide the electrical power to push that huge quantity of water. Nevertheless, to Arthur and Hank, and of course to Michael, the crushing worry was whether it would all work full-scale once construction was finished and the system turned on.

✢   ✢   ✢

Other projects remained on target during 2014. By mid-year, the new national university complex was completed. Jane had moved into her new office. Her navy career over, Rose moved into a fully equipped environmental laboratory next to Jane's office. Since Jane had brought a full staff of complementary personnel with her from Seattle, unfortunately she did not have a position for Adriana. However, with Rose's pleading, Jane was able to use her quite considerable influence to land a position for Adriana with the Chief's transitional team. That group was in effect moving the White House to the Denver State capitol building. With the Colorado state government "on leave," the executive branch of the federal government would be operating out of the state's facilities. Adriana would be reporting directly to the Chief of staff's trusted senior administrative assistant, the very one who had managed the secret compilation of the Master Plan three years prior. It was quite interesting that when Rose introduced her good friend Adriana to her other good friend Jane Stricker, their meeting was cordial enough yet seemed to be an all-business encounter. When Jane, as a favor to Rose, introduced Adriana to the Chief for a private interview, Jane felt considerable trepidation. Adriana had grown into a beautiful, elegant, thirty-year-old young woman full of poise and confidence. Perhaps feeling a twinge of jealousy, Jane was still not certain of her innermost understanding of her technical confidante and lover, the Chief of Staff of the President of the United States. It was a complex relationship with a complex man, to say the least.

✢   ✢   ✢

By January 2015, Michael was working out of George Blake's office in Los Angeles. A few days after another somber holiday season, he had given up his role in the Santa Barbara operation. After wishing Rose "Happy New Year" salutations, it was right back to work. Santa Barbara had been a complete technical success, but as Michael knew it was on a very small scale compared to the challenge he was now facing in Los

Angeles. With the cutoff of water supplied from Northern California to the South, Michael had turned operational control of the Santa Barbara desalination plant over to local authorities. The plant would provide water to local residents until their move to Colorado was complete. Along the entire California coast, rising sea levels increasingly flooded coastal towns. Despite the dangers from recurring wildfires, residents had been moving inland to friends' and relatives' homes positioned on higher ground along the coastal mountains.

Michael had been very select in positioning the large desalination plants in the Los Angeles area. He did not want them too close to rising sea levels and frequent storm areas, nor back too far in the LA Basin in case that area flooded, nor up too high in the ring of mountains surrounding the basin. Nor did he want them too close together in case of a serious earthquake striking a particular area. He and George Blake finally settled on twelve locations extending from the city of Thousand Oaks twenty miles north of downtown Los Angeles down to the city of Irvine forty miles south. Since each of the dozen huge plants required the withdrawal of ocean water to be then transported via pipeline a few miles to higher ground, Michael made sure the windmills placed in the ocean to provide electrical power to operate the driving pumps could withstand the hurricane-force winds and waves of a Category 5 storm.

Michael also designed extensive solar panels just east of the mountain areas that would not only provide an assist in the water transport to Colorado but also serve as backup power for transporting seawater to the desalination plants. Both of these power sources—ocean windmills and desert solar panels—would also serve as backup in operating the desalination plants themselves. The primary source of electric power for those large plants was a fifty-mile-by-fifty-mile combination grid in the LA Basin itself. It would utilize thousands of both elevated solar panels and forty-foot-high windmills. Their foundations would be firmly entrenched in the ground but extend high enough into the air, including their spinning electricity-generating turbines, to operate in the event ocean levels ever filled the floor of the basin.

☆　☆　☆

"What was the number again, Michael?" George Blake quizzed. "The number of gallons per day needed in Colorado?"

"Well, they said with conservation they could get the average American family down to fifty gallons per day. That's a total of fifteen billion gallons domestic water per day. Then commercial and light industrial will need another five billion."

"So next year we are going to provide them with seven billion from here," George said.

"No … ten billion from here, four billion collected from rainfall through the Rockies, and six billion left over after irrigation requirements, transported from the Great Lakes and the Mississippi. I trust they will have the treatment plants completed in time in Colorado to meet drinking water standards," Michael replied.

"Well, this water should be pretty good. There shouldn't be any toxic metals like cadmium, chromium, or lead. Maybe some bacteria can get into the pipelines. They should not need clarifiers and maybe just a little bit of chlorine. That about right, Michael?"

"Yes, right, but I guess our worry is not the Colorado situation but the pushed-up timetable. Within a few months we need to start testing our systems here and be ready at the end of the year for a full load on all the equipment and power sources. George, they are counting on us at the start of 2016, you know …?" Michael's voice inadvertently trailed off.

"And your level of confidence?" George asked. "From top to bottom, we all have had complete confidence in you and your ingenious designs and the perfection you achieved in Santa Barbara. But every once in a while, Michael, I glance into your face and see you somewhere else. Could it be that faraway girlfriend of yours … or is there something I don't know?"

Taken off guard, Michael had to think fast. From his office colleagues to his boss, George Blake, to the notables in Washington, he had consistently exuded nothing but confidence. From lonely evenings working with his experiments in the engineering laboratory at Montecito University, devising his theories, writing his thesis on efficient power, to the perfect operation of the Santa Barbara plant, he had complete confidence in his ideas. His follow-up experiments always worked. It was a wonderful combination of advanced physics and exquisite chemistry. What he had not been revealing were his innermost fears that plagued many scientists and engineers— would it work as designed at full scale? Would it work when other variables are introduced that cannot be designed into laboratory procedures or even at the small Santa Barbara plant?

"Sir, everything about this project—I know and you know that it's going to work. But you caught me off guard; I'm sorry. I have to admit that I'm guilty of a wandering mind at times. Yes, I do think about that girlfriend. I met her about three and a half years ago, and I have only seen her once since, and that was two years ago" Michael said softly with his eyes now looking straight down, knowing that at this stage he dare not admit to George his profound fears of failure.

From behind his desk, George responded in a reassuring fatherly tone, "I understand, Michael. I understand."

*   *   *

It was too good to be true. Was it fate, luck, prayer? All three? Throughout the year 2015, new residences were being constructed and finished on time. New residents had been given moving dates by accessing a sophisticated computer program administered by the Department of the Interior. Transportation into Colorado by planes, cars, buses, and trains was efficiently moving an average of seven hundred thousand people a day. A clearly written pamphlet inserted through the mail slot in the front door was awaiting each new arrival. It indicated the password to their new computer inside, described how they access "new dollars" and the amount allocated per person, listed the services to which they were entitled, and outlined the "job" they were assigned, whether at home or at a nearby location.

Daily television coverage from Denver's one TV station, operated by the national government, devoted hours to the nation's horrific climate conditions region by region, to progress of the new construction, to progress of the move, and most importantly—without reference to political affiliation, religious belief, or philosophical persuasion—obsequious gratitude to the Savior and his Master Plan.

At the moment, there was sufficient power and water. Excess electricity from the nation's nuclear generators was being diverted to receiving stations set up north of Denver. The Great Plains' aquifers still had plenty of water left for current irrigation needs. The warmer weather in Nebraska and Iowa was extending the growing season and leading to record soy, wheat, and corn harvesting. For a short while longer, there was enough water trapped in the Rocky Mountains despite the lack of snowfall and substantially less rainfall. There was no shortage of water during 2015, but the day of rationing was approaching rapidly.

*   *   *

Jane, Rose, and Adriana were settled into their new quarters and positions in Denver. Rose repeatedly attempted to "hook" a ride on military aircraft flying between Denver and Los Angeles to visit her beloved Michael. But even with her associate and close friend Jane Stricker's influence with the president's Chief of staff, each effort ended in dismal failure. Conditions in this new world were different. Commercial aircraft were grounded. No one who arrived in this "New America" was permitted to leave. Nor could Michael leave his assignment, not for one day.

The six outsiders in the Group of Eight were gloating over their plush, refurbished apartments in downtown Denver, although the Oracle was still spending as much time as possible contemplating the future course of nature's events in his favorite spot high in the Rockies, the old mining town of Aspen. The vice president had already moved to a private, secure home in the foothills a few miles west of downtown Denver. The president and his Chief of staff were monitoring all aspects of the plan all day long, every day, from the Oval Office. They were to stay in hot, muggy Washington, DC, until New Year's Day, 2016. That date was designated to be the official "opening day" in New America. It was the day the Master Plan was to be fully implemented. The "Captain and his First Mate" were to stay with the sinking ship until everyone reached their destination of safety. The plan was working. Now it was up to Michael.

☆   ☆   ☆

By the end of July, all twelve desalination plants had been fully constructed. Great care had been taken to ensure that all footings to support the huge heating and distillation units were secure enough in the ground to withstand earthquakes up to a powerful magnitude 9.0. Michael's novelty was tied to two unique design features. One was how ordinary turbines placed on windmills and on solar panels could generate electricity much more efficiently than any other known technology. The other related to pressure and temperature piping configurations that separated salt out of the seawater at ten times the rate of other technologies given the same power input, or alternatively, five times the separation rate using half the power. It did not matter anymore that his technology also produced a more environmentally friendly waste brine. Dreams of a pristine California environment were now irrelevant.

The schedule set for the months of August and September was twofold in purpose: one was to check the integrity of metal pipe fittings at all twelve plants; and the other was to test the electrical output of all the thousands of turbines located in the ocean, in the basin, in the backup areas, and finally along the route to Colorado. The plan for October was to double-check the complicated connections in the system and then start up each operating plant one at a time under Michael's supervision. Assuming that all went well, during November each plant would start desalinating and sending a small amount of water down the first hundred miles of pipelines. Michael did not want to go full blast until he was assured that all equipment was in proper operating order. The word in New America was that clean Pacific Ocean water would be miraculously flowing full force into Colorado in time for the president's triumphant arrival on New Year's Day.

By Thanksgiving, a relieved Michael enjoyed a festive turkey dinner with his proud parents. They were among the last to leave California for Colorado. To date, Michael's scale-up had proceeded according to plan, but on December 1 Michael realized that he had forgotten one thing; he was witnessing a dramatic change in the climate of his nation, yet there had been no contingency built into his schedule for a localized natural disaster. His only hardship so far had been to deal with the oppressive heat. Fires in the mountains and encroaching sea levels had posed little threat to his project.

Hurricanes seldom roared up the West Coast. They typically turned inland toward Texas from Mexico. This one was different. On December 12, heading east off of San Diego, the storm at Category 4 suddenly started to veer northwest toward Los Angeles, catching the U.S. Weather Bureau by surprise. Michael and his team had little time to prepare. Fortunately, the equipment damage was minimal. At least the hurricane gave evidence as to how sturdy the desalination plants had been built. But the downtime in cleanup cost nearly a two-week delay in the start-up program.

George Blake found a dejected Michael staring off to the Pacific. He tried to hide his own concerns. The higher ups were counting on clean water flowing by the time of the president's arrival in Denver in a few days. Would the new systems work at full scale? Could they withstand further natural disasters? "Michael, have faith. And after all this goes well, you have that beautiful young lady love waiting for you. Have confidence."

"Yeah, you say have faith. I don't know, George, what I believe anymore. Is the Lord really with me? … And that young lady. I don't think I know what love is all about anymore – it's been almost three years since I've been with her. And confidence … my dad said 'do it right', but how do I know until I push those start buttons?"

After a day off for his entire team to mark the Christmas celebration, it was back to work. A worried Rose found little time in Michael's hectic schedule for more than sending brief "hellos" and text messages of support.

On December 27, 2015, all systems looked "go." It was time. Michael gave the word: crank up Unit One to full capacity. The ground shook. It was not the unit. It was a magnitude 6.8 earthquake centered in the middle of the LA Basin.

Michael screamed, "Hit the red buttons!" and his operators smartly shut down the unit immediately. Fortunately, there were no strong aftershocks—just a typical series of smaller shocks in the magnitude two range. Michael ordered an inspection of all twelve units for possible damage. A few minor equipment repairs and all was well again. On December 29, Unit One was turned up full blast. Michael held his breath. It was his defining moment. Would the scale-up work?

It did—perfectly. Units Two, Three, and Four followed. On December 30, Units Five, Six, Seven, and Eight fired up without a hitch. On December 31, 2015, Units Nine, Ten, Eleven, and Twelve went on line. The thousand-mile-long pipeline power system was miraculously pushing billions of gallons of water uphill to its final destination without an interruption. On January 1, 2016, the full design capacity of ten billion gallons per day of desalinated Pacific Ocean seawater was flowing into Eastern Colorado. It worked!

Chapter Eight

Perfection

December 31, 2015

"**R**ose, darling. Happy New Year! I'm exhausted, but thanks for calling early 'cause I may fall asleep before midnight."

"Oh Michael, we are going to have a very, very happy new year. Have you received the news yet from Denver?"

"Yes, I know. Everything is working. The water is flowing. You can take a shower there, Rose ... in our clean Pacific Ocean." His faint laugh was barely audible.

"I know. I can't wait. I'm going to do just that. Michael, dear Michael. Congratulations! The word is around. You are a hero." Rose giggled in sheer joy and followed with, "A hero ... Michael, you are an amazing guy!"

"All I know is that I'm a very fatigued engineer, very lucky myself and very fortunate to have a great team working with me ... but Lord knows when I'm going to see you. I miss you very much. I'm thinking of you constantly."

"And I miss you ... but don't you have the rest of the news?" Rose asked.

"What do you mean?"

"Then they haven't called you yet! Hey, darling, some others in addition to the Lord do know when you're going to see me next."

"Come on, Miss Rose. There you go again, you tease. What do you mean? Don't tantalize me."

"Okay, I'm sorry. You will probably get the call tomorrow. The president and his Chief of staff are arriving tomorrow afternoon—New Year's Day. It's going to be a big celebration. He wanted everything to be working and orderly in New America at the start of the year 2016, and your water system was the last peg to fit in the puzzle. It has all come together on time. The Chief called Jane Stricker about two hours ago and told her that your boss will stay behind in Los Angeles to oversee the desalination plants while you are coming to the national university in Denver, the National University of New America, to be appointed a full research professor of water technology! Michael, do you hear me?" Rose thought their phone connection was cut off. There was a frustrating silence.

Finally, "Rose ... I'm speechless. ... I don't know what to say ... I ... uh ..."

"What you're going to say when they call you tomorrow is that you are deeply honored and accept the appointment. Oh, darling, like you said this world is turned upside down, but we are going to be together ... together at last. Oh, I love you so much."

* * *

With his nation in dire straits, the last thing the president expected when his plane touched down in Denver on New Year's Day afternoon in 2016 were streets lined with admirers. His motorcade slowly made its way from the Denver airport to the state capitol past adoring crowds. The Colorado state capitol building had been converted into the new temporary White House. Certainly there was nothing to celebrate concerning the state of the nation, but the Chief of staff did plan for a 4:00 PM outdoor televised address by the president to the citizens of New America. The brief ceremony was billed as a testimonial to the successful transition to Eastern Colorado, that the nation's citizens were now all safe at last, and that the president wanted to give thanks. Truly, the Savior had delivered.

The president felt relieved. The Chief felt ecstatic. The enthusiastic crowd lining the streets and filling the Capitol grounds clearly let their emotions flow. They were joyous, and they were grateful. After the president's short televised address thanking all his citizens for their splendid cooperation in making this difficult transition a success, he turned to his Chief of staff and calmly said, "Good job, Chief ... better than expected. Now let's get organized tomorrow morning in our new facilities and invite in the Group of Eight for lunch. We need to think about our next steps."

"Yes, sir ... and the vice president?"

"Yes, her too. What if I were to die next week from mountain fever?" The Chief did not think that remark funny at all, but it was nice to see a smile on the face of the president. It was probably his first in four years. "And by the way, Chief, don't forget tomorrow to call that young man in

Los Angeles. We want him here soon. What he has done to get all this water moving to Colorado has been phenomenal."

☆   ☆   ☆

The private dining room in the state capitol building was much larger and more ornate than the president's intimate dining room in the White House. It took several minutes for the Group of Eight to become acclimated to their new surroundings. With the joyous mood and a few cocktails, however, it did not take long for the group to feel quite comfortable.

The Oracle felt redemption over what at first seemed like radical fringe thinking. He was not a scientist, but taking clues from his most trusted environmental adviser, Richard Compton, he was able to take bits and pieces of seemingly unrelated events and project them ahead. His forecasts of how minor vagaries of nature foreshadow major climactic changes always turned out incredibly accurate. Today, however, he was not gloating over his accuracy, nor did he feel relieved that the president of the United States had accepted his dire forecasts ahead of the general curve and had been able to rescue America. He remained in his typically solemn mood. He believed that environmental conditions would continue to worsen for the foreseeable future.

Richard Compton, after consuming two cocktails, appeared quite relaxed. He felt that he had made a major contribution to his country. While now assigned to a prestigious professorship in charge of the largest department in the new national university, the Department of the Environment, he wanted nothing more than to spend a nice vacation with his good friend, the Oracle, up in the mountain town of Aspen. But no time for that. The environment was in turmoil.

The two most joyous members of the group were Arthur Schnell and Hank Abrams. They had worked extremely hard the last four years in order to make the transition to New America so successful. Certainly this was the time to enjoy themselves and partake in a little gloating. On the other hand, two members of the group still seemed on edge. John Heyward and H. Stewart had concocted a new economy for New America. By this time, they wanted to actually believe that their contrived system would work. Obviously, they both publicly professed that it would. But privately, they wondered if they had merely created *a truthful myth*—that everyone would actually believe their make-believe system was a real one, a correct one that would work. Only time would tell.

The Group of Eight outsider, Alexis Graham, continued to feel left out and perplexed. She had successfully persuaded the president, probably over the Chief's objections, to invite her to attend the Group of Eight meetings in order to be better informed and in order to provide alternate opinions. Ironically, she found that not once did she have to offer a contrary opinion because over the last two years everything regarding the transitional phase spelled out in the Master Plan had worked to perfection. Nevertheless, in both her heart and mind, she felt uneasy about the Chief's influence on the president. She thought to herself, "Am I being unduly harsh? Could the Chief's motives actually be pure? I'm not sure, but I doubt it."

"Gentlemen, Ali, this is fun, but let's get started. These are very busy times." The president continued speaking after all were seated and the main course served—of course, no meat or fish but lots of fruits and vegetables and featuring soy burgers as the main protein portion of the meal. "It's very difficult for any of us to believe just how successful everything has worked out so far. ... Sure, I said 'Bingo' five years ago, but none of this could've happened without your diligence and perseverance. I am blessed to have you and thank you all from the bottom of my heart. Let's review everything, in order. Richard—the environmental situation around the country; Arthur—the housing situation; Hank—the water and energy situation; and John and H.—the economic setup. Then after that, I have something further to add."

An hour later it was back to the president. "The Chief has advised me that the post-transitional phase in the Master Plan was written in rather vague language. I believe he has a very legitimate concern. That is, how do we preserve order in New America now that everyone is here? Later this afternoon I'm meeting with my Chief counsel and his entire staff. I want to propose so-called 'Guidelines' for how our citizens are to live and carry out their responsibilities. Since this is a temporary situation legally, I don't want them to feel as though I, the Chief executive, am imposing laws, or even something so harsh as what would be called 'rules.' So in my mind I will call them 'Guidelines.' After I follow up on this with the Chief and my legal staff, I'll be back to you to explain."

Except for one attendee, the first luncheon meeting of the Group of Eight in New America ended at 3:00 PM January 2, 2016, enveloped by a general mood of elation. But Ali had a new thought, a disturbing thought: "The Chief—'laws, rules, guidelines'—this can't be good." She breathed a deep sigh.

✿ ✿ ✿

"Gentlemen, please sit down," said the president. The Oval Office in Denver looked almost exactly the same as the Oval Office in Washington—good planning by the Chief. In addition to his invaluable Chief of staff, the president had invited his Chief White House counsel and his top three legal assistants to the five o'clock meeting. "You have all read and studied the Master Plan, probably many times. It contains a great amount of detail regarding the physical aspects of providing housing, utilities, health care, a working economy, and so forth in New America. It was very exact in the transitional phase; that is, how we would transport three hundred million people to Eastern Colorado. What was left vague, because we simply could not take the time to think about it back then, was the social order that would be required in New America. Obviously, in the national emergency I declared, the federal government is the responsible party. We are assuming that everybody is taken care of and everybody is treated equally. That said, on the other side of the coin, every individual person here in New America has an equal responsibility as well to … to make the system work. Everyone has to be playing the same game. Every game has rules. Every society has laws. Order must prevail." Everyone in the room was paying rapt attention to the president.

"Now the complication. Temporarily, we do not have a legislative branch of the federal government, or of the Colorado State government. Obviously, legislatures are established to make laws, the executive branch to carry them out, and the judicial branch to interpret them when there are disputes. Remember, we did tell the Supreme Court that we wished to use them and their federal judges to interpret the rules of New America. But gentlemen, who establishes the rules? I don't want to call them 'laws,' since I should not be the one making laws. That's presumptuous. That would make me a dictator. So what I am thinking is … let's not have anything called 'law,' or not even 'rules.' What do you think if you gentlemen along with Arthur Schnell and Hank Abrams write a preliminary set of 'Guidelines'? We will have the Chief and his staff review them, approve them, and then publish them as 'Official Guidelines of the National Government.' I'm afraid that, in order to establish and preserve order, this will have to be a soup-to-nuts situation. From the number of hours worked per week for each and every able adult, down to what days and what time trash is to be placed outside on the curb."

Not having been trained as an attorney himself, the president felt a little uncomfortable in his prolonged discourse. He seemed somewhat to be meandering and speaking off the top of his head. But the Chief and the attorneys in the room loved it. To the Chief, it was essential to maintain strict order in New America. A new social, political, and economic system containing such a high-density population would not survive long without clear-cut authority from the top. There was no room for dissent. The rules had to be clear, and everyone had to follow them. To the Chief counsel and his staff, nothing could be more exciting. It was an opportunity to draft laws, regulations, and rules from scratch. And it's okay if the president prefers to call them *Guidelines* for political purposes—that's fine; they would be "Official Guidelines with the weight of law."

✳   ✳   ✳

His energy level was usually boundless, but he had found the last two days fatiguing. It was only 8:00 PM, and after finishing dinner with the president, the Chief planned to stop by his office briefly. He simply wanted to check his mail before turning in early for the night. He did not expect the visitor sitting in his office waiting for him. "Ali, what a surprise! What are you doing here so late? You are to be separated from the president as much as possible …for security."

The vice president remained in her seat across from the Chief's desk and smiled calmly. "Relax, Chief. I just wanted a quick update as to what your legal team came up with to … you know, maintain order." The Chief looked ruffled. This was not planned for nor was it pleasant. He worked for the president, not the vice president. "Why is she meddling?" he wondered to himself. Only because the president had strongly recommended that he keep the peace with Ali did he feel a mild obligation to give her any answer at all.

"Look, Ali. It's just preliminary. You know that America is a law-and-order country. And you heard the president state how unusual the situation is with so many people moving into a relatively small area. We simply asked the legal staff to draft some simple rules. We're going to call them 'Guidelines' so as not to be too officious … but you know that people simply have to know what their everyday duties are and what is expected of them. This is a big ship to run, and everyone has to know their role and do their part in an orderly fashion."

"And if everyone doesn't happen to like a Guideline or two?

"No, no. They will be quite simple ... not a problem," the Chief responded, trying to hide his growing agitation. "Why is this intruder in my office, uninvited, at eight o'clock at night?" he growled under his breath.

"But if someone does happen to violate a Guideline? Will there be enforcement? By whom? Will there be a penalty?" The vice president remained persistent.

"That's it!" he screamed under his breath. "Ali, please. As I said, this is all preliminary. Everyone understands we are in a national emergency. It's for their safety. It's temporary. No one is going to violate a Guideline. We will have complete cooperation." The Chief wanted no more conversation. He gathered the mail from his inbox and proceeded toward the door. "Let's go, Ali. It's getting late. You have to drive up those hills in the dark to your home. Good night."

✳   ✳   ✳

Michael was elated. He had spent the entire month of January teaching George Blake all the operating details in running the desalination plants. Michael's team had also completed a perfectly written operating manual describing Michael's novel technologies. On February 1 he was provided with an all-electric new car for his journey to Denver. He would follow one of the water pipelines along the way, checking on its performance. His only inconvenience was stopping every four hours and recharging his automobile's battery for two hours at one of the solar or wind-power facilities. He felt incredibly relieved and gratified that over the past month the entire water system was working exactly as he had designed. The scale-up was a complete success. And it was good to know that George and the team left behind would be able to run the system with full competence. Both Michael's people and equipment would be fully protected by a military presence. Now the most important thought running through his mind was that he would at long last be united with the love of his life, his "Miss Rose."

"Michael, finally! I have been calling and calling, but I guess the cell phone transmitters along the interstates don't work anymore. Where are you?"

"Don't despair, darling. I'm driving north from Colorado Springs. I'll be at the university in a couple of hours ... meet you there?"

"No!" Rose responded with almost a hint of unintended despair in her voice. She knew he might not like the "Code of Order" he was about to receive. "First go to the reception hall and get your Guidelines. Then ask for directions to Green Street just off campus, Building 4, where my apartment is, and I'll look for you just outside the front door. Call me when you see the building. It has a big number '4' on the wall just above the door. Oh Michael, I can't wait to see you. I'm going to make sure my roommates are out for a walk. We all have Saturdays off from our duties. You and I have the weekend. I can't wait!" Her voice was now rising excitedly in joyous anticipation. "And don't take time to sign autographs, you big hero. Your picture has been all over the TV news."

"Wait!" he demanded. "Guidelines, apartments! I was told nothing except to report to the front lobby of the national university just west of downtown Denver. I thought everyone was living in these nice new two-story spacious residences. I—"

"Michael ... no," she said, her voice dropping again. "There are exceptions for certain people critical to the emergency plan. I know who you will be living with and where your apartment is. Oh, I'll explain it all when we're together. And the 'Guidelines'—they're necessary for us to have a systematic way for everyone to live in these emergency conditions. ..." She paused.

So many mood swings. After all these hours, days, and weeks anticipating a wonderful reunion, the two closed their conversation with almost a sense of brooding. "What kind of regimented life is this to be in New America?" Michael wondered to himself.

"There is no 'Guideline' for two distant lovers coming together in New America, at least not yet," Rose mused to herself, happy but bewildered.

✻   ✻   ✻

"Thanks for coming over to my office on such short notice. You know, Arthur, that after the president, you have the most important position in America. You have truly performed a remarkable service in getting New America set up and getting everyone relocated here. Listen, I want to continue to help you in any way I can."

"Well, Chief, the Guidelines are still confusing to many even though everyone is trying to cooperate. I suggest that you think about your legal team trying to rewrite them in clearer, more simple language."

"Right. I agree. We'll get on that right away. Also, before our next Group of Eight meeting, tell me ... everything going okay with food and housing and so forth? I'm not hearing any complaints, but I just want to be sure."

"Well, actually it's incredible. Everyone loves their spacious new one-floor residencies. Sure, for the wealthier, it's a comedown in size and less privacy, but they have every modern convenience. For the less wealthy, the majority, it has been a step up. So they are very happy. You know Americans love diversions and entertainment. While we only have one television station, our government channel, twenty-four hours a day we're showing reruns of popular movies, top game shows, and great sports events ... and as you know these are all on large-screen, high-definition TVs. Also, the large-screen personal computers that we have installed in each home are of top quality. Oh yeah, even though the Internet is limited to what we allow in the Guidelines, they serve as a great communication tool among family and friends ... and also they're full of challenging games to play. I should also mention the Parks and Recreation program is going well too. Kids and outdoor people have plenty to do."

"Good Arthur, good." The Chief smiled. "And how about the food situation? It's been good here in Denver. How about out there?"

"Beyond belief," replied a smiling Arthur. "Fruit and vegetables from California have all dried up, but we're still getting some in from South America through the Baltimore Port and transported by train out here. Our fruit trees have been planted, and by summer everyone will have fruits and vegetables growing just outside their doorsteps. As you know, the grain situation is phenomenal. We're getting lots and lots of corn, wheat, and soy. All those meat and fish eaters ... well, they may be privately suffering, but I've heard no complaints. Our few fish farms just can't supply enough, so fish may not be in anyone's diet in the future. But everyone accepts the gravity of the situation. Oh, and by the way, the nutrition experts on my agricultural staff have sent over suggestions to your legal staff. They want to add to the guidelines directives on what they should eat each day and in what quantities. You know, the best way to promote good health care is through good nutrition and good exercise."

"Yeah yeah, I could go for that myself," the Chief responded blankly.

* * *

It was sounding almost too good to be true. Nevertheless, before the next Group of Eight meeting scheduled for mid-February, the Chief wanted to check all bases so there would be no surprises for the president at that session. He held a brief meeting with Hank Abrams, who assured him that water was flowing from both the Pacific Ocean and the Great Lakes in full force. Adequate electricity was being generated for home use and for transportation. Solar panels installed on the roofs of every building in Eastern Colorado were doing their job. The guidelines called for up to, but not to exceed, three hours of all-electric heat in each residence each night and one hour each morning if the 6:00 AM inside temperature fell below sixty-two degrees. There would be no need for electricity to run air-conditioning systems other than for home refrigerators and commercial freezers. Temperatures might reach ninety degrees in the longer summer days, but the high altitude would keep the air dry and the warmer temperatures quite bearable.

The Chief had one more important meeting prior to the gathering of the Group of Eight. "John, H., good to see you both. How are your apartments? Everything okay with your office setups?" The top economic advisers understood the guideline specifying equality but were rather enjoying their actual status as almost royalty. Their three-bedroom apartments could only be described as "luxurious."

"Incredibly good, Chief," answered a jubilant John. "We love the apartment next to the university, and the staff you have assigned to us is going overboard to make sure we have everything we need."

"I concur, Chief. I concur. All is well," added H. with a polite smile.

"Okay, good. And the job situation, the money system?" Getting to the heart of the matter, the Chief seemed to be begging a positive answer.

"Well, I'm sure it was an initial shock to many to be assigned work right in their own homes, but what everybody has in common is that they feel saved from personal disaster. They're cooperating with whatever task they are assigned to do. All those trades people who worked so hard to get the existing buildings out here renovated and to build all the tens of millions of new ones that have been constructed have been reassigned to our assembly plants. Electric cars and buses, appliances, replacement parts. There's plenty to keep them busy, and you know as an old college prof that I don't like to be called a 'czar,' so I am very happy operating behind the scenes just teaching the lawyers what to write into the Guidelines about the economic system."

"Bravo, Professor. And you, H., … your national bank?"

"Chief, I have to tell you. The transition to the new dollar has worked perfectly. Everyone seems happy that we froze asset values based upon the old money at appraised values. The new dollar backed by our gold and silver reserves is holding up very well. So we can continue to bring vital imports into the country from foreign sources. We still need some raw materials such as steel from Brazil and South Korea and so forth. Almost nothing is coming in from China anymore since we're trying to assemble everything we can right here. And I have heard no one complain of the wage levels we have set and the price levels we have established. For the consumer, we have dramatically reduced their need for disposable income since they are getting free housing, electricity, water, education, and health care."

"Bravo, H.," grinned the Chief, sinking back into his fine leather office chair and whispering to himself, "*Perfect, perfect.*"

* * *

Michael was astonished. Signs pointing to the national university were abundant and clearly marked. The new buildings were beautifully designed and constructed. The grounds looked impeccably groomed. Locating a parking space, he thought to himself, "So this is where the top brains in the country are going to be doing their work. I guess I should feel fortunate that Rose and I are included." Entering the lobby of the reception hall, he was immediately recognized. "Michael, you're here at last ... welcome," said a judicious-looking middle-aged woman introducing herself as the university receptionist. "I have a complete package for you. Please step over to this private office and look through it. If you have any questions, please let me know."

"Thank you, ma'am. The only question I have is how do I get to Building 4 on Green Street?"

The largest of the contents inside the large parcel that Michael was handed was a thick booklet with bold black letters written over the entire front cover: "**New America—Guidelines—2016.**" No time for that, he thought. It probably contained the code of behavior or order or whatever Rose had called it. Several one-page letters were included. One was from the newly appointed dean of the university welcoming Michael and requesting his presence in the dean's office 9:00 AM Monday morning. The dean expressed his gratitude to Michael for his marvelous engineering achievement and indicated that at the meeting he would inform Michael of his title, assignment, and place of work. Another letter indicated the apartment number and location where he would be living. It was just off campus, but not on Green Street. It gave the names of the two male roommates with whom he would be living. "Enough!" he muttered out loud to himself. He felt as if he had transitioned from a joyous free-spirited drive of a thousand miles into some kind of a straitjacket; something he had never experienced before. Maybe everyone else arriving in New

America had similar feelings at first, but he had a special mission of his own to concentrate upon. He hurriedly put everything back in the envelope and raced out through the lobby door toward his car with directions to Building 4 on Green Street in his hand.

✻ ✻ ✻

"I see it, Rose, I see it. Building 4."

"Find a parking spot. I'm running down right now," Rose exclaimed excitedly.

A few moments later: "I don't want to hear about guidelines … apartments … assignments. I just want to look at you … my darling, Miss Rose … to hold you … to love you."

"Oh Michael, it has been so long," Rose said softly, her heart fluttering, tears streaming down her flush cheeks. "I love you. I love you." Hugging and kissing him again and again, she lead him upstairs.

✻ ✻ ✻

It was a jovial Group of Eight at the "New" White House—more like a dinner party than a dinner meeting. Even the vice president could not escape the mood. She carried a continuous smile on a radiant face despite her secret misgivings regarding the underlying motives of the Chief. The room's uplifting mood was only tarnished for a brief period of time as the Oracle and Richard reviewed the continued harsh environmental conditions around the nation. At least they ended their report more upbeat and on a good note: Conditions in Eastern Colorado were just as the Savior had eloquently portrayed in his "Bingo" address—slightly higher temperatures, but not oppressive; some rain, but no hurricanes or tornadoes. The national pestilence plaguing the nation was under control here. Warmer temperatures and a longer growing season combined to create an agricultural boom.

Hank Abrams expressed ebullience at how well the power systems were working—plenty of electricity being generated from solar and wind sources, no burning of fossil fuels, sufficient quantities of treated water. Everything was perfect.

Arthur Schnell reviewed the many facets under his vast responsibilities. Home care, medical facilities, and nursing homes were all working better than possibly imagined. Home-schooling programs and satellite schools were being well received by the public. On Sundays, school buildings were turned over to church leaders. Services were packed. The quality of the millions of residences, thousands of convenience stores, and hundreds of recreational areas were all receiving excellent grades. No one was complaining about the food. Everything was perfect.

John Heyward and H. Stewart, fingers crossed under the dining table, spoke in glowing terms about the success of the economic system they had created. Thousands of bankers who had moved to New America, despite whatever assigned duties they might have been given, were applying for the limited number of positions available with the new prestigious national bank. Everything was perfect.

The question came up as to how well the newly clarified Guidelines were being received and followed by the citizens. The question also arose as to whether there was a need for a national police force for the city of Denver and for Eastern Colorado. Operations outside the boundaries of New America for the enlarged military forces were perceived to be doing as well as could be expected. Limited food choices and harsher conditions obviously were not enjoyable, but military personnel knew that they were performing a valuable national service. They were diligently protecting properties and facilities in all the outlying regions and in the coastal areas. When not being ravaged by storms, the big cities across America looked like ghost towns except for the military convoys on patrol.

The president closed the meeting in his usual calm demeanor: "Gentlemen, Ali. Again, I extend my deepest thanks to you all. You're doing an absolutely marvelous job. We have saved our people from further harm. Guidelines ... let's not disturb a good thing. Everyone seems to be cooperating. Everything is working as planned—orderly. Let's not further change the Guidelines that are already being well accepted ... and let's not create any type of police presence. There is no room for bad or inappropriate behavior. We're sailing smoothly now. Let's not disturb the sails. Everything is perfect."

*　*　*

It was mid-March and time for the Chief to broach a new subject with the president: "Let me update you on a subject that is infringing upon my daily schedule. As you know, we have assigned newspaper writers, TV commentators, and other members of the press the task of writing research papers and other reports pertaining to climatic conditions for our university professors, but I'm receiving over a dozen e-mails and telephone calls daily protesting the fact that we have only one radio station and one television station devoted to the news."

"Ah hah," interrupted the president. "They think the tradition of their free press is now subjugated to our propaganda. They hear nothing but pessimism talking with and listening to the Oracle concerning how long the global warming will last. Then they talk to some of the climatologists at the university, some of whom express optimism that all this could turn around in ten or twenty years. So what is it with the ones you are in contact?"

"I think, sir," replied the Chief, "that while a consensus figure could be around fifty years before we see a reversal … uh … in other words, despite the fact that we're getting Man's carbon out of the air—all that other carbon from the melting permafrost—it's going to take many years before there's enough dissipation of that carbon for a climate reversal to happen. But, you know, even if it were only ten years, these media people are scratching their heads as to how can they be productive. They feel stymied if the public is only hearing what we put out."

"So what do you suggest?"

"I suggest, Mr. President, that I schedule a meeting with all the major media Chief editors and have you do a little persuasion. Tell them how valuable they are in producing new stories about the climate and the harsh conditions around the country. The more we show and tell news stories about heat, drought, hurricanes, tornadoes, and so forth, the more the public accepts these ongoing emergency conditions. And think about it—it has turned out that life is not so bad here. I believe you can turn on your magic to keep these people in line."

"Perfect, Chief. I can do it."

✻ ✻ ✻

"Again Ali, again? Another unannounced visit?" The Chief fumed, obviously ignoring the courtesy normally given to a vice president of the United States. "You get into my office because of your position, but I would appreciate a call in advance."

"Please … calm down. I just want to ask you a simple question," Ali softly responded. "It has gotten back to me, even in my secure, secluded home and office up there in the foothills, that last week the president met with over a dozen media leaders. Right?"

"Right," the Chief answered disdainfully, not elaborating.

"Well, the word is—but of course you must already know this—that the president did a masterful job of persuasion. For now, the press seems perfectly willing to let you go on with this system of government control you have created. But my question is this: Why not return to the three branches of government? Everyone accepts the fact that we are in a national emergency, but this is not like a war. We cannot fight this environmental calamity. We have done what we can by eliminating manmade carbon emissions. We have to wait it out. Why not restore the Congress to make your so-called guidelines, and why not have our court system interpret them when disputed?"

"Why, Ali? Why? I have the feeling that you don't trust me, but you do trust your president, don't you? There's no need for 535 members of Congress to argue over our guidelines. Everyone accepts them ... and since there have been no disputes, we need no court system. So I don't see what you're driving at." The impertinent Chief had just about enough of this dialogue and turned away.

"Okay, Chief. I'm leaving. You and your Savior have achieved a state of perfection. You are to be congratulated. But it will be interesting to see what happens as more time goes by." With the Chief now scrambling through papers on his desk, Alexis Graham, a brilliant woman and the Vice President of the United States, strode briskly through the doorway. Neither said "goodbye."

Moments later the Chief called his senior administrative assistant on his intercom. "Do me a favor, please. Anytime you are aware that the vice president is in the building, let me know immediately ... and uh, that assistant you have, the one who did such a great job during the transitional phase—what's her name? Adriana? Send her in here.

"Adriana, please sit down. The time has been flying by, and I'm sure I thanked you when the president and I arrived in Denver for all the great work you did in smoothing the way. I just wanted to tell you that again. And oh, also to ask that you follow up on something for the president. For obvious security reasons, the vice president is rarely in the same location as the president, but in all the hustle and bustle of getting settled here, he forgot to ask her to keep him up to date with her daily schedule. They both should know at all times where the other is. Please call Janice Jones, the vice president's administrative assistant, and ask her to send Ms. Graham's daily calendar to the president. Uh, of course since everything comes through me to the president, Janice should send it directly via e-mail to my address. Okay?" the Chief paused, lighting up with a warm smile.

"Oh, yes, sir. I understand. I'll do it right away." Adriana rose from her chair across from the Chief's desk, but before she could turn away the Chief followed up: "Oh, one more thing, Adriana. You were here for several months before we came and now almost four months later ... are you getting along okay? Is there anything you need?" Adriana knew from Rose's friend Jane Stricker that the Chief was quite a charming man. She now had a first glimpse of it. She smiled back and looked directly into his eyes and softly replied: "Thank you ... thank you for asking. Yes everything has been just perfect."

"Well, fine then. But you just let me know if anything comes up that I can help you with."

"Yes, I will do that," Adriana replied sweetly. There was a pause as they looked at each other for a moment. Then she turned and slowly walked toward the door. The Chief did not take his eyes off of her the whole way. After she departed, he sat back in his chair and let his mind wander: "One minute I have this agitating vice president here, and the next minute I have this lovely creature staring into my eyes and beautifully swaying out of my office."

* * *

As charming a man as the Chief obviously was in most circles, he also was a workaholic. He was on top of everything. The president felt fortunate to have him as his top aide and to have him available sixteen hours a day. All aspects of the Master Plan were working better than expected within New America, but the Chief was also staying on top of two daily reports from external sources. One was from the ever-operating Pentagon in Washington, DC. It reviewed the status of all the major ports located along the coasts of the United States, the downtown protection of hundreds of vacant American cities, and the cleanup status of the continuing environmental damage inflicted upon the nation's landscape.

The other report was from the Environmental Protection Agency, now operating out of the Pentagon. Utilizing the military's assistance, daily surveillance flights were observing hurricane damage, tornado damage, and earthquake damage. This information was being relayed to the Environmental Department at the national university for assessment. As the Oracle had predicted, the adverse impacts of climate change that had taken place so abruptly continued to worsen month by month.

The Chief's wife was now living with him in their spacious apartment in Denver. He saw little of her. After all day in his office by the president, it became imperative to find evening times and places to review environmental reports with his two top climate advisors—Richard Compton and Jane Stricker. He cleverly arranged to meet privately with Jane each week at a secluded location to review her reports. Jane continued to feel deeply ambivalent heartstrings tugging away—one pulling toward service for her country and the other toward this inexplicable romance.

✣   ✣   ✣

Continuing through the springtime season, *perfection* continued to be the best description of the status of affairs in New America. Michael was in touch with George Blake every day. Amazingly, through occasional earthquakes, hurricanes, and flooding from the ocean, the entire desalination system was holding steady. Michael credited the extra care in making sure all support foundations for the solar panels, for the windmills, for the turbines, for the pipelines, and for the desalination plants were deeply anchored. In late June, members of the major media working at the university scheduled an interview between the president and Michael. While Michael was well known as the engineering hero who delivered clean water to New America all the way from the Pacific Ocean and whose technology assisted in delivering so much water from the Great Lakes, he had not agreed to personal interviews for television viewing. But the president persisted. He convinced Michael that he must put his humility and shyness aside for a few moments to be acknowledged for the great service he had performed for his country.

As ever, Michael displayed his outward poise and rose to the occasion. Without sounding the least bit arrogant, he explained to the president on camera that he had complete confidence in his innovative technologies. While there might have been some typical engineering concern as to whether his systems would scale up to such a large size, he acknowledged the great teamwork of all those involved that helped make it possible. Now Michael's face, as well as his name, was known to three hundred million grateful Americans. Never did he show any signs of his inner insecurities that his novel technologies could work at this incredible scale. Nor did he reveal the slightest hint of his current internal discomfort—dismay of the complete government "guideline" control over his new life in New America.

Not everyone else was happy either. Perhaps it was a very small percentage. At least three persons for sure out of three hundred million. Certainly there were tens of thousands still grieving over damages or injuries sustained before they came to New America, and certainly not everyone was in perfect health in New America. Nevertheless, all those who arrived and survived felt blessed. These three shared mixed feelings. Alexis Graham could not hide her feeling that the president's Chief of staff was manipulating the crisis to his personal advantage. Jane Stricker could not hide her feelings of discomfort over her illicit relationship with the Chief. She also felt distraught that she did not have enough evidence yet that something else was going on with climate change beyond the melting permafrost. And Rose in her separate apartment from Michael—so close but yet still so far apart.

✻   ✻   ✻

New America, summer 2016

"Please don't be discouraged, Michael, please," Rose pleaded. "As close as Jane is to the Chief of staff, I have begged her over and over again to ask him to change the guidelines or make an exception for us. He told her he does not want to make any exceptions … that would open the floodgates of special privileges. But yes, there will eventually be a new Guideline for couples who want to live together. He tells Jane that he understands male-female attractions quite well, and that with the millions of people here, new relationships will develop and the guidelines will be amended to recognize that. The problem is that housing was assigned on a very exact basis so we could have an orderly transition."

"But Miss Rose, I have now been here for six months. We see each other every day at the university—at professional meetings, coffee breaks, sometimes lunch, sometimes dinner. We watch movies together. We take walks and hold hands. Thank God we sneak some minutes alone when our roommates are out, but this cannot go on. I want to hold you, love you, sleep with you, wake up with you. 'Guidelines,' you say? No, they are hard and fast 'rules.' You and I could go to a church service on a Sunday and have a pastor marry us, but then we couldn't live together. The Guidelines only allow us to live where we have been assigned and with the roommates we have been assigned. This is crazy. Am I alone in this?"

Rose replied forcefully to his question, responding in dutiful, nonstop, clear language. "Yes! You are alone. I felt embarrassed asking for an exception. Michael, the president of the United States has saved our nation's people. No one is questioning his plan. No one else is asking for an exception. We must have an orderly society. It's the only way it can work.

This is not the Wild West. This is not doing whatever we want to do. I know it won't be long before new marriages will be recognized. There will be a new Guideline on how to change residences and partners—"

"Darling, stop! I understand." He didn't understand at all, but the last thing he wanted to do was argue with her. He looked annoyed, but they had come too far. He wanted to change the subject. "You are a very smart woman, and you are thinking logically with that sharp brain of yours. But you know, Miss Rose, that warm heart of yours needs some attention … snuggle over here for a big hug."

Rose suddenly changed her mood, let out a deep breath, and followed with a hearty laugh, replying, "Better than that, darling. You know that walk-in closet down the hall from your office where we have sort of 'accidentally' met a couple of times? Well, we could arrange to meet there more often on our coffee breaks."

"Miss Rose, why do I love you more each day?" Michael smiled bravely, hiding his inner frustration.

"Because I bring you good news!" she exclaimed, lighting up.

Michael turned his head sharply and looked closely into her eyes. "No bad news first?" he countered.

"Nope, no bad news. Are you ready, love?

"Go!"

"Okay. The Guidelines—your 'rules'—permit university professors and their associates one week of vacation every six months.. Now you probably know that all those thousands of former ski lodges and condos up in the Rockies are now being used as recreational areas. Usage is drawn on a lottery basis. Michael, darling, my number came up! For the last week in August! And I had a choice of accommodations." Michael was awestruck as he continued to stare at her. "She is amazing," he thought to himself. She continued. "And so guess what? I chose a one-bedroom condo in Aspen. Pack your duffel bag, handsome, and stop complaining."

☆　☆　☆

The summer passed, and all was well in New America. In complete contrast to the environmental devastation surrounding it, the climate was perfect. The afternoon temperatures in the autumn were in the mid-seventies, the evenings cool and clear. A few welcome rain showers, but no serious storms.

Thanksgiving was shaping up to be the best since the Pilgrims' first. The harvest of corn, wheat, and soybeans was incredibly plentiful. The nation was grateful for its survival. However, the national government in Denver faced a serious challenge. At first it seemed a trivial matter, almost humorous, but Americans love their traditions.

The main entree at a traditional American Thanksgiving dinner was of course a turkey. But in New America, there was no meat. No cattle farms. No hog farms. No chicken farms. No turkey farms. As a meat substitute, soy burgers had become the norm for Americans, but to Arthur Schnell that seemed like a poor substitute for turkey in a Thanksgiving Day dinner. The decision went to the top.

The Group of Eight met on November 1. The normal updates were dispensed with. The group discussed the missing turkey situation for nearly two hours. Finally a dejected-looking president offered a solution: "Well, okay, here's the answer: Those folks from England hundreds of years ago settled a new land. They called it 'New England,' and they celebrated their good harvest roasting a bird that was in great abundance and in close proximity—the turkey. Well, now our folks from America have settled a new land that we have called 'New America,' and we should logically celebrate our great autumn harvest with a food now being picked in abundance. It is to be the symbol of our new Thanksgiving Day meal."

He then smiled and slowly rotated his eyes around the room, momentarily glancing at all other eight faces. No one moved in their seats or moved their eyes away from the president's. "Okay, I won't ask you to guess. What did we plant beside every single residence that we built here? What food has just ripened on those trees? Should we not associate it with the fruits of our labor? So that's it. Don't laugh, it's *the apple*. It's nutritious. It's now abundant. It's the people's symbol reflecting the great fruits of their labor to get everyone here safely. So have whatever you want for the first course, second course, but we will celebrate at sweet dessert time with apples served anyway you want—apple pie, apple cake, apple slices with cinnamon. Chief! Create a new logo—a perfect shiny apple. Flash it on TV in between shows. Get it printed in bright red on the top of every issue's front page of our national newspaper between now and Thanksgiving."

It seemed that the president could have gone on and on. He was on a roll. He really liked his idea. But he finally paused and asked, "So what do you think?"

✴ ✴ ✴

The next challenge the national government faced was important but quite a bit more serious than a symbol of Thanksgiving. While America was no longer considered a Christian country, the overwhelming majority of its population stated that they believed in God. Within that majority, an overwhelming percentage believed in Jesus Christ as the Son of God. Over the course of the year 2016, school buildings had been overflowing on Saturday evenings and all day Sundays with religious services for Christians, Jews, and Muslims. The problem now was the coming holiday. With a tradition that many more Christians celebrate the birth of Christ by attending church services Christmas Eve and Christmas Day, how could the large increase in numbers be accommodated? The Guidelines had inadvertently omitted this happenstance. The last thing the Chief wanted was any kind of dissenting dialogue between the national government and leaders of any organized movement, whether it be political, social, labor, educational, or religious—no controversies.

This time, the issue was not to be brought to the attention of the Group of Eight. Unlike the question of Thanksgiving's symbol, this solution would have to be solely the president's decision; the word of the Savior. The follow-up and implementation would fall to the Chief and Arthur Schnell.

As it turned out, the solution was not so difficult after all. Large-attendance facilities such as Denver's baseball and football stadiums as well as the cavernous convention center had been empty and unused all year. They would just need cleaning. The government would set up preaching platforms, portable toilets, and trash receptacles at all recreational parks. Parking spaces would be designated as far as a mile away. But the real key was that from 6:00 PM Christmas Eve to 9:00 PM Christmas night—twenty-seven straight hours—the national television channel, the only one in New America, would broadcast religious services from all these sites. Christians could celebrate at home if they chose to avoid the crowds. The president would introduce the services with a statement that "the government was not establishing a religion." It was merely compassionately honoring an American tradition for a short period of time during a national emergency when there were no other alternatives.

Christian church leaders soundly and enthusiastically endorsed the president's plan. It all went well that Christmas.

*　*　*

9:00 PM, December 31, 2016

The Chief made one more call before leaving his office. "Jane, I'm obligated to take my family to a New Year's Eve party shortly. I know that these special occasions are hard on you. You must trust me to work things out for us. "

"It's okay, Chief. A bunch of us boring faculty folks are throwing a party. I'll try not to be thinking of you," Jane replied part sarcastically, part melancholic.

"Jane, please. Look what we have accomplished. It's unbelievable. You know what kind of work schedule I have … and yet we have found time almost every week for some treasured moments together. Please have patience."

"You're right. I'm sorry. I don't want to sound dejected. I know how busy you are. I just feel very lonely some evenings when I can't be with you. But I think I understand."

"Now that's better. Let's just toast each other to a very Happy New Year."

Alone now with his thoughts, the Chief sat back in his chair, reflecting several minutes upon this remarkable year. How could it have all gone so perfectly? Building this gigantic infrastructure in a space just half the size of one of our fifty states. Eliminating all fossil fuel emissions. Eliminating all cattle methane emissions. Safely transporting tens of millions of Americans to New America monthly. Assembling millions of battery-operated transportation vehicles. Harvesting a record quantity of food crops from the Great Plains. Installing electricity-generating solar panels on the roof of every single building. Constructing and placing tens of thousands of windmills generating electricity. Transporting billions of gallons of clean water every day uphill from the Pacific Ocean and the Great Lakes. Opening up hundreds of large recreational parks. Providing vacation space and recreational activities in the mountains. Building a new national university and staffing it with the brightest brains in the country. Shifting the key elements of the federal government from Washington to a national government in Denver. Assigning living quarters and jobs to every American. Importing necessary basic raw materials from abroad. Creating a clean-energy, all-electric power grid for the economic system. Having a new banking system that worked. Providing adequate educational programs and medical facilities. Increasing the size of the military and having them competently guard the coasts of America and the vacant cities of America. Satisfying the spiritual needs of Americans by providing space for worship. Providing entertainment through television shows and Internet games.

He then began to wonder what could go wrong. New America was surprisingly and gratifyingly *perfect*. As long as outside conditions continued to worsen, he mused, the Savior could continue to convince all Americans that they need not fear—they were safe in his New America. No one more accurate than the Oracle himself continued to predict dire climate conditions. The Savior would continue his brilliant oratory, but the Chief thought that no one other than himself could maintain order. Perfection might not last without discipline. Just in case, control the media, the Internet, and the press corps. And the Guidelines, yes, and through the Guidelines. They were working. America had truly achieved a transformation. It was a new society, like none other before. Full cooperation, no controversy, no dissent. The people listened and they were led. As the Chief rose from his desk and walked toward the door, he felt a sense of relief and then satisfaction. As he closed the door behind him, he was himself transformed, feeling another emotion—engulfed now with an overwhelming sense of *power*. It felt good.

Chapter Nine

Abrupt Rifts

New America, 2017

It happened quickly. Fast and brutal. Six teenagers entered a convenience store and demanded that the clerk hand over all the cigarettes in the store. The clerk, an ex-policeman from New York assigned to this position, replied that there were no cigarettes in New America. The guidelines don't allow them for health reasons. The teenagers then demanded he hand over all his marijuana. The clerk responded that it was for medical use only. A doctor's prescription was required. Suddenly two of the boys grabbed the clerk, reasserting their demands. The clerk obviously resisted and fought the boys off. From behind, another boy lifted a heavy bottle and smashed it upon the back of the clerk's skull, knocking him to the floor, unconscious. The teenagers broke the locks on the medicine cabinets, found the marijuana, and ran out of the store with that and everything else they could carry. Later, the clerk told government officials that the teens seemed to be high on alcohol when they entered the store. The incident did not appear on the government-run TV news station. The clerk did not know who the boys were, and in the absence of a police force there was no investigation.

The Group of Eight could not think of everything. As long as *fear* was the overriding emotion influencing behavior, the national government could achieve full compliance with its Master Plan and its detailed guidelines. But the new psychological mood was "Have no fear—everyone is safe." After a full year in New America, could it be that almost a sense of complacency was beginning to take hold? It was time to start acting like Americans again, or rather, like humans again.

In a free society, citizens can do whatever they wish inside the law. A certain number of them also do what they want outside the law. The first fissures in New America began to occur early in the year 2017 with the convenience store incident. Indications of addictions to and the pleasures of what Americans commonly called "recreational drugs" began to surface. Large supplies of cocaine, marijuana, heroin, and methamphetamines had been brought to New America. Almost all criminal drug dealers who had been previously in jail were placed on parole upon arriving in Eastern Colorado. Now they were busy devising schemes to smuggle in illicit drugs. Users were at all levels in the new society—workers in the new national government, faculty at the new national university, skilled workers who had become bored with appointed work assignments they considered below their standards, unskilled workers seeking a diversion, and teenagers seeking new thrills.

Results of the growing drug use became obvious. Arthur Schnell estimated that less than 15 percent of the population was engaged in any type of regular indulgence, but he felt deeply embarrassed. "Chief, this is a surprise to me. I don't know where all the supplies came from and what quantities are slipping in now, but I'm receiving reports daily of car accidents, sloppy workmanship, absenteeism, store thefts, and vandalism in the parks. Drug dealers are accumulating 'new' dollars in hopes of achieving wealth when all this is over. I—"

The normally charming Chief interrupted harshly, "This can't be! A month ago we weren't hearing any of this. I called you to my office, Arthur, because it's not just drugs. I'm getting reports of alcohol abuse too. Why is this happening? The guidelines ban drug use except for marijuana for approved medical purposes, and alcoholic drinks are to be served only at home."

"I don't know," replied Arthur sheepishly. "Maybe there is growing boredom with the entertainment we have provided them. ..." The Chief gazed away, perplexed. Arthur added another thought, *"Or maybe we have created a perfect society for imperfect humans."*

☆　　☆　　☆

The next Group of Eight dinner meeting was held in early February. For the first time in over a year, there was no festive cocktail hour. The president was already seated at the head of the dinner table when everyone arrived. He was clearly unhappy. There was no polite salutation. "You know, I find this annoying. We rescue everyone from certain devastation, and now it is just one reckless incident after another. Is this the thanks we get? Without a free press, we have kept this news suppressed, but I'm afraid word will get around. It will be inaccurate, and it will be grossly and unfairly exaggerated. Okay, enough. Let's go around the table. I want to hear from everybody. Arthur, let's start with you."

A shaken Arthur pulled his notes from his coat jacket and placed them next to the plate in front of him. He knew this was coming. "I have a list. Let me start with the growing drug problem." He proceeded to describe several scenes of inappropriate behavior occurring in the streets and parks, such as the yelling of obscene language late at night, visible nudity and sexual acts, and reckless driving. He stated that there were over a thousand incidents called into his Office of Civic Affairs during the last week of January.

"Similar to the drug problem, we're seeing the growing abuse of alcoholic beverages. As you know, these beverages are not part of our standard food program, so citizens use their new dollar earnings to buy alcoholic beverages at our food and convenience stores. The supply is obviously limited since we have reduced our overseas imports and there is no wine production in California anymore. We are producing more local beer with all the wheat we have, but since inventories of wine and hard liquor are declining, there is a growing demand for them. So we are getting an increased number of reports of theft, smuggling, and worse—increased drunkenness on our streets and in our parks." He went on to describe specific incidents that went beyond distastefulness to outright horrific, including a drunken teenager striking and killing a young child when he lost control of his brand-new electric mini-car. "And I'm sorry to say this, but I'm hearing rumors that some homes are being set up to become mini-distilleries for producing vodka."

Everyone around the table found eating their dinner difficult while listening to Arthur's accounts. The Chief silently fought off his dismay by saying under his breath, "It's only a very small minority." But Arthur's report turned even more dire.

"Do you want me to go on, Mr. President? I know I'm taking a lot of time."

"Go on, Arthur. One more from your notes there," answered a sullen president.

"I'm really uncomfortable with this one. I had not wanted to mention this to anyone until I obtained more information. The subject is guns. We all know our Second Amendment rights. Our guidelines here in New

America under our national emergency simply restrict the right to *carry* guns. They can be owned but are to be kept in safekeeping within one's own home. But what we did not know was that not everyone came to New America. Sure, we left the military out there along with civilian personnel to operate our power, port, and transportation systems, but we did not know about the ones who stayed behind in remote areas. I'm talking about the thick forests in the Deep South and in the high mountains north of here … up through Wyoming and Montana. I, uh … apologize for this, sir…" Arthur now looked most uncomfortable. "It's the militia groups that stayed behind. These are the people who have traditionally been free-spirit antigovernment people—mostly right wingers carrying semiautomatic weapons. "

After a long pause, the Chief said, "So just leave them there. They're not bothering anybody, right?"

Arthur immediately responded, "Well, if they were truly independent, right, just leave them there. Two problems: One is that they're not as independent as they originally thought. They need more food, clothing, drugs, alcohol, medicines, and cigarettes than they can produce on their own. There are indications of a growing black market. They are getting involved in helping foreigners get drugs into New America. They are getting paid for it in euros, a currency you know is worth a lot more than the U.S. dollar, old or new. "

"But you said 'guns,'" quizzed the president.

"That's the second point, sir," Arthur replied. "They are using their new earnings from dealing drugs to buy guns smuggled in from overseas, slipping past our military. They still have the warped philosophy of government's role as being extremely limited in scope and power. They think the citizens of New America should be fully armed when the time comes to rebel against their government."

That did it. Everyone stopped eating. This was not palatable dinner conversation. The president looked appalled. Under his leadership and vision, his nation had escaped a sudden abrupt change in climatic conditions. The transition had gone far better than anyone could have imagined. The first year conditions in New America could only be described as "perfect." Was the Savior now conceivably looking at another abrupt change? Rebellion?

"Inconceivable!" the Chief exclaimed. "You're talking about a small group of radical nuts. Extremists. The overwhelming majority of our citizens understand the need for a benevolent government to take care of them. We can deal with this … and we can also deal with these alcoholics and druggies. It is a small percentage. Maybe now is the time to discuss the creation of a national police force; one that can deal with all these disconnects quietly, behind the scenes." The president stared at his Chief appreciatively, this able assistant who had always been right on every issue.

The normally detached Oracle actually stood up from his chair and cried out, "This is not what I had bargained for! Doesn't everyone understand? Our planet is in peril. Don't they understand? How can they be so selfish?" When he received no response to his rhetorical questions, he retreated into his seat again. Chin up, forehead frowned, his noble face reflected signs of scorn, frustration, and rejection.

The vice president then followed his lead. She rose from her chair, hands out in front of her, and began to speak clearly and articulately. "Gentlemen, I am the uninvited guest—the president's backup. I have contributed nothing to this famous, this distinguished, Group of Eight. Like you and our nation's citizens, I'm indebted to our president for taking bold action in the face of a calamity. My quiet campaign to the president and to the Chief has always been that there should be alternative plans set to go if certain things go wrong. But we have been on a one-track course. We have created a society the likes of which has never existed before in the course of history. It worked fine for a short time. The president persuaded the last doubter, as long as *fear* was the sole motivator. Now we are beginning to see how some people at times can behave—true ever since our human genesis.

"I am hearing the words 'embarrassment,' 'incredulity,' 'rebellion,' 'national police force.' How long did you think this perfect society would go on? Is it not time to put our brightest minds together to formulate strategies that can deal with a whole host of social issues? That's what you did, Mr. President, to deal with the climate crisis—this smart group right here. Now, to go forward, if we're talking about a presidential task force, I would be glad to coordinate it, moderate it, or lead it." She slowly nodded her head around the table, searching for affirmation and support from the eyes of each face into which she momentarily stared. The Chief's first impulse was to stand up in rebuttal, but he deferred to the president as he thought he should counsel the Savior privately. The last things he wanted were controversy or a new task force.

"Thank you, Ali. Let me digest what you have said. It's getting late. I have to think about all this. Unless there's something else of urgency— Hank, I trust our power and water systems are still performing well?"

"All is well, Mr. President. Don't worry," Hank responded softly and assuredly.

"And Richard, any change with what is going on out there?"

"No sir. Unfortunately, the trend-line climatic conditions continue to degrade," a composed Richard Compton calmly replied. The dispirited Oracle looked down in silence.

Dropping his voice down a pitch into a quiet, deep monotone, the crestfallen president rotated his gaze to the other end of the table: "John, H., economic system okay?" Obviously, the president was looking for a short response.

The two economists smartly refrained from bringing up some disturbing points, none of which had yet reached a critical stage. "Yes," John announced. "The system is working. A few minor issues, but we can discuss them another time."

✻ ✻ ✻

As the months passed, the Chief continued to convince the president that together they had chosen the best course. No publicity of alcohol and drug abuse or criminal behavior or smuggling of guns. No creation of a national police force. Only the creation of a secret database collecting the names of individuals and their misdeeds. The two chose a strategy contrary to the norm. Instead of punishment, wrongdoers were being secretly offered additional "new dollars" to entice them into orderly behavior. "Play it down" was the strategy. However, the Chief went overboard—he began to play it down even to his superior. In his role as Chief of staff screening the president's communications, the Chief "purified" Arthur's written reports to the president, which enumerated incidents occurring that were illicit within the guidelines. He also did his best at the Group of Eight meetings to interrupt whenever Arthur began to express concerns that the numbers of reported misdeeds were trending upwards.

However, the Chief was not able to filter out the report on the economy that John and H. were prepared to give at the May meeting. In preparation, the two had marveled that it had been over five years since they conjured up this dream economic system. Over and over again, they had desperately tried to convince themselves that it would work; that they were not creating a myth. In the past, every nation that printed money in excess of the value of goods and services actually in circulation at the moment created the monstrous economic circumstance called "rampant inflation." That is, the price attached to a good or service would rise if the demand for that product or service was greater than its supply. In New America, because of scarce production facilities serving three hundred million people, supply would obviously be limited except for those products and services deemed most "essential." Prices for those essential products and services would remain constant as demand and supply would be in balance. For all other products and services, prices would be held constant, as would workers' wages, by government edict. The result would be that regardless of demand, people would only be able to purchase the available supply of "nonessentials."

Thus, instead of a market allocation of products and services according to supply and demand and its correlating price mechanism, demand in New America would simply be forced to dissipate if supply ran out. Consumers would just have to do without whatever the government deemed as discretionary, nonessential goods and services.

This dissipating demand would be reflected in the consumer's wallet, not necessarily in his mind. Conventional economic wisdom would then prescribe that in an economy of this nature, employment would suffer. Standards of living would decrease because jobs would not be created to produce any goods or provide any services other than for what the government decreed as essential. In New America, however, there would be no unemployment. Upon arrival, the government had prescribed assigned duties for everyone, from cleaning the streets to serving as the dean of the prestigious national university. In addition, justice and equality would be attained by all citizens as everyone was paid the same for an hour's worth of work.

How wonderful it sounded whenever John and H. had explained the system. Full employment. Stable prices. Free housing. Free medical care for all. An international currency backed by gold and silver in order to import any required essential goods from abroad. How could it get any better?

At the end of their glowing presentation, the president smiled and addressed the now famous economists. "Awesome. This is the best news I've had in months." A welcome pause ensued. Then …

"Uh … what were those little hitches you mentioned a couple of months ago?" the normally taciturn Hank Abrams asked. The Chief cringed. He had not reviewed their report in advance, but he had asked John and H. to keep their presentation positive for the president. The Chief could deal with any minor economic problems himself as they arose.

"Oh, I was just getting to that … just a few small things," replied John. "For instance, we think that part of Arthur's problems with home and store theft is that some people want more of an essential item than others, say bread; or they want some nonessential item in short supply, say a DVD, so a few persons may steal for them."

H. jumped in. "Yes, another instance is that all of us are always concerned about our health. There are only so many scans, tests, and medical procedures available. Well, I don't like to admit this, but there are some very skilled physicians who feel that their time is much more valuable than a lower-level assistant getting paid the same, so they don't want to do as many procedures, and we're finding the maintenance and replacement parts on all this expensive diagnostic equipment have been lagging because the manufacturers and service people don't get paid like they used to. We have lots of other examples … uh … for instance—"

It was high time for the Chief to interrupt: "Gentlemen, Ali, it's time to move on. We have other material to cover. I can follow up on all the situations you're talking about John, H. I will call you tomorrow to set up a meeting."

✳　✳　✳

It was mid-summer when the Chief accepted the fact that incidents with drunkenness, drug abuse, theft, and shortages were impacting more than just a very small percentage of the nation's population. It was also time to realize that other problems were brewing, such as government workers accepting favors in return for informally relaxing certain guidelines for selected people. In the old days, this was called "graft," "corruption," or "bribery"—not rampant yet, but he had to get on top of the issue quickly.

However, the key factor in his waking up to the new reality was a secret report submitted to Arthur by an administrative assistant who was a former FBI informant. The report gave a detailed account of the strong link now formed among a number of unsavory groups. One group was the hundreds of thousands of illegal immigrants who had been "middle men" in the old days. They were the ones paid handsomely for moving relatives across borders, creating false documents, and providing a flow of money and goods for the estimated twelve million illegal immigrants then living in the United States. Another was the antigovernment militia squads implicated in the importation of drugs and guns into New America. Another group was comprised of former members of organized crime who had been shuffled along to Eastern Colorado. Many had reunited in clandestine meetings. Another was a collection of gangs, mostly teenagers and young men, who still believed that loyalty among their own members was the highest value attainable.

The document described how leaders of these groups were meeting together and cooperating on plans to smuggle more drugs and guns into New America; plans that included which government workers could be bribed to suppress reporting. It was impossible to know how serious this effort was, how big it was or could become, but it was real. Now the Chief was truly concerned. All that he had worked for, all that was achieved. He could not take the chance that what was perhaps a small inconsequential criminal effort could be tolerated and possibly mushroom into something much larger and ominous.

✧　✧　✧

National university, September 2017

"Jane has been telling me some very strange things lately. She swore me to secrecy, other than with you, of course." Rose paused and glanced toward Michael's eyes to see if he was paying attention. They were just finishing lunch in the university's main dining hall.

"Yes? And?"

"Well, Michael, she said her secret admirer, the Chief, has been confiding in her that there have been a number of abrupt changes in what he and the president thought was a very orderly society here in New America."

"Yeah? Well like what? 'Abrupt' did you say? We have been waiting for over a year now for the Guidelines to change allowing marriages and, can you believe it, for changes in living quarters so that one can live with his or her own new spouse … and you know the deal, the big new marital Guideline will not be in effect until December."

"No, no. Jane is not talking about adjustments needed in legitimate matters in order to maintain our orderly society here. She's talking about incidents of crime, drug abuse, over indulgence in alcohol. Even violence. She said that there have been several incidents where men—probably they were psychotics—shot three, six, even a dozen people to death…."

"Wait, Rose. We haven't seen anything like that on the news."

"Right! That's part of the secrecy. Our government doesn't want the public getting upset over incidents of crime that may be taking place. Remember, we're all accepting the Guidelines voluntarily. There is no enforcement mechanism, no penalties, no punishments, no police."

"Okay, Rose. I bet it is probably a very small number of happenings. After all, everyone exhibits bad behavior sometimes, and a few cross the line, for whatever reason, into immoral behavior and a very few into illegal behavior."

"Yes, fine, Michael, no problem if it's a very minimal situation … but Jane says that the Chief believes it's growing rapidly, that it might be a reversion to old America and—can you imagine—without a police force or courts or jails. Now! Hold onto your seat, or my hand—can you believe this? You know Adriana works for the Chief. She has leaked to me that the Chief has created a database of the names of all wrongdoers, that they are being enticed, or another way of saying it, being bribed, into good behavior. But listen, Michael. Any repeat offender will be physically removed to somewhere remote … and by some more-or-less secret service–type department that the Chief has created."

"Rose, my Miss Rose, darling. This all sounds deep, dark, and mysterious, but I'm looking at the time, and I must get back for my next meeting. Let's get to something more important. I'm fed up with these stupid Guidelines. Are your roommates out tonight? Mine will be home watching TV."

At first, Rose thought her secret stories of intrigue were being too easily dismissed as being unimportant or uninteresting, but then she thought Michael was right. Their relationship was the most important thing in the world right now. She replied sternly, "Darn, mine are in tonight too," and then continued softly, "So that means we meet in our favorite closet at six o'clock?"

"I can't wait. And then we will have dinner by candlelight and a long walk. There's a full moon tonight. … Love you."

With her cheeks aglow, Rose responded endearingly: "I love you too, Michael. Only four more months and we will be married and able to walk home together for the first time."

✳   ✳   ✳

As was the daily norm, the Chief met with his boss in the late afternoon to review the day's events and the plans for tomorrow's activities. The president maintained a very public stance each and every day, especially attending educational programs and special events for the elderly. In every speech, formal and informal, he reassured his followers that they were safe and secure. The president's public strategies were carefully worked out with the Chief. One was to be sure to insert into each appearance a reference to the disastrous impacts caused by the abrupt climate change and how dangerous it still was outside New America.

Another strategy was to utilize all the pent-up talents of hundreds of professional entertainers and celebrities to conduct live performances each weekend at the sports stadiums. The key tactic was that while admission was free each person attending was asked to donate one dollar toward helping the dependents of all those courageous military personnel out there braving storms and heat to guard America and rebuild damaged properties.

"Chief, I think your ideas are working. You know I don't like seeing reports from Arthur on the number of incidents of bad behavior and crime. You know I don't like violence. You have done a great job with Arthur in taking good care of the victims of these misdeeds, keeping their complaints about them submerged, and I agree with you that we will keep away public reporting of any crime. I want to refrain from establishing a national police force as long as we can. I'm convinced that the strategy you suggested to keep reminding the public how bad it is out there across the land, and how good it is here, is keeping the vast majority in line."

A gracious appearing Chief responded, "Sir, it's you. You're the one who has maintained your incredible oratorical skills and powers of persuasion. I'm simply behind you to suggest some additional ideas for your already brilliant strategies." It was important for the Chief amidst a host of brewing problems to maintain the close confidence the president had in him. A little flattery would not hurt.

As the two separated to attend their respective dinner engagements that evening, the Chief reflected upon the wisdom of continuing to keep some of his other ideas from the president. The Chief had not yet informed him of his secret knowledge of the consortium smuggling guns and drugs into New America. Nor had he informed him of his idea to deport second offenders, nor of his idea to form a new secret service organization within the national government. Yet he feared that eventually there would be a leak—and the president would find out. His dilemma was whether to tell the president and see if the Savior had a second "Bingo" or just keep matters in his own hands.

✵   ✵   ✵

The tone was harsh; the glances fierce. "I called your office in advance. I told your assistant I was coming. Chief, you've been trying to bottle me up. You have tried to keep my schedule full by having me attend an endless number of secondary appearances. Well, you're not going to get me out of your hair. I know what's going on, and I don't like it."

"Come on, Ali. Get off it," the Chief sarcastically replied. "You know your role. You are to stay in the background, off premises, for the sole purpose of taking the president's place if he is incapacitated. I've done as he requested—by keeping you informed of major developments and having you attend the Group of Eight meetings."

"That's not it!" Ali angrily responded. "There is no nation in the world without a free press, unless it's a dictatorship. Open information and debate is America's great tradition. There's no nation in the world where rules are even democratically promulgated and complete compliance expected without the enforcement backup of police and a justice system. Worse—here there is no democracy. Your rules are arbitrary. And I know you know it—this is not the president's doing—it is your handiwork. And now, poor you, you are discovering reality. Information is trying to get out, but you are suppressing it. "

"Ali!"

"I know about your secret police. I know about your deportations to camps high in the mountains. You have to come clean, Chief, and we have to make changes."

The Chief sat back, withdrawing his attack mode, changing his approach, and then calmly posing the question, "All right, Miss Smart One. Just what would you do?"

For the first time, the vice president sat down. She thought pensively for a moment and then cautiously stated, "Well, obviously you and the president did not like my new task force idea, so let's just say it's you, me, and the president. I agree that in a national emergency, public safety is of the first priority, and to do so requires order. Those two goals were achieved last year. But now we have to preserve order in a nation that has been traditionally free. So I would suggest that we loosen the reins a little bit. Let there be a startup of a private, free-press newspaper … a private, free-media television station. Allow some reality to surface. Then let's put a modest police presence into each community and let the citizens know that violation of the Guidelines is not to be tolerated under our national emergency. Tell them that alleged violators will be prosecuted, judged, and punished if found guilty. In fact, change your official Guidelines to National Emergency Laws to create the right impression. Also, Chief, convert your secret police organization to a public one that will openly pursue the cartels smuggling guns or drugs into New America. Should I go on?"

"No. That's enough." While the vice president had been talking, the Chief thought further confrontation with her would be futile. She was a stubborn one who was not going to quit. Maybe a soft, condescending strategy would work better. "I like your idea of just the three of us working this out. The president is a very intelligent man. He's the one who first thought only Eastern Colorado would be safe for all of us. With your input, I'm sure we can work this out with him. He's down in Colorado Springs today. I'll set something up for the three of us before the end of the week. I would appreciate your keeping the nature of this conversation private."

Ali was taken back. "I don't trust the man," she was thinking to herself. There had to be some new motivation why he would change his mood so suddenly. Her last thought leaving the Chief's office was, "Okay, I'll play along. At least I'm in the game now." Meanwhile, as Ali closed the door behind her, the Chief's private thoughts were firm and forceful. "I know the lessons of history—give an inch and they want a mile. No way!" Through the intercom he called out, "Adriana, I need to see you right away!"

✻ ✻ ✻

It was a beautiful Saturday afternoon in late September. The four of them sat in the park in brilliant sunshine, enjoying a perfect temperature. It was becoming almost impossible to imagine that outside of New America it was chaos. Michael was called back into his office by one of his associates. It was Adriana who then turned the conversation to matters of state. "Jane, I know you really get uncomfortable with this, but believe me I am really trying my best. He—"

"I know," replied a smiling Jane. "He likes beautiful young women. That's why I get confused. He keeps telling me he loves me, but I'm not so gorgeous, nor so young."

"*Au contraire*, dear Jane," piped in Rose with a giggle. "You are much younger than he is, and I think you are an exotic beauty." All three girls laughed heartily.

"Seriously, though," interjected Adriana, dropping her smile. "I don't know what his intentions are, but he does keep dropping hints. Of course, he doesn't know that I know about his intimate relationship with you, Jane. But believe me, I'm not interested. I have a lot of neat young guys to hang out with. I'm not looking to preserve my job by doing any untidy favors for my boss."

Jane gazed directly into her eyes. "Ad, I'm very happy to hear you say that, and I know you mean it."

"Okay, you two. I'm little Rose over here outside this web of lust and intrigue. You both have been telling me stories about what's going on with this guy. What's the latest with all this secret stuff—drugs and guns and secret police?"

"Well, let me tell you the latest I know," Adriana said. "The Group of Eight is having their next dinner meeting this coming Monday night, October 1. Yesterday the Chief and the president met with Vice President Graham. We were told not to mention this meeting to anyone. Apparently, the vice president left the building looking quite perturbed. I'm guessing maybe she was not being listened to or did not get her way. The Chief came back to his office with a nice, big, smug smile on his face. So I guess all the secrecy goes on. I see the reports. The number of bad incidents continues to rise. The Chief is adding lots of new personnel to his security organization. I'm supposed to be keeping track of their raids, and of course I'm sworn to secrecy. How can I keep it from you two? I don't know where all this is leading ..."

"Yes," said Jane. "That's the point. We don't know where all this is leading. No one does. It's just that the Chief is trying to steer it with as little outside interference as possible. You know, actually, girls, he was with me late last night. He does confide in me in his weaker moments."

"Women power," laughed Adriana. Rose blushed.

"Hmmm, right. I guess they do need us for more reasons than one," Jane derisively responded. "But he does seem to be determined to protect the president from criticism. He believes that in times of a grave national crisis, there can only be one leader, one decision maker, that dissent would cause delays and disorder. But what is really bothering him are the misfits, the disorderly ones exhibiting bad behavior when they really should be grateful. And of course, the criminal element. They have to be dealt with accordingly, and he wants to do that behind the scenes so that no one gets too nervous and upset about it."

Rose added quietly, "I guess what has to be done, has to be done. Jane, you and I know too well the dangers out there and what is going on with this crazy climate. As they say 'safety first.'"

"The only thing, ladies, and I lose sleep over this, is that sometimes I get a hint that he is manipulating the president ... that perhaps what he really wants underneath it all is the power to control the ultimate destiny of this nation just the way he sees it."

"I think I sometimes see it the same way, Jane," added Adriana in a sullen tone of voice.

☆　☆　☆

Word traveled quickly. There was silence on the government-run television station and no reporting on the government-run radio station. By word of mouth, however, the news was contagious. It was late October and dark at 8:00 PM. Several hundred visitors were finishing dinner at the "vacation" lodge half way up Pikes Peak. Over the sound of the background dinner music was heard the gruesome noise of failing engines. It was unseen; too late. The plane crashed directly into the lodge. Seventy-nine persons were killed. Another 125 were injured. The story spread quickly that dozens of smashed boxes of pistols, rifles, and semiautomatic weapons were strewn about the area. Hundreds of bags of cocaine, heroin, and methamphetamines littered the disaster scene. The plane was attempting to smuggle guns and drugs into New America from somewhere in Mexico. Engine failure prevented it from flying over the last high mountain peak prior to a clandestine landing site in the plains of Western Kansas.

☆　☆　☆

The Chief wanted to maintain the regular monthly schedule of the Group of Eight dinner meetings. One was to be held the following week in early November. However, the president overruled him—a rare happenstance. The president wanted nothing of Ali's recommended task force, and he had been meeting with her and the Chief over the last few weeks merely to pretend that he was listening. But now he needed the comfort of his team—the team that had so competently supported him over the last six years. He also needed to show them that he was firmly in charge.

This time the mood was different from any previous meeting. Joyous during the first year, the mood was sullen so far this year. The atmosphere for the first time was contentious. The vice president appeared flustered. The Oracle was obviously perplexed. Richard Compton looked out of place—there was no climate science about this meeting. The two economists, John and H., were nervous. Arthur Schnell, the man with the awesome responsibilities in charge of domestic affairs, appeared fearful. With so much disquieting talk, the Chief obviously looked perturbed; he wanted all bad news kept submerged. Only Hank Abrams seemed composed—his energy and water systems continued to operate flawlessly.

"This plane accident is not the only tragedy!" Ali almost shouted. "Every week I hear reports of violence, but the problem with this one is that so many people are talking about it and forwarding e-mails. It combines a violent tragedy where many innocent lives were taken with exposure to the increasing problem of drugs and guns. Mr. President, I have been begging you privately, and now I'm asking you in front of your whole team: expose the truth, allow the news, create a visible police force; let the people know these things are not going to be tolerated."

"Ali, Ali," the unmoved President calmly replied. "Let me assure you. I have been listening to you ... and this evening I want to listen to everyone. Very shortly, I know I'm going to have another revelation on how to handle this. Now Arthur, review with everyone the statistics from your latest incident report."

"Yes sir," a clearly worried Arthur replied, yet somewhat buoyed now from the president's seemingly imperturbable demeanor. "Uh ... now, these are only the incidents reported to my Office of Civil Affairs. It could be that only half of all events that take place are reported. We are certain that there are a lot of domestic happenings within residences where the victims don't report; neither neighbors nor the public knows about them ... and therefore they can't report them. Okay, personal attacks or property damage from drug abuse: up 20 percent in October over September and up twenty-five times the number over last February. Alcohol related: up 16 percent over September and twenty times from February. Shootings resulting in death: plus 24 percent and up thirty times. Robberies: up 40 percent and up one hundred times. Rape: up 5 percent and up ten times. Domestic violence: up 12 percent and forty times. Assault and battery not involving guns drugs or alcohol: up 30 percent over September and up three hundred times over February. I think a lot of that last statistic is a result of restless teenagers carrying on."

"Can you give me the actual numbers, Arthur, on the shootings?" a dejected Oracle asked.

"Yes. In our nation before the abrupt climate change, we were experiencing about fifteen hundred homicides a month. Last February we had only thirty-five reported, and who knows how many unreported. That number rose to 842 in September and 1,050 so far in October; that's the plus 24 percent over September and the plus thirty times over February that I read off before."

"Well then," the president said calmly. "Let's face the facts. These are alarming trends. We have to be concerned. But the stance we have to take with the public is that the total number of incidents within our total population of three hundred million people is still statistically small. I am not going to panic. … I think you used the right word Arthur: 'restless.' Our people are not doing what they had been accustomed to doing. They are safe and secure. The government is taking perfectly good care of them. Some of them are just getting restless and going overboard. I will work out a plan. In the meantime, in my next televised address, for the first time I will make reference to the fact that there have been a small number of misdeeds carried out by some of our restless citizens … that victims are being compassionately cared for, and not to worry—the government is rehabilitating the transgressors, and any repeat offenders are being kept off the streets.

"A grateful society does not need the presence of a police force. The people believe in me. I'll also refer to the terrible tragedy at Pikes Peak and mention that some former members of old crime organizations were trying to pull a fast one. They were attempting to make a quick profit by selling some guns and drugs to our honest citizens. It was an unfortunate tragedy where their plane's engines failed and accidentally crashed into a government-sponsored vacation lodge. All the victims' families are being looked after."

Initially worried that the plane crash and tonight's revelations would reveal the gaps in his reporting bad news to the president, the Chief breathed a sigh of relief. The commander-in-Chief kept his cool. Maybe he was only hearing what he wanted to hear. Arthur's statistics were probably less than half the true number of incidents occurring.

John and H. looked greatly relieved. All the attention on crime allowed them to escape reporting their disturbing news. True, their economic model worked perfectly the first year. Lately, however, they were receiving an increasing number of reports concerning incompetent job performance—reports of vast shortages of nonessential but desirable goods and services; reports of a small but increasing number of shortages of essential goods and services, other than wheat, corn, and soy products. Reports of graft and favors within the government were also steadily increasing. Also disheartening was the continuing increase in the number of reports in the health-care sector. Growing shortages of medical supplies were worrisome. Among caregivers, there seemed to be a spreading sense of complacency within the medical profession. The quality of care seemed to be diminishing.

John and H. did not yet want to admit a flaw, but it was just possible that their new economic system lacked the powerful motivating factors of innovation, entrepreneurialism, private gain, performance distinction, and individual advantage.

✳   ✳   ✳

The president's approach worked well. In his public addresses, he squelched the rumors and corrected the misinformation that was circulating among the public. "Yes, there have been incidents of misdeeds, but the number was relatively small. Be assured that your government is right on top of the situation." Nothing to worry about. The Chief would have preferred that the president avoid the subject publicly and just let his secret police do the job. He finally disclosed to the president that he was building a small "Anti-Crime Force," operating behind the scenes to deal with wrongdoers and that it was working fine. He did not disclose how large it actually was becoming or how fast it was growing. Ali felt little relief that the president was giving marginal credence to her recommendations. She was growing concerned but had no idea how large the Chief's secret service organization had already become. Her distrust of the Chief continued to mount, while poor Jane and young Adriana remained perplexed. On the other hand, as December approached, there were at least two hearts that were growing very happy. Finally, the new guidelines pertaining to marriage and living assignments had been finalized. They were to take effect December 15, 2017.

✳   ✳   ✳

"Michael, Michael. This is it! Sweetheart, can you believe we can finally get married? I feel like a million 'new' dollars, backed by gold. I'm the happiest woman alive. We have waited so long." The two were walking hand in hand after having dinner together in the university's only intimate dining hall. Of course, by this time hundreds of favors had graced the national university from the national government. The intimate Schnell Dining Hall included dinner by candlelight, linen tablecloths, and ample supplies of fine French wines. One had to actually make a reservation a month in advance to obtain seating. Department heads and their top associates had preference. Rose continued her one-way conversation as they walked, squeezing his hand and pleading, "Well, I love the smile you're wearing, but aren't you going to say anything?"

Michael stopped and put his arms around her, squeezed her tightly, and then pulled partially back and looked directly into her inquiring eyes. He finally found the words: "Rose, you remember the night we met in Washington. We didn't have to speak…. There are no words to describe how I feel. My roommates are gone for the night—out inspecting windmill turbines tomorrow morning. I kept it from you as a surprise. Come with me."

"Wait!" Rose felt her heartbeat surge. She kissed him on the lips passionately, tears beginning to flow down her warm cheeks in the cool December air.

At breakfast the next morning, they settled it. They would marry in the small interdenominational chapel that had been built beside the university. It would be in the early evening of Christmas Eve. They would make special arrangements for their parents to arrive from their outlying residences and stay overnight in the university's guest rooms. Jane would have enough influence to arrange that. Jane would also have enough influence to arrange that the regular dinnertime at the university's intimate dining room would end early. After all, it was Christmas Eve, and faculty members would want to get home early. The challenge was to entice the dining staff to stay late to serve dinner for the wedding party. Probably some French wine would do it. In addition to their parents, Adriana would be invited to bring a date, and, well, Jane could bring a faculty friend. Also included would be the roommates they had lived with over the past many months as well as some of their closest colleagues at the university. It looked like a total number of twenty-two. They could handle it. Since new living quarter assignments were not to take place until January 1, they would arrange to take a one-week honeymoon at one of the government-operated lodges by a beautiful mountain lake. The rooms were surely all booked by now, but again Jane could exert her influence. No problem.

The two literally ran at full speed to their university offices that morning, holding hands, laughing all the way.

✿　✿　✿

The president and the Chief called it the "Goodwill Plan." The Chief had prevailed. There would be no free press. There would be no visible national police force. With his unmatched oratorical skills and powers of persuasion, the president would appear weekly on the government television station and the government radio station. He would provide updates on the horrific environmental conditions across the country. He would bless the heroic efforts of the military forces protecting the nation's assets and repairing property damage. He would laud the engineers and volunteer workers laboring under the harshest conditions in order to bring water, power, and imported goods to New America. Then, as he did last month in his televised address, he would continue to admit that there were always a small band of troublemakers and that the government was expending every effort to counsel and rehabilitate them. Nevertheless, for the citizens to feel safe in this "Land of Goodwill," a newly initiated "neighborhood watch" of volunteers would be on guard to act as a deterrent. There would be no mention of the Chief's Anti-Crime Force that would take care of repeat offenders. Behind the scenes and unannounced to the public, there would be the unwritten part of the plan—the part regarding the Chief's special forces dealing harshly with the hardened criminal elements smuggling in guns and drugs.

The atmosphere in the room at the December Group of Eight meeting was in stark contrast to the prior meeting. It was almost joyous again. The president no longer needed their comfort or advice. Arthur would not be requested to report on crime statistics. Deferring their verbal comments again, John and H. would be asked to circulate a written report that could be read after the meeting. There would be no mention of their concerns during the dinner meeting. The president's media "chats" would allay any civil unrest. Despite rising rates of criminal incidents, the Chief's Anti-Crime Force along with the new neighborhood watch groups could easily handle the statistically small number of disorderly incidents.

The last hour of the meeting was devoted to preparing plans for another festive holiday season. Lots of special music was to be programmed for the one radio station, and plenty of taped holiday shows for the one television station. Daily live performances by top celebrities were planned at the stadiums. And preparations were underway for religious services similar to the success enjoyed last Christmas.

Throughout the upbeat dinner meeting, only one face failed to show a smile. It was Ali Graham's. The vice president could not take her eyes off the Chief the entire evening. "What was his face revealing? What was that look in his eye?" she wondered to herself. "Is it arrogance, smugness? It would do me no good to petition the president again or take an open stance again with this now happy group. They're making it seem like everything is under control, and they have thrown me one small bone—the neighborhood watch. But something is missing. All those calls I'm getting from governors and from congressmen. There is no emergency within New America … only in the old. But where now is America's freedom?"

*   *   *

During that festive holiday season, another joyful group was able to submerge the fractures growing within this perfect society called New America. The French champagne and red Bordeaux flowed freely on Christmas Eve in the university's intimate dining room. The wedding was perfect. A week of bliss followed for the two lovers, resolving to cheerfully accept whatever would happen next in this now upside-down world. They understood that so much in life was out of their control, but regardless, they would use their intelligence and determination to help their fellow man in any way they could, just so long as they could stay together—forever.

Chapter Ten

Revelations

New America, 2018

Richard Compton maintained his contacts with the National Weather Bureau, the National Hurricane Center, and those in military intelligence dealing with climatic conditions. Almost all coastal cities and those situated nearby on large inland waterways were mired in flooding of one to three feet; higher during high tides and deluged during violent hurricanes—on the West Coast, Seattle, San Francisco, Los Angeles, and San Diego; on the East Coast, Boston and New York. The military was still able to operate port facilities at inland Philadelphia and Baltimore for the importation of "essential" goods. The navy was having a difficult time protecting its large facilities at Norfolk. The southern third of Florida was submerged twenty-four hours a day with up to two feet of water. Thanks to Michael's foresight in Los Angeles, his windmills were sturdy and holding. His solar panels were elevated enough to avoid incoming tides. The dozen huge desalination plants were high enough to avoid flooding and strong enough to withstand hurricane-force winds and violent earthquakes. Through the end of 2017, it had been eight consecutive years that climate change delivered more adverse impacts upon America than in the preceding year.

"Thank you for seeing me, Arthur, on such short notice," Richard said upon entering Arthur's office and scanning his cluttered desk. "I know how busy you are keeping up with all these reports."

An inquisitive Arthur replied, "No, Richard, It's good to see you. I need a break. What's up? You know I don't think we have ever met privately. "

"Well, I know that you're the man in the middle. After that first perfect year, I understand you're getting tremendous pressure from the public while at the same time the president is assuring everyone that all is okay."

"Yes, all the work getting ready to squeeze a few hundred million people in here and then to get them all here and get settled in …" He laughed heartily in a vain attempt to relieve the obvious pressure he was feeling. "And then after the satisfaction we all felt during that great first year … to now experience the mess that is developing."

"That's just what I want to talk to you about. You know that this was all to be temporary. The wisdom of most climatologists claimed five, ten, fifteen years to see the greenhouse gases retreat. But you know, on the other hand, the Oracle has always been predicting much, much longer, and I agree with him." Richard paused. Arthur sat up in his chair and gazed at him intently. Richard continued, "I am concerned for our nation. It was a wonderful plan to move everyone here, to the safest place. But just think, Arthur; you have three hundred million Americans squeezed in, most of them having been free to travel anywhere they desire, do whatever they want, and you know, 'to enjoy the blessings of liberty and the pursuit of happiness.' Arthur! If we're all stuck here another fifty years, we're going to implode. I'm here to tell you that the Oracle and I study the climate reports every single day. It's not going to get better for a long, long time. You're in charge of civil affairs. You know what's happening already. But all of a sudden, it seems like the president doesn't want to get off his party line that 'all is well here, other than a few isolated incidents,' I know you know that that's not true. It seems that he no longer even wants to discuss the economic system John and H. set up. I sense that just in the short time we've been here, there are indications of failures. I—"

Putting both palms out across his desk, Arthur stopped Richard. "Wait! Wait! I know exactly what you're saying. I don't want to sound fearful, but I talk to myself constantly about trying to remain upbeat. Yet I'm afraid we have created a society where most people truly believe that the government taking care of their full needs is a good thing. But like you say, is it?"

"Yes, but whether it is or isn't, philosophically, the point now is that not everyone believes it or wants it. That little minority—sure they moved here out of *fear,* but they miss their cherished freedoms and their sense of self-reliance that they have been accustomed to. I'm afraid, Arthur, that minority is growing. And then, of course, you have all the ones breaking the rules, the guidelines. As you have reported, their numbers are growing rapidly. At what point do these numbers no longer become statistically small?"

Arthur sat back again and stared hard at Richard for a moment and then spoke softly, "You know, I'm just an old environmentalist from Montana; secretary of the interior. Ha! I thought I would just be looking after the national parks. Now look at me, in over my head. And you … you're a college professor; a teacher. How are you so astute in the matters of human behavior? Perhaps that's what we've missed in the Master Plan."

"I am human, Arthur. I'm human. The two of us—we have to be more than just environmentalists. I want to help you in any way I can."

✳   ✳   ✳

"Come in, Rose. Hi. Come over to my conference table and sit down … and don't tell me about your great honeymoon again. I'm jealous, and I've heard enough," Jane giggled.

"Hey, okay. I'm all business. What's up?"

"You know Fred Wosnicki, the astrophysicist from MIT? Some call him a 'stellar physicist.' He'll be down in a minute. Rose, dear, I've been hinting at this for a long time, and now I have to tell you. I finally have enough data to bring you and Fred into this. I have a rough theory, but I need the your help to challenge it … or verify it—

"Oh, Fred, come in. You know Rose, my trusted associate and dear friend. She's not only beautiful, but she is the best atmospheric scientist I know." Rose blushed. Jane was really turning it on.

"Sure, Rose. How are you? Heard you just got married. Congratulations."

"Oh, thank you very much. I'm fine, and you?"

"I am very well … wish I were half my age so I could have competed against your famous husband." He laughed. "Oh well, I can't wait for the professor here to let me in on the secret that she keeps hinting at. Since she trusts you, Rose, I suppose I won't get it out of you."

"Relax, Fred. Rose doesn't know yet either. That's why I asked you both here. I'm finally ready to tell you what I suspect, but I need your assistance. First, let me say that if I'm even halfway right, and you two finally put all the pieces together with your expertise to confirm, the outcome will just be so dramatic." Jane dropped her voice, her smile gone. "I uh … can't imagine. I'm going to trust that we keep this project confidential. My theory changes everything."

"You have our attention, lady. Lay it out," Fred said.

✳   ✳   ✳

Arthur took another long stare at Richard, who now sat back, realizing that he had just offered to help, but how? Arthur then suggested, "You know, John Heyward has a good friend over at the university, another economics professor. His name is Charles Green. I understand that he is very good in sociology too—civil affairs—and has a Nobel Prize for describing human behavior in both an economic sense and a societal sense. What would you think if we met with John and Charles and got their perspective? We would include H. too."

"Count me in," replied Richard.

Moments later, Charles responded to Arthur's request of John Heyward. "Sure, John. I'm free to meet with you all at five o'clock. The conference room by my office. See you then." Charles pushed "END" on his mobile phone and looked back at Michael. The two had become good friends and often lunched together at the main university dining hall. "That was my friend, John Heyward—you know, the economist from Wharton on the president's team of advisors. … He wants to meet with me later today. Must be important … three other members of the president's select team will be with him—Arthur Schnell, the secretary of the interior, H. Stewart, chairman of the National Bank, and Richard Compton, the environmental professor from Princeton. I wonder what's up."

"Charlie, I've known Arthur for some time now. Would you mind if I stopped by to say hello to him? Haven't seen him lately."

"Sure, Michael. Come by my office at five this afternoon."

✳   ✳   ✳

Jane's look now changed to one of firm determination. "Okay, let's get started. Carbon dioxide, methane, water vapor, solar wind, ocean oscillations. Here's the story. We all know the conventional wisdom on how 'gradual' climate change suddenly turned 'abrupt' back in 2010. If a line was crossed from Man's excessive fossil-fuel burning and the result was that the permafrost suddenly melted at a much faster rate than previously forecast, a vast amount of carbon dioxide and methane, two of the major greenhouse gases, would escape into the atmosphere and heat it at a greatly accelerated rate.

"I happened to be the one studying the permafrost across northern Canada and the Arctic lands, so I was the one who warned the president's advisors and then the UN's IPCC. Thank goodness we took action in time. But then, I began to research where all the carbon went. It wasn't evenly dispersed. It was hanging over the equatorial areas, heating both sea and air. Perhaps that's why hurricanes starting becoming so severe. Those warmer middle-of-the planet ocean currents headed north and accounted for the higher temperatures Rose was recording in the North Atlantic."

Fred and Rose sat frozen, listening to Jane and wondering what was coming next.

She continued, "I then began to observe, and this is where I need the help of you two. Three other factors came into play: First, there appeared to be a gigantic increase in water vapor in the Northern Hemisphere, over both the Atlantic and Pacific oceans. As you know, water vapor is by far the largest of all the greenhouse gases. So the water vapor is in the north and the CO_2 is in the south. Second, I happened to overhear one of you astrophysicists mention a very unusual positioning and intensity of the solar winds. Third, I did some research on the so-called 'El Niño, La Niña Effect' of ocean patterns out in the Pacific, and my studies are showing the possibility of these patterns being responsible for much higher temperatures in our Western states. Can you imagine if all this came together at the same time? Rapid heating in North America the last ten years, right … but now, the northern water vapor is dissipating at a far more rapid rate than the southern carbon dioxide. The solar winds could go back to their normal patterns at any time. The Niño/Niña ocean oscillations could go back to more normal patterns anytime now … and then?" Jane stopped and smiled broadly as Fred and Rose sat in disbelief.

"And then …" Rose said quietly, "our climate could revert back to normal almost immediately if all three of those came together at the same time. A complete reversal!"

"Unbelievable!" Fred gasped.

"Now, let's not jump ahead too fast. What are you studying now, Fred, and what about this solar wind?" Jane calmly asked.

"Well, I'm out in space studying the planets right now, and I've been confused about this solar wind situation. You know, plenty of scientists have been studying the sunspot activities, and since we've been in a lull recently, it is thought that lower activity results in less radiant heat coming to earth—a cooling effect. So that's why global warming has been blamed solely on Man's carbon emissions."

"Explain that please, Fred," Rose inquired.

"Okay. From here, sunspots appear as dark spots on the sun, yet each one is about the size of the earth. They result from the mechanical motion of the sun's hot gases rising up from the deep while cooler molecules on the surface are falling back down. A magnetic field is created from this motion, and it sort of becomes a magnetic bubble. Sunspots are fluid and move and change quite often. Since the bubble, the sunspot, is relatively cooler you would think that less sunlight and less energy would come to earth. But it's the opposite. When sunspot activity is high, solar activity is high … and that higher energy skirts around the spots and shoots out into space faster, bombarding our atmosphere with more UV light radiation. However, the conventional wisdom is that sunspot activity doesn't have as much impact as Man's burning of fossil fuels and clear-cutting forests."

"And the solar wind, Fred?" Jane queried.

"That's related to sunspot activity, but different. The solar wind is there all the time in varying degrees. It's an extension of the sun's outer surface, the corona. It represents charged particles moving out rapidly—maybe 250 miles per second—and each second may hold one million tons of mass."

Staring intently at Fred, Jane looked astonished.

"We think that near the sun's equatorial zones, stronger magnetic fields form closed loops and hold some of the gases from escaping compared to the weaker gases escaping from holes in the corona closer to the sun's poles. Strong solar wind is usually associated with strong sunspot activity, since combined they mean that higher solar activity going on—a double-barreled effect bombarding the earth and causing more warming. But again, since we've been in a long cycle of less sunspot activity, like 10 spots a year as a low, versus a high of 150, solar activity would not have contributed to our abrupt climate change—"

"Unless …" interjected Rose, then pausing.

"Unless what?" Jane pumped.

"Unless you heard what I heard," Rose continued. "That some unusual pattern might have taken place where, despite the down cycle in sunspot activity, new holes in the corona occurred near the sun's equator and huge winds escaped as never recorded before, at least until Fred's group started keeping track. Listen, Jane, with Fred's help I can get on it right away."

"Great. Now also Rose, tell me about this ocean oscillation business."

"Well, I'm beginning to think I should have paid more attention in class. My atmospheric science all this time has me paying attention to air and water currents and to their temperatures, but I remember now that there are about nine factors that contribute to climate change—the strongest link of the earth's average temperatures being related to solar activity. My profs taught that solar activity has a lot more to do with global warming than man's CO_2 emissions. They thought the latter was of little consequence—in other words, the opposite of what the scientific consensus has been telling us the last twenty years. But then you have to bring in the all-important oscillations, and the two don't always match."

"Okay, I'm confused," offered Jane.

"Jane, ocean temperatures are not evenly distributed. Rolling patterns up and down occur, called 'oscillations,' where unusually warm or cold waters take turns coming to the ocean's surface. This surface water has a major impact on the earth's atmospheric temperatures close to earth's surface. The warming phase in the Pacific oscillation is called 'El Niño,' while the cooling phase is called 'La Niña.' Let me remember back; in the 1940s, '50s, and '60s, we experienced high solar activity—"

"That's exactly right, Rose. That should have caused global heating," inserted Fred.

"But," exclaimed Rose, "we also had at that time a very strong, unusually long La Niña. The net effect on balance was slightly cool, and then came the 1970s when solar activity sharply fell off while La Niña was still there. So we had cooling and cooling effects in the two climate barrels—a decade of very cold weather. Then the oscillations changed in the 1980s and continued through most of the '90s, to the warm El Niño cycle. Solar activity was then high; therefore we had warming and warming effects in both barrels ... so global temperatures went up. World-wide fossil-fuel burning and forest degradation also increased, so many scientists automatically associated the warming trend with Man's activities."

"Rose, ironic that in the ten years before our abrupt change, 1998 to 2008, the world was all charged up about gradual global warming when actually worldwide temperatures were falling on average, even though they were higher in North America."

"Right, Jane," Rose replied. "During that period, solar activity slackened a lot while the warming El Niño cycle weakened. Double cooling effect."

"This is like a roller coaster ... constantly changing," sighed Fred.

"Except, Fred, a roller coaster's ups and downs are engineered, so we can see the curves, the hills, and valleys and know the speed. But, as you said before, the solar wind and solar sunspot cycles are uneven in length of time and in degree of strength. They're unpredictable. The same with the warm/cold ocean current oscillations. Their length of time and degree of strength are variable and unpredictable, and then the results are not spread evenly throughout the globe."

The three brilliant scientists sat quietly for a few moments, dazed. They were deep in thought and then broke out into laughter simultaneously. There had to be some humor in the fickleness of human destiny.

"Right, so who knows what's really going on, or what's to happen next," Jane finally spoke. "But that's why you are here. We are going to find out."

✳   ✳   ✳

A week later, Michael arranged lunch with his friend Charles Green again. Another esteemed professor joined them, Edward Stern, department head of neuroscience from the University of California, Berkley.

"It was good to see Arthur Schnell again, Charlie," Michael said as they sat down for lunch, "although he looked a little haggard."

"Yes, that was quite a distinguished group that came to see me. But to tell you the truth, I think they all seemed a little worn out. They wanted my impressions of the economy they created here in New America and how human motivations affect its performance. Like we here at the university, they are obviously seeing some problems."

Edward laughed. "So what did you tell them?"

"I told them to be glad it's temporary. This system couldn't last for long. Then they all looked at me and gave the impression that they thought it's far more than temporary. That's when I gulped. Then they asked me what I thought was missing … like the human element."

Michael was enjoying this conversation, on something other than engineering. He welcomed new knowledge like a sponge. He was learning.

"Oh, like you and I talk about all the time," said Edward.

"Right, Ed. They have built no human motivation into this economic system. On the technical side, they are not allowing for any growth or ability to supply what is demanded longer term. Growth has to come from exploited labor, which we gave up over a hundred years ago, from motivated productivity enhancements, which we Americans specialize in, except here in New America, and from investment coming from profits or loans. Well, here there is no motivated labor pool, no productivity inducements, and no investment, nor profits, nor loans. They have created a make-believe economy where everybody produces the exact quantities that they think everybody needs and then they print the money to pay the workers. Then they control the price of wages and goods and services so there will be no inflation. Brilliant, say for a one-year economic system, but when you do that for very long, the strength of demand of what people really want versus the availability of supply ... well, the two forces become quickly distorted. That's why we're seeing all these shortages now. Full employment, price stability—nice, but soon shoddy workmanship, no growth, and product shortages—not so nice."

"And so how does it normally work? I have always heard of booms and recessions and even the Great Depression. How is it supposed to work?" Michael wondered out loud.

"Michael, you seem interested. Why don't you come over to my dinner meeting at one of your favorite spots, the Schnell Dining Hall, next Friday evening? We have a little group discussing these issues on an interdisciplinary approach. Ed will be there."

"Sure, love too. Just so I'm not home too late for Rose. I'm a newly married man, you know," Michael responded with a gracious laugh.

"Right on ... and to answer your question real briefly, managing an economy is not easy, but on the demand side, the first assumption is that the population is growing, and between the newcomers and the existing population, there is an ever-increasing demand for more products and services from all sectors—government, industry, commerce, and consumers—to meet a broad range of needs, satisfactions, conveniences, health, whatever. Second, to provide sufficient availability, there have to be incentives to produce. For example, when the workers finally took over in Russia after their revolution in 1917 under Lenin, they believed that two hundred years of mistreatment would be erased if each worker produced from his ability and shared with each citizen according to his needs. Ha! They discovered quite quickly that the doctrine of Karl Marx's was contrary to human nature, and in no time they abandoned it, since production dwindled. And guess what? They then put incentives and rewards into the system in order to raise production. When Lenin died six years later, he had repudiated everything he had fought for in helping to lead the revolution.

"Unfortunately, instead of turning to the modern Western capitalist system with fair human rights and working conditions for all workers, Stalin was intent on increasing production at all costs. So an 'incentive and reward' motivational system became 'produce or die' instead. Cruelly, millions went to Siberia to work *and* to die."

Michael finished his dessert and could only say, "Wow!"

Edward smiled. "Human behavior," he whispered to himself.

"So ideally," Charles continued, "a central bank should be in the background monitoring the supply and demand balance; providing the right amount of a medium of exchange—money—an amount equal to the needs of the supply/demand balance. Of course, an economy can easily get out of balance. Could be bottlenecks in supply, or overconfidence and overexuberance in demand. Then the central bank can try to ameliorate any adverse impacts of the natural adjustments, which usually serve to get the economy back in balance. It can control the money supply downward to dampen inflationary factors in a booming economy or upwards to spur demand in a falling economy. It can adjust interest rates up or down on its loans to member banks. It can buy or sell U.S. Treasury securities on the open market to increase or decrease the liquidity, or lending ability, of its member banks." Then with a big laugh, Charles said, "And they get criticized for doing too much, or not enough, depending on which social/political foot you are standing on, because economics is fluid, not always predictable, and, as often quoted, 'not an exact science.'"

"Well, Charles, you said your economist friend from Wharton, the now renowned John Heyward, is a technical expert, so maybe from our dinner meetings, where we are going to discuss the human side, you will be able to pass some wisdom on as to how to keep this economy here moving ahead instead of backward."

"Edward, my friend, I'm afraid that when they came to see me last week, I told them that there appeared to be little hope of that. Our president likes the idea of a benevolent government running the human machine. My old friend, John Heyward, is facing a dreaded dilemma."

✻   ✻   ✻

By the middle of springtime, the Chief was busier than ever. He refused to visit with the president's medical team despite the pains he was feeling in his upper arms and chest. He tried to ignore what he shrugged off as digestive upsets and constant fatigue. He simply wasn't eating right or getting enough sleep, he thought to himself. His romantic interludes with Jane had tapered off. Once-a-week bliss was down to once-a-month rush. She was completely absorbed with some new project, and he was deluged with a steady stream of reports, the bulk from his secret police, officially known as the Anti-Crime Force. For him, the lust was dissipating. Nature was dictating a new course for his mind and body. For her, she was too engrossed in her special work with Rose to ponder over lonely nights. She was far from despondent.

The May Group of Eight dinner meeting carried on just as it had for the past many months—less jovial, but not outwardly tense about the state of affairs. The president had now made it clear that all "whining" was to be confined to written reports that the members would take home with them, not to be read in advance and discussed. Richard Compton would continue to report on climatic conditions, indicating no improvement in the trends. He withheld his personal concerns over the state of affairs in New America that he had unloaded on Arthur. Arthur would summarize crime incidents and violations against the Guidelines without a show of emotion. John and H. would briefly mention that some products were in short supply and that they were working on it. Hank would enthusiastically paint a glowing picture of the two continuing bright spots: First, clean, "green" energy had become a full, complete reality. America was showing the way. Second, the utilization of salty seawater for domestic purposes was now practical on a mass scale; there was no mention of costs. That factor was unimportant in New America.

The last two in the group remained mostly silent, always somber. It was as if the Savior and his Chief had come to enjoy the Oracle's gloomy pronouncements of long-term adversity. To the Savior, it meant a referendum for his continued undisputed, benevolent leadership. To the Chief, it meant eternal power, if only he could contain the transgressors.

As for the vice president, her growing reticence was actually concealing a new force in the works. It was not the growing number of transgressors among the citizenry, but rather the alliance she had formed with key governors and certain members of Congress. Their mental state was becoming a mirror reflecting the growing discontent against a small central government bureaucracy controlling every aspect of American life, national emergency or not.

✻   ✻   ✻

"No, it's okay. You go ahead. Jane would like me to stop over tonight for a few hours to work on that special project I told you about."

"You sure, darling? It would be the third Friday night in a row with these guys."

"Michael, it's fine. I'm very happy that you are learning all about that economic and political stuff. It's way over my head. How 'bout we both get home by ten?"

"That's a date, lover."

The Friday night meetings were now taking place at Charles Green's apartment. His two assigned roommates were also bachelor professors from the university. Stanley Adler was famed for his political science teaching at Georgetown University in Washington, DC. Jonathan Bellwether was renowned in the field of religion at Southern Methodist University in Dallas, Texas. In addition to Michael, the other "members" of this group of intellects were Edward Stern, neuroscience from Berkeley, and G. J. Ruch, a distinguished professor of philosophy at Harvard.

"Charlie, why don't you finish up on economics? You've taught us all about supply and demand, inflation and deflation, money and banking. You also know so much about the human element. Can we go there?" Edward suggested.

"Sure, but you cut me off if I get too long-winded. Most people find economics boring," Charles replied with a laugh. "Well, okay, let's start with human motivation. What factors induce people to buy ... anything? Or to work? Obviously, there was a time when we had to satisfy our essential human needs. We were hunters and gatherers so that we could provide food to eat and survive. We needed to protect ourselves, so we found or built shelters. Then in the favored geographical regions, we turned to agriculture about ten thousand years ago and suddenly found the time to formally develop language, write, read, converse, and think. We became 'civilized' and started to trade goods—clothing, containers, tools, weapons. Then, to facilitate all this exchange of desired goods that made life easier, we developed a middleman for all these goods—money—and you know the rest to this modern day.

"So once the basic survival needs are met, we naturally seem to want more. Intangibly, we have inquisitive minds. We want to learn more about everything. Tangibly, we want to acquire more tools, more conveniences—not only more, but better—so the quest is on. One economist made it simple by saying we first survive, then we seek comfort, and then we seek happiness in the broadest and most diverse sense. Theoretically, the harder we work and the better techniques we use to produce, the higher our standard of living becomes. The less we work, or through natural disasters, disease, or war, then the lower our standard of living. We professors like to live well and be happy, so that's why we are against 'war.'"

That brought a laugh out of everyone. "Now here is where it gets complicated. I'm sure Edward will explain this later better than I. We want more and better goods and services to make life better—easier, more convenient. So we work to produce them. We then get paid for our work so we can buy them. But no two workers are exactly alike. We live in a world of paradoxes. Similar and opposite. Plus and minus. Good and evil. Love and hate. Security and adventure. Workaholic and lazy. Aggressive and passive. And so on.

"Some workers are better working alone; some find their group association and its values the most powerful motivator. Some cherish rewards for a job well done. Others don't like to be pressured. Some take pride in their work. Others drag their feet. Some need supervision, while others are better on their own. There's a whole diversity of needs: status, achievement, comfort, more money, better working conditions, fringe benefits, freedom, self-growth, excitement, avoiding boredom, sense of competence, psychological advantage over others, the thrill of competition, the rewards of cooperation. And it varies by cultural background and by age. Younger people will work hard and look to future rewards, while older people are looking toward security. And then there is morale, a subjective feeling of things going well that seems to promote better performance."

"And so," Michael interjected, "it sounds so complicated. Don't we all just want to live in the appropriate manner we individually desire, to be treated as we think we should be fairly treated, and to be rewarded one way or another that reflects our contribution and ability?"

"Brilliant, Michael; well spoken. You are learning fast," replied Charles. "But remember, that is your personal outlook, and it is a good one. As I said, we are all different regarding the actors that motivate our economic behaviors, but what we find are common threads, and you have found three of them: the way we prefer to live, the way we want to be treated, and the way we are rewarded for our productivity."

"And those common threads here in New America, Charlie. What are they holding together?" queried G. J.

"Not much. As I started to say this evening, technically we have created a mythical economic system that in truth can only work for a very limited time. The most obvious downside is the fact that we are now witnessing tremendous shortages of many goods people feel they need. On the psychological side, as we have been discussing motivational factors, many workers are bored and their workmanship is shoddy, making the supply side of the equation even worse. They have nice spacious apartment-style residences with gardens outside, but many do not prefer to live that way. They have no say in how they are treated, even though our benevolent government is taking good care of all their basic needs. And rewards and recognition for their work—none!"

✧   ✧   ✧

The same June evening at the home of Alexis Graham: "Thank you for coming. I am very sorry we cannot accommodate all 585 of you. I appreciate your selecting an informal leadership, the Group of Twenty. I don't know how you did it, but I commend you." The vice president was referring to the 435 House members of Congress, the hundred U.S. senators, and the fifty state governors.

Some were seated and some standing around her spacious living room as the vice president continued, "And I believe that we should use a guise for this meeting, that it's my birthday celebration. And of course the president wouldn't have been invited up to this hillside location of mine since we have to be separated for security reasons. I suggest that we also keep the real content of this gathering to ourselves. You all know of the Anti-Crime Force being run out of the president's office. It purports to have as its sole mission the tracking down lawbreakers—guideline violators—but I must tell you that it is also a form of secret police, garnering information on anyone suspected of potentially disrupting this 'perfect' society. Each of you and your colleagues—beware.

"Now, you all know that I have been personally disturbed for some time now at the lack of balanced input as to how we run this state of national emergency—a program that includes me, the vice president, in merely a symbolic role, and one that completely excludes all of you. So let's begin the task tonight of working out our own plan. I know you cannot keep your frustrations to yourselves much longer."

✧   ✧   ✧

"And gentlemen, we have created another myth that we are being told is the truth," began G. J., the Harvard guru of philosophy. "It is our political system here. True, a strong leader has to be in command of government resources during a national emergency, but to create what they have called a 'New America' and expect us to live here for perhaps many, many years … then *order among disorderly men* cannot be achieved without either a democratic system formulating laws by majority rule or a dictatorship backed up by coercion. That, my friends, has been the political history of mankind from day one. From democratic tribal councils of the wise elders or conversely the ruthless tribal Chief to the plurality of constitutional America or conversely fascist Nazi Germany—all created enforceable rules. In New America, we have only the president's so-called voluntary Guidelines. It's unprecedented. It can't work."

"Stan, you're the political science expert. Do you concur?" Charles asked.

"Right on. That's exactly what I taught at Georgetown," replied Stanley Adler.

G. J. Ruch continued, "What I think the president must have been reading six years ago was Winston Churchill, but today, Plato and Socrates. Those two giants of early intellect, four hundred years before Christ, theorized in *The Republic* and *The Statesman* that the perfect state could only be attained through the training of a very few wise and good men who would rule all others with justice—justice achieved through their search and attainment for wisdom, truth, and reason. They would be the enlightened ones. Sadly, however, they ended their discourse believing that such an endeavor was merely a 'striving,' that such perfection could probably only be achieved in heaven, and that secondarily, laws would have to be formulated and applied to govern the people, and those laws would often be unjust. In New America, I believe that our president is trying in his heart to create 'just' laws—his Guidelines. A noble ambition, I must say."

Michael again interjected. His engineering mind was always creative, but this was deep. "Okay, so are you saying we don't have a democracy here, or a dictatorship, but the impossible imagination by our president, who is called the Savior by many, that he thinks idealistically that he is this perfectly good statesman who can rule wisely with absolute justice?"

"That's exactly what I am saying," responded G. J. calmly and coolly. "The ancient Greeks would call such a man the 'Philosopher-King.'"

The room became quiet. Minds were racing. Charles rose to find more of that special beer available only to the illustrious faculty of the national university.

"Well, we're on a roll now," Charles said lightly as he returned with his arms full. "We might as well hear from everyone." Michael glanced at his watch. It was already 9:50, and he had promised Rose he would be home by 10:00. But this was too good to skip out on. He had been bothered by the arbitrary guidelines since his arrival, and by his lack of physical and academic freedom. He had been given an assignment—do that and nothing else. And he remembered what his father lectured to him about many years ago: "Everyone is going to tell you their 'Truth'—don't accept any of it without your own verification."

"I think my input will be brief," the soft-spoken teacher of religion, Jonathan Bellwether, began. "We previously discussed the fact that today's great religions replaced tens of thousands of years of beliefs in the pagan gods of the natural world. Multiple gods were associated with the key elements of life—sun, water, fire, food, and love. As the 'civilized' world grew just a few thousand years ago, and as scientific knowledge was gained and shared through better-developed languages and writing, pagan gods became less associated with physical phenomena. Their influence dwindled. The new gods of the 'supernatural' were revealed over a mere few thousand years. Most of these new religions were part philosophical, part mystical. They were associated with Man's behavior, his intangible soul, and his spiritual relationship with a divine being. Taoism, Buddhism, Confucianism, Hinduism, Judaism, Christianity and Islam—founded roughly 1800 BC to 600 AD. They all set forth specific ways, in the form of suggestions, morals, rules, and laws, to foster orderly relationships among Man on earth and between Man and his deity. Remember that, at the time, 99 percent of the population would be considered 'poor' by today's standards, and the ruling 1 percent 'very rich.' Therefore, the second aspect of these religions or philosophy/religions would be that of providing hope of a better afterlife for the impoverished masses—heaven, reincarnation, whatever ..."

Michael wasn't sure what to believe. With the advent of science based upon repeatable, discernable observations, certainly the pagan gods were no longer relevant. The new gods' credibility had to be taken first on the reported words and deeds of one or a small group of men, such as Abraham, Moses, Jesus, or Mohammed, and then secondly on a full belief that their divinity was to be accepted as a matter of simple faith. Some scientists could not accept belief in something that could not be observed, seen, or proven. Other scientists, amazed at the delicate and precise order of the universe, firmly believe that only a supernatural power could have created such wonder. Others could not believe that bodily death was one's end, that there would be absolutely nothing afterward. What a comforting feeling to believe in a peaceful afterlife! Others, agnostics, were not sure what to believe. Others, avowed atheists, believe that there could be no god, especially no all-loving god, while witnessing so much natural horror and manmade violence on earth. To them, life was a physical/chemical/biological happenstance.

Jonathan continued his turn, "Now then, we also know that America was founded on the principle of religious freedom. Today, the overwhelming majority of Americans want to believe in something bigger than themselves. They like the idea of an all-knowing, all-loving God, and they commonly pray to Him for guidance and hope. Here in New America, the government has continued to remain hands-off. It has to the best of its ability accommodated religious gatherings.

"The only Guideline restrictions have been in the disallowance of building worship facilities due to lack of space and the limited hours we can use schools, stadiums, and public areas. Like everyone else, I am worried about the growing crime rate, alcohol abuse, drug abuse, and the breakdown of productivity, but my biggest concern, and it is shared by most in the clergy, is that so many people, in referring to the president as the 'Savior,' have actually come to believe he is truly a deity. Gentlemen … another myth."

Interesting. It was now past ten o'clock, but Michael stayed to listen to Edward Stern's take on the mind and its influence on matters at hand. Professor Stern was considered the leading academic in America in the burgeoning field of neuroscience.

"Thanks for putting me on last, Charlie … and after all this beer, is anyone listening?"

"You bet I am!" Michael cried out and then laughed. His inquisitive mind could not get enough, and this segment was on the "mind."

"Okay, like Jonathan, I'll be brief. Charlie, put me on first, next time." Edward laughed back.

"Charles was right on in so many ways. Our behaviors are diverse, and they are complex. But they do emanate from the nature of our brain, the center of our nervous system that controls everything we do. Without a microscope, our physical brains all look pretty much the same, but microscopically, we are all different, and sub-microscopically, very different. That visible, tangible, physical brain contains billions of neural cells, each one with thousands of individual sites at both the beginning and ending that emit and receive chemical messages. Considering that we are each born with a unique set of genes, not all of which may work in accordance with design and which are continuously bombarded with different outside environmental influences, it's a miracle that we work as well as we do. It's an intense factory of chemical and electrical energy up there, comprising only 2 percent of our body weight but consuming over 20 percent of our calories. From that physical machine, we go to the intangible, invisible, subjective 'mind,' that intense consciousness still not yet fully understood.

"But again, like in our economic behavior, we look for common threads. We all have the five senses of sight, smell, touch, feel, and taste. These sensations are first electrochemically transmitted to the middle part of our brain, where initial behaviors are emotionally generated in response, including the famous 'fight or flight.' In humans, messages via neurotransmitters then go back and forth to the large front part of our brain, where our neurons give us the ability to reason and reflect before taking action or deciding on inaction. Behaviors reflecting love, hate, jealousy, revenge, power, and so many others tend to be primarily emotionally based. Those among us who reflect longer try to ameliorate those emotions, those passions, with thoughtful reason—'reason' being the ability, the experience to comprehend the consequences of certain actions or observations, with the follow-up resulting in behavior that benefits everyone in one's surroundings. And then unfortunately, in the neurologically impaired or immature brain, some thoughtful reflections become distorted to what we call the 'irrational,' followed up with behavior that is deemed harmful.

"Nevertheless, we do have common threads. The urge to compete is counterbalanced with a need to be cooperative and compassionate. Each person weighs whichever potential action one feels or reasons as more advantageous to one's individual needs or one's group needs and behaves accordingly. Furthermore, since we are social beings raised in a particular historical culture, we mix our unique individualism in with our group cultural values. It all gets stirred together. Here in America, we are accustomed to independence and self-reliance as important values to most of our individual and group thinking. So naturally, once the strong motivation to be safe settles down, we experience a general uneasiness as a common thread among us, even though certainly there are many who accept and like being taken care of. The emotion of *fear* is now being overshadowed by other emotions and by rational thinking, by irrational thinking, and by diverse cultural values. Where this leads to next, I'm not certain. We don't have much historical experience in herding so many people together who in general have such advanced, sophisticated minds. One last thing: History has taught us, and it continues to be valid this day, that within each group there is a propensity for a strong, aggressive leader to emerge. Probably goes back to our biological evolution when survival came first. It's called the 'dominant male' theory." The intellects in the room momentarily fell silent.

"Well, I know this," Charles finally offered. "Our positions here as educators at the national university were created to pass down our knowledge to the people, and also to be available to the government in helping make this new nation work. Gentlemen, I submit to you that the government has not used us one iota in that second mission. That visit to my office many weeks ago by several members of the president's team was useless. There has been no follow-up. I don't know if we have Plato's 'statesman' in charge, or a deity, or a dominant male, or just a great orator, but it is time we develop our own plan ... the National University Plan."

* * *

"Michael, it's after eleven. You're over an hour late. I rushed home from Jane's."

"I'm sorry, Rose, it's just ... it's just all so overwhelming to me. I don't like this New America."

"Well, maybe then you should just learn to accept things the way they are. Everyone is safe, and that's a good thing ... and besides, what we are trying to discover is whether the climate can change back again in a much shorter time than fifty years."

"Yeah, fat chance. The Oracle has never been wrong."

"Michael! That's an affront! Jane and I are no dummies. There is a chance that we're on to something."

"Okay, okay. Are you 'smarties' reducing the fifty-year forecast to twenty, to ten, to five?" Michael retorted, raising his voice and reflecting a long evening of stimulating but inconclusive intellectual dialogue.

"I don't know. I don't know!" Rose replied with a hint of anger in her voice for the first time ever in their relationship. "We have much more to do. So what's *your* answer? You and all your beer-drinking professor friends ... talking about what? Out-of-touch theories? Michael, we've covered this before. I know you cherish your individual freedom, but 'order' here in New America is paramount. The president is the one in charge, and we know through Jane that the Chief is cracking down on the criminal elements. Where is your patience? You have to abide—"

"Okay!" Michael knew when to back off. Abruptly, he turned away, mad at Rose's harping on "order" and left the living room without further reply. It was the first time in their marriage they went to sleep without a hug, without a kiss; no lovemaking that night. Frustration had set in.

* * *

It had been five months since Richard Compton paid his unexpected visit to Arthur Schnell's office. The follow-up visit they made along with John Heyward and H. Stewart to Charles Green's office had hardly been rewarding. All they heard from Charles was resignation that their perfect society was beginning to crumble. Nevertheless, a new bond had formed. The four, half of the Group of Eight, were meeting clandestinely for several months on a weekly basis—a Saturday night "social." Were there no answers? The president seemed to place himself high on a pedestal. He had withdrawn from hearing them out at the monthly Group of Eight meetings. He appeared to be oblivious to how severe the general discontent was becoming. His demeanor was all smiles. The dinner meetings had become like social gatherings of old friends who had successfully weathered a storm together. Conversely, the Chief never ceased to scowl, going overboard to let everyone know he had everything under control. And then there was the Oracle. He had grown increasingly taciturn, frustrated that anyone could have anything on their mind other than working to save the planet. And so the now-impotent Group of Eight condensed into a new "Group of Four"—two environmentalists and two economists—dedicated to becoming an action group that would formulate a practical follow up to the original Master Plan. "Phase II," they called it.

✻   ✻   ✻

Meanwhile, the resolute vice president continued to surreptitiously communicate with her esteemed "Group of Twenty." These were all-powerful politicians formerly accustomed to pomp and privilege but more importantly to having a strong say into how government was to be run. Now on the outside, they were searching for a commonality they could rally around. The vice president was persistent in setting a goal upon which they all could agree. Debate—yes; but come to an agreement—imperative. What was their primary complaint, their primary frustration? In the final analysis, they agreed that it was lack of democratic free expression as to how New America should be governed. In traditional America, its founding fathers agreed that *justice* was the goal and that a constitutional democracy was the best way to achieve that virtue. In New America, their aspirations were to defend its borders against a new enemy—a dangerous climate—and within its borders to secure the blessings of liberty and justice for all. They tagged their plan with the code name "RIFA," for the "Re-Institution of Free America."

✿   ✿   ✿

The bond of love was too strong. This silent treatment could not go on much longer. The two ate their Saturday morning breakfast without a word, without a look. And then it happened again—they both reached for the orange juice pitcher at the same time. Their hands touched. Their eyes met. Just like in Seattle seven years ago, except this time they embraced and kissed, and Rose cried.

"Michael, I'm so sorry. I know you have been unhappy with how life is so prescribed here. I ... I—"

"No, darling, I'm the one who should apologize. I'm sorry I took my frustration out on you last night ... never again. I've thought it over. If you and Jane are really on to something, then go after it with all your devotion and energy. Life is full of surprises; let's pray for a good one. Now, let me bring you into something I haven't told anyone about yet. You know that my water and power systems are more efficient than the prior technologies, but certainly if economics were truly a factor, it would be at a ridiculous cost to create so much electricity with my solar and wind-turbine technology. It should be a major supplement, not a pure replacement. Well, you know, if we ever get out of this place and return to our past lives and a normal economy ... Listen, Rose, I've been working alone on a project behind the scenes, quietly, outside my assigned position."

"Michael, that's the way I like to hear you talk. Sweetheart, your eyes are lighting up, and you're getting me excited."

"Yeah, well. You know the old story. We have enough coal in this country for four hundred more years, but it's hard work to mine it, and its burning is dirty. So sure, use solar and wind on a large scale where that makes sense, but when we return, our big growing economy should also use all that coal if it were to become easier to mine, and if it could burn cleanly." Michael paused and walked across the room, smiling and gazing out the window.

"Michael!" Rose exclaimed.

"Right!" he turned back and exclaimed in return. "I have found a way to do both!"

✿   ✿   ✿

A week later, Rose excitedly rushed into Jane's office and quickly closed the door behind her. "I think I finally have enough data. It did happen, Jane; it did happen!"

"Wait, wait, slow down; tell me," a grinning Jane responded.

"Okay, listen. Up in Fred's lab I reviewed and tabulated data from thousands of satellite photographs along with thousands of UV light readings at dozens of recording centers spread throughout the United States. From 2008 through 2016 inclusive, there definitely were fifty to a hundred large holes in the sun's corona, *at its equator*, that allowed a vast amount of solar wind to escape, even though sunspot activity was about average and the solar winds escaping at the sun's poles were about average. This unusual phenomenon had to certainly be a major cause of the sudden heating effects we were feeling by 2010 on."

"And now; what is happening now?" Jane asked excitedly.

"It looks very different. I have to get the data completed, but it appears that we have a significant fall-off in activity. But we are still warming, so maybe it takes a period of time for the changed activity to take effect, or maybe there's something in the oceans still going on. ..."

Rose's face exploded with a look of determination. "I'm almost there with that part ... I'm almost there. Give me one more week. I think the ocean oscillations and water vapor situation will all tie in. Jane! What will we do if this all fits together?"

"Okay," Jane responded, more calm now as she had to soak in the sudden revelation. "Remember now; our first step has been just to confirm what happened to set the abrupt change in motion years back. If we prove that out, we then have to determine just what is happening now and what it means for the next few years. When we finish, my plan is to take this information to the Chief. Why play with it among the university faculty? We should go right to the top decision makers."

✾ ✾ ✾

"Hi Dad, you always told me to call you if I needed advice. You said you would never impose your own views on me, but for me to be an independent thinker. Obviously, I spent my college days and the last ten years engrossed in the engineering field. I love it, and I guess I'm pretty good at it. You always thought one should do what one is good at and what one loves to do. That combination is best. You also warned me not to automatically accept what one tells you about an important subject without following up with your own independent confirmation. You also told me to be diligent in my work. Don't get arrogant—be sure to get it right. I've tried, Dad, but sometimes I wonder if I've been just lucky that my ideas have worked. I don't know.

"Well, Dad, I've been pulled out of my field lately. Away from desalination, wind, and solar power to studying geothermal energy. Other than around active volcanoes, it doesn't make much sense. Thank goodness I'm doing some neat work on the side. It was uncomfortable at first, but you know I have felt uncomfortable, in sort of a very vague way, ever since I arrived here two and a half years ago. Despite the successful flight to safety and how perfect most people thought everything was here for a while, it seems that there has been something almost sinister in the air this whole time—at least for me. It's about the way we are living—like we are expected to behave like programmed robots. But you know that I've learned a lot recently … a lot from my professor friends at the university. And I've learned a lot from my dear wife, Rose. She is teaching me that there are new possibilities out there—in a technical sense, though. She hasn't yet experienced the intangible side. She is in what I call the 'majority element'; those who accept our current human condition and will play by all the rules yet hope for a change in climatic circumstances so we can go back to the way we liked to live before—with our freedom of choice.

"Then there is the 'diverse bottom element.' It is all those who are bored, or aimless, or abusers, or cheaters, or criminals, or selfish, or lazy, or accept being pampered in a nanny society, or just don't want to be so orderly in an ordered society. Then finally there is the 'restless free element,' the ones who cherish the idea of free thinking, debate, personal freedom, self-reliance, personal growth, opportunities, and a chance to excel. I guess I'm in that last group, and I'm growing more and more restless.

"The group of enlightened professors I have been associating with is putting together a plan that plays on these factors of that 'free' element, but one that would also enlighten the middle element while bringing order to the bottom element. I really don't like to place everyone into such layers—we are all so different—but I'm just trying to simplify things to make it easier for you to understand. The profs are going to submit their plan to the dean of the national university and then petition the president to seriously consider its merits. But I just don't know, Dad. We have a leader, as you know, referred to as the Savior, and he just might not listen to anybody. And I'm also concerned that once a petition is presented to him, a myriad of vested interests will get into the game with competing recommendations and challenges, and we could end either with chaos or the opposite, where nothing gets accomplished. So I'm working on it, Dad. Maybe I can do something that brings it all together. I don't know. Well, have to cut it off now and get to my projects. Thanks for listening, Dad.

Say 'hi' to Mom. I look forward to more of your advice. Talk with you again soon. Love you. Take care."

✻ ✻ ✻

The Group of Twenty gathered again at the hillside home of the vice president. This time the pretense was a birthday party for the Speaker of the House. It seemed perfectly appropriate for high-powered politicians accustomed to fund-raising dinner parties to gather and converse about the state of affairs while celebrating a birthday. After all, in New America where they had nothing to do, it was logical they would indulge themselves in social parties and meaningless debate. The vice president wanted no suspicion of anything more until the group finalized their plan and was ready to present it to the president.

"Now let's talk one at a time. Shhh!" Ali exclaimed. "I'm trying to take notes of what you are saying and can't do it with you all shouting at the same time. We know that social and economic disorder is spreading, but beyond our calls for order, freedom, and justice are we agreeing that we should present a list of specific 'grievances,' or 'recommendations,' or 'demands'? Remember that my idea of leading a 'task force' was already shot down, so let me hear from each of you."

"Grievances!"

"Recommendations!"

"Demands!"

"Suggestions!"

"Ideas!"

"Considerations!"

"Amendments to the Declaration of National Emergency!"

Ali knew that it would not be easy to arrive at a consensus among this politically savvy class of liberals, moderates, and conservatives. But time was running out. She must arrive at a plan they could all back. They were politicians skilled in practicing the art of the possible. Concessions would have to be made.

✻ ✻ ✻

"I have it, Jane. The data!" Rose spoke excitedly with a clear voice into her mobile phone. She was in her lab just down the hall from Jane's office, but she couldn't wait to tell her.

"Okay, okay. I have a lecture to give at two. Call Fred. See you both in my office at three o'clock."

Jane's office, 3:00 PM: "Yikes, okay, first things first. We're proving out the sudden-warming theory first. We're there!" Rose then tried to calm herself and began speaking more slowly and professionally. "First, the studies are clearly showing that coincidentally the warm current oscillations in both the Atlantic Ocean and the Pacific Ocean occurred at roughly the same time beginning in 2010. Secondly, the currents are both warmer than usual and larger than usual. These are big, big El Niños. Thirdly, they have continued in that pattern until about six months ago; and they are gradually tapering off. Next, yes, Jane, I have confirmation of your suspicion of a much larger amount of water vapor, the biggest GHG, over North America during this time frame than ever possibly calculated before. That phenomenon is a much larger factor in the warming of the atmosphere than the added carbon from the melting permafrost. It was the larger amount of water vapor from both the ocean oscillations and the melting permafrost." Rose hurriedly cited statistics and then looked up from her notes. Both Fred and Jane stared openly first at Rose and then at each other. Their minds were racing.

"And Fred, can you confirm Rose's conclusions?

"Yes, Jane, absolutely. The unusual holes at the sun's equator were there. An incredible volume of solar wind definitely provided a direct impetus to the sudden melting of the permafrost and subsequently to the ongoing warming. Rose has done a magnificent job piecing together my data."

"So! Part one, Professor," Jane addressed herself out loud. "Part right, part wrong: I warned of the sudden permafrost melting. I was right. I blamed it on man's carbon emissions and thought that the additional release of carbon would abruptly exaggerate the warming. I was wrong there. The Oracle believes that since carbon dioxide stays in the atmosphere a long, long time before it comes down and is reabsorbed into trees and oceans we are going to have global warming for at least fifty more years."

"But!" a grinning Rose exclaimed.

"Yes, okay, the future—Part two. Rose, you said the warm oscillations were fading away … and the water vapor?"

"That too! Back to normal. We're also seeing more cloud cover—that leads to cooling. And more wind—that leads to cooling also."

"And you have been examining the unusual equatorial solar winds. Any conclusions yet?"

"Also fading away. That only leaves the residual carbon gases, the weakest warming effect, now that water vapor, ocean oscillations, and solar activity are in retreat."

Rose stared at Jane right in the eye now, wearing a grin a mile wide. Jane stared back with no expression, looked down at the reports on her desk, looked up again, and then rose from her chair, hugging Rose as tightly as she could.

✢   ✢   ✢

"Michael, oh sweetheart. We have it! The real reasons for the abrupt climate change and the reversal soon to come! I love you! I love you!"

"Rose … darling. This time I'm going to sit down. I'm going to listen and believe every word you say, and then carry you into our bedroom!"

"That's a good plan," she replied softly.

"Just one question first. What is Jane going to do with this little piece of news?"

"Well, as I will explain to you, it may take about three years for enough cooling to take place before it's safe enough to go back to old America, so Jane thinks she will first spring it on her lover, her confidante, the Chief. That way the president can keep things orderly. Until then, our work is our beautiful, little secret."

Chapter Eleven

Clash

Year 2018 [continued]

Mid-summer witnessed a continuation of the progressive increase of discontent in New America. The perfect society had not lasted for very long. The Chief was not sure of the reasons for misbehavior, but he continued to pursue his strategy of utilizing Neighborhood Watches for petty wrongdoings and his secret police for criminal activities. Clearly, the president's view overlooking illicit behavior as insignificant was unsavory to the Chief. Signs, placards, and small marches were becoming more frequent, but sometimes the more vocal critics seemed to suddenly disappear. The president was unaware of such tactics.

The meeting with the president was arranged for August 2 at 2:00 PM. The dean of the national university and five of his leading professors had petitioned the president to present their National University Plan for improving conditions in New America. Also scheduled to attend was a collaborator with the professors, the young engineer hero whose technical breakthroughs had brought clean water to Eastern Colorado. Since the president's Chief of staff arranged all communications for his Chief executive, it was logical that he was the one to greet them at the entrance to the conference room.

"Gentlemen, good afternoon. Good of you all to come. Please be seated." After a few minutes of mannerly introductions, the Chief looked at his watch. "The president seems to be a little bit delayed, so let's get started. You know he has a hectic schedule. I'll take notes and you can leave your written 'petition,' or rather your plan, with me."

The dean and his compatriots looked somewhat unnerved, but they had no choice. Turning to his most eloquent spokesman, Stanford economist Charles Green, the dean nodded. "Charlie, go ahead and let's get started."

"Sir, I'm sure you know the state of affairs in our great country. From a climatic point of view, horrific on the outside, placid on the inside. Not so with the state of the citizenry. We recount our university charter to address the concerns of a society compressed into a small area for the sake of personal safety. For that initial transition, wonderfully successful, we are eternally grateful. No question, a matter of great weight—to care for the citizens during an emergency—falls upon the executive branch of our federal government. Nevertheless, to the point here today, the executive branch should be aided by the top scholars in our land. We petition you here today, sir, to allow us the right to exercise our ordained responsibility to assist you in your benign governance.

"Our recommendations for your wise consideration are fourfold. They are broad in scope and encompass the general areas of freedom, religion, politics, and the economy. We need not enumerate grievances that are growing among all layers of society, throughout the territory of what is labeled 'New America.' We are sure you are well aware of the grievances. Our petition addresses solutions."

The scene bordered on the pathetic. The Chief seemed disinterested despite a pen dangling in his hand, looking down at his notepad. The personal presentation was being made to a president who was not present. Charles continued.

"First, in the general matter of freedom, we call for a second, privately owned and operated television station, a second, privately owned and operated, radio station, and a second, privately owned and printed, newspaper. Each would be free of any review or censorship by the government. We realize that such freedoms carry the risk of some dissent or criticism of the government and its policies and its rules; that is, its 'Guidelines'—originally delicately described as 'benevolent' now more often referred to with sarcasm. However, we also rationally understand that during this period of national emergency, the executive branch of our federal government must be the final and supreme arbiter. We are certain that our people recognize that fact and will submit any final determination to your wise judgment, as only you have all the facts and resources at your disposal and command. The people simply want the fundamental American right to be heard, to be listened to, and to have their opinions, judgments, and concerns be respectfully taken into account.

"Second, our religious community holds the utmost belief that religious freedom has been preciously preserved in New America. They are eternally thankful for that liberty. However, they unanimously believe that their constituents' faith cannot prosper under the physical restrictions placed upon their gatherings. On their behalf, we petition that a third television station be freely established to carry twenty-four-hour-a-day church services under programming purely established and operated by all religious denominations as they shall among themselves agree. We understand that numerous requests have been made for air time to the government czar in charge of broadcasting by certain religious leaders. All such requests have been denied. We understand that the present broadcasting schedule only has space for government-sponsored news and reports and for government-selected entertainment shows.

"Third, obviously the uniform layout of tens of millions of residences in New America resulted in a completely integrated society. We are certainly not recommending the allowance of people moving to whichever area they want. That might end up with neighborhoods characterized by race, color, age, or religion. But what we are witnessing is the coalescence of groups of neighbors wishing to live by more flexible guidelines better suited to their particular neighborhoods. We believe such liberalization would result in a less discontent, perhaps even a happier, populace. To accomplish this better state of local affairs, we petition that you establish regional neighborhoods with local mayors elected by the local citizenry, whereby local interpretation of certain, preselected guidelines be allowed, whereby a local police force be established, and whereby limited retention facilities be made available for flagrant transgressors or criminals."

The president still had not shown up. Michael was growing increasingly agitated that the Chief seemed to be hardly listening. He also thought that perhaps the National University Plan was so broad that the president might not be ready to accept so many challenges to his emergency period omnipotence. Charles did his duty and continued, his voice dropping in enthusiasm.

"Fourth, our economic system obviously requires a boost from the supply side. Products always deemed convenient by most Americans are now rarely obtainable. Products classified as 'necessary' are also becoming increasingly scarce. A black market is growing rapidly for certain goods illicitly smuggled in and paid for in all kinds of nefarious ways. With no savings, with no private or bank loans available in the system, growth is not possible. With no system of incentives or rewards for increasing worker productivity, the quality of what is being produced is becoming increasingly shoddy. Accordingly, to redress these deteriorating conditions, we hereby petition you to modify the present economic system with the following modest adjustments: a) establish a national economic board comprised of government, university, and former economists who will assess those products most in need; b) allow the national bank to loan 'new dollars' to existing or new enterprises that can produce such goods, and allow such enterprises to set their own prices for selling them, subject to earning no more than a 10 percent profit; c) allow workers to produce more than the government-set standards, and if such goods or services can be sold in free-market exchanges, allow the workers to keep such excess in the form of 'new dollars,' which of course are backed by gold and silver reserves at a set redeemable price.

"Sir, this set of requests represents the beginning of what we trust is the national university's input into helping our supreme government manage through a long period of grave national emergency conditions while also preserving certain fundamental liberties so long enjoyed by the great American populace. We pray, sir, that you will give our initial petitions the utmost care and consideration."

Charles looked up from his prepared notes, sadly recognizing his futility—he had been aimlessly, fruitlessly talking all this time to a "sir" who had never entered the room.

✻   ✻   ✻

"Chief, the president is not returning my calls to his direct line. Is he all right?" Ali demanded, although surprised that the Chief directly responded to her telephone call rather than letting one of his assistants answer.

"Yes, of course he's okay. He just wants his calls screened since he has been feeling overwhelmed with so many requests. What can I do for you?"

"Chief, you know who I am. You are not to be an obstructionist. You must know I have been ignored for much too long. I want a meeting with the president as soon as possible."

"And the purpose?" the Chief asked sharply.

"That's my business. I am the Vice President of the United States," Ali retorted in return. "I will be bringing the Senate majority and minority leaders, the Speaker of the House, the Chief Supreme Court justice, and the governors of our two largest states."

The Chief was silent.

"Call me back, Chief, before day's end, or we march in tomorrow morning."

After reluctantly agreeing to call her back, the Chief sat back and reflected a long moment, tapping his pen on his desktop. "She has been an obstinate thorn in my side for a long time, but now she has the aid of her colleagues. If there is discontent among them, then the best way to dispel it is to avoid a confrontation. Let them blow off steam. This is not a third-world county where they come in with guns blazing and pull a coup. The president can handle this." He rose slowly and walked toward the president's office.

☆   ☆   ☆

The meeting tone was one of complete cordiality. Ali was the spokesperson for the visiting group of luminaries. She was direct but not strident. "Mr. President, it need not bear repeating ... you know how indebted we are, and the entire nation is, for your foresight and courage to bring us here to safety from the ravages of the dreadful climate change. Our simple message is this: if we are going to be here for the projected length of time that has been forecast, it is time now to re-institutionalize free América to its traditional values of open government. We realize, as a practical matter, that we cannot re-form our fifty states within the boundaries of Eastern Colorado. We are not asking for that. But we do seek to have the political wisdom and skills of our fifty governors appointed to a new Council of Ministers. ..."

The Chief sat stone cold. The president raised his eyebrows but continued to politely listen, sitting straight, pressing fingertips together under his chin.

The vice president continued. "We propose that the Council of Ministers also include the full body of the last elected Congress, all 535 of them, less the number of incapacitated or deceased. We would then round the number up to an even six hundred at the time of a next election. We propose that the council be initiated now with the present electives and that a first election be held three years from now ... and then a new election every four years thereafter. We suggest dividing up Eastern Colorado into thirty neighborhoods so that present ministers and future candidates would be assigned and elected accordingly. In the future, this division would allow for local amendments to the present national guidelines. For the present time, the fundamental duties of the Council of Ministers would be as follows: first, to review the present guidelines and recommend changes for you to consider; second, to advise and consent on all future new or amended guidelines set forth by you; and as the elected representatives of the people, propose and vote on new guidelines or future amendments to the present guidelines.

"Understanding the need for your 'Declaration of National Emergency,' by which we all live, we generously respect the requirement for your executive leadership. Accordingly, we propose that it require a two-thirds majority for the council to pass or amend a Guideline and then to give you the right to veto both national and local Guidelines unless a three-fourths majority of the ministers overturn your veto. All disputes in interpretation would be reviewed and settled by the Supreme Court, as originally promised before we came here but never implemented."

Ali paused and sat back, completely composed. The room was silent. The Chief wondered if that was all. Everything she said so far was about politics, or was there more? Yet, fooling with the 'voluntary' Guidelines, the rules, was dangerous. At least she didn't bring up the idea of calling them "laws." He stared coolly at her, waiting.

"Sir," she petitioned, "we respectfully submit this plan to you. We trust that it be viewed by you not as consideration to take under advisement, nor conversely as a demand, nor harmfully as a threat to your authority, but as a simple representation of the people's will to be governed in their daily life here under a system of *consent*. We need not remind you—I'm sure you are well aware, sir, of the growing discontent we are witnessing here in New America, on our streets, in our homes, in our places of business. We believe that our reforms are simple and direct. They address the current grievances as we and our citizens see them. Mr. President, we await your favorable response."

The president maintained his famed "calm, cool, and collected" demeanor. As usual, it was disarming. "And Ali, in your prudent judgment, is it you and the wise Congress and the Supreme Court and the fifty governors who bear these so-called grievances? Or is it also the good and noble citizens of our great country?"

Thinking quickly, Ali wanted to make sure she got it right. "Sir, as our forefathers taught us, we are merely humble servants of the people, elected to express their will. Of course, there are no polls taken in New America, but we are quite certain that we are speaking for the vast majority."

"So then, the will of the people … yet am I not to take *your* plan under advisement, or view it as a demand, or as an encroachment—just do it, right? Ali, gentlemen, you can't have it both ways. I, too, am an elected official … elected as the people's Chief executive of their government. Your plan offering me wide latitude in veto power may sound grand—even generous—but I too have the right to listen to the people and determine in my own rational mind what legitimate grievances they may hold. That's what I shall take under advisement. Not your plan, but the people's will, in my own way. Now, is there anything else you came to see me about?"

The Chief looked down and placed his index finger to his forehead, musing to himself, "Brilliant … every time, this man is brilliant."

It was difficult to discern who was staring who down the hardest in this moment. Finally, to break the tension, the Chief justice spoke for the first and last time, "My good sir, this was not meant to be a day to present oral arguments. You have heard our position and have our document … pure and simple. We shall continue this matter another time. Thank you, Mr. President, for agreeing to see us on such short notice."

Alexis Graham left the room without a good-bye to anyone.

* * *

The Chief's job was not finished. Another group had been demanding to meet with the president. The Oracle spent little time in Denver, often retreating to his Aspen "think tank." Richard Compton, increasingly disturbed with life in New America, was spending most of his time trying to figure out future climatic conditions. But the little known Group of Four had been meeting on a regular basis. It was obvious to them that the Group of Eight meetings had deteriorated—away from their original mission of providing detailed action points to fill in the president's grand vision. It even seemed at this point that their detailed written reports, which were circulated to the entire group, were being callously ignored by the Chief and unread by an oblivious president.

The four finally summoned the courage to confront the Chief and demand an audience with the president. The Chief felt it best to continue his strategy: Let them come in and vent, but don't let them know they are not getting an inch of control. They may want to present arguments for more civil liberties, but if one concedes any amount then the seekers will always want more. Stand firm. If they want changes to the economic system, fine; give them some small concessions as "trials." On the other hand, if they offer any suggestions regarding the criminal elements or alcohol and drug abuse, then fine; listen to them as long as their recommendations can be carried out through the Chief's so-called Anti-Crime Force and his Neighborhood Watch informant program.

Again, the president appeared to be late getting to the meeting. The Chief again suggested that the group get started while indicating that the president's busy appointment calendar must have him behind schedule.

With Richard Compton, John Heyward, and H. Stewart looking on, Interior Secretary Arthur Schnell was designated to present the two main topics covered by the group's plan. "Well, Chief, we trust that the president will be here soon. I'll leave this summary of our improvement plan here on your conference room desk in case he misses anything. How much time did you allot us?"

"Oh, you have a full hour. It's two o'clock. Plenty of time. Proceed," replied the Chief.

Arthur continued, "Our plan breaks down into a section on civil affairs and a section on economic affairs. Implicit in our title is the tenet that we genuinely believe that the structures we originally conceived and adopted when we created New America need some serious improvements. I will address the problems we see in our civil affairs and the recommendations we have for improving them. John and H. will address our growing economic problems and the steps we see required for improvement."

All eyes went to the door, but still no appearance by the president. The Chief was pleased to hear that the recommendations appeared to be specific and not a general call for more political freedoms as expressed by the university group and the vice president's group. "Well, Arthur, go ahead; get started. Along with your summary here, I'll catch the president up on whatever he misses."

Left with no choice, a disappointed Arthur Schnell, a dedicated champion of the welfare of his country's natural resources balanced with the welfare of his country's citizens, enumerated the growing problems of civil unrest, of careless drinking, of incidents of drug abuse, of neglect in taking care of buildings and facilities provided to the people, of teenage vandalism, of petty theft, and most troubling, of the lawlessness of a criminal element committing violent acts while leading illicit drug, alcohol, and gun cartels. The salient recommendations to address these problems primarily revolved around enhancing the duties of the neighborhood watch teams to include verbal and written dissemination of the Guidelines addressing inappropriate, civilly illicit behavior and illegal criminal behavior.

In addition, the watch groups and the national government's sparse Anti-Crime Force would be backed up by the creation of a local police force equipped with night sticks patrolling the streets after school hours and all during the night. Arrests could be made by the local police with cases going for prosecution to an expanded unit of the Anti-Crime Force located in the national government's civil affairs office in Denver. A second set of recommendations referred to the creation of local councils that would send written requests suggesting guideline amendments to Denver for possible consideration. A third set of recommendations, also pertaining to the Guidelines, would come directly from the Group of Eight.

"Rather innocuous," the Chief thought to himself. "Perhaps even helpful, other than submitting potential changes to the guidelines from any kind of local councils. Not too bad," he mused.

John and H. carried the economic portion of the improvement plan. They shared their concerns about attempting to create an economy that would have none of the flaws suffered by past generations of every civilized society on earth. Admittedly, they did initially recognize that while the structure they devised might work quite well in a short-term emergency situation, maybe it was just a hope and a prayer that it would be suitable longer term. Now they knew that they had deluded themselves with the dawn of New America and its novel economic policies put in play. They were foolish for forgetting that their system was devised for only the short term. They were overly optimistic.

Now they felt embarrassed that that "perfection" only lasted one year. Supply was now their main concern. Accordingly, their primary recommendations for the president's consideration in their plan were to introduce two new incentives intended to increase production of essential goods and services.

The first entailed an elaborate scheme for anyone in the public to submit written suggestions to the national government outlining how production of prescribed "essential" goods and services could be increased. A pool of winning best ideas, cut off at one hundred, would be created. Then ten final winners would be selected by random drawing. The winners would each receive a package of awards worth one million dollars, part in the form of free extended vacations at the best mountain resorts, part in the form of a gift of the newest model electric automobile, part extra spending cash in "new" dollars, and the remaining approximately nine hundred thousand dollars in gold and silver reserves that could be converted to "old" dollars when the emergency was over.

The second incentive was a redeemable point bonus system for both individual workers and those working in groups. If government-set production quotas were met or exceeded for pre-listed essential goods and services and the government increased the available supply of imported basic raw materials, productive workers could accumulate awarded bonus points and later redeem them for available upgrades in new computers, cars, appliances, mobile phones, and mountain vacation packages.

While the Chief was half-listening, feigning patience, he thought to himself that all this sounded very complicated and unnecessary. He recognized that many goods and services were increasingly in short supply, but that was a problem for the economists and the government to ameliorate, not the citizen workers. Other than the increasing numbers of transgressors he was forced to deal with, the Chief believed, as did the president, in their basic tenet for new America: "The populace should be grateful, content, and productive in a secure society designed solely for their personal benefit."

At five minutes to three, the door opened and in walked a smiling president. "Richard, Arthur, John, H.! Good to see you. I'm so sorry I'm late. I have one meeting after another these days, and another is coming up at three o'clock. It's been hectic, but well worth it. I've been meeting with school-aged children on a regular basis, counseling them to study and learn world history, social studies, and the natural sciences—about all the tragic natural and man-made events of the past. You know how important it is for them to become model citizens, of course, following the valuable educational portion of the Guidelines we have established for them. Oh, it's about three. Chief?"

"Yes sir, I'll finish up with the gentlemen. They have a full report for you to peruse at your convenience ... and there is a nice summary here. I'll leave it on your desk tonight."

The so-called "Group of Four" sat in silence for a moment, completely chagrined. They had never said a word to their president, the one who had purportedly agreed to meet with them on this day to listen to their recommendations for improving New America.

✻　✻　✻

"Jane, tell me again. Why can't you wait to tell me your news until we meet together Thursday night? Okay, okay, I'll meet you at you-know-where tonight at say, nine o'clock. It's been a long day, but I'm afraid I have to listen to another one of the president's long monologues on leadership. He has to reassure himself every few days that he is doing the right thing, and I'm his sounding board and confidence booster. See ya later, sweetheart. Wear that French perfume I smuggled in for you." The Chief rose wearily from the sofa across from his desk. He dropped the report he was reading back on the top of his littered desk. It was from the director of his secret police. He could not keep up with all the reports flowing in documenting activities of his Anti-Crime Force, the ACF. Neither Arthur Schnell, in charge of civil affairs, nor the president were aware of the growing number of plain-clothed, armed squads of secret police supplementing the modest number of uniformed ACF. He took his notepad and walked slowly toward the president's office.

✻　✻　✻

"Hi, Chief. I have some dinner here for us. Remarkable, but I think today was the end of it. We now have three reports—ha! They call them 'plans' for me to just go ahead and wave my approval wand. Don't they know? One is self-serving the politicians—ah, that Ali! The second is way too broad, from those ivory-tower eggheads. And the third from my own team—too plain—no creative thinking.

"You know, this bit about some discontent, a little wayward behavior, some crime, more religion, more citizen participation—it's bunk! That talk of Arthur some time back about guns and rebellion—poppycock! I brought everyone here to safety, except the ones left to guard our properties and protect our borders. They all came voluntarily. It was not a death march. It was a life march! And here … here … look at what we have! We have built a just society. A fair society. A peaceful society. A compassionate society. *Everyone here is equal!* When Plato and Socrates said the truly 'just statesman' might only be found in heaven, and that the next best thing is a society governed by just laws, well, good lord, we have come very close to their ideal state."

The Chief was doing his best to pretend to pay close attention to the president's philosophical ramblings.

"All right, so we have a few people who have succumbed to Adam's problem, tempted by a goodie and committing a misdeed. We have to spell out some rules—softly put, the Guidelines—unfortunately, for this little minority. You have an effective Anti-Crime Force to handle that, and it is so gratifying that almost everyone respects their assigned place in life here.

"So yes, I have studied all the significant leaders of the past. The tribal Chief surrounded by a council of elders for sage advice could be brutal or could be compassionate. It probably depended on the circumstances necessary for survival. If you want to call me the tribal Chief surrounded by my group, then fine, but I rule the compassionate way even in the face of danger to my tribe. Then we had a transformation in how we looked at nature and the supernatural. Abraham and Moses led their people to a promised land and established rules of orderly living for them. Jesus objected to the sanctimonious ways of his religious leaders and enjoined his disciples to find a new way, granting forgiveness and seeking everlasting life with his Father in heaven. Mohammed was inspired by God's messenger to create a more just society, and he persuaded his followers majestically. It is so unfortunate that a small number of his followers to this day believe that nonconformance or disobedience to Allah is not dealt with through persuasion but through death.

"Yes, and we had many centuries thereafter where leadership was exercised by a small number of kings and queens who were recognized as superior, sometimes even divine. Sure, some were benevolent, but many fell into the old temptation of securing the 'goodies' for themselves and their close followers, often exploiting the common people—food, taxes, hard work. Nowhere is there more recorded history of that kind of exploitation than in Russia. The 'Roman Caesar' was the 'czar,' exercising absolute power. Peter the Great turned his country away from an Asian influence toward a European one and built the first large factories, but he did so by extracting extremely hard work from farm peasants and factory workers. The czars continued that exploitation until 1917 when the leadership of the workers inspired them to unite and revolt against the czarist system of leadership. Oh, how unfortunate, Chief, that the next leadership of the workers' groups, the soviets, was the new Communist Party. For the next thirty years, the treacherous, callous Stalin was so intent on increasing production to catch up with Europe and America that he exploited millions of workers, with so many dying as a result. Tragic."

The Chief was trying hard to sit up in his chair and pay attention to his boss's monologue.

"Now then, using our expanding, brilliant minds, we did have a period of Enlightenment. Lots of debate in Europe about the nature of Man, and monarchies, and even the young American experiment with giving the people the right to elect their own government leaders—democracy. Oh, and then another tragic reversal—the madman Hitler, an incredible orator, developed a social/political philosophy of genetic superiority of a selected white class, his own, and attempted to take Europe and Russia by force. One of the classes he blamed Germany's problems on was the Jewish. He exterminated six million of them. Unbelievable cruelty! And so we went to war to take him out, in 1945, and sadly the wars continue to this very day as more cruel, corrupt, selfish leaders exploit their peoples for wealth, power, social ideology, political ideology, or religious ideology. Is it not a delight that every so often a more just society becomes transformed with relatively little violence. I am thinking Mahatma Gandhi in India in 1947 leading peaceful protests against British rule. Just unfortunate the Indian Hindu and Muslim factions then spoiled his dream. Then just the opposite transformation with Mao's Cultural Revolution in China, forcing millions of people to move and lead unhappy farm lives in rural areas they didn't own. Hey, I better not forget Saddam Hussein. A little dicey how we took him out, but there was a leader of very recent times who did not hesitate to kill tens, perhaps hundreds of thousands of his own people, maybe not of his religious sect, but nevertheless, of his own nation. He even authorized the use of deadly chemical poisons to kill thousands of women and children in horrible deaths.

"Ah, yes, probably history does not say too much about the magnanimous, benevolent leaders of the past—not exciting enough. So many millions have suffered at the offensive maneuvers of those leaders set out to exploit or conquer others for their own personal gains. The historians naturally follow those earthshaking events. Just look at our own nation. Every child knows Washington, Lincoln, and Roosevelt and the Revolutionary War, Civil War, World War II. But those great leaders also had other motivations—Washington, the humble first president entrusted to lead a new system of government designed to secure justice and liberty for the then-classified 'citizens.' Lincoln, the preservation of the full United States and the freeing of the black slave class. Roosevelt, the regulation of a depressed capitalistic economic system in order to protect investors and bank depositors and provide new benefits for the working class and unemployed. Then we had Martin Luther King Jr. and Lyndon Johnson leading the way to passage of new legislation that opened doors for all Americans to be treated without discrimination in their civil affairs. And Ronald Reagan, the Great Communicator, who helped restore Americans' confidence in themselves to build a stronger economy for their own country while decrying Communism's failings. Unfortunately, he stressed the idea of self-reliance and less government involvement too much. That philosophy eventually led to a greedy, self-serving environment that did not best serve the people's needs. Remember, Chief, that's why I was elected way back in 2008—to transform our nation into having a munificent government serving our people with all the good things they cannot do for themselves."

The Chief had patiently listened to many of the president's private monologues but was beginning to think this was one of his best. He was glad he forced himself to pay attention.

"And you know that really is the crux of the matter, Chief. And that's why I've succeeded so well in the past ten years and why I will continue to succeed far into the future. I understand the true nature of Man. We have basic needs to live, grow, and survive, and then we have many additional needs to be satisfied, like good-quality health care, better nutrition, high standard education, proper entertainment. In our great country, everyone should have equal entitlement to the best. Competition, greed, status, class, envy—they are all sins of the past. We are good by nature—compassionate, caring, unselfish; not evil or sinful. With proper, inspirational leadership, we can all get along. Did you hear me, Rodney King?" The president finally smiled with that last comment. He was enjoying his own dissertation of the history of Man.

"But Chief, don't get me wrong. I am not telling you I am an all-wise, absolutely enlightened, perfectly just, purely benevolent leader who has created a government under me that provides everything for everybody. I am not forcing mandatory labor upon anyone with the threat of punishment. I am not exploiting my people. I have simply taken care of their basic needs like housing, food, education, and medical care and assigned something productive for everyone to do in order to contribute to their own well-being, and in doing so I have provided for all those things they cannot best get for themselves. From that point on, they must take responsibility for their own lives. Yes, I have persuaded them to come into the system, but I have not brainwashed them. Chief, we will continue leading and running our new America as planned. You will feed our friends some nice words. Our problems are minimal. The Guidelines don't change. And Plato, I say to you, I think there is a loving God up there, my creator, watching over the exercise of my free will, and I think He believes that I am very close to your ideal 'just statesman.'"

✻　✻　✻

Monday night, September 3

"So, my handsome Romeo, you have been so busy lately, and quite tired. Are things any better? I miss your bear hugs." Jane was well aware of the two opposing tugs within her mind and body, constantly at battle fighting their internal war. A smart, reasoning mind purely devoted to her science versus her emotional outpourings of affection for this man—whatever the consequences. Cool neurotransmitters versus warm hormones. But tonight was to be all intellect—she had something of the utmost importance to tell him.

"No better … in fact, worse. Now we have groups of malcontents pouring in to tell the president how he should make things better. The president is extremely honorable, intelligent, and well-meaning, but perhaps he has a naive, or should I say overly idealistic, view of human nature and our natural behaviors."

"How so?" Jane asked.

"Oh, he believes we humans are good guys, except for a few transgressors who can easily be rehabbed, and as long as we are properly led, everything will be just rosy … and he knows that he has the oratorical skills and powers of persuasion to be that leader. The only problem is that we are not all that simple in our behaviors and our beliefs and our motives, so I must keep pacifying the old politicians and your professor friends who have been expressing their discontent lately and at the same time increase my police forces to handle the rule breakers. … Whew! But I will do it. I'll get it done."

"Well now, my good man, don't I just have some great news that can end all your troubles."

"Yeah, right, sugar—the Martians are coming to rescue us."

"No, seriously," Jane maintained her warm smile.

"Okay, okay, but first, it's been a few weeks. Jane, I know you think I've become more detached, but I find you irresistible. Tell me your good news after."

"But, Chief!"

"You were never one to argue, my sweet Jane. You look so beautiful tonight. Later."

* * *

"Chief, I do love you. When do you think we can get married?" Jane asked half playfully, half seriously. It was the same statement and question she had asked him a dozen times before.

"Of course, love, of course. When things settle down."

"Ha! Things will never settle down. If I transferred my professorship from Seattle to Georgetown, would you marry me then?"

"Jane, be serious. We may never see those towns again for the rest of our lives."

"So, you have forgotten already why I asked to see you tonight instead of later in the week?"

'Oh yeah. You have some good news, huh?"

"Chief, this is for real." She leaned across his body and whispered clearly in his ear, "Global warming is ending. Global cooling is beginning."

The Chief lay motionless in the bed. That was the *last* thing in the world he wanted to hear. With the Savior's leadership gifts and his own powers of rule making and enforcement, why change? New America was his forever. Once the criminal elements and the voices of discontent were controlled, this new nation would be his land of private privilege and endless power. "Jane, what in the world are you talking about?"

They both sat up. "Chief, we can end New America and go back to the great civilization we had before. Soon!"

He stared at her blankly. She continued, "Oh, I know you can't believe it—the Oracle and so on. But we have made new discoveries. Why are you looking so astonished? Certainly you want the old way of life restored."

"But Jane, we started out with a paradise here, and then some things started happening. But I can fix—"

"Chief, Chief! This is not, nor ever will be, paradise here. We want our freedom back! Do you hear me? The climate change is making another abrupt change. It's cooling. In three years we can all go back!"

This was Jane Stricker, an eminent scientist, talking. He began to think maybe he should listen.

"Who else knows, Jane? Who else?" The Chief asked sternly.

"Virtually no one. Just the two scientists working with me on the project. I thought you should be the first one we tell. It has to be handled correctly. It's earthshaking news." Jane thought she understood now. The Chief could not show elation when the news was so utterly surprising. Shock and disbelief precede acceptance.

The Chief simply stared straight ahead. No matter about climate change, he thought. Power takes precedence.

※　※　※

Thursday evening, September 6

"Michael … strange. I've been calling Jane for three days now. She hasn't been to the university and she is not answering her cell phone or her e-mail. She left no messages with anyone on the university staff. Last I heard she was going to see the Chief and tell him the incredible news a couple of days before they had planned to rendezvous. I'm worried. Fred has heard nothing either."

Reflecting for a moment, Michael responded by thinking positively. "Well, darling, you know that Chief has that very special retreat up in the mountains. Maybe they are doing a little celebrating up there together."

"No. I checked that. I called Adriana. The Chief has been in his office full-time the last three days. Curious, though. She said the Chief was acting much cooler to everyone. Said he has been quite tired lately and not as jovial, not his usual charming self with the girls in the office. All he has said in the last two days is 'Good morning' and 'Good night.' Michael, what should I do?"

"How about her apartment? Could she have the flu or something and not want to talk to anyone?"

"I checked that out too, just before you came home tonight. You know she lives in that luxury apartment the Chief set up for her ... by herself. I had her neighbor who has a key peek in. She's not there."

"Well ..." Michael thought long and hard. "I know Arthur Schnell in charge of the civil affairs group, and of course Adriana works for the Chief who oversees the Anti-Crime Force. He must be the one we know who saw her last. We could ask one of them to begin a search."

"Oh, Michael," Rose said softly, almost despairingly, "you know all the stories we've been hearing of persons suddenly disappearing. We had been assuming they were people arrested for repeated criminal behavior or persons trying to sneak back to their former homes. But Jane?"

☆　☆　☆

Flashback, Tuesday morning, September 4

The long walk Jane made in the mornings to the university was a pleasant one through a beautifully landscaped park between her special apartment building and the entrance to the elegant campus. A narrow maintenance lane traversed the park's grounds. It was very sudden. A dark car with its silent electric engine pulled alongside from behind. Jane was pulled into the car through an open back door in less than three seconds. She could not see her assailants, and her screams were quickly muffled. No one spoke.

When her blindfold and gag loosened, Jane found herself in a small room with no windows except for a small opening in the upper middle part of the one door. It was comfortably furnished with a small living section, a single bed, and a kitchenette. Like a small studio apartment from her early college days, she thought. She looked out the small window framed in the door. Mountains. "I'm in the mountains!" she exclaimed to herself. She turned the door knob. It was locked. She raised her voice: "Hey … hello … hello!"

Time to think. Was this a joke? Were her associates going to come and wish her "congratulations" because maybe the great news had leaked out? No. Fred and Rose were sworn to secrecy except for telling Michael, and he could be completely trusted. Had the Chief decided he needed an escape with her because the good news had finally sunk in? No—why such rough handling? Besides, he had complete access to a luxury mountain retreat, and this little room had no view windows and only a single bed. Then she touched her arm. It felt quite sore. It was black and blue. It had happened so fast, and they were so forceful. They hurt her arm when she tried to resist and gagged her mouth harshly. They said nothing. They were professional. This was no good-natured, friendly kidnapping.

She looked out the window again. In the distance, before the nearest mountain, stood a large building. There appeared to be a wire fence around it. There were at least a dozen people walking around aimlessly inside the perimeter. This was not a resort. It looked like it could be one of the mountain detention centers rumored to be where the national government's Anti-Crime Force took repeat offenders.

"No!" she screamed out loud. Her startling thoughts continued. "The Chief controls the Anti-Crime Force, and he has hinted to me in weak moments about his secret police squads. I never wanted to pursue that gruesome subject with him. Did he do this to me? Why? Why?"

She saw the handbag that she had been carrying over her shoulder on the way to her office. She opened it quickly. Everything was there except for her cell phone. This is the time in a person's life when fear dominates one's emotions and uncontrollable trembling begins.

✻   ✻   ✻

Friday, late afternoon, September 7

"Hey Rose, I'm in my office." Adrianna spoke as quietly as she could into her private cell phone. "Any word yet on Jane?"

"No, Ad … nothing. I'm so worried about her."

"All right, listen. I never told you about this before. It seemed unimportant. First, give me the timeframe. When did Jane meet the Chief?"

"Well, they were to have one of their little love affairs at her private apartment last night, Thursday, but she rearranged it earlier … to Monday night."

"And no one has seen her since?"

"Right," said Rose. "I went to see her in her office Tuesday, mid-morning. She wasn't there, no one had seen her, and she left no messages."

"Okay, now stay calm, Rose. I bet she went off to the mountains into deep thought and just wanted to be alone. Maybe she had a falling out with her lover-boy. But since the Chief was the last one with her, here's what I want to tell you. The Chief records all his calls for one week and then destroys the recordings. He does that to be sure his orders are carried out. You know he has these two directors who are supposed to know about everything that is going on. One is in charge of his uniformed ACF—you know, the Anti-Crime Force. The other is hush-hush, but of course I see a lot of the correspondence and know about all the e-mails and calls. Anyway, I'm thinking I can come in tomorrow morning and listen to his recordings of this week before he destroys them Monday. He is going to some function with his wife tomorrow morning. It's Saturday, and no one else will be in."

"Oh, Ad …"

"Rose, don't worry. No one will know. I'll tell building security I'm just coming in for an hour to finish a report. Maybe Jane had conversations with the Chief over the last few days … or maybe the director of this secret force had conversations. I'm certain he knows of the Chief's love affair and protects the situation and the parties involved."

"Okay, Ad; please be careful. Call me as soon as you leave the office tomorrow."

☆   ☆   ☆

Saturday, September 8

"Rose, where are you?"

"Just about to go on our usual Saturday morning walk, but with my phone on, waiting to hear from you."

"No! You and Michael stay there … in your apartment. Don't leave. I'll be right there." Never before had Rose heard such a serious tone of voice from her friend Adriana.

"Michael, wait. Ad is coming over now. She sounded so edgy. She must know something about Jane."

They almost didn't know who it was when Michael opened the door. Adriana was wearing a large hat with none of her long hair showing, and sunglasses, and she was draped in an oversized raincoat.

"What the?!" exclaimed Rose.

Adriana hurriedly entered the room, closed the door behind her, and quickly removed her hat, coat, and sunglasses. She appeared shaken. "Okay, calm. Sit down. Sit down. Let me compose myself." Rose and Michael complied. They could only stare at poor Adriana with disbelief and unbearable anticipation.

"What, Ad? What is it?" Michael tried to ask with less emotion.

"Let me start from the beginning." Adriana spoke more slowly now, sitting on the edge of the sofa, looking down as though trying to memorize and then recall a sequence of events. "Our dear Jane. Okay, first I reviewed all the e-mails on the Chief's computer in his office for the last week. Nothing. I reviewed all his correspondence for the last week, including back and forth with his secret director. Nothing. Then …" She looked at Rose and Michael and began to tremble.

Michael reached over and rested his hand on her forearm, trying to express some form of comfort. "Yes," said Michael softly. "Go on."

"I listened to his recordings. You know, the ones I told you he keeps for a week. His first assistant and myself are the only ones who know about them, and where he keeps them." Adriana then reached into her handbag and removed a small electronic recording device. "This is my own recorder. You won't believe this … but I recorded what the Chief did with Jane."

Rose jumped to her feet. "What? Is she okay? Is she safe? What do you mean?"

"She is safe. She is not hurt. You will hear it all. He kidnapped her."

Michael finally lost his cool. "What? Is he crazy? A jilted love affair?"

"No, no, worse," replied a now more composed Adriana. "On Monday afternoon, she called him to move Thursday's rendezvous to that night. He objected, but she said she had something important to tell him that couldn't wait."

"Right," interjected Rose. "She was going to tell him about the climate reversal so it could go right to the president to deal with."

"Yes, I'll get to that," Adriana said. "On Tuesday morning at seven o'clock, the Chief called his director of that secret group, whatever he calls it, and told him that his mistress, Jane, would be walking to campus about eight o'clock, to intercept her, and without being seen, take her blindfolded to Camp Twenty-Nine, not to harm her in any way even if she resisted—to place her in the special single facility that has amenities and keep her there, locked and secure, until further notice. No one is to hurt her, and she is to be made comfortable and well fed but have no outside contact. The follow-up conversations the next four days were about the Chief making sure she was all right and getting good care, and inquiring about her reactions. This director guy, Joseph, said she was unharmed but emotionally frantic and kept demanding to know why she was there against her will and who was behind it. Joseph said that the story was being fed to Jane over and over that perhaps it was a mistaken identity … that it would soon be resolved. But she had been selected out of a group photograph as being a leading figure in a major drug-smuggling ring. This Joseph then asked the Chief yesterday what the real story was, and the Chief replied that she was creating false information about climate change that would be damaging to national security—treason."

Michael and Rose sat in disbelief, mouths wide open, eyes locked on Adriana's puzzled face. "What? Why? That's crazy!" Rose lamented.

Michael did not hesitate. Science, engineering, climate change, natural disasters—all that was familiar experience to him. But New America—this was different, unreal, unnatural. Collecting his thoughts rapidly, he answered, "Because he doesn't want to go back to the old way. He has a leader who thinks he has proselytized Americans into thinking we now live in some kind of paradise. The Chief knows different. He doesn't want dissent. He doesn't want the old way because he has complete power here. That hush-hush group you talked about—Ad, I know what they do, and they have now done it to Jane. They are America's new secret police."

"But what do we do, Michael? That bastard! How do we get Jane back?" a forlorn Rose blurted out.

"Wait, there's more before I let you listen to the full conversations. I know where this Camp Twenty-Nine is. I found maps in the Chief's desk. After we go through the Eisenhower Tunnel at the old Continental Divide there is a big valley on the other side. The lake there is nearly dried up, but we have our government vacation retreats all spread out there. Well, down at the end, there's the old town of Breckenridge, one of our resort retreats. Just past there over a small mountain is another valley, completely empty of human presence, except for Camp Twenty-Nine. It is a holding facility for criminals … and poor Jane.

"There's more—I've waited until the end. You didn't ask why I came incognito. I have another conversation recorded. It's the Chief telling Joseph that this Jane person has two other professors or associates working with her who are involved in this climate scheme but that he didn't think to ask her for their names Monday night, and for Joseph to get the names from Jane, right away. Later, Joseph kept replying that Jane would not reveal the names even after trying to trick her into telling. She didn't seem to be buying the possibly mistaken drug lord identity story."

"Oh my God!" Rose gasped. "If he *is* a madman, he will want Fred and me too!" The three sat back in silence now, all thinking to themselves how incredulous this chronicle of events had become.

"Let me think," Michael said. "Let me think. We have to warn Fred."

"Who is Fred?" Adriana asked. "What is this climate stuff all about anyway that the Chief wants to muzzle?"

"The four of us were sworn to secrecy, Ad—myself, Michael, Jane, and Fred Wosnicki, a professor working with us. Ad, we have discovered that the warming has ended. Cooling has begun … slowly. You will be able to return to New York in about three years."

It was Adriana's turn for a jaw to drop in disbelief. Moments later, she responded, "So the Chief didn't make up this story about a scheme of nutty professors without a reason—his beloved New America. So I get it now, and that confirms my theory that I should not have been seen coming to your apartment … and that you guys are also in jeopardy."

Chapter Twelve

The Trap

Sunday, September 7, 2018

In a classless society stripped of distinctive privileges, except for a few persons high in the national government or national university, and one without a free press, stories of missing persons become just short-lived, word-of-mouth rumors. Government control over Internet and e-mail content prevent wide-scale dissemination. In the case of Jane, however, the halls of the entire university were shaken. By early Friday morning, notices were up on all the bulletin boards. Over the weekend and first thing Monday morning, the dean had made countless phone calls to the Office of Civil Affairs, the Anti-Crime Force, and even to the president's office. No sign of Jane. No word.

Michael asked Rose to call Fred to tell him the story, swear to secrecy, and demand he stay indoors. Adrianna spent the weekend with Michael and Rose. By Sunday evening, the three had agreed on Michael's plan as the best course of action. Adriana divulged that it was obvious to those in her office that the Chief had constant run-ins with Alexis Graham, the vice president. Michael reasoned that she might be the only high-ranking person who could stand up to the Chief and also have influence with the president.

"Ad, since you've met her many times, do you have her private number and know where her secure home is located?" Michael asked.

"No, I don't, but I can go back to the office again. I have access to it. I'll tell security I still need another hour to finish the report I'm working on. I've done that before, so it won't raise any suspicion."

Adriana was back less than two hours later. It was approaching 9:00 PM. The three of them scurried to Michael's car, making sure they were not being observed. The narrow road up the foothills was pitch dark. Almost an hour later, Ad made the call. "I'm sorry for calling you so late, Madam Vice President. I know it's almost ten o'clock on a Sunday night. This is Adriana Sanchez. You may remember me. I greet you in the office when you arrive to meet with the Chief and also for the Group of Eight meetings."

"Oh ... yes."

"Ma'am, we are approaching your home in a minute. I'm sure you have a security detail at your gate. We need to see you. It's urgent!"

"Miss Sanchez. Who is 'we'? Who is with you? How do you know my private number and where my property is?"

"I'll explain everything. You've heard about the missing professor?"

"Yes, the dean called me yesterday, quite upset. Is this—?"

"Ma'am, she was kidnapped. We know where she is. It's the Chief!"

✻ ✻ ✻

"Michael, I'm stymied," the vice president said. "But I do like your plan the best of all the ideas we've considered. I now remember meeting you when you received the president's award last year. They said you were quite brilliant." Ali smiled to break the tension.

"Well, ma'am, thank you. Seems like lately I've been learning a lot about some non-engineering matters, like how humans tend to behave, or misbehave. I do think when a person is selling his services for personal profit, and then feels squeezed, he is going to lean toward an action that best preserves his advantage. I think he'll play along and come to our side."

Rose and Adriana gazed at Michael in admiration. "Worth the try," Ali replied. "Now, it's past midnight. You three are staying here tonight. First thing tomorrow, you call wherever you are supposed to be on Monday morning and say you are running a fever and are staying home until it passes. I'll make my calls as we agreed. I'll see if I can get my contacts here an hour before I arrange for him to be here. We need time to get them all briefed."

✻ ✻ ✻

Monday afternoon, September 10

The vice president had a large conference room at the rear section of her home. Ali had arranged for her full Group of Twenty—governors, members of Congress, and the Supreme Court—to be there. They had all been told the full story. Initial reactions of astonishment now turned to looks of determination.

"Joseph, so kind of you to come on such short notice, but as I mentioned on the phone, I have a serious security problem, and you are the person I need. Please come back to my conference room in the rear. I'll show you the problem."

"I'll see if I can oblige, ma'am. I don't have much time. My boss has been calling me."

"He knows you're here?"

"No, ma'am. I'll call him when I leave so I can explain to him what your problem was and whether I fixed it."

"I'm sure you can, Joseph. I'm sure you can," Ali replied with a slight smile on her face.

When Ali opened the double doors to the conference room, all twenty-three persons were standing, speechless, all facing the startled director of the Chief's secret police.

"Come in Joseph. In your job, you probably know them all, but I'll introduce them formally to you."

Joseph could do no more than nod as each was introduced. No hands were shaken. He was most taken aback when Rose was introduced as Professor Jane Stricker's associate at the national university. He had her name and picture in his cell phone. She was next on his list. By Friday afternoon she had been identified as one of Jane's accomplices in the scheme the Chief had described to him.

"Joseph, Rose here has something to tell you. It's very important to the future of our nation."

"You probably know who I am by now, and Joseph, I know who you are. Our sense of national order, with our people all squeezed into this small area and with none of the personal freedoms as we knew them, is beginning to completely unravel. A rebellion may soon be approaching. I know you work for the president's Chief of staff. I know you have been placed in charge of a civilian-dressed, secret police force directed to quietly suppress not only criminals but dissenters. Do you want to sit down?"

"No, uh, no," Joseph replied weakly, trying to hide his obvious consternation.

It was now Michael's turn to be proud of Rose.

"Joseph," Rose continued, remarkably poised in her assertions to the director of the secret police, "there is no scheme involved in the fact that our climate is making another rapid change. Jane Stricker has her facts straight. Our nation is beginning a cooling period. We will all go back to where we came from within three years. You may release her now."

"I ... I ... don't know what you're talking about."

The vice president took charge: "It is time we all sat down. Joseph, you have a long distinguished record with the FBI. You have served our country well behind the scenes, fighting organized crime and protecting our law-abiding citizens. You are receiving extra compensation and other benefits very few persons enjoy right now. I won't enumerate them. I am asking you to recognize the truth and to serve the best interests of our country again. You will be rewarded. Listen, Joseph! Apprehending proven criminals—yes! But how many repeat offenders of some very simple Guidelines have you moved to your retention camps? How many vocal dissenters have you moved? How easy was it to move Jane Stricker last Tuesday morning to Camp Twenty-Nine?"

Now sitting, Joseph's face turned white, but he remained silent. He had been trained not to respond under interrogation. Ali continued, "I have a recording that I'm going to play for you now. You should recognize your own voice."

Less than five minutes later, Joseph finally responded, his head bowed, "Okay, I'm trained to do what I'm ordered to do. I have always assumed that whatever the Chief organized was a directive to him from the president, always in the best security interests of the United States and now New America. It appears that the Chief has overstepped his bounds. I'm sorry. What do you want me to do?"

With that, everyone in the room relaxed into their chairs. The first part of Michael's plan had worked.

✼ ✼ ✼

"Yeah, Chief. I'm driving back to my office from—would you believe—the vice president's home. Her security team reported intruders last night, and they want my help. Nothing was stolen, so they think maybe the organized crime guys are looking for information on them."

"That's strange. What would she know, Joseph? Was the vice president there? My girl who is assigned to following her schedule is sick today."

"Yeah, she was there. A little upset, but okay. She thinks I'm in the security group for the ACF. Listen, Chief, will you be in first thing tomorrow morning? I have something to show you, but I don't want to use a courier."

"Right; make it eight thirty. I have stuff at eight and at nine," the Chief replied curtly. "Oh, and one more thing. Is Jane Stricker still acting ornery?"

"Yeah, that's what her guard said this morning. Maybe I'll have to get up there and let her know again that we're still trying to investigate the drug thing as fast as we can."

"Okay, and make sure she is well taken care of. I'm still thinking about what to do longer term with these university quacks; and to think I was having an affair with one. You told me you've identified the others. Have you tracked them down yet?"

"Not yet, Chief, but I think we're close. I'm told they were hiking up in the mountains over the weekend and not back yet."

✻ ✻ ✻

Tuesday morning, September 11

There was only one way for the vice president to see the president without going through the Chief. That was to be in his driveway at 8:00 AM, awaiting his departure from home to office. With the security teams of both officials innocently cooperating, Ali was in the president's limousine in no time, sitting alongside the president with Michael, Rose, and Adriana in the opposite seat. The vice president held the indicting recorder in her hand.

✻ ✻ ✻

At 8:30 sharp, the Chief responded to the firm knock on his door, "Come in, Joseph."

The door opened. A figure entered. Complete astonishment. With his eyes wide open and jaw dropped, the Chief was speechless.

"Hi Chief. Not much freedom up there in that camp of yours. Sure glad to be back," Jane Stricker replied with a soothing voice and wide smile. Her hair and makeup were perfect. She never looked better.

"Ja-a-ane!" the Chief stammered. She approached his desk and sat down comfortably across from him.

"You look like you're surprised to see me. What's the matter, Chief? You didn't like what I told you last week? Oh, I know. You're upset—it's only the second time I've ever been to your office."

"No, no. It's just that I've been worried. Your dean has called several times saying a professor has been missing from work, and then we found out it was you. I've been calling your cell phone constantly. I've alerted my Anti-Crime Force. I've been looking—thank God you're okay! Where were you?"

Rising from his chair, he began to come around his desk to greet her, but she quickly stood up, stepped back, and raised her hand toward his chest.

"Your retention center, Chief. Camp Twenty-Nine."

"What in the world are you talking about, Jane?"

Another knock on the open door. "Oh, excuse me, Chief. Sorry I'm late for our meeting."

"No, come in, Joseph," Jane quickly countered. "Sweetheart, this is the kind gentleman who kidnapped me last week on your orders and was so nice to rescue me late last night."

The Chief was now completely flabbergasted. He had to think quickly. "Joseph! Did you make some kind of stupid mistake? This is my good friend, the famed Jane Stricker … from the university."

"Yes, but this is the one you told me had hatched a crazy scheme about the climate; that something was going happen to threaten our national security. Remember? You told me to kidnap her and take her to the mountains and keep her in seclusion."

"Joseph! Of course I said no such thing! What is this nonsense?"

"Not nonsense!" echoed a firm voice from the doorway. Alexis Graham, followed by the president himself, then Adriana, Rose, and Michael all entered the room. Ali, with recorder still in hand, continued, "Better sit down, Chief. We have something for you to listen to before we arrest you for kidnapping."

✧　✧　✧

An hour later, Ali requested that the president open the wide patio doors in his office overlooking a large courtyard. As he did, he heard one unified sound, repeated over and over. The sound was a word, one word of respect—a clearly defined "sir"! He immediately recognized them all: the over five hundred members of Congress, the governors of the fifty states, and the nine justices of the U.S. Supreme Court. The Chief justice stood in front of the large group with a placard. It read in bold letters: **"FREEDOM with ORDER and JUSTICE."**

"Ali, I have been feeling very tired lately. I keep talking to myself. Perhaps I've been touting my own philosophy too much. Maybe I need to rethink things a little, or maybe I'm dead right and just have to go out there and do a better job of persuading them. ..." His voice trailed off. "But at least I do now know that my Chief of staff went overboard in trying to make my dream come true. I sought the truth, but maybe it was a myth. Ali, I need your help. Will you stand beside me?"

The president waved to the now-silent group outside, gave a thumbs-up sign, and retreated to the leather chair behind his desk. As he slouched down in his seat, a compassionate vice president felt empathy toward this well-intentioned man who tried to do his best; one who had lost sight of America's first priority after security of person—individual liberty; one who now seemed paralyzed, not sure of the right road ahead.

"Of course, sir. I'm with you."

Chapter Thirteen

Lessons Learned

Denver, September 15, 2018

Congress called itself into session—in the former Colorado State Capitol building in downtown Denver now occupied by the national government. The vice president presided over the Senate. Both houses unanimously passed the 2018 Amendment to the 2012 National Declaration of Emergency. It called for joint action among the governors of the fifty states, the Congress, the Department of the Interior, the national university, and the president and vice president to create a Plan for Return. The plan would encompass not only how Americans would begin to return to their prior residences on an orderly basis in approximately three years but also how life would be reordered in New America during the next three years. Full national elections would resume in the year 2024. The president signed it without an objection.

Beginning immediately, the three equal branches of federal government would be reconstituted. During any future national emergency or further amendments to the current one, the Chief executive's powers would be enhanced in order to effectively deal with the situation but always with the timely advice and consent of the Senate. In the current emergency, the vice president would henceforth have full authority to act for the president whenever the two deemed it appropriate.

Within a week, Alexis Graham issued five executive orders. All included the signature of the president. The first eliminated the Guidelines and substituted "laws" to be passed by the Congress. The second eliminated all electronic restraints that had been placed upon the freedom of Internet usage. The third established a privately owned and operated television station, a radio station, and a newspaper, all free of any government censorship. The fourth reorganized and integrated the so-called "secret police," the Anti-Crime Force, and the neighborhood watches into one uniformed police force. There would be no tolerance for criminal acts, smuggling, black markets, drug abuse, and alcohol abuse. With the right of freedom comes the obligation of responsibility. In accordance with traditional legal practices, alleged wrongdoers would be arrested, prosecuted, and punished if found guilty, with full information regarding the cases openly available to the public.

The fifth order established the eleven-member Joint Council of Economic Advisors. Stanford's Charles Green would be chairman. John Heyward and H. Stewart would be members. Their immediate task would be to create incentives and rewards within the economic system to stimulate more supply and higher quality. They would also study how to phase out the stifling wage and price controls without triggering inflation. And finally, they would explore ways to make sufficient credit available in order to allow entrepreneurs to increase the production of goods and services most in demand by the nation's citizens. The council's charter directed the group to attempt to find the perfect balance between private interests and the public good during the transition period. It also directed the group to be sure to eventually return the economy to its traditional free-market system under appropriate government regulation in order to prevent unfair practices.

✢ ✢ ✢

Sunday evening, September 23

"Michael, I could not have accomplished this without you. Your plan to set up the Chief and put him in his place worked out perfectly. I never trusted him. He let his personal ambition run away to extreme ends." Ali laughed. "His lust for power turned out to be stronger than his lust for your dear friend Jane. I'm afraid he never really loved her. He enjoyed the romance, but he wanted to be close to her knowledge as well."

"Oh, I think she is getting over it real fast. She will be just fine," Rose interjected. "She sure had a terrifying experience, but she is a strong person and back to what she enjoys best—working in her lab. Michael and I pray that her next romance is the real thing."

"Yes, I hope so. Well, you two are probably wondering why I called you over to dine with me tonight, other than to say 'thanks' for the tenth time. You truly are hero and heroine."

"Don't forget Adriana. She was the key," added Rose.

"Don't worry. She will be properly recognized and rewarded. And talking about people—you may not know about the Oracle. His friend Richard Compton will be on my environmental advisory staff, as you two will be also, but the Oracle ..." Ali laughed again. "At first, he refused to believe your team's findings, Rose; he never thinks he is wrong, you know. But now all your calculations have been fully confirmed by the full university Science Department. He is a very noble, well-intentioned man who has contributed a great deal to humanity, looking forward to returning to New Orleans when everything settles down, but, well ... now he is still secluded up in Aspen, predicting an explosion of a supervolcano—whatever that is—any day now."

"Theoretically possible, but highly unlikely," said Rose. "It's an explosion of exceptional violence throwing up hundreds of cubic miles of ash. The typical volcano first erupts out of the ground and builds a mountain prior to subsequent eruptions. A supervolcano is so big that it destroys mountains and then settles back down into the earth's surface."

"Interesting, Rose. Go on."

"The Oracle is probably thinking about Yellowstone in Wyoming. There have been no super-volcanic eruptions in our recorded history anywhere on the planet. It's thought that the last one was at Yellowstone some six hundred thousand years ago, an explosion a thousand times the size of the Mt. St. Helens explosion in 1980. Yellowstone actually sits on top of the biggest volcano on earth. I mean all that superheated rock for hundreds of miles down below, with hot gases and water vapor at the surface. Who knows? With about two thousand little earthquakes a year being recorded at Yellowstone, anything can happen someday. A big explosion would be catastrophic; but my geologist friends say there are no signs of an impending big explosion."

"Well, anyway, with the poor president now frozen in indecision and with the distraught Oracle still predicting doom—such honorable men of the greatest esteem, but ... I suggest that we move on. I want to discuss with you both what we have learned from all of this. You two are quite wise for your years. It seems like an oxymoron, but it's like we have been living with a myth, but one nearly everyone thought was true for a while. The abrupt climate change, sure, was reality, but after that ..."

"Not one truthful myth, ma'am, but several," Michael added when the vice president paused. "If people are living and behaving in accordance with a belief and accepting it as real at that point in time, then to them, it is the truth. If that belief is later proven wrong, then you have *a truthful myth.*"

"Okay … go on, Michael," said Ali.

"Ma'am, from what I've learned, living matter, whether it's the organic earth, or you, or me, or our total society, thrives best when it strives to be in balance. Since change is constant, that delicate balance keeps changing during its lifetime. Between birth and death, we have to constantly adjust in order to maintain any sense of short-term equilibrium. The sun and its planet earth were created some four and a half billion years ago. We are already halfway to extinction when the sun burns itself out, but that's a long time, right? So for now, humankind *can* thrive if we strive for and maintain our sense of balance. There will be no utopia here. No perfect society. Our human natures, our large brains, for the short time we have been here, are both inquisitive and acquisitive. It is a myth to think that a central government or authority, whether benevolent or malevolent, can long hold us in submission. Some men will follow without reservation, but most want freedom of thought and action. Corrupt, totalitarian governments are our scourge. It is a myth to think that some men will want to selfishly acquire illicit power for themselves without also trampling upon others. Religions call such men 'evil,' but they are also mentally imbalanced or extremely selfish in securing their own advantage, so they brutalize others. I've learned that a thriving society must seek a balance in offering freedom for the many while securing order among the disorderly few, with equal justice under the law for all.

"Same with economics. It was a myth to try to create a thriving society with directives and controls. The government thought we could forget our basic nature—to strive to acquire better goods and services for ourselves— or our nature to grow in knowledge, inquiring to know more about virtually everything. The government thought we could be static and content for the next fifty years as long as it took care of our basic physical needs. Some of us very much need help from the compassionate nature of a generous, just society. Call it want you want—progressive liberalism or compassionate conservatism. Too much or too little government involvement can be and should be an ongoing lively debate in our democracy striving to find the right balance at any given time. Nevertheless, with a good educational foundation and good mentoring, the great majority of us want to be self-reliant and responsible and learn how to succeed on our own. And the environment, ma'am … Am I talking too much?"

"No, no. Go on, Michael."

"Well, 'truth' in science is forever on a learning curve too. I know we don't like to accept the vagueness that everything is 'relative'; that what is 'true' today may be disproved by a new scientific theory tomorrow. At any exact point in time, we like certainty—repeatable, verifiable facts. Remember ten years ago when the scientific majority opinion convinced the environmentalists, the press, and the politicians that the climate science was 'done.' Yet what happened recently is that what we thought was a truth, you know, carbon dioxide is a greenhouse gas, the average world temperature was going up in the 1990s, Man was burning an increasing quantity of carbon-emitting fossil fuels, so therefore it was logical to blame Man for global gradual warming and for the abrupt warming here in North America. It was a truthful myth, now dispelled. Man was only part of the story. There are so many variables affecting climate change; most impossible to predict. The lesson is that we must encourage brilliant scientists like Jane and Rose to keep digging into learning more and more. Keep open minds. Our environment is tremendously complex. It is constantly changing. Ecological balance is difficult to sustain for very long, so we must have our best minds discovering, discovering ... and ensure that our citizens be diligent in exercising the cleanest environmental practices currently available. I know that when we all go back to our former lives my solar and wind and desalination technologies, and even my recent discoveries for clean-burning coal, will not yet compete equally, cost-wise, with hydroelectric power, natural gas, domestic oil, and nuclear power sources. In time they will. We will need to utilize all these technologies and move relentlessly toward balancing jobs, efficiency, economics, and environmental safeguards. We can create a strong economy powered by a combination of clean energies and independent of foreign sources."

"Very good, Michael. I understand. I like your expression of the need for balance in a rapidly changing world. You know, back home they used to call me a 'progressive liberal,' and I really was in matters of political equality, equal opportunity, and the environment. On the other hand, that passion for justice for the underdog has to be balanced with safeguarding our liberties and not allowing the strong hand of government to overstep into the realm of intrusion. I support the idea that it is the federal government's role to help the truly disadvantaged, ensure equal opportunity, set fair rules of play for society, and be the referee to ensure compliance ... but not to be a player on the field. I understand the importance of a sound economic foundation, with equal opportunity—Martin Luther King Jr. in one of his last sermons spoke about the issue: 'If a man doesn't have a job or an income he has neither life nor liberty nor the possibility for the pursuit of happiness." Our Constitution is an incredibly great treasure, national emergency or not. Hey, I keep Patrick Henry's famous 1775 speech right here on my table—you know, 'Give Me Liberty, or Give Me Death.' Listen. ..."

Ali reached over and picked up a small book with a dark, worn cover. She opened it to a book-marked page and continued: "'Should I keep back my opinions at such a time, through fear of giving offense, I should consider myself as guilty of treason toward my country, and an act of disloyalty toward the majesty of heaven, which I revere above all earthly kings. Mr. President, it is natural to Man to indulge in the illusions of hope. We are apt to shut our eyes against a painful truth, and listen to the song of that siren, till she transforms us into beasts. ... Is this the part of wise men, engaged in a great and arduous struggle for liberty?' And later he states, 'I have but one lamp by which my feet are guided; and that is the lamp of experience. I know of no way of judging the future but by the past.'

"Now isn't that something, my young friends," Ali said, half stating, half asking.

"Yes," a now relaxed and composed Rose replied. "I think in my ardor to learn pure scientific truths so that I could help mankind—mankind treated as one entity—I overlooked what Michael discovered. We are complex, diverse beings, each of us with our own unique mind and personality. We all have differences but also some common, cherished values. As Americans, our nature is to debate and argue, to be independent thinkers, and most of all, to be free of outside control. We appreciate help where and when needed, but we also want to be individually responsible. I think the national emergency will have some long-lasting benefits to us as civilized humans. When the situation warrants, we all help one another. We like to work, and we also like to serve. We have also learned to live here in Colorado without class discrimination and bias. Just as the founding fathers sought to create a more just society, this experience will further that cause."

"Yes, my dear Rose. We will go back to our squabbling and finger pointing, but I'm putting my trust in achieving that necessary balance between raging, vocal, peaceful activists advocating for good causes and the orderly discipline of that wonderful Constitution we are so lucky to have. You're right. We will have our differences in thoughts and opinions, but we will be civil. Now just maybe I'll run for president in 2024," Ali said with a wide grin.

"Ma'am, I like that idea. When you win, would you keep one more thing in mind?"

"Sure, Michael, what is it?"

"Well, just be aware that we will be facing more emergencies in the future—climate, accidents, earthquakes, whatever. Could we please have a national emergency act formulated in advance so that the responding powers of government provide safety, order, justice, and freedom for all?"

The three laughed heartily. Candles lit, dinner served, wine poured, the compatriots now became politely silent, quietly smiling and relaxing into a dream world of satisfied deeds and enthralling thoughts … and praying, despite Patrick Henry's admonition, that hopes of a better America ahead would not be an illusion.

Chapter Fourteen

And ... One More

America, three years later, early morning in Denver, September 11, 2021

Upon their early rise at daybreak, Michael and Rose began to joyfully celebrate the first birthday of their beautiful son Alexander Adriano. For friends Ali and Ad, there was no mystery as to the origin of his first and middle names. In addition to her new duties as a caring mom, Rose was busy keeping up with the timing and impacts of the abrupt cooling climate change. With Jane's confirmation, her earlier predictions were proving to be right on target. An orderly transition of moving the people of America back to their homes safely was in process. Other than the treasured moments of delight spent with his love-struck family, Michael was fully engrossed in leading a joint technology team under the Departments of the Environment, Interior, Energy, and Commerce. His mission was to plan and help implement the best combination of currently available and new technologies for clean, efficient, and economic water and energy systems.

The president remained loyal and honorable but was an increasingly lonely man—alternating between moods of personal exaltation and melancholy. Without hesitation, he continued to delegate many of his Chief executive duties to Ali. His calendar was primarily filled with personal appearances and eloquent speeches to schoolchildren, encouraging them to study hard, be diligent, and become good citizens of the future.

The vice president performed most admirably. She had set personal ideologies aside in the interest of finding a middle ground to govern well. She came to understand that almost all the diverse elements in American society had something positive, well-meaning, and important to contribute. Balance the best of past experience with progressive ideas for improvement. She liked that *e pluribus unum*—"out of many, one." The radical ends of that diverse American spectrum were entitled to their rights of free speech, and she listened politely to their rants. She also made it clear that she was intolerant of criminal behavior and civil disobedience. Minds thinking in the world of fantasies, or of radical ideas for a new society, or even in the realm of neurological dysfunction were minds that could be dealt with firmly but humanely. In America, the majority rules without trampling on the minority. The Revolutionary War was over—the ballot box ruled now.

The Plan for Return that Ali was leading was working smoothly. She often pondered over the differences and similarities of the two plans— the Master Plan and the Plan for Return. Both started out working so smoothly. The president's, formulated ten years earlier, had been based on the factor of fear. This one was based on joyful anticipation. Both are great motivators, but perhaps the early success of the president's plan was understandably uncertain in its potential outcome. It was something so novel. He was to be greatly commended. If only he had granted more participation, although the vice president was never quite sure how strong a role the villainous Chief had played in the president's obstinacy.

High in the Rocky Mountains, the secluded Oracle, as well intentioned as ever for his concern for humanity, continued his forecasts of environmental doom. He wrote voraciously for his daily blog and never did get back to New Orleans. He recalled that before the abrupt climate change, which he had so correctly predicted although for partially the wrong reasons, the world could not come together to prevent even gradual climate change. Back in 2009, China was building a new coal-fired electricity-generating plant every day yet at the same time imploring the United States to contribute 1 percent of its gross national product to helping the less-developed nations of the world deal with the adverse impacts of a gradually warming climate. He also lamented that at the December 2009 Copenhagen conference called to set new limitations on man's carbon emissions, the polluting nations failed to agree on mandatory reduction standards. Only in Europe was there a strong commitment to reducing carbon emissions, ever higher taxes on gasoline consumption, almost full reliance on nuclear power plants to generate electricity, and mandatory use of electric public-service vehicles within city limits all contributed to the effort.

Missing in the laments of the Oracle was the very peculiar fact that the abrupt climate change so obviously begun in 2010 only impacted the North American continent and the Arctic region above it. The Oracle had predicted imminent disaster everywhere. The rest of the world continued to experience melting glaciers, higher sea levels, and warming temperatures, but on a very gradual basis. The European Union continued its laudable program of sending several billions of euro aid to Africa every year to help mitigate the adverse impacts of less fresh water and declining agriculture caused by severe droughts. Both in Africa and the coastal lowland areas of Southeast Asia, huge migrations of populations were occurring, gradually moving to more hospitable areas climatically. Unfortunately, this natural event in the long course of human history was not happening without upheaval, dissent, and occasional violence.

In Denver, Jane Stricker, along with her expanded team of scientists, continued her leadership role in studying the complicated interplay of man-made and natural releases of greenhouse gases, retreating glaciers, melting/freezing ice formations, water vapor volumes, cloud cover formations, wind patterns, ocean oscillations, sunspots, and solar winds. The national university was going to retain its title after the transitional period. In the future, it would be a celebrated scientific academic center solely dedicated to studying environmental trends and predicting natural events. It was important that the nation be optimally prepared in the future for all kinds of natural calamities—fires, earthquakes, volcanic eruptions, floods, tornadoes, hurricanes, and even, yes, for periods of extreme warming or cooling climate change.

Jane's university colleague and new friend, Charles Green, was going to become dean of the Economics Department at the University of Colorado in nearby Boulder when his five-year term as chairman of the Joint Council of Economic Advisors expired. Charles had been a confirmed bachelor his entire adult life but seemed to have genuinely fallen in love with this incomparable intellect and irresistibly delightful woman. Jane Stricker felt the same way about him. Had requited true love arrived at last?

Already transitioned to New York City to again be a liaison for new arrivals was heroine Adriana Sanchez. Reporting directly to the vice president's own Chief of staff, this beautiful, vivacious young lady was enjoying the close protection of a contingent of handsome young marines. Life was good again.

✻   ✻   ✻

The other side of the globe, 9/11/2021

The small island of Dire, two hundred miles off the coast of India, had been largely uninhabited for centuries due to an unidentified plague that occurred in the late 1600s. But now its population was over one hundred thousand residents. All were members of a clandestine new extremist movement known simply and mysteriously as "21." Very little was known about their radical ideology or their leadership. It was thought that they were exiles from the radical Taliban and al Qaeda groups that had been chased underground or to remote mountain areas by Pakistani and American armed forces prior to the United States recalling all its overseas troops in the year 2012. However, of what little that was known about the sect there seemed to be no religious motivation in any dialogue overheard by outsiders. They did not publish newspapers or send indoctrinating messages over any public means of communication. Since both European and American foreign intelligence services had been terminated, no reports of potential terrorists were getting to the president of the United States, busy enough getting all his citizens safely away from the devastation of the abrupt climate change impacting the North American continent. Even the United Nations had become void in its knowledge of changes in radical movements. Ever since its headquarters moved out of Manhattan in 2014, the world organization had become fundamentally insolvent and pathetically impotent.

The best information about Dire came from published reports in China, whose Communist Party had been abolished in 2015. That great nation made a successful transition to democracy without bloodshed. Despite official censorship, enough information about the merits of democracy leaked out to the younger segment of the Chinese population, who were benefiting from rapid economic progress. And as the Chief had correctly noted, "Give a little bit of freedom and they will hunger for more." The old guard had suppressed democratic movements earlier by force, but by 2015 the newcomers in power no longer had the support of the Chinese military establishment to savagely put down reform movements.

The concern now was to protect the new Chinese democracy from outside terrorists. The Western democracies lacked the understanding, will, and courage to face terrorism and looked away. They had other problems with which to deal, but the new Chinese leaders understood the lesson of America's 9/11: "Be vigilant—not everyone respects you, and some even hate you." It was learned that the leaders of a possible "movement" in Dire spoke in terms of the merits of absolute rule. The names Alexander the Great, Caesar, Peter the Great, Napoleon, Trotsky, Hitler, Stalin, Mao, and Saddam were repeated frequently in glowing terms. Expressions were overheard by Chinese intelligence agencies like, "Minds are meant to be controlled, not freed; if not by persuasion, then by force—once and for all." There were no indications of any type of military facilities above ground, but satellite photos revealed some scattered digging activities. Daytime pictures revealed no unusual shipping activities other than known commercial vessels stopping there to release containers of food, medicines, tools, and small appliances. It seemed curious to Chinese intelligence gatherers that so much food would be coming onto the island when there were already extensive agricultural and livestock areas apparent in their photos. Night photos did show small unidentified vessels traveling in and out of Dire's small port unloading mysterious cargo.

Surveillance, yes—be vigilant—but the prime hope with Chinese authorities was that this anomaly was just a case of a cult of misfits, basking in some old glory of past conquerors. Nearby in democratic India, the government was oblivious to the peoples and leaders of offshore Dire. Muslim Pakistan was still the main concern and threat to Hindu India.

The island had no airport. Electricity seemed to be generated by a large number of wind farms operating on land and at sea. Chinese intelligence also gathered that the name "21" was short for an incongruous set of long numbers, reading like a computer's serial number—"419110191121." None of this information was passed on by the Chinese to the insular American government.

✳   ✳   ✳

Elsewhere in the world over the past ten years, some advances were made while some regression was apparent. Without the United States as a scapegoat anymore, Venezuela elected a new president and returned to a prosperous democracy, thriving for the benefit of all its citizens. Its vast exports of oil were being shipped to the petroleum-thirsty economies of India and China. Oil revenues were being smartly reinvested in universal education and diversified economic projects benefiting the long-term prosperity of the Venezuelan peoples. Brazil, Columbia, and Argentina all expanded the diversity in their economies and enjoyed slow but steady progress. Unfortunately, in several smaller countries in Central and South America, malevolent dictatorships still flourished from time to time for the selfish benefit of the limited few in power, until the next armed democratic revolution tried again to oust them. It was regrettable that larger Latin countries or the United States did not help the democratic reformers who lacked the advanced weapons easily available to the next cycle of anti-democratic rebel movements. The world was still awash in the production, selling, and smuggling of deadly arms.

The Middle East remained embroiled in its perpetual cliché— "volatile." The best news was that major wars were precluded through a balance of nuclear weapons. On a smaller scale, it was somewhat like the former American/Soviet détente. The Hamas and Hezbollah dared not attack Israel any longer as Israel moved small tactical nuclear weapons to it borders and displayed them to be easily seen. Nor did Israel dare first-attack its adversaries, as Iran was completely nuclear-armed with tactical warheads attached to short-range missiles deployed at multiple sites. Without any further negotiations or outside influences, Palestinians simply declared Gaza and portions of the West Bank as their legal state. In the absence of rocket attacks, Israel cancelled its economic blockade. However, establishing Jerusalem as a neutral, religious, international city was still a dream for the young, school-aged kids to figure out.

Iraq did the smart thing and declared itself the Unified States of Iraq. The Kurds were given the north, the Islamic Shiite sect the south, and the Sunni sect the middle. Bagdad was declared an international city. The nation's democratic national government located there was chartered to provide military and police protection and for fairly dividing the nation's oil revenues among its three states on a per-capita basis.

Iran continued to be in turmoil. The strong clerical right, declaring its near divinity, was able to continue to dominate the military. Peaceful revolutions that had occurred years earlier in Eastern Europe and the Soviet Union and the recent peaceful transformation in China were impossible to accomplish in Iran. Dissidents continued to be jailed and treated harshly. They could not persuade the military force surrounding the clerics to their side. Whether the motive of the clerics was to restore a great Persian empire or to spread the gospel of Islamic states mastered by theologians were not certain. What was certain was that the nuclear deterrence capabilities of Russia, China, and Israel were made crystal clear to Iran and prevented any further influence of autocratic Islam. It was held in check except for continuing expansion in a number of weak African states.

Africans continued to suffer in great numbers under horrific social, political, and environmental circumstances. Without U.S. medical and food aid, the spread of disease and famine increased and human conditions worsened. Corrupt governments dominated over half the African populace. Natural resources were exploited for the benefit of the few, not efficiently processed for the benefit of the many. Drought in areas close to the expanding Sahara desert caused difficult relocations and conflict. European aid sometimes helped ameliorate the desperate situation, but the die was cast. Conditions were getting worse, and ethnic divisions only aggravated an already sad state of affairs for the struggling common man over a large part of the African continent. Michael's plea for "balance" fell on deaf ears in this part of the world.

An interesting alliance had come to pass during the past five years. By 2015, the stern leaders of Russia began to retire, enjoying the vast personal wealth they had acquired after the fall of Communism and the breakup of the Soviet Union. During the 1990s, younger generations had been prematurely euphoric over the fall of autocratic Communist rule and the promise of democracy. Unfortunately, without any historical experience with the workings of free institutions or free-market capitalism, their dreams were quickly snuffed out. Corruption, greed, and secret battles over entitlement to the nation's vast resources of oil and gas reserves put a hold on genuine democratic reforms in a nation whose entire existence had been previously dominated by all-powerful "czars," "premiers," "general secretaries," and "presidents." By 2015, however, the tide had changed. Democratic reformers were able to hold sway and spread the petroleum wealth into more diversified industries. Natural gas exports to Europe for heating oil use continued, but a major new trading partnership was inaugurated. Democratic Japan expanded bank credit to fledgling Russian enterprises, while Russian consumers began to enjoy the flood of modern electronic devices and appliances made in Japan. In return, Russia was able to provide natural resource–deprived Japan with minerals, metals, and petroleum. Russia had replaced the United States as Japan's main trading partner. The peoples of both nations benefited.

It was a far different story in Afghanistan. When the Americans pulled out, the militant Taliban faction regained control. Prior advances in the status of women, education, and political freedom all suffered a reversal. The Taliban alliance with al Qaeda renewed the latter's prior strength, but the followers of Osama Bin Laden no longer had their sights set on America. America had become impotent in world affairs. Plans for attack were centered solely on heavily fortified, fully prepared Israel. The problem for the al Qaeda leaders was that infiltration was impossible; the only attack would have to be a nuclear, biological, or chemical one from the outside. To accomplish that would require the military support of rockets or planes from Iran, and the Iranians wanted nothing to do with a completely devastating, massive nuclear retaliation from Israel. Al Qaeda was in checkmate.

✣   ✣   ✣

"Remember darling, those wonderful sleep-in Saturday mornings? And now we're up before six."

"Michael! Do you want to send this little guy back?" Rose grinned as she squeezed baby Alex against her chest.

"No way! We are so blessed. After a long, hard week, could we just go to bed an hour earlier on Friday nights?"

"Yes, darling … good idea. Now here—your turn to change diapers."

A few minutes later at breakfast, Michael glanced at the just-delivered morning newspaper. The date printed at the top was "September 11, 2021." A side headline read: "Lessons—remembering 9/11." Michael glanced at Rose filling his cup with more coffee. He gently touched her extended arm.

"Rose. Today … it's twenty years."

"What is?"

"Since the Islamic extremists slammed airliners into New York and the Pentagon and almost another into the Capitol or the White House." Michael's voice seemed far away as he stared out the window, now showing the first light of dawn.

Rose attempted to reassure him. "With all our problems over the last ten years, no one thinks about that anymore. Who knows what's going on, anyway? Don't you worry, my love; I'm sure the rest of the world and its extremists have plenty of their own problems to worry about. No one is thinking of us anymore."

"I don't know. Afraid I'm a natural worrier. I hate to think I'm a full-time skeptic, but I guess maybe I am … from in college when I didn't think the state guys were right when they said we could get enough water to Southern California from the north. That's when I started working on my turbine and desalination ideas. And then I was worried to death I wouldn't be able to scale up. Then I was worried when I came here, and everybody and everything was 'assigned' and then told that everything would be just fine if we obediently followed the government's Guidelines. Even today, while Ali and her team seem to recognize the need for balance in their responsible approach between individual needs and society's needs, I fret that creeping government could eventually kill the goose that lays the golden egg. And 9/11. How do we know who is out there patiently waiting for the right time to hit us again … or worse? We have no overseas intelligence anymore or even overseas military bases. The lesson was supposed to be 'Always be prepared,' but we're not."

Rose laughed. "Oh, so now I will add you to my list of persons to comfort. Little Alex gets a hug from me every time he cries. Okay, here I come, love. You get the next comfort hug."

"I'll take it. I'll take it." But Rose's hug didn't help much. In a morning of supposed celebration, Michael continued to be despondent. He thought about good and evil, evil and good—men can see it in different ways.

* * *

As Michael and Rose fussed over getting up so early in the morning, far away on the island of Dire the time on this September 11 was now five o'clock in the late afternoon. The two men were about to be served an early dinner on the veranda of their small, modestly appointed beach cottage they called "Headquarters." They conversed in near-perfect English. Antoine spoke first as they seated themselves at the humble table in front of them.

"Is everything ready, my good friend in arms?"

"Yes, my comrade; we have two hours left for full delivery, full dispersion, full impact. Everything is in place," Aazim replied calmly. "I will give the final order as we finish this meal. ... It will be 7:00 AM in Los Angeles, 8:00 AM in Denver, 10:00 AM in New York, 3:00 PM in London, 4:00 PM in Paris and Rome, 6:00 PM in Moscow, 7:00 PM here in Dire, 10:00 PM in Beijing, and 11:00 PM in Tokyo."

Antoine smiled and reflected upon the flag waving gently on a short pole planted into the nearby sands. As twilight was approaching, the tightly squeezed numbers were barely discernable: 419110191121. He spoke to his friend Aazim, "No fancy name for us ... just an obvious fact. They were so surprised in '41 when the Japanese hit them, and they just could not believe what happened when that first plane hit twenty years ago on 9/11/01. Idiots. They never learn. They are lost in their human rights. And here it is 9/11 again, and their sole purpose is to get themselves back to their comfortable homes. Ha! Another surprise for them. Nonetheless, dear Aazim, our strategy is right; our timing is right. We must take them out before they come out into the world again."

* * *

Born and educated in Paris, Antoine had felt disenfranchised from the time of his earliest years. His father was an international banker who spent most of his time in Zurich, Switzerland. His mother was rarely sober. Every time the family did have a chance to dine together, his parents argued incessantly about politics, economics, and social status. His father argued for pure laissez-faire capitalism. Each person should try to make as much money as possible and responsibly take care of himself and his family—the highest human endeavor. Elected government should only provide for police protection and national defense. Conversely, his mother argued for full government involvement—economic socialism and full social care, cradle to the grave, for all citizens. Equality in all ways for all persons meant "justice"—the highest human endeavor. Before he understood sex appeal, poor Antoine wondered how these two ever came together into the state of marriage.

In college, he stayed late rather than go home to an absent father and incoherent mother. This circumstance led him to fall into membership with a clandestine, radical group of college students whose ideology was primarily one of anarchy. No one should ever tell them what to do. Their biggest challenge, however, was coming up with a practical plan for eliminating government altogether while at the same time preventing street mobs from running loose. After graduation, Antoine resigned from the group—it seemed to him that their ideology would lead to chaos. He took a banking job his father opened up for him. Within a few years, he was transferred by happenstance to a group within the bank that was helping small governments around the world obtain legitimate financing for the legal purchase of weapons; weapons of all kinds, sizes, and degrees of power. He began to think again about his parents' arguments and about the radical ideas of his college associates. Even after a horrific war initiated by the madman Hitler, the world was armed to the teeth and only adding more armaments. This was madness, Antoine thought. He began to think further: "Disarm them all by controlling them all." The seeds had been planted to grow a brand-new ideology—one act of violence to end all violence.

"I look back now," said Aazim, continuing in his calm tone of voice, "and am amazed that we have accomplished this incredible preparation in such a short time. We have thought of everything. Success is assured. I remember our meeting eight years ago again, Antoine, a few years after our first meeting in Paris, in what was it, 2008? You said that you wanted to control all the guns and weapons of the entire world. I said that I wanted to control all the peoples of the entire world. I asked you if you were a pacifist and praying for everyone to destroy their weapons. You laughed and asked me if I was a religious fanatic who wanted everyone to kneel down to the one true god."

Antoine laughed heartily but nervously. They were so close in time to the fateful command, and yet this man, Aazim, had so remarkably trained himself—his steel mind, his calm breathing, his steady voice, and his entire body—such wondrous repose. "Aazim"—"the determined one" in Islamic languages. It may have been his daily yoga or meditation sessions; but whatever, Antoine was full of admiration for his good friend and accomplice.

"I still do not understand all those banking mysteries, but Antoine, somehow you were able to transfer billions of dollars from secret Swiss bank accounts into our account, and I'm certain those super-smart bankers and dumb multimillionaires don't even know it yet to this day. Incredible, dear Antoine, incredible!"

"Yes, if I can put aside humility for a moment, it was a good trick to put my hands on all that money. But better yet, dear friend, was that I could use my relationships with some very special arms dealers to get what we have now. The typical deal is guns, rockets, tanks, even planes, but the arsenal we have … that's what is incredible."

Both men turned very serious now, as though a heavy weight had just penetrated sharply into their fast-moving minds. Aazim spoke more sternly, "'Chemical, biological, and nuclear.' Those three words have been thrown around now for twenty-five years—WMDs, weapons of mass destruction. In all the capitals of the world, they have been the big fear; that some radical extremists will get hold of them and terrorize the peace-loving peoples of the world or upset the money-making trading of the capitalists or interfere with the scripted order of the dictatorial power holders. But it has not happened, my good comrade … not quite yet."

"They are all complacent now, my friend—other than the ever-vigilant Israelis surrounded and outnumbered by millions of Arabs and Persians hell-bent on their annihilation…. The time is now ripe," Antoine added, moving aside his half-eaten dinner plate and fumbling to look at his watch. It was now six o'clock. One hour to go.

✻   ✻   ✻

New York City, 9:00 AM, 9/11/21

"Johnny, you show up without fail every morning right on time to take me to the office. You know how much I appreciate you and all the other marines, but can I ask you a question?"

"Certainly, Adriana, I mean ma'am. Fire away."

"Well, I know I'm part of the vice president's staff, but I feel so safe here in New York that I don't quite understand why I need protection. Don't get me wrong—I'm having a blast with you guys. But it doesn't seem like we would be targets."

"First of all, ma'am, security is our routine. We protect embassies, we protect bases, and we protect strategic locations. The marines are always out in front. We helped the other service branches protect New York City here for the last six years while everyone was in Colorado. And now you, ma'am ..."

"Oh, come on, Johnny, you can call me by my first name even when you're on duty," Ad interrupted him, smiling warmly.

"Right, okay, Ad. I was saying that we protect you as part of the normal, traditional security for the president and the vice president and their staffs. We always have to be on alert for the crazy nuts who carry a grudge. You remember John Kennedy and his brother Bobby, and then there was Ronald Reagan. You just never know ... and then we are always getting reports. ..." Johnny paused, wondering if he was permitted to reveal any more.

"What kind of reports, Johnny?" Adriana quizzed.

"Oh, just reports that foreigners may be infiltrating our borders. We can't secure them 100 percent, you know."

"Well, we've always had illegal immigrants getting in."

"Right, but even though we don't have overseas intelligence any more, our internal intelligence tries to keep track of terrorist organizations infiltrating."

"And?"

"Suspicious, because they are different ... not the nearby Cubans or Mexicans, but I don't know of anything we should be alarmed about. They have not been identified as our old nemesis, al Qaeda. So relax, Ad. We still have all our satellites and electronic surveillance systems in place. See you tonight with the crowd at Louie's."

As Adriana left the company of her handsome, sturdy guardian and began entering her office building in Lower Manhattan, she paused. She turned and gazed in the direction of the former Twin Towers, those American symbols of soaring prosperity that crashed to the earth twenty years ago at this time on this day. "Never again, I pray," she said to herself as she turned back and walked inside.

✻   ✻   ✻

"What makes us different, dear comrade Antoine, is that we have thought of everything. The others all thought they were invincible, so they overextended themselves without thinking it through. Alexander went too far without enough resources. The Romans rotted from within. Napoleon overreached. Stalin butchered millions to produce more goods but did not understand how to sustain a stilted economy. Hitler was crazed with his supremacy doctrine and stupidly lost sight of the long cold road into Russia and of America's strength. Saddam thought he could do it by bluffing his adversaries and by buying the loyalty of a hundred thousand protective guards with wine, women, and wealth. After two thousand years of fighting, the Europeans grew weary and are now pushovers. They have become like the violent Vikings who are now the pacifist Scandinavians. ..."

"Go on, my friend," Antoine said quietly.

✻   ✻   ✻

He was reflecting on how he came to hear of Aazim. It was in Tehran at the time the Supreme Ayatollah was dissatisfied with the simple bomb-making and rocket-launching knowledge Iran was buying from North Korea. He wanted to secretly purchase knowledge on producing small, tactical nuclear weapons from the French. He thought such weapon flexibility would amount to a major advantage against his rivals—the Sunni-sect Muslims, the Wasabi-sect Saudi Arabians, and the hated Israelis. Aazim was Iran's Director of Foreign Intelligence at the time.

Educated in Geneva with post-graduate studies at Columbia in New York, he was trained in intelligence gathering in Moscow and exposed to weapons information smuggling from North Korea. Aazim understood conflict at an early age and early in his career was exposed to many fundamental differences in varying cultures. He pondered over the relative strengths and weaknesses of each. America had its big-government reach, progressive liberal wing loudly debating with the limited-government, free-market capitalists of the arch-conservative wing—with the silent majority in the middle. Democratic Europe was continuing on its no-growth, part-free, part-socialistic course with no specific roadmap to follow. The weak European Union publicly championed universal human rights but did nothing about it outside its borders and did little within its borders when it came to Muslim immigrants. Its military budget diminished each succeeding year while its health care budget soared.

Aazim saw the mixed results of a partial and incomplete rebellion against centuries of harsh rule and corruption in Russia. Democracy was finally gaining ground after a false start at the time when the Communists lost power, but to Aazim the outcome seemed hardly worth the effort. There was still rampant corruption and little justice. In North Korea he witnessed the results of an inefficient, autocratic government that could accomplish nothing on its own and could not effectively help its people prosper.

He began to put all the pieces together at the time he met Antoine. The problem with all these past and present societies was that they lacked one coherent philosophy that could work effectively for the long term. There were too many opposing factions in the so-called "free" societies or "mixed" societies. In the autocratic societies, the leadership was so selfishly corrupt that its stay in power could not be sustained; their course was always radical idealism, eventual triumph, subsequent disillusionment, and finally defeat. Then the cycle would repeat. Only his native Iran had it altogether. Ingenious, except for the fallibility of man. Here is where the broadly educated, worldly exposed Aazim ran into his dilemma.

In Iran, the nation's constitution was modeled after the Constitution of the United States, a country that had stood strong for over two hundred years before its recent slip into mediocrity and isolationism, consumed by its climate crisis. But the Iranians were smarter; they added the Supreme Ayatollah at the top of their constitution, and he had a direct link to God. Hence, all the American-style bickering and misdirections were eliminated in Iran, where the faithful were taught that pure obedience to God was of the highest calling in one's life. A divinely linked theology overseeing a subservient, secular state appeared ideal to Aazim, for a while. He began to notice, however, that from time to time there would be calls for modest reform whenever it appeared that some of the educated class wanted more say in running the government. A permanent autocratic leadership promoting universities and allowing an elected parliament to participate had to eventually run into dissension. There was unrest. Democratic reformers who went too far were always prosecuted and punished.

Perhaps the system was not so perfect after all. Aazim began to think that it was not pure obedience to God that he was practicing, but obedience to varying religious scholars often espousing contradictory interpretations of Islam. He thought it began to look like America, Europe, Russia, and China—debating or fighting within each society over which doctrine is "true." Within Islam, was it Wasabi, Shiite, Sunni, Sufi? Was it secular Turkey or fundamentalist Iran? He began to have doubts about the self-proclaimed divinity of the Ayatollah, and he even began to have doubts about believing in a religion at all. There simply was too much disagreement—in Iran and everywhere. The world needed a new foolproof ideology.

✻   ✻   ✻

Dire, 6:00 PM, 9/11/21

"Well, okay, I will go on. Thank you, Antoine. You are a good listener. So you and I see the world as weak. They say that some 80 percent of Americans believe in God. In Muslim countries, of course, they say it's 100 percent. Europe is so secular that the churches are nearly empty. In Russia and China, religion is a doormat. It's all so arguable. Who knows the truth? Good and evil, God and the Devil, faith and hope. Forgiveness, salvation, obedience, heaven, hell … these are all just empty words to me now, illusions. Some humans need to draw from a strength they believe is bigger than themselves, even if they can't see it, so they try to experience it or hope for it. Others cannot believe in an all-loving God when they see hatred and violence all around them. You and I, Antoine, have agreed that the best we can expect is that we do all that we can with these expansive minds of ours. And when our physical end comes, our vital energies will flow on forever, somewhere; and whether anyone else or any supernatural intelligence is aware of that energy is beyond our human comprehension. In the meantime, we break away from the mold, leave the dissension behind, and do our very best to change the world to the way we see it."

"Ah, dear friend, we see it the same way now. But will *we* agree five years from now?"

"No, Antoine. I'm afraid perhaps we might not. The question at that time will be which one of us will become dominant, and will it be voluntary or by gentle force?" Aazim let out a hearty laugh while his quite serious "good comrade" continued staring out at the flag. "Some things never change," Antoine mused, sensing the contradiction inherent in their mission.

"Well, Aazim, we do agree that all six billion of us here on earth are of different minds. At least it's good that you and I are in concert on one thing right now: Mankind on this planet has messed up. They just can't seem to get it right. We'll do it for them and be convinced that it's the right way, the truth … forever and a day."

"Well spoken, Antoine. The world society we create with our tens of thousands of disciples will be the right one ... and it will last. We will have avoided all the mistakes of the past. Our wisdom, learned from the ages and the annals of human experience, will prevail. We will rule from the perch of complete dominance, but there will be justice for all. Anyone who dares to disagree at least will be without weapons—your dream, Antoine." The two men glanced again at the beauty of the setting sun and then at their watches. Fifteen minutes to go.

✻　　✻　　✻

Denver, 6:45 AM, 9/11/21

"It's going to be beautiful day today, Michael. The forecast is for perfect temperatures and nothing but blue sky. Let's plan a long walk with Alex in the carriage and a nice picnic in the park. And tonight we have his first birthday cake."

"Sure, but first let me finish reading the paper and checking the news on TV, and on the Net too."

"Wow, you really are caught up in this, aren't you, love?"

"Sorry, Rose. I just can't get it off my mind. All these years of listening to one extreme—thinking everyone in the world is nice and they just need some help and compassion; and then to the other extreme—suspecting everyone of possibly doing harm. At the university with Ed Stern and his neuroscience team, I learned so much about human behavior. While we are individually controlled by our complex and diverse brains, they believe that each one of us has innate capacities to be either violent or compassionate or both. It depends on the circumstances at the time, the mental health of the mind, and the environment and culture we individually have been exposed to over our lifetime experiences."

"Sounds quite deep, but reasonable, love. But this morning? Like what are the chances?"

"Yeah, this morning. I just have the strangest feeling. I mean, I don't believe in premonitions, Rose, but I just feel someone out there is thinking 9/11, twentieth anniversary, and has violence in mind." Inattentive to Rose's inquiring gaze, Michael proceeded to scan his newspaper, search the Internet for news reports, and tune in the TV news. He was fully engrossed now in what Rose surely hoped was a fast, fleeting figment of his imagination. Their young family was so happy now, and to her it was as though America was being reborn and she was right in the heart of it. Her little Alex was going to have a very bright future.

✣　✣　✣

Dire, 7:00 PM, 9/11/21

"What are the numbers again, Aazim? We have capacity for how many of us underground in our tunnels? For how many years?"

"Antoine, my dear comrade, you are the numbers man and master planner. I am supposed to be the one who carries it all out. But okay, let me review everything for you. I think you are a little nervous.

"Our tunnels will hold all ninety thousand of us on this island. In the unlikely event—even though remember we have thought of everything— that we somehow receive a retaliatory blow or accidently receive fallout from our own WMDs, we can sustain ourselves with enough food and water underground for three years. Our other ten thousand disciples are spread around the world, set to deliver and then quickly return by all the private vessels we chartered. At the time of the shock, one thousand of them will deliver our ultimatum to surrender to the capitals of 150 countries. It will be clear that we have the only antidote to the sickness and weakness of their suffering populations. Blackmail will work. Five thousand of our best disciples—of course vaccinated—will have already spread the biological devices throughout those countries. Entire populations will be sick and weak within twenty-four hours. Unfortunately, the severely immune-impaired may die. To all the physicians in all those countries, it may seem like a severe influenza pandemic, but in this case they don't get better without our antidote."

"So the whole world gets the atmospheric shock followed by the bug … except the United States," confirmed Antoine, now looking even more somber in his unwavering gaze at the flag.

"Right, that is the truth. It still amazes me, my good comrade, that you were able to smuggle nine nuclear shock bombs and the short-range mobile missile launchers. In a few short minutes, we will bring them out of hiding and rocket them high above Western Europe, Eastern Europe, Russia, the Middle East, India/Pakistan, China/Japan, Africa, South America, and of course North America. The enormous shock waves will knock out all electrical devices for up to six months, except of course the strongest one over the United States—for up to two years. Perhaps we are going overboard there, but just to be assured of our complete victory and their complete annihilation—the world we shock, sicken, and heal; the United States we super shock and eliminate. Despite its current weakness, it is the only country with the ingenuity, resources, and sense of determination that might not submit to our demands for complete surrender."

"We kill them all. How many?" a now even more soulful Antoine inquired.

"Ah … you, the great man of enlightened Western Europe. You forget your numbers, but are you remembering your conscience? You have read enough prophecies of doom. You Westerners create those crazy, violent movies. You dwell on science fiction. You are all confused. Behind that facade, in real life, you must not feel it is wrong to kill if the means justify the ends. All Americans, three hundred million, will die rapidly and grotesquely as the black clouds of chemical dust sweep the land. Our number, if you have forgotten, is four thousand—four thousand disciples smuggled into the country, each dispersed and armed with the chemical weapon and its antidote for their safe escape. The Americans survived their brief battle with what they called 'abrupt climate change,' while the rest of the world muddles along with their gradual change. It is not a problem for us to be concerned about. This time, dear Antoine, America has no 'Savior.'"

"But you must know, my dear Aazim, that these are untried weapons. We have no experience, no guarantee they will all work … or that any will work." For the first time in the last two hours, Antoine breathed a sigh of relief. Maybe nothing will work as planned. He moved his cold stare away from the flag in the sand and fixed his eyes on Aazim's. The two men smiled softly at each other. Barely audible, Antoine spoke. "It is time, my good friend … make the calls."

✣   ✣   ✣

New York, 10:00 AM, 9/11/21

"Adriana, it's Johnny. I'm coming back for you. We have a shelter. There's a top red alert. Something shot up into the sky, and our detection systems are going berserk. I want you to—"

✣   ✣   ✣

Denver, 8:00 AM, 9/11/21

"Michael, I was just talking to Mom on my cell phone and it went dead. Did you hear that boom and feel that rumble? Sound barrier? Earthquake?"

"Rose! The computer and TV screens just went blank. The kitchen light is off. We've lost electricity."

Rose looked perplexed. Michael shuddered with fear. Picking up Alex in his arms he walked to the balcony and opened the door. Rose followed them onto the deck.

The clear early morning blue sky was beginning to take on a blackish tint far to the west, with the wind blowing it slowly toward the east…. The two stared in wonderment of what it all meant.

Epilogue

After experiencing the shock waves that knocked out America's electricity, we are hopeful Michael, Rose, and their young child survive the ensuing chemical attack.

After witnessing Antoine's last minute pang of conscience, we pray his uncertainty as to whether the weapons of mass destruction would actually work does culminate in a favorable outcome for the peoples of America and the world.

And finally, we trust that positive steps are undertaken in the coming years to resolve our human conflicts peacefully, without violence. We have enough natural calamities, such as the vagaries of climate change, with which to eternally contend.